To Catch a Viscount

Heart of a Duke

USA Today Bestseller

CHRISTI CALDWELL

To Catch a Viscount
Heart of a Duke Series

Copyright © 2022 by Christi Caldwell

All rights reserved. No part of this book may be reproduced in any form by any electronic or mechanical means—except in the case of brief quotations embodied in critical articles or reviews—without written permission.

The characters and events portrayed in this book are fictitious. Any similarity to real persons, living or dead, is purely coincidental and not intended by the author.

This Book is licensed for your personal enjoyment only. This Book may not be re-sold or given away to other people. If you would like to share this book with another person, please purchase an additional copy for each recipient. If you're reading this book and did not purchase it or borrow it, or it was not purchased for your use only, then please return it and purchase your own copy. Thank you for respecting the hard work of the author.

For more information about the author:
www.christicaldwellauthor.com
christicaldwellauthor@gmail.com
Twitter: @ChristiCaldwell
Or on Facebook at: Christi Caldwell Author

For first glimpse at covers, excerpts, and free bonus material, be sure to sign up for my monthly newsletter!

Printed in the USA.

Cover Design and Interior Format

Other Titles by Christi Caldwell

HEART OF A DUKE
In Need of a Duke—Prequel Novella
For Love of the Duke
More than a Duke
The Love of a Rogue
Loved by a Duke
To Love a Lord
The Heart of a Scoundrel
To Wed His Christmas Lady
To Trust a Rogue
The Lure of a Rake
To Woo a Widow
To Redeem a Rake
One Winter with a Baron
To Enchant a Wicked Duke
Beguiled by a Baron
To Tempt a Scoundrel
To Hold a Lady's Secret

THE HEART OF A SCANDAL
In Need of a Knight—Prequel Novella
Schooling the Duke
A Lady's Guide to a Gentleman's Heart
A Matchmaker for a Marquess
His Duchess for a Day
Five Days with a Duke

LORDS OF HONOR
Seduced by a Lady's Heart
Captivated by a Lady's Charm
Rescued by a Lady's Love
Tempted by a Lady's Smile
Courting Poppy Tidemore

SCANDALOUS SEASONS
Forever Betrothed, Never the Bride
Never Courted, Suddenly Wed
Always Proper, Suddenly Scandalous
Always a Rogue, Forever Her Love
A Marquess for Christmas
Once a Wallflower, at Last His Love

SINFUL BRIDES
The Rogue's Wager
The Scoundrel's Honor
The Lady's Guard
The Heiress's Deception

THE WICKED WALLFLOWERS
The Hellion
The Vixen
The Governess
The Bluestocking
The Spitfire

THE THEODOSIA SWORD
Only For His Lady
Only For Her Honor
Only For Their Love

DANBY
A Season of Hope
Winning a Lady's Heart

THE BRETHREN
The Spy Who Seduced Her
The Lady Who Loved Him
The Rogue Who Rescued Her
The Minx Who Met Her Match
The Spinster Who Saved A Scoundrel

LOST LORDS OF LONDON
In Bed with the Earl

BRETHREN OF THE LORDS
My Lady of Deception
Her Duke of Secrets

REGENCY DUETS
Rogues Rush In: Tessa Dare and Christi Caldwell
Yuletide Wishes: Grace Burrowes and Christi Caldwell
Her Christmas Rogue

STANDALONE
Fighting for His Lady

MEMOIR: NON-FICTION
Uninterrupted Joy

PROLOGUE

London, England
Spring 1829

ANDREW BARRETT, THE VISCOUNT WATERS, was suffocating.

But then, polite events hosted by respectable members of the peerage had that effect on him.

He despised betrothal balls.

In fairness, he detested all *polite* affairs.

That was why, at that particular moment, during this particular betrothal ball, he found himself in the Viscount Wessex's gardens, avoiding the crush of respectable guests, who'd all gathered to celebrate the upcoming nuptials of the viscount and viscountess's daughter, Miss Marcia Gray, in what would be the match of the Season.

One of the *ton*'s diamonds would wed an illustrious marquess with one of the oldest titles in England, a proper fellow with a commitment to his title and deep pockets. Because of that prestige and those deep pockets, he was the catch of the Season.

That's what all the *ton* was saying.

And frankly, as long as they weren't saying anything about Andrew, he should have been satisfied.

Oddly, however, a restlessness had driven him from the ballroom to the viscount and viscountess' gardens.

With a bottle of champagne in one hand, Andrew loosened his cravat with the other as he walked the length of the graveled path.

He stopped beside the watering fountain and took a long drink.

"You know, it is rude to go sneaking about someone's home and stealing their spirits."

Those words filtered from below, and a memory slipped in of the first time she'd put that charge to him. Back when she'd been a young girl, and he'd been a pup still at university, playing at adult.

Andrew glanced down at the earthen floor.

His gaze collided with a familiar stare, in a very unusual place. Those large eyes belonging to an even more familiar person. His connection to her cemented by his brother-in-law's close friendship with her father.

"Marcia Gray," he murmured.

As if it were the most natural thing in the world for a respectable young lady—the focus of the night's gathering—Marcia inclined her head and greeted him. "Andrew."

She scooched herself out from under the stone bench, grunting as she did so, until she sat before him on the ground and glared up at him. "If you were a gentleman, you'd offer me a hand."

"No one would accuse me of being a gentleman," he said, and raising the bottle to his mouth, he took a long drink.

"No, that much is true," she conceded, studying that decanter.

Following the direction of her stare, he held it out.

The lines of disapproval at the corners of her narrow mouth dipped farther as her frown deepened. "It really *is* bad form to take your host's spirits."

Andrew propped a foot on the stone bench, and resting an elbow on his knee, he leaned down. "And tell me, is it in good form to go sneaking off and hiding during one's betrothal ball?"

Just then, the thick clouds parted overhead, allowing the glow of the full moon's light to illuminate her face and reveal the deep red blush blazing across her cheeks.

"I'm not… hiding."

"Avoiding your betrothed on the night your match is formally announced hardly seems promising," he drawled. He started to add another teasing comment about her not being at the side of her future bridegroom… but stopped.

The glimmer in her eyes, troubled and sad, reached him.

Ah, damn.

"Second thoughts?"

"No!" she said quickly. "None. How could I have second thoughts about marrying Charles?"

Easy, the way Andrew saw it. Charles, as she referred to him, or the Marquess of Thornton, was outrageously fat in the pockets. Respectable in ways Andrew had never been and would never be. And an absolute bore.

Nay, Thornton could never be good enough for Marcia.

He'd just trusted she was cleverer as to have realized it.

He studied Marcia as she studied the fountain at the back of the gardens.

It wasn't his business.

He should go.

But she was a friend.

A woman whom he'd known since his early university days, back when she'd been a girl.

"Do you love him?"

"Yes," she said. "He is kind and respectable and well-read and kind—"

"You said that one already."

"And he's a devoted brother to his three sisters, and he has a stellar reputation and a wonderful sense of humor."

"*Thornton?*"

She nodded.

"As in the *Marquess* of Thornton?"

Marcia let out a sound of exasperation. "Yes, as in my betrothed."

He snorted. "This would be the first that I've heard anyone claim the fellow has a sense of humor." At least not the kind of humor that was clever enough to leave a fellow laughing.

She wrinkled her nose. "Well, he does."

"Do you know what it sounds like to me, Marcia?"

The lady hesitated and then shook her head.

"It sounds like you're trying to convince me as much as yourself that he's the love of your life."

In reality, she was too young and too innocent to know that there was no such thing as *the love of one's life*, or even love.

There was lust.

There was grand passion.

And those base desires merely tricked people, like his siblings and their spouses, and the woman before him, into believing that love was real.

Except now he wished he hadn't spoken those words as Marcia's eyes grew stricken.

Oh, bloody hell.

The last thing he could afford to do was lead the girl to break her betrothal. To do so would anger his family and hers, and there'd be questions about why she'd ended it.

With a curse, he reached down and plucked her up from the earthen floor and set her on her feet.

"I do love him, you know," she said.

"I know," he said instantly, even though he didn't know any such thing.

In fact, he didn't know a deuced thing about her relationship with Thornton, nor did he wish to.

What he wished was to drink his champagne and tup a lonely wife and, for a brief moment, sate his own loneliness.

Andrew briefly contemplated the stairs from the garden to the grand ball taking place and then looked at a motionless Marcia.

"It's just..." she began, wringing her wrinkled white lace skirts.

The white had begun to show grass stains where she'd gone crawling about that would likely be noted by guests, and as such, he could not be seen with her or near her or exiting the gardens with her or entering the ballroom anywhere close to her.

Perhaps it was their family's connection. Or perhaps it was that he'd known her since she'd been a girl, a girl who'd been just as vexing as the woman now standing before him, but he found himself asking anyway.

"It is just…?"

"We've never embraced."

Oh, bloody hell.

Grass stains on her gown and now talk of whom she'd kissed or, in this case, not kissed.

"No one's ever claimed Thornton is any sort of rogue," he volunteered helpfully.

Or rather, he'd attempted to be helpful.

"No. I know he's not a rogue." The way she'd spoken that word indicated she clearly took affront with fellows who possessed Andrew's reputation.

He bristled. "Many say rogues make the best husbands."

Marcia gave him a look. "You don't truly believe that."

"No." Absolutely, he did not. "But many do."

"Well, I'm not one of those people, Andrew."

He stole a glance upward, confirming that they were still alone and mentally sorting how he could make his escape, when she began to pace.

"I'm logical when it comes to love," she said.

"When there's nothing logical about love?" he asked, unable to help himself.

She jabbed a finger his way. "Precisely, Andrew. Which is why, when I was being readied for my betrothal ball this evening, I had a moment of panic."

"I'm sure all couples have their reservations, Marcia. I'm sure you'll be as happy as every other happily married lady in London." Who, with the apparent exceptions of his sisters and mother, appeared to be not at all happy.

"But what if we're not, Andrew?" she implored. "To make a mistake on something so important…"

This… this was decidedly not a promising union. He opened his mouth to say as much, but caught that distracted and worried glimmer in her eyes once more.

For a second time, he couldn't bring himself to muster the truest words about the likelihood of a forever happiness—because there was no such thing.

Even his mother and sisters, all in love with their spouses, had known the greatest misery on their paths to that wedded state.

"Do you know what I think?" he asked softly, and Marcia's gaze crept over to his, a hesitation in her eyes and in the little shake of her head.

"I believe if you believe in love, and if you believe you love Thornton," he said, "then ultimately, you are going to have the very happiness you seek with him, Marcia." He brought his hand up for what he intended to be a supportive, sibling-like pat of her cheek. Except his palm stilled upon her satiny soft skin, and his touch became a caress, fueled by the unexpected heat and warmth of her.

Marcia's thick golden lashes fluttered, and then she closed her eyes and leaned into his palm.

Being a woman whose family, through Andrew's brother-in-law, Edmund, the Marquess of Rutland, had a connection to Andrew, she and he invariably always landed at the same functions. He even had distant memories of Marcia as a bright-eyed girl, hiding in corners of ballrooms and parlors, watching affairs, and oftentimes, he'd thought, spying on him.

But then, she'd been a girl. Now, as he slipped his eyes over her heart-shaped face, bathed in the soft glow of the moon, he appreciated for the first time that the golden-haired girl had in fact become that Norse goddess, Sif.

Granted, an innocent goddess. And an almost married one at that.

One with a nipped waist but surprisingly generous hips and a bosom the perfect size to fit in a man's hands. Despite himself, his gaze lingered on her modest neckline and the slightly olive-hued skin belonging to a woman unafraid of the sunshine.

He found his search shifting higher, but still to a less-safe place. Her strawberry sweet mouth: crimson red, with a slightly fuller top lip than bottom, lent an alluring pout to the flesh.

Desire grew within him, and his breath grew slightly ragged.

The girl had grown up, and at nearly five or so inches shorter than his six feet three inches, he'd need to just tip his head down a fraction, and he'd have her delectable mouth under his.

Since he was a rogue, he didn't seek to deny himself the feel of her. Nay, desire stirred within, and he lowered his head, bent on tasting of her.

Smack.

He stilled as a noisy kiss landed upon his cheek.

"You are the best of friends, Andrew," Marcia said with a wide, innocent smile that reached all the way to her fathomless brown eyes that definitely did *not* glimmer with passion. "Thank you. I should return."

With a jaunty little wave, she collected her skirts and rushed back to the betrothal ball and her betrothed… and away from what would have proven to be a disastrous act on his part.

CHAPTER 1

London, England
Spring 1829

CHARLES WILL BE HERE.
He is coming.
Why wouldn't he?
He is just late.
He is always late, after all.
Granted, Marcia just hadn't expected he'd also be late—to their wedding. A wedding that was supposed to begin at ten o'clock.

Out of the corner of her eye, she caught another flash of movement as her father, Marcus Gray, Lord Wessex, the man who'd adopted her nine years earlier, stormed back and forth, frantically pacing the vestibule of St. Helena's Church.

All the while, Marcia's mother sat at the front of the dark stone church with its rows of long stained-glass windows; periodically she stole glances back at the entrance of the church.

A feeling of unease pitted in Marcia's belly.

Her four siblings chatted and squealed and giggled happily and noisily around their mother.

The normalcy of her sisters and brother at play drove back some of the discomfort of being a bride, standing at the back of a church, waiting for her bridegroom to arrive.

Waiting along with all the members of Polite Society assembled in those narrow, uncomfortable-looking pews.

Except, why… isn't he here, a voice niggled at the back of her head.

Stop it! She fought the urge to clamp her hands over her ears and tamp out the thoughts and fears that had taken shape.

Charles loved her, deeply and truly.

There was certainly… *some* justifiable reason for his delay.

Marcia forced herself to turn and steal another peek into the church at Lord Stormont, the tall, slender gentleman at the front of the church. He stood with his arms clasped behind his back and periodically looked down the long length of the aisle.

She found comfort and reassurance in that.

Because surely if Charles wasn't coming, his best friend wouldn't be standing at that altar, waiting for him to arrive.

He is coming.

Sometimes Marcia repeated those three words in her head in a clipped, firm way. Other times, she sang them silently, to try to distract herself from the discomfort of waiting.

Nonetheless, the mantra remained the same.

He is coming.

Just as she continued to believe that, a ticking clock somewhere in the hall chimed, marking the passage of fifteen minutes… and then another fifteen minutes.

There could be any number of reasons for why he was late.

Charles was responsible for four sisters, two who were out for the London Season. He was often squiring the spirited, noisy, and always endearing ladies to everything from *ton* events to ices at Gunter's.

They were notorious for arriving after the expected hour.

With a grin, he'd often lamented about that to Marcia and then had smiled in that wistful, devoted, loving-brother way that had always touched her heart and reminded her of the manner of man he was and how fortunate she was that he'd offered her marriage.

Yes, there were many reasons for why Charles hadn't yet arrived.

And she couldn't even think of one why he wouldn't come.

Her father, the man who'd raised her, abruptly stopped pacing just at her shoulder and stared in the direction of her own unblinking gaze.

"He is coming, Papa," she said tightly.

"I know," he returned with such firm conviction that she glanced over, believing him. "I'm sure there is a reason for his delay."

"*Their* delay," she corrected. Because that mattered. Surely. Charles' difficult-to-corral sisters had to be the reason behind his absence.

"Yes, yes, that makes sense. I am sure…"

As his words trailed off, Marcia followed his stare to that tiny crack in the door.

Whispers had broken out in the church, a noisy buzz like the swarm of bees that pollinated her mother's favorite lavender bush.

Marcia's palms grew moist inside her gloves, and her mouth went dry, her throat becoming even more parched.

Through the crack, she saw a servant in the livery of her future husband's family, a young footman whom she recognized from the dinner she and her family had first attended at Charles' household.

A servant, but no Charles.

Marcia trembled.

"I… am certain he has merely come to announce that Thornton is on his way," her father said.

She wanted to believe him, but wondered if he even believed that assurance or whether he'd sought to convince himself.

"Of course," she murmured and stared after him as he hastened off, slipping out of the vestibule to go meet the servant.

The servant was now speaking with Lord Stormont, who she could tell, even through the tiny slit in the door and distance between them, appeared to pale.

Her father reached the pair and said something to the men. As the footman handed him a note, Marcia looked away.

Then, Marcus released a black curse, one that made her ears go hot, and she looked through the crack in the door at the man who'd been a father to her in every way but by blood. She found his stare on her.

His cheeks had gone even more wan than Lord Stormont's.

She curled her toes sharply against the soles of her diamond-encrusted silver slippers.

She caught the sides of her white satin gown, the neckline

adorned with the same jewels that were on her footwear, and crushed the fabric, knowing she was hopelessly wrinkling her wedding dress.

Also knowing it mattered not at all, because there'd be no wedding.

This day or *any* day.

Her father returned. "Marcia," he whispered, his voice ragged. "I am so sorry. Thornton is not coming. There will be no wedding."

She'd gathered as much, but hearing her papa speak those words aloud added a realness to them that hit her like a kick to the belly, and she doubled over from the pain of it.

An agonized groan split the quiet of the vestibule. Was it hers or her father's?

Mayhap it had come from the both of them.

It was deuced confusing trying to sort through the buzzing in her ears.

Marcia raised tear-filled eyes to her father's. The crystalline sheen that hazed her vision made his face a blur. "Take me out of here, Papa," she pleaded.

"Of course," he said hoarsely, and then, like the hero of a father he'd always been, he caught her by the arm and proceeded to guide her out.

Her breathing grew more and more shallow as she at last gave life to the reality of what had happened this day.

What her betrothed had done.

The betrothed who'd loved her.

Who'd vowed to keep her safe and fill her every days with laughter and to always be the reason she smiled.

Who'd promised there wouldn't even be a need for him to wipe away her tears, because he'd allow her to know only happiness.

A strangled half laugh bubbled past her lips, and she caught the miserable sound with her hand.

She was aware of her father quickening the pace he'd set for them.

Then they were at the carriage, and he was handing her up and promising to return and shutting the door with a firm click.

At last, Marcia was alone.

She remained seated on the red velvet squabs of her parents' gleaming black carriage and stared unblinkingly at the tufted bench opposite her.

She'd taken the ride to the church in this carriage just an hour ago, though it seemed forty years ago. As the vehicle had rolled through the crowded London streets, she'd reflected on the fact that it was the last time she'd ever make a journey in her family's carriage. At least as an unwed woman. For when the ceremony concluded, she'd be handed up into another conveyance by another man.

Marcia's eyes slid shut. In the gardens on the night of her betrothal ball, she had almost kissed Andrew Barrett, the Viscount Waters.

Andrew was a notorious rake, of course, but also a gentleman, whom she'd known since her arrival in London when she'd been a small girl.

That almost kiss should have been her first clue that her marriage to the Marquess of Thornton was destined to be doomed.

Alas, it hadn't been a stolen kiss in a moonlit garden that had seen her ruined.

Nor had it been a wicked rogue with a notorious reputation.

Rather, it had happened in the halls of St. Helena's Church, with all the *ton* watching as she was jilted by an honorable, charming gentleman.

This time, as moisture dampened her cheeks, she didn't attempt to stop the flow of her tears.

What now?

CHAPTER 2

A BOTTLE OF BRANDY HAD BEEN a terrible idea.

In fact, the only good idea Andrew had had last evening was welcoming back to his townhouse the lush, warm companionship of two of London's most notorious widows.

Even so, his head raged from the tribulations of too much drink and a lack of sleep and the vigorous sex he'd enjoyed with his company.

He forced his eyes open and promptly winced as the brightness of the morning sun penetrated the fog.

Based on the brightness of those rays, it was very nearly noon… or later.

Andrew closed his eyes and let his head fall back on the pillow.

No point in forcing himself to rise. There was hardly any reason to—

He stilled.

Oh, shite.

Was he going to be late?

With a warm, naked body pressed against his side, Andrew forced his heavy eyes open again, and this time, the sun's rays glaring through the gaping curtains nearly blinded him.

By the height of the sun in the morning sky, he was indeed late.

Nonetheless, Andrew reached over the lush body pressed against his other side and fumbled around the nightstand for his timepiece.

Raising the gold watch fob, he consulted the time.

Noon.

Yes, he'd missed it.

Though he wouldn't be missed by the respective parties or their families.

His own family, however, was another matter.

"Never tell me you're looking to end our fun now." A husky voice, belonging to Lady Scarlett, his latest lover, made even huskier by desire and sleep, cut across the morning quiet.

Meanwhile, his other bed partner wrapped long, talon-like fingers around his shaft. Already sprung hard that morn, the flesh grew harder and jumped under her touch. "He wouldn't think of it," Lady Charlotte purred, squeezing him with her clever hand.

A hiss slipped out.

He'd worry about the matter of his disappointed family after he took his morning—or in this case, *noontime*—pleasure.

The thing of it was, people spoke of love, but this was the purest emotion there was—raging, hot lust.

He reached for both women.

This was all he wanted.

Knock, knock, knock.

And also what he was going to be denied that day.

The hell he was.

"Go away," he shouted.

Knock, knock, knock.

"It's me."

The annoyed announcement came from none other than Benedict Adamson, the Earl of Wakefield, a chum from his Eton and Oxford days. The two men, born to wastrel fathers, had bonded as young boys, who'd been jeered by their peers for their disreputable sires.

That, however, was where all similarities between him and Benedict ended these days.

"Tell him to go away," Lady Scarlett panted, biting down hard on the lobe of his ear.

"I'm not going away," the earl called, his voice muffled by the panel.

Andrew was a dissolute reprobate capable of a great many sexual feats. Alas, plowing a lover while his childhood chum pounded and pounded away outside his door escaped the prowess of even

Andrew.

With a curse, Andrew set each lady aside.

Both women let out sharp cries of disappointment.

"He's not going away," he said, giving them each a stroke on a breast. "We can resume our fun later this evening."

Lady Charlotte pouted. "You are assuming we'll want you," she whined, swinging her long, thin legs over the side of the bed.

Andrew hopped up onto his knees and nestled the back of her neck. "I know you will," he said silkily, suckling her flesh and earning a breathless laugh that instantly became a breathy moan.

Knock, knock, knock.

"Waters," Benedict called, an impatient warning there. "It's urgent."

With a sigh, Andrew placed a kiss on Lady Charlotte's right shoulder.

"Just a moment," he shouted at the panel and swiped up his breeches and shirt from the floor.

"Why do you bother with a bore like Wakefield?" Lady Scarlett pouted as she pulled on her gown.

"Really," his other companion intoned. "He's a dullard."

He narrowed his eyes into thin slits. "Have a care." He knew precisely what Wakefield was. He also knew that when the other boys had beaten him and mocked him for the crimes of his father, Benedict had proven a staunch ally, lining up at his shoulder and beating his detractors back.

"We've displeased you," Lady Charlotte said with some surprise in her eyes. "I thought you should agree with us. He *is* a proper bore."

"Ladies," he said when they'd finished dressing. "Thank you for the lovely time."

Andrew opened the door, and the earl, tall, bespectacled, and with not a blond hair out of place on his always sensible head, stepped aside so the ladies could pass.

A blush on his cheeks, Wakefield averted his eyes to the ceiling. "Ladies," he greeted.

Lady Charlotte paused and smoothed her palms over the front of the earl's dark sapphire wool coat. "Perhaps we might convince both of you gentlemen to enjoy—"

"Many thanks, but *no*," Benedict interrupted, his voice garbled as his gaze climbed even higher.

"That is disappointing," Lady Charlotte purred, patting his cheek and then motioning for her friend to follow her.

The moment they'd gone, Benedict shut the door.

"Benedict," Andrew called in greeting, "to what do I owe this early morning pleasure?"

"It is not morning,"

"I was speaking metaphori—"

"It is afternoon." The other man grabbed his timepiece and tapped the glass front with the tip of his respectably gloved finger. "Twenty minutes past twelve o'clock, to be exact." His friend paused to frown at the doorway the young widows had just stepped through. "I'll have you know it's bad form entertaining one's mistresses at one's family townhouse."

"It's even worse form to interrupt a friend in the middle of a good fucking," he drawled, and Benedict's color blazed several shades redder. "But here we are."

"You needn't be crude," Benedict mumbled.

"Is this why you've come?" he asked. "To lecture me on my behavior?"

"I have long since ceased to try."

"Yes, and I appreciate that you abandoned your attempts."

When they'd been around twelve or so, Benedict had proposed in the quiet of those midnight hours while the rest of their house had slept at Eton that they transform themselves. That they dedicate their efforts to becoming respectable and being men of honor.

Andrew had scoffed.

The other man had tried and succeeded in becoming everything their respective—but not respectable—fathers hadn't been.

"What is the urgent matter that merited interrupting my morning pleasure?"

"Do you mean your morning pleasure that likely was a mere continuation of your last evening's pleasure?"

Andrew grinned, and his friend rolled his eyes.

"You are late," Wakefield said.

"I don't—"

"Oh, don't give me that nonsense," Benedict interrupted. "Miss Gray."

He stared too long.

"As in Marcia. As in—"

"I know who Marcia is," he said, interrupting whatever lecture was forthcoming. "I considered going, but then didn't want to make a scene by arriving late and detracting from the happy affair and all. I intend to put in a belated appearance at the wedding breakfast."

His valet at some point had already filled the washbasin, and Andrew padded across the room.

"You were not the only one who would have been late," Benedict muttered.

Andrew paused, water sluicing through his fingers as he looked questioningly over at his friend.

"Thornton," the other man bit out.

Andrew noted something harsh in Wakefield's voice when he spoke that name… which was odd as Wakefield and Thornton were both friends and partners in a number of business investments.

"Never tell me the fellow was late to his own wedding." Marcia would have hated that. She deserved far better.

"He's late to everything," Benedict said.

"I didn't know that."

"Oh, yes."

"Hmm." Andrew would have expected punctuality to be amongst the man's many respectable—and tedious—habits. He splashed more water on his face.

Benedict beat a hand against his side, his features tense and his eyes harder than he'd ever recalled.

Andrew paused mid-rinse. "What is it?" he asked quietly when an odd heaviness settled over the room.

"He didn't arrive," Benedict bit out as Andrew resumed scrubbing the stench of women and sex from his person.

"Didn't arrive?"

His friend gave him a look. "You don't know?"

"Know what?"

Benedict crossed over and held out the paper Andrew had failed to see in his hand until now. "The papers did not waste any time in printing a"—Wakefield's lip peeled in a sneer—"special edition. It was being circulated while we all waited at the church."

Reaching for a dry towel, Andrew dried his hands and accepted the newspaper.

Scandal

One of Polite Society's most respected, most coveted young ladies is nothing more than an impostor. Everyone was well aware that...

Andrew skimmed his gaze over the front of the page. It appeared Marcia's mother, the Viscountess Wessex, had taken a lover long ago, and Marcia was a product of that relationship.

He paused, lingering his gaze a moment on the gentleman in question's identity—Lord Archibald Hamilton, *the Marquess of Atbrooke*.

His jaw tightened. The Hamilton family, from the marquess on down to his sister, Lady Carew, were vipers, and it appeared Marcia's mother, Lady Eleanor, had been just one more victim of theirs.

With a grunt, Andrew tossed the scandal sheet aside. "Atbrooke's back from his time in the penal colony." That was a shame.

"That's *it?*" Wakefield demanded. "That's all you have to say?"

"What else is there?" What the papers wrote about Marcia Gray was irrelevant. "It doesn't matter." He knew who she was as a person, and she was all that was good. Who had sired her mattered not, and whoever disparaged her could go hang.

"It matters to Polite Society." Wakefield spoke like he was a tutor schooling a young charge.

Andrew shrugged. "It doesn't matter to me, then." He dunked his head in the basin to wash his hair.

"Well, it isn't about you, Waters," the other man snapped. "It's about Marcia, and it mattered to Thornton, because he left her at the damned altar."

Andrew whipped his head back, spraying drops of water upon the other man's immaculate garments. "What?" That shocked question exploded from him.

Wakefield gave a tight nod. "He jilted her."

Andrew cursed. "Thornton can go to hell."

"Yes, and he undoubtedly will," Wakefield said. "But this is not *about* Thornton. It is about Miss Gray, and she is going to need the support of those who care about her." He gave Andrew a pointed look.

"Us?"

"Yes, us!" That exclamation came filled with annoyance. "She is going to need respectable members of Polite Society to be there, supporting her through this."

"I'm not respectable," Andrew felt inclined to point out.

"You're a viscount with a respectable title and an even more respectable family. That will do. And she values your friendship." There was a sharp quality to that statement that was gone in the other man's next breath so that Andrew suspected he'd imagined it.

"You always were the better person and friend." To Marcia. To him. To everyone. Wakefield was a bloody paragon. "But I—"

"No 'buts.' Wherever Marcia is, we need to be. Is that understood?"

At that directive and a warning look from Benedict, Andrew inclined his head. "Now, may I see to my morning dress?" he asked dryly.

"Of course."

As Wakefield let himself out, Andrew gave his head a wry shake. How naïve and innocent his friend was. He thought a showing from respectable members of the *ton* might somehow ease Marcia's hurt at Thornton's betrayal and her broken heart.

Andrew, however, was the last person who could help any lady, let alone Marcia, with that futile endeavor.

CHAPTER 3

WHEN MARCIA HAD MADE HER debut amongst the *ton*, she'd been heralded a *diamond*.

The papers had praised her as being *the* lady with whom all bachelors in the market for a wife that Season should strive to make a match.

And she'd hated it.

She'd not wanted them to see her as a potential arm prize for some man, elevated for reasons that had absolutely nothing to do with who she was as a woman.

Only, in the matter of a moment that morn, Marcia had gone from a diamond amongst Polite Society about to wed, to an object of scandal and gossip—and derision.

Shut away in her father's offices nearly two hours after she'd been left standing at the altar, the irony was not lost on her.

She wanted to turn back the clock.

She wanted to go back to the time when the *ton* had spoken only favorable words about her, before… *this*.

Seated tensely on the edge of the sofa, Marcia tangled her fingers together and squeezed her hands in a solitary, single fist. As the blood drained from her knuckles, she forced her gaze up, forced herself to look at her father.

He stood at the hearth, his hands clasped behind him. The last time she'd looked over at him, she'd found those hands shaking. Since then, he'd hidden them behind his back.

Which appeared to be what her parents excelled at—hiding things from her.

She made herself slide her gaze over to her mother.

She was paler than even her husband. Her lips appeared to have gone bloodless.

What most accounted for her mother's misery this day? The fact that Marcia's heart had been broken and her wedding called off by the bridegroom? Or rather, was it that Marcia had learned the truth about her past, and the secrets of her birthright had all come out in the papers at the very moment Marcia had been waiting for her bridegroom? Waiting in vain.

Now, she knew why. Now the whole world knew why.

Marcia stared vacantly at the folded paper on the corner of the table. Folded as the sheets were, only partial words proved visible, a kaleidoscope of black ink and partially completed sentences.

Scandal

Marcia Gray, the daughter of Lord and Lady W.

To think Society declared her…

But it did not matter. Marcia had already committed to memory each word splashed upon those scandal sheets.

Scandal

Marcia Gray, the daughter of Lord and Lady W. Or that was what they would have had you believe.

To think Society declared her an Incomparable.

The shine is certainly off this diamond, as her family's secrets and the truth of her birthright mark her as nothing more than a pasty fake.

With a rush of movement, her father stalked over and grabbed that newspaper. Wordlessly, he returned to the hearth and tossed the pages atop the logs on that grate.

The lightly burning fire immediately licked at the corners, painting them black, and they slowly curled before catching in a fiery conflagration.

As if burning them might somehow undo the truth and make all of this go away.

Her parents still hadn't learned, had they?

The truth always won out and found its place in the world, while secrets and lies were vanquished.

"Is it true?" she asked quietly when it appeared neither her father nor her mother would find the courage to speak. "Is Lord

Atbrooke... my father?"

Her mother's lips flattened into a pained-looking line. Then, slowly, she nodded. "He is."

"Why didn't you tell me?" she whispered. "Why didn't you tell me about *any* of this?" That same question had dogged her since she'd first seen her name printed in the special edition that waited for them on their arrival from the church.

If possible, her mother turned a deathly shade of white.

Her father was immediately at her mother's side. Taking a seat beside her, he caught her fingers and gave a light squeeze.

Marcia stared on at that tender touch, a loving show of support between husband and wife.

I almost had that...

Her heart shuddered and ached in her chest all over again as she grappled with what she'd lost. At what she'd been so very close to having. "I had a right to know," she said, her voice catching. Marcia pressed a fist against her breast, thumping it once. "I had a right to know," she repeated. "And not to find out from some"— she slashed that same hand in the direction of the hearth—"*gossip* column."

Husband and wife shared a look. They had an unspoken language between them, while Marcia was left sitting there, attempting to decipher the indecipherable exchange.

Then her father drew her mother's knuckles to his mouth, kissed lightly and held her fingers there a moment longer before mouthing the words, "I love you."

Her mother looked over at Marcia once more. Some color had returned to her cheeks, and the uncertainty and agony in her eyes had faded.

But then, love did that, she thought bitterly.

It made one feel one could do and be anything.

"I never told you the truth... about the man who sired you," her mother began.

Marcia firmed her mouth. "No, you haven't." Instead, she'd let Marcia believe there'd been some grand soldier who'd been the love of her mother's life, who'd gone off to fight Boney's forces, only to never return. A laugh that sounded bitter to her own ears spilled from her lips and poisoned the air. "I think we've confirmed as much this day. That is, unless you intend to say that the Marquess of Atbrooke was in fact a soldier at some point."

Her mother turned white again. Her fingers shook, and her father covered them with his other palm. "No," her mother said quietly, her voice steadier than those trembling digits. "He was never a soldier. He was a…" She paused, as if searching for proper ways to describe the man partly responsible for giving Marcia life. Suddenly, her mother straightened, and she brought her shoulders back and her chin up. "He was a scapegrace. He was the worst sort of scoundrel. A terrible cad." She spoke like one at last freed by the ability to speak freely.

At last, it made sense. Before her mother had loved her father, she'd loved a rogue.

"He seduced you," Marcia said as understanding dawned.

Her mother's lips curled inward until they formed a thin, flat line, like she was biting them on the inside. She gave a slight, tight shake of her head. "No," she finally said on a faint whisper so soft that Marcia thought for a moment she'd merely imagined it.

Marcia's brow dipped. "I don't—"

Her mother held her eyes, and something in those blue depths froze the words on her lips as the same pit of dread that had formed in her belly that morn and swelled at the church grew all the more.

"He… took advantage of me… in a different way."

Marcia wished her mother hadn't spoken. And she proved a coward in that instant, not wanting the details of that day, but forcing herself to take them in anyway. "I don't understand." She didn't wish to, because she didn't want to find out that any of this was somehow even more sordid than she'd first believed.

Her mother drew in a deep breath. "He… forced me, Marcia."

She sat there, motionless, with that admission ringing in the silence, scarcely daring to breathe or move out of fear that if she did she'd splinter into a thousand tiny fragments of absolute nothingness.

"What?" she whispered, despite knowing how very wrong it was to ask that one word, to expect her mother to repeat something so ugly, something that, by her pale features and haunted eyes, had clearly ravaged her to speak aloud.

"I—"

"Nnnnn." Marcia cut her mother off with that unintelligible utterance, the only approximation of a word she could manage in that moment. She surged to her feet and pressed her fingertips hard against her temple to blot out the words that now sat there. But no matter how firmly she dug and how much she rubbed, they remained.

Her breath came low and shallow, or was that her mother's? Perhaps it was her father's? Or mayhap, it belonged to all three of them.

"I was alone," her mother said, recounting the story of her conception. Rather, the true story of it. "Outside in the gardens during a ball. I had been… planning to meet your father." She paused, her features stricken. "That is, I was planning to meet Marcus when Lord Atbrooke came upon me. After… that night, I fled back home to Grandfather. I told him everything. He supported me and crafted a story to explain my having a fatherless child."

Those last parts of the telling came with such ease that she might as well have been recounting a remembrance from a long-ago picnic.

Had Marcia really wanted the truth? Had she really insisted her parents provide her with those details? Now, she regretted it with every fiber of her being.

She'd imagined there could be nothing worse than discovering that her life as the daughter of a young widow and a war hero had been as false as the fairy tales her mother had once read to her.

She'd been wrong.

This.

This was so much worse.

A humming filled her ears.

"No," she whispered, scrabbling at her throat before she realized what she was doing. Marcia forced her hands back to her lap.

Her real father had been no hero but, rather, a fiend who'd… raped her mother, gotten her with child.

Oh, God.

Her entire life had been conceived from ugliness.

She froze as something else her mother had revealed this day hit her.

The night she'd been attacked so viciously, she'd been intending to meet Lord Wessex, the man whom her mother had truly loved.

Instead, she'd found herself raped and carrying the child of a man she loathed. *And now they have you present every day as a reminder of what Mother suffered and what they lost together.*

Hugging her arms close, Marcia hunched over, desperately seeking to escape the pain and misery cleaving her from the inside out.

"Do not do that," her mother ordered, her voice raspy and harsh, and she stormed over with an angry rustle of skirts. She took Marcia firmly by the shoulders and gripped hard. "I love you."

"We love you," her father said quietly as he came to his feet and moved just close enough to stand at his wife's shoulder, but far enough away to not intrude on the moment between mother and daughter.

"I know," she said.

But how could she know that for sure now?

How could she be sure of anything?

How could her mother's love even be true? How, when she was the daughter of a man who'd raped her?

"That was the single worst day of my life, Marcia," her mother said, her voice catching, her eyes, so like Marcia's, reflecting the pain of remembrance. "But from something horrible came something... came *someone* so wonderful. It brought me you, and you gave me life, and you made me whole."

Tears filled Marcia's eyes, and she bit her lower lip.

Her mother's voice grew more earnest, making it impossible to believe anything other than the words she spoke. "You made me love, laugh, and smile again... and I ceased thinking of him. I ceased thinking of how you were created and only that you were *you*."

"Do you truly think I believe you've not thought of... him or that night again?" she asked, her voice hollow. "That you didn't see me and also... s-see"—her voice broke—"him?"

"No," her mother cried, gripping and releasing the sides of her dress. "That is, I did think of it, Marcia. They were… they are nightmares that, no matter how many years have passed and how many will, tangle in my thoughts and resurface. But I found my way. You gave me life. You sustained me, and I'd not have you think—"

"That I wasn't wanted?" she asked quietly.

Her mother sucked in a breath. "*Of course* you were wanted."

"By both of us," Marcus said, his voice firm and resolute. "You are not Atbrooke's daughter. You are *my* daughter. My child. You are as much my life and my world as your mother's." His throat bobbed, and a fresh wave of tears stung Marcia's eyes at the power of his profession, one she was wholly undeserving of. "I would give my life for you, Marcia, and someday, when you have a child of your own, you will understand that. You are my daughter, forever and always."

Only, that was as much a lie as every other one that predicated this moment.

Surely her mother and father knew as much.

Just like that, the bubble of illusion she'd allowed herself to catch the string of popped, and Marcia found herself landing hard back on earth with the real truth. The inescapable one.

Unable to meet her parents' eyes, wanting to escape this moment and the agony of the truths she now knew, Marcia slid her gaze over to the window, fixing her stare on a lone ray of sun that streamed through the curtains and slashed upon the hardwood floor.

Hands came down to rest upon Marcia's shoulders, long but so very delicate fingers gripping her. "You are wanted. And you are loved, Marcia. I need you to never doubt that. Ever." There was a faint entreaty in her mother's words, and Marcia reluctantly slid her stare back over to look at her mother dead-on.

"I don't doubt you love me," Marcia said softly. "Either of you." Her parents' shoulders sagged as if in relief. "I know you do." Somehow. For reasons and in ways that Marcia didn't and couldn't understand.

"Of course we do." With a sob, her mother threw her arms

around Marcia and held her close, and Marcia held her back.

All the while, Marcia stared blankly over the top of her mother's shoulder at the doorway.

How much had been taken from her mother and father. How much her mother had suffered, and what was worse, she'd had Marcia as a living, breathing, constant reminder of that evil act.

She felt her father's stare and looked to the man who'd been her father in every way but one. His eyes glittered with grief and sorrow… and love. There was that, too. Not the requisite hate she'd expect, the sentiment he and her mother were entirely deserving of.

And somewhere deep inside, surely they felt that emotion, too. Because how could they not? How, when, in this instant, with all she'd learned, she despised herself so?

At last, her mother lowered her arms, ending the embrace and stepping away.

"Do you have any… questions for me, Marcia? If you want to know anything, you need just ask. It was wrong of me to keep all of this from you."

Did she have any questions? What questions could she possibly have? The man who'd sired Marcia was a monster. Knowing that as she did, what else was there to learn?

"I know this is a lot," her mother said softly. "I know you will have other questions, and I promise you can ask me anything, and I will share everything. You were owed this long before now. I just couldn't—"

"I know, Mother," she said, quietly interrupting. And… she did. For how could she have wanted to speak of it? What woman would wish to?

Her mother looked as if she wished to say more, but couldn't figure out the words. And then she leaned over and placed a kiss upon Marcia's forehead, in the same way she'd done when she was a small girl, and her mother had been putting her to bed. "I love you."

"I love you, too," she said automatically.

Her father kissed her forehead in a way that matched his wife's, in the same way he always had, too, as if he were her real father.

But he wasn't.

Her father was a monster.

And it was his blood that she shared.

She fought to keep her features even and her breathing steady, not wishing for them to hear it was not. Wanting to be alone.

Needing to be alone.

And then, mercifully, they both left.

The moment they'd gone and closed the door behind them, she stood for a long while.

Or mayhap she stood for mere seconds. Time had ceased to mean anything.

She doubled over and fought for breath, sucking in great, heaving gasps of air. Trying to fill her lungs and exhale. Suddenly, the task of breathing proved impossible.

She'd believed that learning she was in fact a bastard and Charles breaking off their wedding while she'd been waiting at the church to be the worst kind of agony.

Only to discover how very wrong she'd been.

In her mind, she saw the man who'd sired her violently forcing himself upon her mother.

She squeezed her eyes tightly shut and moaned, fighting that vision as much as fighting the truth of her existence.

She wanted neither.

A light knock sounded at the door, and she wrenched up so fast, the muscles of her neck screamed in agony. Her heart pounding, she rubbed at the aching muscles. "Yes," she called, her voice so very steady. How *was* it so steady?

The panel opened.

Her sisters and brothers—Maisie, Flora, Lionel, and Clarion—hovered in the entryway, each of them in possession of the same flaxen curls as she, Mama, and Papa had.

Only, they were four children who'd been conceived in love. They were not a black stain upon the happiness Marcia's mother and father had known.

Six, seven, eight, and nine, they were near in age to her own when she'd first come to London, back when she'd known only the lie and had believed wholeheartedly, as only an innocent child might, that the man who'd sired her had been a hero, and he'd loved her mother as much as she had loved him.

To be that innocent again.

"Hullo, little ones," she said softly when the always precocious lot proved remarkably silent and subdued.

It was the first time she could recall any of them being so still and so quiet.

The sound of her voice seemed to penetrate whatever stupor had befallen them.

After they entered the room, with one of her brothers closing the door behind them, they joined her.

Flora cleared her throat. "We have come to speak with you about something."

Maisie nodded.

Marcia stiffened. Had they been listening at the door? Her pulse raced, and bile stung her throat as her thoughts grew twisted and—

"We are going to kill him," her sister said with a remarkable calm for such bloodthirsty words.

Oh, God.

Marcia's heart pounded all the harder.

They knew. They knew the truth. All of it. All the worst and ugliest parts.

Clasping his hands behind him, Lionel jutted his small chest out. "Happy to do it. After all, a blighter who'd jilt you deserves a good killing."

"I have to do it," Clarion said. "I'm the eldest brother."

Flora gave an emphatic nod. "We're all going to shoot him. But I'm going to do it first, because I'm the better shot."

Lionel frowned. "Hey." And as her brothers and sisters launched into a debate about who would have the honor of killing Charles, it hit her. Her younger siblings weren't speaking of the horrors their mother had shared a short while ago, or the words in the newspapers but, rather, the scandal of Marcia being jilted at the altar.

A relief so heady filled her that it left her nearly dizzy. She composed her features in a suitably solemn mask for their offering and cleared her throat to be heard over the din of their quarreling.

"I said ahem." That managed to break up their argument, and her brothers and sisters went silent. Marcia inclined her head. "I am most grateful for your offer. However, I would ask that you not."

"Because you think I'm not a good shot?" Flora demanded, folding her arms mutinously.

If she had been capable of smiling, her sister's annoyance at having her shooting skills questioned would have been the moment.

"Oh, just the opposite. I don't think for a moment you—"

"Hey."

"Or you," Marcia added over Lionel and Clarion's matching interruption, "wouldn't be capable of felling him on any dueling field." She shook her head. "But I don't want that."

"Because you still love him?" Maisie asked hesitantly.

Did she still love Charles?

She stared wistfully at the seat where he'd gotten down on a knee and asked her to marry him after he'd spoken to her father. She thought of how he'd tangled his fingers with hers and raised them to his lips and then pulled out from behind his back a bouquet of the biggest, most gloriously bright hothouse flowers. As big as they'd been, she'd not known how she could have failed to see them behind his back.

But then, that was because he'd been all that she'd been able to see.

Flora tugged her hand lightly, bringing her back from her musings about a simpler time.

"I don't know," Marcia finally said, giving them the first true words she could that day. "Now, run along and practice your swordplay," she urged, knowing precisely how they loved spending their time and how to get them off and thinking about something other than their elder sister's humiliation.

As they went scurrying off, she remained there, haunted by just one question:

What now?

CHAPTER 4

ANDREW INTENDED TO SPEND THIS particular night as he did so many other nights—at his clubs.

Whistling a merry tavern ditty, Andrew danced sideways down the stairs with a jaunty, jig-like step.

His butler, Thomaston, stood at the foot of the steps, his features creased with their perpetual lines of worry.

"Thomaston, my good man," Andrew called down. The fellow, who was the son of his late father's butler, had proven to be just as loyal and just as good as the one who'd preceded him. So good that Andrew could never sort out why he'd not found higher-paying work in a more respectable household. "Readied my carriage, have you?"

"Yes, my lord. I've seen to it."

"Ah, you are worth your weight in gold, my good man." Waiting as he was to see Andrew off.

"Thank you, my lord," Thomaston said when Andrew reached the foyer. The butler then cleared his throat. "However…"

Oh, bloody hell.

Warning bells chimed.

"Company arrived for you. I took the liberty of showing him to your office."

Him.

Usually, a pair arrived—a pockmarked fellow and a taller, even tougher-looking brute.

He stilled.

He'd prefer good, respectable creditors to the manner of men who held his vowels.

"Lord Rutland awaits."

Lord Rutland, though his swell of relief quickly receded. Lord Rutland almost always paid a visit only when Andrew was in trouble.

His brother-in-law inspired only slightly less terror than the men often sent to *discuss* Andrew's debt. And only because Andrew knew the marquess loved Phoebe so hopelessly and so desperately that he'd not off Andrew—no matter how much he wished to do so.

"*Ahem.*" Thomaston again made a throat-clearing noise.

"How does he look?" Andrew ventured.

"His usual way, my lord."

As in menacing. As in snarling and growling. As in Andrew was in deep shite.

Andrew stared at the front doors, briefly contemplating escape. Very briefly. He knew better, however, than to further raise the ire of the notorious and ruthless Lord Rutland.

Cursing quietly, Andrew shifted course and headed for his office. The moment he reached his rooms, he paused long enough to muster a sense of unaffectedness, donned a grin, and drew the door open.

"Brother-in-law," he called jovially.

Seated not at the front of the desk but, rather, behind it as though he were in fact the master of this domain, the Marquess of Rutland steepled his fingers and leaned back in Andrew's chair.

"You're expected at Lord and Lady Wessex's," Rutland said without preamble.

Leave it to Rutland to get to the heart of it. "Let me ask you this." Walking to the drink cart, Andrew began pouring himself a glass. "You had quite the reputation before marrying my sister. Visiting the same clubs and haunts I enjoy now." He held the snifter out to his brother-in-law, who narrowed his eyes, but otherwise gave no indication of interest in that offering. Oh, well. More for Andrew.

"But I wasn't a wastrel," Rutland said bluntly, his graveled voice dripping with disapproval and disgust.

Two sentiments Andrew was quite familiar with from any

number of people.

"No, you were just a scoundrel." He flashed a half grin. "Fair enough."

"Do you treat anything with any real seriousness, Andrew?" his brother-in-law asked, and his usual icy tone would have been preferable to this quiet condemnation.

And here Andrew had believed he'd ceased caring what others thought of him.

Andrew's patience snapped. "Do you truly believe my being around Marcia Gray will somehow *help* the lady's reputation?"

"I'm not talking about Miss Gray," Rutland murmured.

"Then what are you—?"

"I'm talking about your life in general, Andrew," Rutland cut in. "You're still drinking and wagering and whoring like you did when I first met you, and it's time that you think about someone *other* than yourself." With that, his brother-in-law stood. "You've missed the past two events the lady has attended. I expect you, at the very least, to be at her family's ball this evening." His wasn't a request but, rather, an order, and without so much as a curt goodbye, he left.

After he'd gone, Andrew shook his head. "Lovely talk," he muttered. Grimacing, Andrew sat in his office chair and slowly sipped his brandy, welcoming the warmth it provided.

His peace proved short-lived.

A new set of footfalls sounded outside.

Bloody hell. What now?

Thomaston knocked and ducked his head inside. "You have additional company."

"Who now?" Andrew exclaimed, tossing his hands up. "My mother? My stepfather? *Huntly?*"

Two men appeared at Thomaston's shoulder, both of them some six inches taller than the butler's five feet eight inches.

And Andrew was proven wrong. He did prefer Rutland's company... to this.

Bloody, bloody hell.

"Mr. Creed and Mr. Tavish, my lord." There was an apology in his butler's eyes. "I insisted you were not receiving visitors, but they insisted you would see them."

Behind him, Creed cracked his knuckles, and Andrew's gut churned. He'd put his skills against any gentleman in the fighting ring. But neither was he so arrogant to believe street fighters from East London played fair.

"That will be all, Thomaston," he said. The moment the other man had seen himself out and drawn the door shut behind the pair, Andrew jumped up. "My good friends," he called in warm greeting to the scowling pair, "to what do I owe—"

"We ain't yer good friends," Creed growled.

Andrew touched a hand to his heart. "Now, I'm deeply wounded. With all the years between us?" Since Andrew's Oxford days, to be precise. That had been the moment he'd begun seriously wagering… and losing. And occasionally winning big. That was what kept him in the game and why they'd tolerated him as long as they had.

The pair strolled over, and he tensed when they stopped directly in front of his desk.

"Good friends don't let their friends go unpaid," Tavish pointed out.

"Ah," Andrew said, lifting a finger. "But I never claimed DuMond was a chum," he said, referencing the owner of Forbidden Pleasures. "We, on the other hand"—he gestured between himself and the pair—"share a history." It wasn't untrue. How many times had he invited them to join him for brandy in his offices? Andrew headed over to his well-stocked drink cart and reached for a bottle of whiskey and three tumblers.

"We ain't 'ere for drinks," Creed growled.

Andrew had been convinced, as long as he'd known the man, that the fellow had come growling into the world instead of crying.

"Ah," Andrew said as he stopped before them. "But that doesn't mean we can't share one since you are here."

They exchanged a look and then settled themselves into the winged chairs opposite him.

"Yer luck's been even worse than usual, Waters," Tavish said as Andrew splashed several fingerfuls into first one glass and then the other.

That was how he'd gotten on with these men who inspired terror in all, including Andrew, through the years. He treated them as social equals, which he expected was a good deal different than the usual calls they paid.

Andrew snorted. "You don't have to tell me, my good man." The tables had never been kind, but the occasional hand that smiled kept him coming back, looking for that next big hit. He handed each man a glass and then poured himself one. "To my luck turning."

"I'll toast that." Tavish lifted his glass and touched it to Andrew's. "I don't want to break your legs."

Andrew grimaced as he drank. "Trust me," he said after he'd swallowed down that long sip. "I don't want to have my legs broken. How long do I have?" He looked between them.

Creed and Tavish shared another look.

"A sennight," Tavish finally said. "Mayhap."

A sennight.

And then what?

Lord knew Andrew couldn't count on his brother-in-law to bail him out. Not again. Not after all the times he'd done so before.

"Mayhap your luck is changing this night," Creed grunted, as if uttering more than a syllable had physically pained him.

"Alas, I'm afraid if it is; it'll have to wait until later this evening," Andrew muttered.

"Oh?"

Andrew inclined his head. "I have to put in my visit to the respectable sorts first." He paused. "My brother-in-law."

"Ohhhh." Both men gave matching murmurs of understanding.

For all knew Rutland.

Rutland had only ever won at the tables, whereas Andrew and most other men were big losers. Rutland had never been indebted to anyone, but had held the debt of most, including Andrew's late father.

"You can find yourself a fancy wife," Tavish put in, and then both men promptly laughed.

Andrew joined in, appreciating that brief spot of amusement. He wasn't above an emotionless entanglement if it meant a big purse and some woman who was content with a title and no fancy illusion of love and romance. No respectable lady, however, with the dowry the size of which he needed would waste her name and future on him. Not that he could or would ever blame her.

"Yes, well, there is always that option," he said. Shaking his head, he followed his pronouncement with a mouthed, "No, there's not."

The hulking pair erupted with amusement once more.

But then the pair stopped, and gone was all hint of affability. In its place were the menacing threats they really were.

Creed set his glass down hard on the edge of Andrew's desk and then dropped his palms on either side of the tumbler and leaned forward. "DuMond's been patient, and he's not going to be any longer. He wants you to know that."

Yes, DuMond had been. But the owner of a gaming hell was only patient when funds were occasionally coming in, not when they were *never* coming in.

And there could be no doubting that Andrew had been on a long run of losing.

"Are we clear?" Tavish growled.

He inclined his head. "Abundantly so."

Andrew was going to have to come up with some serious coin—and fast.

Or his life was likely forfeit.

CHAPTER 5

Over the years, Andrew had found himself facing any number of disapproving individuals.

He'd enraged any number of lovers when he'd broken off their relationships.

And, of course, he'd made cuckolds of even more neglectful husbands.

So being the recipient of all manner of annoyances and anger was not an unfamiliar way to find himself, even where his family was concerned.

Seeing them lined up alongside their respective spouses in a row, all frowning with disapproval, however, was.

As he descended the steps of Lord and Lady Wessex's crowded ballroom, he briefly considered the exit behind him and then the group gathered below.

His elder sister, Phoebe, the Marchioness of Rutland, glared at him. "Do not even think of it," she mouthed so perfectly that no audible sounds were necessary for him to understand her.

Throughout his life, Andrew had been threatened with duels and employed his skills from Gentleman Jackson to defend himself from sometimes bigger and stronger men.

None of that was anything when compared to the furious party waiting for him.

Forcing a grin, he tossed his arms wide as he approached that same lot who'd ordered him to stand in support of Marcia at these dull affairs. "Hello to my dear fam—"

"You are late." His brother-in-law Rutland's growl cut through the din of the ballroom as Andrew at last reached them.

"Ah, yes, but crush that it is, I daresay my appearance—"

"Or lack thereof," his sister Justina put in with an annoyed mutter.

"Or lack thereof"—Andrew pointed a finger her way in agreement—"was noted."

Justina rolled her eyes.

"*Ahem.*" He looked to his mother, who had her arms folded, and managed a sheepish grin.

"Mother!" Andrew dropped a kiss upon her cheek. "How very good it always is to see you, and it's unexpected, as I thought you were set to leave." With that, he swept her up and whirled her about, earning a small laugh. His mother often traveled to the Cook Islands, as his sister Phoebe did with Rutland, so it oft seemed Andrew was the lone member of the Barretts who never went anywhere.

"We were set to go," his mother said when he'd set her on her feet. "We still are. Nathaniel and I, however, decided it would be best to remain behind awhile…"

Following Thornton's public shaming of Marcia.

"Nathaniel," Andrew greeted his stepfather, an older, kinder, more honorable gentleman than the lady's previous husband, Andrew's sire.

"I should also add *we* noted your absence," Phoebe said, this time in gentler tones.

"Ah, but it's not really an absence," he said, giving a light wag of his eyebrows. "It was merely a tardy arrival, eh? Furthermore, why does it matter so much if I'm—"

"It matters," Rutland growled, and Andrew swallowed noisily.

Egad, as a young man in university, Andrew had been equally awed and terrified of the dark, menacing marquess, a man with the blackest reputation in London. That hadn't changed. Well, with the exception of the black reputation.

"Ah, this again," he said, shifting his attention around the room.

"Yes, this," Phoebe chided, tapping him on the arm with her delicate wood fan. "We agreed that a show of solidarity is important."

A show of solidarity?

"When did we agree to this?" And for whatever reason did they need to put on that show?

"We didn't. You were otherwise occupied and failed to attend the family meeting. As such, we sent word round."

Ah, yes. Of course.

Understanding dawned in Phoebe's eyes. "You didn't read it."

Andrew put on a good show of indignation. "I'm here, am I not?"

"Probably because Edmund sent round another note this evening ordering you to be here."

"Ah, but Rutland wouldn't go about ordering me to join him," Andrew said, tossing an arm jovially around his brother-in-law. "Isn't that—"

"I would and I did. And, it wasn't a note, which you know."

Swallowing nervously, Andrew drew his hand back. "Er… right." He did a sweep of the ballroom, searching for the top of Marcia's head. His gaze landed on her parents. Both looked wan.

"Is she even here?" he asked.

"She is," Justina piped in. She paused. "Or she has been." Her eyes softened. "The poor dear."

The poor dear.

This pitying her again.

"Thornton did her a deuced favor," he muttered.

His sisters collectively gasped, slapping palms over their mouths and glaring at him over the tops of their hands.

"What?" he protested over their indignation. "He did. The fellow is a stodgy bore and a mama's boy at that." A servant approached, and Andrew plucked a glass of champagne from the liveried fellow's silver tray and downed a quick sip. "Miss Gray would have always been too much for him," he continued when the footman had walked off, "and is better off without him." Andrew toasted the truth of that statement and, in one steady swallow, drank what remained in his glass.

Phoebe gave him a peculiar look.

"Yes, well, that's hardly here nor there," their mother said quietly. "What matters is that it did happen. And it is not just about her having been left at the altar. There's the gossip about her parentage. The girl needs all of the friends and support she might find. So you will dance with her, and you will smile and stand by our side and her family's as they weather this."

Andrew would maintain with his dying breath that the only atrocity would have been had the lady found herself locked arm in arm with Thornton for the remainder of her days. This time, however, Andrew was wise enough to keep his mouth shut. He inclined his head. "My mission is clear," he said with a nod to his stepfather, a minister at the Home Office.

At his poor quip, his sisters groaned.

Rutland dropped another arm around his shoulders and squeezed hard enough to earn a wince and slight yelp from Andrew. "Not really the time for jesting, is it."

It hadn't been a question. Not really. It had been another of Rutland's familiar warning growls.

The man was deuced loyal and had a friendship with the Viscount Wessex that went back some years, the origins of which no one—certainly not Andrew—knew or understood.

Swallowing once more, Andrew nodded. "Of course."

Rutland lightened his grip and then thumped him hard between the shoulder blades.

The music came to a stop, and as the dancers streamed from the dance floor, and a new set of partners took their places, Andrew's family left.

Yes, he was here. He'd shown up at yet another polite affair, as he only ever did when pressed to be there for Marcia. Their families were closely entwined, but it was really his friendship that brought him here.

Andrew did a sweep, desperate for another drink. These events had that effect on a disreputable chap.

His gaze landed on a servant with a silver tray aloft, and Andrew started in his direction.

Nearly there.

A figure stepped into his path, cutting off his pursuit.

"At last," Wakefield exclaimed, exasperation rich in his tone.

"You, too?" Alas, it appeared another drink was not to be this night. Andrew stared wistfully at the servant now scurrying off in the opposite direction, handing out flutes to other more fortunate fellows. "I didn't know my presence was sought by so many."

"It's for her," Wakefield said tightly. "It is important that we show support for the young lady."

"You mean Marcia?"

His friend went ruddy in the cheeks, and he stole a glance about. "It's hardly proper to use her Christian name," he whispered.

Andrew eyed him. "Normally, I'd concur, but this is the same girl who insisted on baiting our hooks because she was better at spearing worms." This was Marcia.

"Well, she isn't a girl, Waters," Wakefield said, sounding about as close to exasperated as Andrew had ever heard the usually measured man. "She's a young lady whose name is now being dragged through the mud, and she is in desperate need of—"

"Friends?" Andrew drawled, lifting an eyebrow.

His friend nodded. "Yes, friends."

"I'd be remiss if I didn't point out that friends generally use one another's Christian names and don't go about referring to one another as 'ladies' or 'gentlemen.'"

"Waters," the other man said, his voice strained.

"Oh fine." He was always the more focused of the pair. "And I'm here, aren't I?" Andrew looked about for the young woman at the heart of their uncharacteristic debate. "Where—"

"She is missing."

When Andrew didn't immediately respond, Wakefield's brows dipped. "Did you hear me? I said Miss Gray has gone missing."

"Smart girl," Andrew said under his breath, and the earl either opted to ignore him or pretend he'd not spoken.

"Someone should check on her"—so that was what this was about—"to see if she's all right, and I—"

"I'll do it," Andrew said with a sigh. Tugging his gloves off, he stuffed those articles into his jacket.

His friend cocked his head. "*You* will?"

What the hell was that supposed to mean? Andrew bristled. After all, he knew better than anyone where to find the lady when she was hiding. "I assure you I'm quite capable, ol' friend."

Nor was he being entirely altruistic. There was the matter of stealing some freedom from the stuffy crowd he found himself amongst.

Leaving a stunned Wakefield behind, Andrew went in search of Marcia.

Everyone was staring.

Or they had been.

When Marcia had been standing with her parents flanking her in the middle of the ballroom, all pitying eyes had been turned towards her.

The jilted bride.

The bastard daughter.

The humiliated, brokenhearted, no longer betrothed.

The unworthy.

What would they say if they knew the real truth about her?

The unwanted.

The spawn of a devil, a daughter who was and would forever be a constant reminder of the night her mother had been assaulted.

Seated in front of the fireplace in her father's office now, Marcia shivered, chilled from the inside out. The fire did little to fend off a shaking that had nothing to do with any real cold, that instead came from a self-loathing so potent, so powerful, it threatened to consume her—and she feared it one day would.

After all, how did one reconcile the hideousness of the person who, in a violent act, had cleaved himself to her and Marcia's mother, a reprehensible act that served as the very basis for Marcia's very existence?

She buried her face against her skirts, the satin rustling noisily, and drew in a deep breath.

The light tread of footfalls in the corridor reached her, faint but still noisy whispers, and familiar. They grew increasingly louder until the moment they stopped outside her father's offices.

Marcia hugged her arms around her knees and tried to make herself as small as possible, trying to will the person to leave, wanting to be alone. Not wanting to talk to anyone.

Alas, she was to be denied yet again anything of which she wished.

The door handle jiggled.

"Locked," one of the young women said loudly.

"Obviously, it is locked." There came another faint rattle. "We know you're in there, Marcia. Open up. We won't be turned away."

"No," the other young woman piped in. "If you don't, we shall leave the townhouse, climb our way up the ivy, and come in through the window. I haven't climbed trees in many, many years, but I will do so this evening. For you."

By the dogged determination in that announcement, Marcia knew the other woman meant business. Such was the way when one found oneself lucky enough to have devoted best friends, as she had.

With a sigh, Marcia hastily pushed the bottle of champagne she'd snuck and her barely sipped-from glass under the sofa.

Rap, rap, rap.

"I'm coming," she mumbled. "I'm coming."

"What did she say?" one of the ladies whispered. "She's running?" The young woman didn't wait for a response, but raised her already slightly elevated voice. "We shall run after you, then, and find you. I'm quite a good runner. I am—"

"She didn't say 'run.' She said—"

Marcia opened the doors.

"She's coming."

Miss Faith Brookfield, daughter of the Marquess of Guilford, beamed. "She's not coming. She's here!" As if she feared Marcia might change her mind, shut the door, and lock it once more, Faith hastened into the room.

Anwen, sister of the Viscount St. James, gave Marcia a look and, with a smile, shook her head.

With hearing loss in one ear, Faith often misheard or failed to hear certain words when they were spoken.

"May I?" Anwen asked Marcia.

"Of course you may," Faith called over with the confidence and assuredness only a best friend could. "Come in, come in."

Marcia stepped aside and let her other friend enter before closing the door behind them.

Marcia and Faith had been friends since they'd been small girls, and it hadn't been long before that same depth of friendship had extended to Anwen, a young lady whom they'd met during their Come Out.

"We have been looking for you," Faith said softly, and Anwen took up a place at the other woman's shoulder.

Ah, this.

Marcia tensed and kept her features even.

This was what she'd come to expect and despise.

It was even now the reason why she'd closeted herself away during her parents' Help Marcia Save Face Ball, as she'd coined it. All so that days after being left standing at the altar, so they might show the world Marcia was unaffected by Charles's defection. But she *was* affected.

And she also knew her absence would be remarked upon and would fuel only more whispers and gossip. Even with that, even knowing her every action would be scrutinized, she'd run away and hid herself.

From the looks.

The hesitancy.

The pity.

And when it came from her family and dearest friends… well, there was nothing worse.

"I'm fine," she assured the pair of ladies, who were more silent now than she remembered them ever being.

But then, no one knew how to speak to her these days.

Her friends exchanged a look. "How could you be?" Anwen whispered and then promptly grunted when Faith tossed a less-than-discreet elbow into her side. "What was that for?" she asked with a glare.

"As if she needs a reminder, Anwen." Faith returned her attention to Marcia. "How are you?"

"I told you, I'm fine." Splendid. Elated. Overjoyed. What did the world expect her to be? They all knew. As such, why did they insist on asking her to put her feelings into words?

"I suspect that is a lie, but we have come to help," Faith declared.

Help?

Marcia resisted the urge to groan. "I do not need—"

"Shh," Anwen urged, touching a silencing finger against her lips. "Now, if you would…" She gestured with that same finger at the leather button sofa that hid Marcia's champagne.

Marcia hesitated too long.

Faith took Marcia by the arm and steered her across the room. Gripping her by the shoulders, she guided her gently onto the floor. "Sit."

She grunted and stared questioningly up at the two women assembled before her, their features serious.

Leaning down, Faith whispered something into Anwen's ear, part of which Marcia made out as, "… the door."

Hurrying across the room, Anwen turned the lock and then rushed back.

Despite herself, as both women seated themselves on the floor beside her, Marcia found herself suddenly intrigued. "What—?"

"Shh," Faith ordered, compelling Marcia to silence.

"Show her," Anwen urged excitedly.

"Show me what?" Marcia asked, exasperated.

Faith reached inside the clever pocket found along the front of her gown, and drawing something out, she stretched her hand slowly out to Marcia.

Marcia leaned over the other woman's palm as Faith unfurled her fingers and revealed…

She puzzled her brow. "It is a necklace."

"Oh, this is no ordinary necklace," Anwen murmured excitedly.

"No?" Marcia studied the gold piece, adorned with rubies, more closely. It was pretty but not remarkable, at least not in the way of the diamonds and baubles that adorned the necks of powerful ladies.

"Tell her," Anwen urged.

"It is…" Faith began, pausing for dramatic effect, "the Heart of a Duke."

Marcia scrunched her brow even more, assessing it more closely. "A… duke's heart?"

"Not a *real* duke's heart," Faith exclaimed, her voice rich with exasperation. "It is said that the wearer of it will win the heart of her one true love."

She couldn't help the snort that escaped. What a load of rubbish.

"Hey now," Anwen chided.

"Forgive me." Marcia bowed her head. But her friends hadn't had their hearts broken. Their lives weren't steeped in sin and ugliness. They still believed in things like happily ever afters and in finding one's true love.

"Anwen," Faith said in a warning way to their friend.

Suddenly, even her best friends' company was too much. "I cannot thank you enough for the gift," she said softly. "My parents have fireworks planned for this evening. They are not to be missed."

Anwen's eyes lit up. "Splendid!"

Both women stood and went to the door.

Faith paused, looking back at Marcia. "Aren't you coming?" Concern filled the other woman's eyes.

"I will," she promised. "Shortly. Go along without me."

Her friends hesitated, but then, with a nod, they rushed from the room.

The moment the door had closed, Marcia's shoulders sagged as she welcomed the hum of silence.

That moment, however, also proved fleeting.

Another set of footfalls sounded outside the room. This time, the tread was slightly heavier, more determined, and not the hesitant, delicate ones of her friends.

Oh, blast.

Her father.

Would her parents not just leave her alone?

Marcia hurriedly lowered herself to the floor, and with the fire in the hearth crackling behind her, she looked towards the entrance of the room. Positioned as she was, with the sofa shielding her from view, she squinted to get a glimpse of this latest interloper.

Click.

A moment later, the person on the other side of that panel let himself in, and then came the muttering in a voice that *was* familiar, but it decidedly did not belong to the man who'd been a father to her these past years.

Carefully pushing herself up, Marcia peeked over the edge of the sofa and looked at the man who'd invaded her father's offices.

Several inches past six feet, and possessed of chiseled cheeks devoid of the facial hair favored by dandies, and Viking gold hair that brushed his shoulders, she'd recognize the gentleman anywhere.

Dressed in a midnight-black jacket and a pair of matching black trousers, with the only white on his body his perfectly tied snowy-white cravat, he could have been a nighttime pickpocket.

As he snooped around her father's desk, moving methodically and determinedly, it occurred to Marcia that she wasn't entirely off the mark in her assessment of him being a nighttime thief of sorts.

Quitting his spot at the sideboard, Andrew seated himself at the edge of the throne-like leather chair behind her father's desk.

He proceeded to tug out drawer after drawer, rustling through each and then closing it with a click when his search turned up empty.

And as he did, Marcia observed him unnoticed.

Coming to his feet, Andrew dropped his hands on his narrow hips and did a circular sweep of the space. "Where in blazes is it?"

It was so very reminiscent of a time long ago—when she'd been a girl, and he'd been a young man on a similar hunt—and if she'd still been capable of smiling, this would have been a moment for it.

How much simpler those times had been. Back when she'd believed the lies about her parents and believed her life to be different… than what it was.

"You won't find any," she called over, and Andrew turned slowly. Marcia reclaimed her seat upon the floor and looked back towards the dancing flames.

Andrew hesitated. "Hullo."

She felt in his words, or rather, in that single word, a reluctant greeting.

The notoriously jovial, boisterous Viscount Waters had suddenly gone quiet, without his normal free fall of charming words and jests… or anything at all.

Alas, such was the way all behaved around her now.

"Hullo," she returned.

There was more of that interminable hesitancy, and Andrew cleared his throat loudly. "Shouldn't you be at the ball?"

"Shouldn't *you*?" she shot back.

"Fair enough," he allowed, and she braced... waited and prayed for him to leave.

Though he wasn't incorrect in his questioning. For Marcia *should* be there. That was, after all, the entire purpose of this evening. Because her family had decided it was best for them to put on a brave show, to show the world that they were unashamed and that her family and their friends were proud of Marcia, and that, for all the words that had been written and truths revealed, they had the support of many.

At least that was what she'd been able to make out of the muffled discourse amongst her parents; her godparents, the Duke and Duchess of Crawford; and the most unlikely of her father's friends, the menacing figure of the Marquess of Rutland, along with his wife, Lady Phoebe, a couple whose relationship she'd never been able to quite make sense of.

Grimacing at that reminder of all she'd heard discussed between her parents' most powerful friends, Marcia raised her glass of spirits to her lips and took a sip of the warm, bubbly brew she'd been drinking before her friends had arrived with that silly bauble.

This was the first time she'd ever had the stuff.

At all prior engagements, she'd always been forced to partake in too warm lemonade and ratafia.

What other wonderful things were they keeping from ladies?

The floorboards groaned slightly, indicating Andrew had moved.

She looked up to find him towering over her.

He nudged his chin at the spot beside Marcia. "May I join you?"

She narrowed her eyes. "Did *they* send you?"

They as in her parents and his family members.

"Here or to the ball?"

"Either."

"The latter," he allowed with an honesty that made her lips twitch, the most she'd managed to smile in so many days now. "But I've come here"—Andrew pointed down at the floor—"of my own volition." His gaze slid to her bottle of champagne, and she followed his stare.

Marcia winged an eyebrow up. "Looking for any spirits?"

He grinned. "Indeed."

"You'll find plenty of champagne in the actual ball." *Please, just go.* She didn't want any more company. Not even jovial, affable Andrew Barrett.

Andrew who'd gone uncharacteristically solemn. He swept a hand towards the floor and asked again, "May I?"

Marcia shrugged and went back to watching the dancing flames.

The last thing she wished for was company.

Anyone's company.

Alas, he settled onto the floor beside her. Drawing his knees up to his chest, he looped his arms around them. "Hiding?"

"Avoiding the crowd," she amended.

"Not that I can blame you," he muttered, and she stiffened. "I'm doing the same."

He was…?

And then it occurred to her. Marcia whipped her gaze over to find his trained contemplatively on the fireplace. He wasn't speaking about the scandal surrounding her name and her wedding day. He was merely speaking about avoiding the crush of guests.

Except…

It wasn't at all the same.

"Charles broke it off with me," she said. It was the first time she'd *spoken* that truth aloud.

"Yes, I heard the news. If I had a glass, I'd toast you." He looked pointedly at the flute she held.

Ignoring that unspoken request, Marcia wrinkled her brow. "Toast me?"

"For avoiding being leg-shackled to that one." He scoffed. "That prig would have made you miserable. I'd say the misery of a little scandal is a small price to pay to avoid a lifetime of misery." With that, he picked up the bottle of champagne, lifted it as if in a little toast, touching the edge of the bottle to her glass.

Crystal clinked against glass.

She stared bemusedly as Andrew proceeded to drink from the

bottle.

But then she frowned when he continued drinking. "Hey now," she scolded. "Do save some." Reaching over, she grabbed her libations back.

He frowned as well. "Hey now, indeed."

Marcia refilled her glass. "And I don't need you attempting to make me feel better," she muttered and then began to recite every last word she'd had thrown her way by pitying family members and friends: "'He wouldn't have made you happy.'"

"Oh, that is a certainty," he said, helping himself once more to her bottle.

"'There was always something off about him.'"

"You know, I was recently saying as much myself," Andrew murmured. He apparently had no idea that she was reciting a list and not speaking for herself.

"'You were too good for him.'"

"Well, you are," Andrew said it so quietly, so simply, she paused. His words penetrated her frustration, and a warmth flared in her chest, in a place very near to her heart.

"This isn't what *I'm* saying," she explained. "This is what everyone keeps saying to me."

He pointed with the bottle, wagging it in her direction. "Listen to the everyones. They know."

They knew?

Who knew anything anymore?

Certainly not Marcia.

"You dropped your necklace," he remarked.

She stared dumbly at him.

Andrew pointed, and she followed that gesture to the spot at her feet.

"No," she said on a rush. "It's just—"

Except he was already reaching out, and in one smooth motion, he looped that chain about her neck. The fire having warmed it, the metal proved surprisingly hot as it fell against her skin.

Her fingers immediately came up to touch the heart pendant that rested there. A silly bauble that her friends had insisted would bring her true love.

"There," Andrew murmured, his mouth near the lobe of her ear. His breath was a soft sough upon her skin that sent the most exciting little shivers traipsing, tickling, and teasing over her skin, pulling a breathy but soundless laugh from her.

Did she imagine the hesitancy as he drew his fingers back, as though she wasn't the only one who'd enjoyed a tingle because of his touch?

"You really should be getting back," he said.

"Why?"

He cocked his head, sending a golden strand tumbling over his brow. Endearingly boyish in his befuddlement, he brushed that loose curl back. "Do you know, you're right. If you don't want to, you shouldn't have to. You should feel free to do whatever you want."

"Are you leaving?" she asked, unable to account for the sudden disappointment.

Actually, she could.

Ever since she'd been a small girl, she'd enjoyed Andrew's company. A rule breaker and a charmer, he always had a smile on.

"Alas, I fear I have to. My presence—or rather, my lack thereof—has been noted."

"Lord Rutland?" she asked.

His brother-in-law's relationship with her father went back as long as Marcia had memories of the viscount.

"The very same," Andrew muttered.

"Made you come, did he?" She brought her shoulders back and an emphatic finger out and up. "He insisted on standing in solidarity," she said in her best impersonation of her father.

"I would have come anyway," Andrew said, a light flush staining his cheeks.

Stretching a foot out, Marcia kicked him lightly in the ankle. "Liar."

He winked, ringing a laugh from her as he stood.

And it was so unexpected, so *foreign* these days, she started at the feel of it shaking her frame.

Marcia stood as well.

"I'll have you know, I *did* enjoy myself," Andrew murmured, dusting a finger down the curve of her cheek, and that place he touched tingled just as that sensitive place at her nape had.

She gave his hand another playful swat. "Liar."

Andrew tangled his fingers with hers, and her breath shuddered as he raised her hand to his mouth and dropped a kiss atop her knuckles. She trembled once more.

"Not this time, Mar."

Mar.

It had long been the childlike nickname he'd given her. In this moment, however, there was a heightened intimacy to both his touch and his use of that single-syllable moniker that left her head clouded.

Suddenly, he released her. "You really should return."

"I can't think of a single reason to."

"I'll dance with you." He spread his arms and dropped a deep, courtly bow. "My dance skills are legendary."

For a second time that night, and in so very long, a laugh escaped her. He might well just be teasing, and he might have made her smile at the orders of his brother-in-law, but she'd be forever grateful for that. Going up on tiptoe, she pressed a kiss to his cheek. "Thank you," she said softly.

He touched a finger to that place her lips had touched. "Whatever was that for?"

"For not treating me as though I'm dying or sick or pathetic."

"I've already told you you've dodged a bullet, love. He did you a favor." With that, he headed for the door. "You'll see," he promised, lifting his palm in a wave.

With that, Andrew left, and Marcia was alone.

Unlike before, however, after her friends' visit, the same melancholy and misery didn't come rushing up to meet her.

Because, for a brief while, with Andrew, the Viscount Waters, she'd simply been Marcia.

Not Marcia the jilted bride.

Not Marcia the bastard daughter.

Not the pathetic creature whom everyone pitied or scorned.

She'd just been herself, and it had felt so very good.

Do you know, you're right. If you don't want to, you shouldn't have to.

You should feel free to do whatever you want.

"Do whatever I want," she murmured, repeating those afterthought-feeling words he'd spoken, advice she'd not noticed in the moment had been advice, or so very valuable and important to hear.

Distractedly, she toyed with the necklace, the silly talisman her friends had brought, and Andrew had placed upon her neck.

And she stopped.

That was it. That was it exactly.

Not for the first time that night, Marcia smiled.

CHAPTER 6

The parade had continued.

Or that was what Marcia had come to refer to it as. The Parade of Suffering.

Or, The Parade of Balls.

It was all really the same.

Polite affair after horrifying affair, Marcia wondered if the purpose wasn't rehabilitating their family's image and making a brave show but, rather, putting her through a public walk of shame.

And yet, following her meeting with Andrew in her father's offices, and after reflecting a good deal on what had been casual words, she'd found herself eager to attend those infernal affairs. For one very specific reason—she was a woman on a mission.

Granted, she was on as much of a mission as she could be when surrounded by overprotective parents, and her parents' friends, and her own friends.

Standing on the edge of the ballroom, Marcie was flanked by her parents, who were flanked by Marcia's godparents, the Duke and Duchess of Crawford. Also joining them were the Duke and Duchess of Bainbridge and the Duchess of Bainbridge's sister and brother-in-law, the Earl and Countess of Stanhope. And the list went on.

Marcia stole a peek down the length of a very long, impressive line of powerful peers who'd lined up once more in a display of support.

Positioned as so many of them were had left a disproportionate number of guests on the side of the dance floor where Marcia now stood. A dance floor largely occupied by the powerful peers' respective sons and daughters.

As if any of this could change anything for her.

No, because there was no changing anything for her. Just as there was no altering the truth of her existence. She'd been born of the ugliest sin, spawned from the seed of an evil man.

The bloom was off her rose, and the world knew she was illegitimate. All that remained were the ugly whispers, not about the one who'd sired her, but about Marcia herself.

Marcia, who'd only ever been polite and good and respectable.

And for what?

What had it all been for?

She'd hardly lived at all.

Well, that was at last at an end.

Or it would be if he would hurry up and show up to one respectable event.

She searched the crowd for that particular peer. To no avail.

"Where *is* he?" she muttered.

"What was that?" her mother asked, pausing whatever she'd been discussing with the Duchess of Crawford.

Marcia fought a grimace. "Nothing. Nothing at all," she assured, and her mother went back to her discussion with the duchess.

As it was, it had grown increasingly difficult to go sneaking off to some corner of her host's households so she could escape it all.

Because, of course, her family had noted her wish to do that.

And they were suffocating her.

Her high-necked gown threatened to choke her, and she resisted the urge to claw at the fabric and rip it away so that she might properly breathe again.

And yet, for all the support they might manage to throw behind her, they still could not stop the unkind words.

As if on cue, the Countess of Witherspoon, one of Polite Society's leading hostesses, passed close, giving Marcia a once-over, and then she spoke loud enough for Marcia to hear.

"With the reputation of that one's mother and *real* father, they should be guarding her that closely."

Marcia's cheeks flamed hot.

At her side, her father cursed and took a step towards the retreating matron.

Marcia gripped his arm. "Please don't," she begged.

"I'll see her thrown out," Marcus gritted.

"Stop!" Marcia exclaimed, and then she lowered her voice. "Please," she implored. Because then that would be talked about, too. "You cannot silence everyone." Lord knew her father had certainly tried, failing still to realize or accept that Marcia would continue to find herself given the cut direct.

"I can try," Marcus said, balling his hands at his sides.

He *would* try, but he wouldn't succeed. "I'd rather you did not, Papa." She held his eyes. "Please."

He looked like a man tortured, and then he gave a tight nod.

Her mother, who'd been oblivious to this latest snub, exclaimed happily, "He's here!"

Marcia's hopes rose… only to flag a moment later.

"Wakefield approaches!" her mother said.

Ah, so this was the next supportive fellow lined up in the Restore Marcia's Reputation Tour.

Wakefield, as in Benedict, one of her other dear friends. Like Andrew, whenever they'd been in attendance at summer house parties, Benedict had always allowed her to join in his and Andrew's fun.

Bespectacled and somber where Andrew was teasing, respectable where Andrew was not, the young earl couldn't have been a bigger foil to the viscount. For those reasons, he was apparently the person favored by her father to stand up with her. His friendship, however, was no less dear.

"Wakefield," her father said when Benedict arrived.

The men exchanged bows.

"Look, Marcia, it is *Wakefield*," her father said, and she fought the urge to cringe with embarrassment.

"Yes, I see that." Marcia looked at the earl. "Benedict," she greeted.

"I thought I might request a set," he said, offering a bow.

She opened her mouth, but her father said, "This one will do. Will it not?"

How eager her father was to rush her off. Marcia donned a smile. "Of course." She placed her fingertips on Benedict's sleeve, allowing him to lead her onto the dance floor for the next set, a quadrille.

Perhaps because he wants to see you married off, to be rid of you, so that you aren't a constant reminder, the insecure voice in her head taunted.

Marcia dipped a curtsy to the other gentleman beside her who, instead of offering the requisite bow to her as his neighbor, presented her with his shoulder in a clear cut direct.

Marcia bit the inside of her cheek. How was it possible to both love her family for supporting her while also hating them for putting her through this? Powerful as he was, her father's protection extended to his wife, but that same courtesy had been shown to the bastard daughter of another man.

She and Benedict met in the middle.

"I'm sorry, Marcia," he said quietly.

She lifted her gaze.

"Thornton is an arse."

A smile tugged at her lips. "I daresay this must be the first I've ever heard a curse from you, Benedict." Unlike Andrew, who'd taught her some of her favorites.

A blush stained the earl's cheeks. "I allow it when the situation merits it."

They were separated once more by the steps of the dance.

When they met up again, she rushed to assure him. "I'm fine," she promised. She gave such assurances so often these days that they actually fell effortlessly—if untrue—from her lips.

"I believe you are," Benedict said.

He appeared visibly relieved—and desperate to not talk about her scandal.

Because it was easier, she allowed him the escape from the uncomfortable discussion that he clearly sought.

Unlike Andrew.

Andrew hadn't hesitated to speak freely of his unfavorable thoughts about her former betrothed and hadn't danced around the topic of her scandal.

As if she'd at last managed to conjure him with her thoughts alone, Andrew was there.

Her heart picked up its tempo.

Finally.

She followed his movements as he strode through the crowd. His steps were lazy. Nay, languid. And long and… She stared intently at him, trying to will him to look her way, because she really did need to talk to him.

Alas, it appeared she wasn't the only one.

A voluptuous woman stepped into his path, cornering him.

Marcia narrowed her eyes. Not that he appeared upset about being cornered.

Just the opposite.

The pair leaned close to each other, with the lady motioning to him and whispering something in his ear.

Some unexplainable emotion she'd never before felt where Andrew was concerned slithered around inside of her.

The exchange between the woman and Andrew lasted only a moment before he moved on, only to find himself stopped once more by yet another lady.

Marcia wrinkled her nose. What ridiculousness was this? She'd known him to be a rogue, but she'd never really paused to witness it in action before now. *It's only because you have a need of him, and he and his assignations are standing in your way.*

"Marcia?" Benedict's voice cut across her musings, jerking her attention to him as they came back to the middle.

"Hmm?" she blurted. "Fine. I'm fine."

He puzzled his brow.

She gave thanks a moment later when the set concluded, and he escorted her from the dance floor. Her gaze landed on her parents, who'd also been dancing and now made their way back from the dance floor. Towards her.

Their gazes were sharply focused on Marcia, and their attention was greater than it had been when she'd been a mischievous girl.

And it was suffocating.

Their attention was briefly called away by the Duke and Duchess of Crawford.

Marcia seized her moment. "If you'll excuse me, Benedict?"

Catching the sides of her skirts, she lifted her hem and darted off, slipping around columns and pillars, using the grand stone hall as her personal hide-and-seek lair, her gaze still on her parents, who were now intently searching. She swallowed a curse and dived behind the curtains of a private alcove.

Or, as the case would have it, a not-so-private alcove.

She gasped as a large forearm looped possessively about her waist and drew her close, crushing her breasts against a hard, solid wall and stealing her breath. A man had captured her.

But then her gaze landed on the man holding her.

Andrew touched his lips to the shell of her ear, and despite knowing he was a rogue, despite knowing he must think she was someone else, she felt her breath quicken.

"I was wondering where you—" He froze. His eyes bulged, and with a curse, he released her like he'd been burned.

"Expecting another?" she drawled.

Even in the dimly lit space, she caught the blush that filled his cheeks. She patted his face the way her Aunt Dorothy had always done to Marcia when she'd been a girl. "The Viscount Waters blushing. I didn't think it was possible." That endearing color deepened. "So," she said, catching the curtains and peeking between the slight slit in the fabric, wondering who he had meant to meet amongst the many ladies he'd spoken to on his way to the alcove. "Who is she?"

"No one," he said quickly. Too quickly.

Marcia slid him a glance over her shoulder.

He blushed. "Lady Robins."

"Andrew! She is married."

"She is unhappy," he said defensively.

She frowned, unable to account for this… disappointment.

There was no end to the number of people whom Andrew had left disappointed over the years.

Never before had Marcia looked at him the way she did now.

And it shouldn't matter. But for some unexplainable reason, it did.

"Tell me, Marcia, what does it matter if a lonely woman wants my company?" he asked.

"It matters because she is married."

"And do you believe those unhappy couples actually have love between them?" he countered, but didn't wait for an answer. "I'll spare you from wondering—they don't. They're miserable. The wives as well as the husbands."

"But they spoke a vow to be faithful, Andrew, and when you make that vow, you honor your commitment."

He opened his mouth to further disabuse her of that idealistic view on commitment, but something in her eyes called the words back.

She was speaking about her betrothed, the blackguard who'd stranded her at the altar. And it didn't matter how much he reassured Marcia that she was better off. She'd suffered a broken heart, and only time could and would heal that. Someday, however, she'd realize how lucky she'd been to be spared a lifetime of misery with a passionless fellow like the marquess.

"You're going to find someone who is going to make you truly happy, Marcia," he said quietly.

"As happy as Lady Robins is with her husband?" she asked dryly. "Or all the others like her?"

"No. As happy as Rutland makes my sister and Huntly makes my other sister. And my stepfather makes—"

"You've made your point. But I won't have those things, Andrew," she said, shifting closer. "I'm not your sisters, and I'm not even my mother. I'm a bastard."

He frowned. "You're a—"

"A bastard," she interrupted him.

"You're a lady," he completed the thought.

"No, I'm not. I'm some by-blow who was conceived by—" Marcia abruptly stopped, biting down hard on her lower lip and looking beyond his shoulder to the alcove wall behind him.

Hearing her speak so about herself, so jaded and harsh and so unlike Marcia, caused a tightening in his chest.

His fingers moved as if of their own volition, coming up to

briefly stroke the curve of her cheek. That skin was so satiny soft and warm, and Marcia's eyelashes fluttered shut as she leaned into his palm.

As he caressed her cheek, he marveled at the feel of her, marveled at the fact that he'd not touched her more in this way. In any—

Egads.

He drew his hand swiftly back. "You're going to marry some respectable, honorable fellow who'll give you love and his good name, and you'll wonder that you were ever so brokenhearted by one such as Thornton."

Did he speak that reminder for her benefit or his? Perhaps it was a mix of both.

Marcia's lashes lifted. "I won't," she insisted with the dogged stubbornness she'd always possessed in spades. "It doesn't matter."

He suspected she'd convinced herself that she actually believed it. But she hadn't.

"I've made some... decisions about my future," she said.

Decisions.

He'd heard the distinct pause in her statement.

Warning bells clanged at the back of his mind that said to slip between the curtains and make a hasty exit from this conversation and ballroom, getting himself far, far away from this young, innocent woman and whatever plan she'd hatched.

"I want to live my life," she said.

"Brava! That is precisely what you should do."

He made to step around her, but she slid in front of him, blocking his path, positioning herself in a way that if he evaded her, they'd be revealed to all who might pass on the other side of the curtain.

"I want to go to fun gatherings."

"This is a fun gathering," he croaked.

Marcia gave him a long look.

"Fun for young ladies," he amended.

She narrowed her eyes. "Don't patronize me, Andrew."

"I'm... not. I'm... just..." Desperate. He was desperate, because he knew precisely where she was going, and he needed to get himself going before he heard any more.

"I am tired of polite affairs, Andrew. I want to experience the thrilling side of London. I want to go to those gaming hells that admit gentlemen and ladies. I want to know what it is to be wicked."

"Gentlemen and ladies do not visit those gaming hells," he gritted out. They were places of evil and ugliness and everything she wasn't.

"You do."

"Precisely," he whispered. "That is it exactly."

"Fine, then I want to see how the other half lives. The disreputable side." She beamed. "Of which I am now a member."

This was why she'd sought him out?

"Marcia," he said imploringly. "You are not in our ranks."

"Not yet," she said with a smile. "At least not physically, but by way of reputation and name... I am."

And damned if she didn't somehow sound... pleased at the prospect.

"Marcia, you don't know what you're saying."

Her smile faded to a dark frown, and she glared at him, and he'd have been properly terrified of such a blistering glower if they were having absolutely any other discussion but this one.

But they weren't.

"Oh, I do. I have always been proper and lived precisely as a young lady should, but what has that gotten me, Andrew? The cut direct by members of Polite Society because of Charles's actions." She paused. "A broken heart." She added that last part more softly, as if speaking to herself.

It wasn't the first time she'd mentioned her betrothal to Thornton, but it was the first time she'd spoken plainly and honestly of her heart being broken. The truth of that left him trapped between a place of wanting to pound Thornton for having dared to hurt her and pulling her into his arms and reminding her that her former betrothed wasn't fit to lick her slippers.

"Marcia," he began gently. "That is precisely why... this, what you propose here, will not and cannot work. Because if you do the thing you're speaking of doing, then you won't have a future. Not one that is respectable," he added.

"Because an honorable, respectable gentleman will not take

me as his wife if I'm engaging in improper activities?" she asked quietly, searching her eyes over his face, and Andrew pounced, so desperate to dissuade her that he'd play on her fears of not finding love again.

"No, they won't."

She grinned, slowly, a devilish, impish smile that sent terror clamoring in his brain. "Perfect."

"*That* is *perfect*?"

Marcia gave an emphatic nod, slightly dislodging the heart-shaped, diamond-encrusted haircomb tucked in her curls. "Because a man who would so judge me is not any man I should wish to wed. And I'll have you know, I have you to thank for this decision I've reached, Andrew."

He was the reason for this harebrained plan? "Splendid."

She frowned. "You're being facetious."

"Oh, not at all. I'm sure your father and my brother-in-law and my parents and your mother would all appreciate the fact that I gave you the idea to sin," he said under his breath and set to work righting the bauble that sparkled even in the dimness of this space. The last thing he could afford was to be discovered with her while her hair was in disarray. This was the one time he'd actually done the honorable thing, but the world would never expect that or believe it. He assessed his handiwork and made a few more adjustments. "There," he murmured, pinning back into place a stubborn curl intent on escaping.

Alas, the curl proved as obstinate as its mistress. He collected that strand once more and then stilled, noting belatedly— dangerously—the silken texture of that perfect coil. He'd always thought it ridiculous those exaggerated ringlets arranged by lady's maids everywhere to mark the virtue of their mistress as clearly as a white gown and white gloves. Only, as he continued stroking that curl between his thumb and forefinger, he assessed those tresses in a new way. He'd proven to be a failure as a rake for not noting until now the shimmer of those curls, or the feel of them. Or mayhap it wasn't just any innocent young woman's hair that so fascinated him but, rather, this particular woman.

Andrew relinquished that tress and yanked his hand back

so quickly he brushed the curtains of the alcove and set them dangerously aflutter.

When he shifted his attention back to Marcia's face, he found her staring... oddly at him.

"I was fixing it," he said, his words running together, and he found himself transported back to the time he'd been an uncertain, stumbling, bumbling young man who'd first discovered women. "Your hair," he clarified when her brow dipped a fraction. "Can't have you going out looking like you do."

She touched a hand to the back of her head. "There's something wrong with how I look?"

"No," he blurted. Anything but. That, however, was the problem. Except... "Yes." He swiftly switched course, and Marcia's brow fell farther.

Bloody hell, end this already.

Andrew took her gently by the shoulders and instantly regretted that decision. The feel of her skin proved even more tempting, even more enticing than those silky strands. He flexed his fingers and hovered them instead just above her shoulders. "Marcia, if we're discovered, and then you're seen looking rumpled, the world will assume... They'll assume..."

She nodded slightly. "*Yes?*"

He'd opened his mouth when he caught the mischievous sparkle in her pretty brown eyes.

Andrew narrowed his. Why, the imp knew precisely what he was speaking about and was having a deuced good time at his expense. "They'll assume I was making love to you," he said bluntly, at last finding his way in this discussion. "They'll assume I had you in some alcove with your skirts up." He gripped that material and crushed it noisily in his fingers. "And your back against the wall." He curved his other hand against the small of her back, guiding her against the wall in question. "As I took you here," he whispered, "just on the fringe of Polite Society."

He'd meant to scare her.

By the way her lips parted, and her breath caught, and her skin flushed, he had.

Only, what he'd also managed to do was conjure for the both of them wicked imaginings of the very scene he'd painted.

This time, unlike before, his fingers didn't comply with reason. He was incapable of unfurling them or releasing her.

Instead, his hands curled reflexively into her hips, and he slowly started to lower his head to claim her mouth.

Marcia's gaze locked with his, and then with a little laugh, she gave a roll of her eyes.

A roll of her…?

She shoved her palms lightly against his chest. "I know what you are doing," she said, her voice perfectly steady and even and… calm. Everything Andrew was decidedly not.

"And what is that?" he croaked.

"You're trying to scare me with your wickedness."

That was the conclusion she'd arrived at? That one. And not that he'd been a moment away from taking her in his arms?

Relief filled him. Good, her erroneous assumption was certainly the far safer one. He forced out a laugh that sounded strained to his own ears. "Did it work?"

The lady stuck a finger under his nose and waggled it back and forth like he was a naughty boy whom she now scolded. "It did not. I shan't be frightened or deterred. You're *Andrew* and the last fellow I'd worry about being amorous around me."

He frowned. The last fellow she'd…?

Well, now. Just what in blazes was that supposed to mean? He rather didn't think he wanted to know.

Alas, he should have expected she'd not let him off so easily, as with her next breath she answered the question that had popped up.

"I'm not afraid of my reputation around you, because there's absolutely no desire and absolutely no passion between us. We're simply friends."

"Friends," he repeated dumbly.

She smiled and nodded. "*Friends.*"

The thing of it was, before this moment—or rather, before these recent exchanges—he would have actually agreed that they were… friends, of sorts. At least as much as a man could be friendly with a woman. But that had been before he'd noted the feel of her curls and before he'd almost lowered his head to take her mouth.

And before she'd asked him to help her sin.

On the heels of that came another grating thought. "And are there certain gentlemen whom you do have to worry about being amorous around you?" His query emerged as a growl.

For God help the blokes, Andrew would take them apart.

Marcia blushed. "Not yet. Though it remains to be seen, with my reputation now what it is, if I'm a subject of different interest."

He'd need to start appearing at far more respectable affairs. That was all there was for it.

"Marcia," he said quietly. "You've been hurt, and I know something about that." He'd made the mistake of trusting an innocent heart to a woman who'd been merely using him to get to his brother-in-law Huntly. The road of love wasn't one he intended to dance down again.

"You do?" she asked softly, surprise rounding her eyes, and he immediately cursed the revelation, because this inquisitive young woman would only ask questions. Only… she didn't, and that was what allowed him to continue so easily.

"I do, and it's why I know in this moment that going out and sullying your name and reputation won't undo what's come before. It won't make the pain go away. It won't bring Thornton back to that day at the altar."

Her features spasmed, and his heart hurt at the visible pain she was still too innocent to attempt to conceal. God, he could happily bash Thornton within an inch of his life for what he'd done to this young woman. And he would have been content to end him if the blighter hadn't ultimately done Marcia a favor when he'd jilted her, sparing her a lifetime of tedium and misery.

"I don't want him back," she said softly.

Andrew palmed her cheek. "I think you might actually believe that, love," he murmured, and as she turned into his touch, he reluctantly released her. "But going to scandalous events will not bring you the happiness you seek."

She might have had her heart broken, but she was still a young woman with dreams of love… and throwing away a chance at the future she truly sought for a grand time of sinning would only deny her happiness.

"Andrew, please," she entreated.

It was all he could do to keep from agreeing just because he'd never heard Marcia beg for anything, and he hated to hear her do so, and he hated even more that he was the one to deny her. But he had to be.

For the both of them.

But especially for her.

"I can't do this, Marcia. I can't do what you want."

Not the least of all reasons being what his brother-in-law and her father would do to Andrew were they to discover he'd helped her in such a way.

Her expression fell, and such tangible disappointment filled her eyes that he found himself wanting to call back his rejection, only so he could restore her smile. But even he, cad that he was, knew better. "I'm sorry, Marcia."

She gave him a long look and then shrugged. "Very well. I bid you good evening, Andrew, and wish you much pleasure with whatever lady planned to join you in this alcove." With that, she slipped off.

He followed her departure through the crack in the curtain, watching after her as she wound her way through the ballroom, staring until she'd disappeared from his line of vision.

Good. He'd gotten through to her. Yes, he'd hurt her, and he hated himself as much as he did Thornton for doing so, and yet, no good could have come from his helping her pursue a wicked path in London.

Only, as he took his leave, giving up on keeping company with any other woman in this ballroom, he couldn't shake the feeling, knowing Marcia as he did, that it couldn't have been that simple to deter her from her goals.

CHAPTER 7

Desperate times called for desperate measures.

And there could be no doubting that Marcia was desperate.

It was why since before her exchange with Andrew, she'd confided in Faith and Anwen—and plotted with them.

For she was something more than desperate... she was determined.

The following night, standing before her friend's bed, staring with Faith and Anwen at the parchment laid out, Marcia couldn't shake the image of military men surrounding a table of battlefield plans.

She hardened her mouth.

Well, in a way, that was precisely what they were.

As young women without the same freedom of movement afforded men—even men of their same age and younger—they had to think out every step.

That was why she was sleeping over at Faith's household for the evening. Her parents were so relieved at imagining Marcia with her friends, surrounded by them and smiling again, that they would never suspect she was up to anything else. She counted on that.

It was the perfect decoy and the perfect plan.

In fact, everything about her planning was perfect.

Except for Andrew's rejection.

"I still cannot believe he rejected you," Faith said in her slightly too loud way, the elevated tone a product of her partial hearing loss.

That made two of them.

"Hush," Anwen chided. "We are focusing."

Focusing. As they'd been since Marcia had sought their continued help with her plan. Had they been any other young ladies, they surely would have sought to talk her out of her efforts. Faith, however, was the daughter of a marchioness who'd opened up her own school for women, and Anwen was one of the founding members of a society of women speaking about and against the strictures placed on women. As such, they were forward thinkers.

"I think this is the one you should have always gone for," Anwen said, leaning across the bed and touching a finger to a name inked on those pages.

The Duke of Rothesby.

Faith made an impatient sound. "A duke will not help. That isn't their way."

"The Duke and Duchess of Crawford are generous enough people," Anwen pointed out.

"Yes, but they are an older duke and duchess, and everyone knows Crawford has always been the stodgy, proper type and not the roguish type more concerned with his own happiness like those"—Faith wagged her finger at the page—"roguish ones. Furthermore, that is the reason Waters rejected you," she said, shifting them back to the matter at hand. "It was naïve for us to expect that he would do it."

It was naïve for Marcia to have expected him to help her.

That was what her friend had meant, but was good enough to not say it aloud.

The thing of it was, she'd been so very certain her connection and friendship to Andrew these many, many years would have meant he'd have not hesitated to help her.

Even now, she couldn't stave off the same disappointment that had dogged her as she'd left him there in that alcove, waiting for the woman he'd planned to meet when Marcia had waylaid him.

An unpleasant taste settled in her mouth, souring her tongue, like she'd tasted vinegar.

That was only because of the fact that he'd refused to help her. That was all it was.

Faith chewed at her fingernail, contemplating the page. "The way I see it, this might be your best option," she said, pausing in that worrying of her index finger to jab it at a different name.

Anwen sat up straighter. "*Landon?*" she asked, frowning at Faith.

"Everyone knows Landon is up for a spot of wickedness, and if he does reject Marcia, Marcia can just ask Rothesby, because those two are always together."

"Those *three*," Anwen pointed out. "Waters is the third of that trio."

"But he's already rejected Marcia."

She frowned. Need they keep reminding her that Andrew had rejected her? As her friends launched into a debate, she cut them off. "I must go."

"We are accompanying you," Anwen said.

Faith nodded.

"You are decidedly not."

"And whyever not?" Faith demanded, folding her arms. "Do you think we aren't capable enough?" She didn't give Marcia a chance to answer. "I assure you I'm quite skilled with my rapier."

At her side, Anwen matched the other woman's posturing. "We *both* are."

"Because I must do this alone," she said, and gathered up her cloak and donned the midnight-black muslin garment.

"Don't be silly. Of course you mustn't. You must have a friend with you," Faith insisted.

"Two friends with you," Anwen added. "Safety in numbers, and all... and..." The young woman's eyes glimmered with their familiar mischief. "I'd quite enjoy living on the wild side."

That was precisely why she'd not allow them to come. They were still respectable. Unlike her. "No," she repeated, drawing her hood into place. As it was, they'd already been far greater friends than she deserved, sticking with her even though she was a bastard. Even when all the world had begun talking about Marcia—and still did—they remained staunchly supportive. They'd been supportive even in this scandalous pursuit of fun.

She'd not repay their loyalty and friendship by putting them in potential harm's way.

But you will jeopardize your siblings, a voice whispered.

Also, allowing her friends to accompany her would only increase the risk of discovery.

"If it is discovered we are all missing, then they will search." Marcia was capable of enough furtiveness that she'd escape notice.

Her friends appeared ready to debate her, but then Anwen caught Faith's eyes, and some silent exchange occurred between the pair.

"Fine," Faith muttered. "But I am helping find you a hack, and you must return here immediately after you've secured the gentleman's cooperation."

"I will," she said, not missing a beat. And she had to. With her parents believing she was safely ensconced in the household of the Marquess and Marchioness of Guilford, she couldn't very well return home at such an hour. Not without raising questions—and suspicions.

And so it was, some twenty minutes later, that Marcia found herself on the surprisingly comfortable squabs of a hired hack, rolling along the streets of London towards the less respectable end.

To give her fingers something to do, she pulled the page she and Faith and Anwen had been discussing for the better part of the evening. She had committed the names to memory long ago, and yet, she unfolded the page and studied it distractedly anyway.

Five names in total.

Two added only because three seemed too few.

Only one of those names had been a serious contender.

She'd expected him to be there for her, the one man she'd thought would find her proposal good fun and welcome her along with him.

Andrew.

Who'd been waiting in an alcove for some other woman when she'd managed to corner him. It shouldn't have shocked or surprised or disappointed her. She well knew what Andrew was. A scoundrel. A rake. A rogue. Those were words affixed to his name in all the scandal sheets, and he'd even made lighthearted jests about them.

And that was absolutely the only reason she'd been disappointed by him.

Because she'd expected him, as a rogue and as her friend, to not have denied her request.

In her mind, there'd been something freeing about the adventure she'd planned to embark on. But since she'd hatched that plot, her imaginings had always included Andrew at her side. And so there'd been no unease about the course she intended to follow. She'd known Andrew would be there and would dispense with any problems and that he'd show her the ways. In fact, she'd imagined them as two chums partaking in the grandest of fun.

But he had said no, and that rejection had hurt more than she'd expected, because she'd never imagined he'd say no.

Being rejected was becoming an increasingly familiar sentiment. She'd been rejected by Charles. By the bulk of Polite Society.

The carriage rolled to a stop, and she forced herself to shove back those maudlin thoughts.

She'd arrived quicker than she'd thought.

Drawing back the curtains, she peeked out at the building awash in light.

She'd not known what she'd expected. Perhaps for the sin of the establishment to be so great that it all but spilled into the streets in the form of its wastrel patrons.

As it was, the streets proved empty but for the occasional gentleman strolling up to the establishment, knocking, waiting, and then being admitted a moment later.

She'd been nervous until this moment.

Why, this street might as well have been any other respectable London street and the business unfolding inside that establishment not so very scandalous or outrageous after all.

Sitting back in her seat, Marcia removed a book from her reticule, and as she waited, she read.

He'd been granted a reprieve from attending Polite Society functions.

There'd been no requests—also known as demands—put to Andrew, requests that he make an appearance and show support for Marcia.

His services had been exhausted, and his family recognized there was no longer any benefit to his standing shoulder to shoulder with Marcia and her family.

Good.

He should be relieved.

Hell, he was.

Why, now Andrew was free to spend his entire nights at his tables and at some of London's wickedest clubs. He should be relieved and concentrating on the cards in his hand. His shockingly good hand.

Alas, another thought kept intruding…

I want to know what it is to be wicked.

From another, that admission would have been wicked, sultry.

From her, the words had been matter-of-fact, spoken in her bell-like, clear voice.

He laid down a card, and opposite him, his friends and two others who'd joined their trio tossed down theirs, muttering and cursing as they did.

This should be distraction enough. His luck had turned.

Alas…

Scowling, Andrew drew his winnings in.

"With that glower, Waters, one would never know you've been winning," the Duke of Rothesby drawled around the cheroot clamped between his teeth as Lord Meadows quit their table, conceding defeat and leaving him with Rothesby, Landon, and Lord Templeton.

Lord Templeton chortled with laughter, and ignoring him, Andrew scowled at Rothesby. "I'm not glowering."

The duke looked to Landon.

"Oh, you're definitely glowering," the marquess said and then shot an arm up.

Almost instantly, a blonde beauty appeared. She looked between Rothesby and Landon.

Simultaneously, the two men pointed Andrew's way.

The voluptuous creature sashayed over and perched herself on Andrew's lap.

"Hullo, my lord," she purred, wasting no time as she placed kisses upon his neck.

As his friends dealt the next hand, he stared blankly out at the crowded floors.

This was what Marcia had wished to be part of and also the *last* place she should ever be.

Rejecting her request had been the absolute right decision. The honorable, respectable one. And he'd made it, a man who was known for being anything but.

It'd been two days since she'd snuck into that alcove and put her favor to him. Two days since he'd sent her on her way. And since he'd seen her.

What Marcia had proposed had been trouble wrapped up with a big crimson bow and was therefore the last thing he needed in his life.

Now, he was free to pursue his own pleasures, and...

And he couldn't keep from thinking that he'd failed her.

And even accustomed as he was to failing others, this felt... different.

Grabbing his snifter, Andrew tossed back a long swallow of brandy.

The young beauty used that as an opportunity to climb closer, straddling his lap so that her filmy skirts climbed about her thighs. Angling her head in the crook of his shoulder, she kissed his neck, nipping firmly.

His body responded as it should.

This was perfect.

This was precisely what he needed.

His breathing grew slightly shallower. Slightly quicker.

She reached between his legs and rubbed the flesh there.

His manhood stirred, as it invariably did, and yet...

His gaze locked on her blonde curls.

They weren't quite golden enough. They weren't sun-kissed shades of—

Cursing under his breath, he disentangled the determined creature's fingers from his person. "Not tonight, sweet."

Mayhap if her hair had been any other shade. A dark brown. A light brown. Auburn. Red. Anything. Just not blonde.

The young woman pouted. "You're sure, my lord?" she breathed, lowering her head to cover his mouth with hers.

Andrew turned, and her kiss landed on his cheek. "Perhaps later," he promised.

Although it was an empty one.

He was distracted this night.

As he had been for several days now.

Andrew helped the young woman off his lap, and she sauntered over to another table, another client. In an instant, she'd happily seated herself upon the lap of a more obliging fellow.

When Andrew turned his attention back to the table, Templeton was ordering another bottle, but Andrew's friends stared baldly at him.

He resisted the urge to squirm. "What?"

"You are not yourself, my friend," Landon said flatly.

No, he wasn't.

As his friend had pointed out, Andrew was the last one to reject a lush beauty. Particularly a blonde beauty with enormous breasts and just as generous hips.

And yet, since an unexpected exchange in an alcove two days earlier, when he'd had a golden ringlet between his fingers, he'd been unable to think about anything but that ringlet. More specifically, that lady.

She'd been so stricken, and he'd seen the disappointment in her eyes.

And hell, he was more than accustomed to earning disappointment from everyone. His mother. Her second husband. His sisters. Their spouses.

There really was no end.

But this had been Marcia.

Young Marcia, now grown up, who treated him not like a shameful rogue, but as a social equal, and who was even now probably sad-eyed and quiet. He'd never seen her that way before that bastard Thornton had broken her bloody heart.

Andrew revealed his latest winning hand to a round of groans and laughter from his friends and a black curse from the young rake Lord Templeton.

In that, Andrew could well commiserate. How many times had he—did he—find himself on the end of losing hand after losing hand?

He tossed back his whiskey. "It isn't every day the cards favor me, and given the state of my wagering lately, I wasn't interested in squandering my win. Or should I say *your* money?"

The marquess laughed, and Rothesby threw a middle finger up, while Lord Templeton slammed an unsteady fist upon the table hard enough to rattle the bottle and the pile of winnings stacked in the middle of the table.

"Damn you, Waters," the young gentleman roared, his cheeks flushed and his voice raised loud enough to penetrate the din of the gaming hell. He earned brief, curious looks from the other patrons before they returned to their own pleasures.

"Hey now," the duke said. Even as there was a hint of lightness in the words, Andrew's friend had layered a hard warning under them for the other man's benefit.

Too inebriated, too desperate, the marquess failed to hear the latter. Lord Templeton jabbed a finger at Andrew's chest. "You're a ch—"

"Whoa!" Rothesby and the marquess raised their voices to be heard over the insult that would paint Andrew into a corner, and the other man proved sober enough to not complete what he'd intended to say.

Andrew quirked a half grin. "What was that?" he drawled, lifting a single eyebrow.

"Having a good bout of luck you are, this time. But you're still your father's son," the other man spat.

Andrew stiffened, curling his hand hard around his glass. Not because he felt any affection for the miserable bounder who'd sired him. Never that.

"Why, you probably have a wife or two of your own." Templeton busted out laughing, cracking himself up with the reminder of what Andrew's father had been—not only a lousy, unlucky gambler and a womanizer, but also a bigamist. "Don't you have anything to say?" the man demanded, his cheeks florid.

Andrew shrugged. "If I did have a wife, I'd have the sense to at least marry a rich one. That way, I would add to the fortune I took from you this night."

Across the table, Rothesby and the marquess roared with amusement.

Templeton's cheeks grew redder, and he shoved his chair back, scraping the legs upon the floor as he stood and towered over Andrew. "Make light of it all you want, have your jest, but at the end of the day, you know I'm right. Me and the rest of the world know you're a wastrel, a pathetic, impoverished viscount who's as morally bankrupt as your father."

"You go too far, Templeton," the duke said quietly. That stern, clipped warning contained all the ducal superiority that terrified the world, and it also managed to penetrate Lord Templeton's rage.

The young lord went even more flush in the cheeks and then dipped an uneven bow. "Gentlemen," he murmured to Andrew's friends and table partners for the evening.

Landon nodded his chin in the other man's direction. "Get the hell out. You're done at these tables."

All that bright crimson color drained from Templeton's cheeks, leaving the young man pale. With that, he wandered unsteadily through the crowd.

"Ignore him," Rothesby said quietly, and as the duke dealt the next round of cards, Andrew looked restlessly around the club.

The truth of it was, Templeton *wasn't* wrong. And Andrew wasn't himself. Of late, he'd been out of sorts. And, at least in the privacy of his thoughts, he could be honest with himself as to the reason behind it.

Or more specifically, the person behind it.

Oh, it had nothing to do with the insults that had been leveled by Templeton. Andrew was well accustomed to Society's opinion of him. That was, Society's *unfavorable* opinion. Every insult written about Andrew, every wary look tossed at him by protective mamas, every disgusted look sent his way by respectable peers was well earned and deserved. Why, even his friends knew him precisely for what he was—Waters' son.

As Templeton had needlessly reminded him and the table that

night, he was the son of a wastrel, a womanizer, and, worse, a bigamist.

That vile reprobate's blood flowed freely in his veins, the life-sustaining force tainted and poisoned by the man who'd sired him. It was why Andrew had taken to gaming and bedding beauties as he had.

It was why, back when he'd been innocent enough to believe in love and to believe himself different than his father, he'd given his heart to a woman whose soul was as black as his own. A woman who'd ultimately been intent on revenge for having lost her lover to Andrew's sister in the name of marriage.

From that moment on, Andrew had given up on the pretenses and accepted—nay, not accepted. He'd fully embraced his reputation and owned his birthright.

Yes, everyone viewed him rightly, just as Templeton did.

That was, everyone except Marcia.

She'd been the only one to see something *different* in Andrew.

And after his exchange with Templeton, Andrew could at last make sense of why he'd been so bothered these past several days.

He couldn't shake the look of disappointment that had glimmered in her eyes when she'd last looked at him. Oh, he was well used to disappointment from others, but the fact that she'd come to him, that she'd sought his help before anyone else's?

Granted, she'd enlisted his aid in learning the ropes of sinning, but nonetheless she'd sought *his* assistance.

No one ever came to him for assistance, for the very reasons Templeton had raised.

Why, even his closest chums, Rothesby and Landon, supported him and staunchly defended him—as they'd done a short while ago with Templeton—but they also knew better than to seek assistance, in any way, from one such as Andrew.

Andrew grimaced and downed the remainder of his drink.

It was better not to see her anymore. Helping her in the ways she'd wished would have gotten him only a bullet square in the chest at dawn by her father.

Andrew shoved to his feet.

The other men looked up with some surprise.

"I am out," he explained. "Quitting while I'm ahead."

"For a change," Landon drawled, and then his smile faded as his features fell into a somber mask. "You know he's full of shite," he said with a greater solemnity than Andrew had previously believed him capable of. "A sore loser and a mama's boy who is unaccustomed to losing."

As Andrew raked over his winnings, he felt Rothesby's intent stare, and then the duke proceeded to do the same. His friends assumed Andrew's moroseness had to do with Templeton's insult. Both men were from illustrious families, and even as the best friends they were, the other men couldn't relate to Andrew, who really didn't give a damn what people said about him or his father. They didn't know that this moroseness was a mere continuation of his earlier sentiments about Marcia.

The marquess took his cue from Andrew and Rothesby and hopped up, joining them.

As they made their way through the club, Andrew absently took in the scene of sin unfolding. Lords fondled young beauties, sometimes more than one or two at the same time.

At one time, there'd been no greater joy for Andrew than that which he'd found in these halls. Now, he felt an ennui. Perhaps because he'd grown older. Perhaps because he'd gotten more jaded. He'd been bored before. He knew the desire to play and sin would return soon enough. It always did.

As Templeton had pointed out, it was in his blood.

They reached the front of the club, where a servant produced their cloaks.

After he'd flung his over his shoulders, he fastened the clasp at his throat and then stepped outside.

At this early-morn hour, the respectable lords and ladies had already sought their beds for the evening, and the reprobates like he and his friends were ensconced at their clubs, seated at tables where they'd remain until the sun began its climb.

Descending the steps, Andrew, Rothesby, and Landon made their way towards their waiting carriages.

"You know," Rothesby said, "Landon is right. Templeton really is a twat. He—"

A figure stepped from the shadows behind Rothesby's conveyance.

All three men stiffened, and Andrew reached for the dagger he kept in his boot… before registering the small figure clad in an elegant black satin cloak. The deep hood concealed the lady's identity, but that cloak proved to be familiar.

He froze.

Impossible.

Absolutely, bloody impossible.

"By God, you are obstinate," he bit out, sheathing his dagger.

His friends exchanged a look.

"I've come to speak with you," she said, her clear, lyrical soprano so unlike the husky contraltos of the women with whom he usually kept company. She was neither sad-eyed nor appeared brokenhearted, but, rather, she looked resolute.

Andrew marched over. "Yes, I've gathered as much. Damn it," he growled. "I've already told you—"

"Not you," Marcia said tartly, and then he narrowed his eyes as she turned her focus on another. "*You.*"

It took a long moment for that word to penetrate. Nay, more specifically, it took a moment to register exactly what she was saying and to whom she now pointed.

"*Rothesby?*" Andrew asked, and in his incredulity, he squeezed several extra syllables into his friend's name.

His friend inclined his head. "I confess to being intrigued," he murmured in that silky, rakish whisper he used with any number of women.

That same whisper Andrew *himself* had used with any number of women.

But fuck and damn, this was entirely different.

Rothesby had used it with *this* woman.

Marcia glanced up at him. "If you will?"

"If I will 'what'?" he snapped.

"Excuse us, my lord."

My lord now, was he? For some reason, even *that* grated.

And she expected Andrew to excuse her? To leave her alone with Rothesby? Over his bloody dead body. "No," he said flatly.

Dismissing Andrew anyway, Marcia turned back to Rothesby—the richest man amongst them. The richest of most men in London. "As I was saying," she said to the duke.

The tall, obscenely wealthy duke. Andrew clenched his jaw.

"I was hoping to enlist your help in a matter, Your Grace."

Rothesby grinned. "I'm even *more* intrigued, my lady."

Oh, this was quite enough.

Gritting his teeth hard enough that pain shot from his jaw all the way up to his temples, Andrew took Marcia's hand in his and tugged her along. "Let's go."

"Hey," she gasped, yanking against his hand.

Retaining his hold on her, he pulled her away from his friends. She resisted.

"Stealing my fun, are you, Waters?" Rothesby called dryly.

"More like saving you," he muttered, resorting to tossing her over his shoulder, earning a laugh from the young duke and an impressively fierce pinch on his lower back from the minx struggling against him.

He cursed. "See what I mean?"

"She looks like a handful. I would be happy to—"

He and Marcia spoke at the same time.

"No."

"Yes," she called over to Rothesby.

"Over my dead body," Andrew snapped, stomping over to his carriage.

As though Andrew strolling the streets of London with a woman flung over his shoulder were the most natural thing in the world, his driver drew the door open.

"My lord," he greeted.

"Evening, James." Andrew deposited Marcia in the conveyance and then climbed swiftly onto the opposite bench.

James shoved the door closed.

"Andrew, I am not at all pleased with you," she snapped, shoving her hood back and revealing a tangle of golden curls that hung like a sun-kissed waterfall about her shoulders. The combs some maid had surely, expertly tucked within those strands had slipped nearly free in the melee, and he stilled at the sight of her, an Athena with the fiery spirit of Nix, a veritable goddess of secrets and night mysteries.

"Are you listening to me, Andrew?"

"No," he murmured. Now that he'd seen her in this siren's light, he could not unsee her.

At least not in this moment.

Later, logic could be fully restored.

Marcia tipped her head at a little angle, and that slight shift sent her cloak gaping, and his gaze fell unbidden to the high neckline of her white silk evening dress.

His breathing came harder, shallower.

Revealing absolutely no hint that she knew the effect she was having on him, Marcia folded her arms and glared at him. "You are being ridiculous."

That managed to right his thoughts.

"*I'm* being ridiculous?" he echoed, his temper flaring, his voice and anger both rising, and he welcomed those far safer sentiments. "This from a woman who took a damned hack to East London by herself and waited, alone, outside one of London's seediest gaming hells. Alone."

"You said 'alone' twice."

"Well, it bore repeating." Some of the anger went out of him. "Marcia," he implored. "What are you doing?"

"I told you, I want to live." She looked up at him with the widest eyes, and the innocence there proved even more sobering.

"If you visit these streets, you'll find yourself doing anything but," he said bluntly. "You'll find yourself killed… or worse." Images entered his mind of the danger she'd escaped only by sheer luck, and he dragged an uneven hand through his hair.

"Worse?" she asked, her voice genuinely curious, and his patience snapped once more.

"Yes," he hissed. "You'll find yourself backed up against a wall by some fellow who isn't so patient and isn't so respectable and who forces himself on you."

All the color drained from her cheeks, leaving her a stark white. Her trembling fingers came up, and she clawed at her throat.

The brittle set to her shoulders, as if she were one ragged breath away from shattering into a hundred thousand pieces, gutted him.

Good. At last, he'd managed to get through to her.

Only, that didn't make him feel good.

"Marcia," he said, the ache in his voice matching the feeling in his chest.

She blinked slowly and then gave her head a shake as if to dislodge the disgusting thought he'd intentionally planted there. She moved her eyes over his face. "You are worried about me."

"Damned straight I am," he barked.

Her eyes softened, and she looked at him in a way no one had ever looked at him before. Abject terror clawed at his brain, and all of him recoiled from that emotion.

"The last thing I can afford is having your father and my bloody brother-in-law believing I've landed you in trouble."

Just like that, the spark in her eyes went out. "Oh," she said, glancing down at her feet. "Of course."

Of course.

Good, let her believe that lie.

The truth of it was he *did* care about her. He cared about her more than he should. Perhaps because they'd known each other for years. Perhaps because that friendship, as she'd called it, went back to when she'd been a small girl sneaking up on him in her father's office when all Andrew had wanted was a stiff brandy.

"Marcia," he implored. "Why are you doing this?"

"I need to, Andrew," she said quietly, her tones as resolute as the glint in her eyes. They bespoke a woman who had no intention of wavering. "If you won't help me, then I intend to find someone who will."

She would. He saw it by the firm set to her shoulders, and by the upward tilt of her chin, and by the fire blazing in her determined eyes.

"I'll tell your father," he threatened.

Marcia didn't miss a beat. "No, you won't."

And he wouldn't.

It was another way in which she knew him, too. And it unnerved the hell out of him that a person did know him enough to know that. It shook him that this young woman, an innocent one at that, did.

"You intend to seek Rothesby's aid?" he asked warily, silently berating himself for what he intended to do if she persisted, unable to reason himself out of it.

"I do."

Not *I would*.

I do. As in she intended to continue her meeting with the duke who waited outside his carriage, baldly watching the exchange between Andrew and Marcia.

He should bloody let her do it.

It wasn't a bluff.

He should just let her go.

But then an image slithered forward like a serpent sliding around his brain—Marcia against a wall in a tableau different than the one he'd painted for her. Some bounder wasn't forcing himself upon her. Rather, Rothesby was pleasuring her, wringing breathless cries from her innocent-no-more lips.

A black haze fell over his vision, briefly blinding him, and he shot a fist up.

The carriage immediately rocked forward.

Marcia's throat wobbled.

For the first time that night, he saw hesitation in her features. "A-Andrew?" A question was there in the uptilt of her voice.

"You want to sin?" he said huskily, reaching for her. He brought her down atop his lap, settling her there. "Then you should be prepared for everything that entails, love."

With that warning, Andrew tangled his fingers in the hair at her nape and brought her mouth down to meet his.

Several times in her life, Marcia had *almost* been kissed.

The day her betrothed had asked for her hand, he'd lowered his lips to brush his mouth over her cheek and nothing more.

And there'd been three instances with Andrew she could—and secretly had—cataloged as the Almost Kiss at Her Betrothal Ball, the Fireside Chat Almost Kiss in her father's offices, and the On the Fringe of Society Almost Kiss in the alcove.

There'd been so many almost kisses with Andrew, or what she'd believed had been almost kisses, that she'd allowed herself to wonder what kissing Andrew Barrett, the Viscount Waters, would in fact be like.

She knew that, as a notorious rogue and black sheep of Polite Society, a scoundrel of the first order, he'd know precisely what he was doing.

She knew he'd be experienced.

She knew she'd probably even enjoy it some.

In all her wonderings, however, she'd been wrong.

She'd been so very wrong.

She enjoyed it more than just *some*.

It was as though she'd come alive for the first time, born of a single flame that licked at every corner of her being, becoming a fiery conflagration that threatened to swallow her in sheer desire and wanting.

Moaning, she tipped her head to better receive his kiss, and he angled her chin a fraction, knowing precisely the amount to shift her to deepen their kiss and better avail himself of her mouth.

All the while, she kissed him back, hesitantly at first.

Then he glided his palm down her body, lingering at her waist, and then cupping her buttock.

She gasped, and he slid his tongue inside her mouth, stroking her in a kiss she'd never known could be a kiss. She'd expected there to be only lips meeting and sparks, but not tongues and pure fire.

There were no words, but then, she didn't think any were possible, or needed, anyway.

There was simply feeling, and she surrendered herself to it.

She dimly registered the crunch of satin as Andrew gripped the bottom of her skirts, and then she felt the kiss of the nighttime cool upon her heated flesh when he dragged her skirts higher.

"Do you like that, love?" His voice emerged as a gravelly, raspy taunt that belied the affectionate word that fell from his lips.

He didn't appear to require an answer. Which was good, as Marcia didn't think she could make her mind or her tongue form words. Nay, her mouth was capable only of this intimate takeover carried out by the man who held her.

And yet, not even her former betrothed had called her *love*. She'd simply been Marcia, and only that, after he'd formally asked for her hand. She'd never been *sweetheart* or *dear heart* or any other endearment.

Until now.

Until this man.

And she well knew that coming from this man, Society's wickedest rake, it was an empty endearment at that.

But her mind didn't care.

Some part of her, a part of her that longed for that closeness still, a part of her she'd believed dead after Charles's betrayal, stirred at that gruff word.

Sighing softly, she surrendered more fully to Andrew and his embrace.

Nay, their embrace.

He gripped her buttocks, sinking his fingers into the flesh, molding his palms to her, and Marcia's breath quickened.

As if of their own volition, her hips began to move scandalously against him, and as the carriage swayed gently back and forth, she rocked her hips in a bid to be closer, in a bid for… something she'd never before known, something she couldn't identify, but something she was so very desperate for.

He grunted, an animalistic dissolution of speech that only further fueled that sharp pressure between her legs.

Then he was guiding her closer, giving her more, pressing her against the rigid length outlined by his breeches.

It was too much, this fiery sensation and yearning, and she turned from his kiss, burying her head in the crook of his shoulder and clinging tightly to him.

And it proved the wrong movement, too.

He immediately stopped what he was doing, and she secretly cried out at that abrupt cessation. She registered that, at some point, the carriage had stopped.

"Is this what you want?" he whispered harshly against her ear. "To be tupped in a carriage like a common whore?"

Her heart squeezed painfully as his cold question brought Marcia crashing sharply back to earth. And mayhap it was because it was this man—who was a friend—who spoke to her in frosty tones she didn't recognize, that she felt a sudden urge to cry.

"Hmm?" he jeered, running his palms over her thighs, which were still splayed over his legs.

He was taunting her.

She bit the inside of her cheek, reminding herself that Andrew wanted no part of the favor she'd put to him, and that was what drove him.

Marcia forced her features into a thoughtful mask and made a show of considering his question.

"Is this what it means to live a sinful existence?" She smiled. "Then, yes." His eyes flared, and she curved her lips into a wider smile. "Thank you for your first lesson, my lord," she said. "This was quite enjoyable, and I am looking forward to more of our time together."

With that, she patted his hand, climbed off his lap, and opened the door herself.

She paused only long enough to peek inside at him. The moon doused the carriage in a white glow, and she took in Andrew's slack jaw and immobile form.

Good. She'd shocked him now. "Shall we say tomorrow at one o'clock in the morning, my lord? Lord and Lady Edgerton are hosting a ball."

"And never tell me, you intend to just slip off?"

"They're my parents' neighbors, Andrew," she said. It would be entirely too easy for her to tell her parents she would be spending yet another night with Faith and then sneak off. "I will meet you at the end of their street."

He stared at her with something akin to dread. "You really have thought of everything."

Marcia waggled her eyebrows. "Everything." Her fingers still shaking from his touch, she attempted a breezy wave. "I shall see you tomorrow!"

And then, with her legs still unsteady, she managed to make her way across the street to Faith's household.

CHAPTER 8

Andrew had made many mistakes in the course of his twenty-eight-year existence.

He shouldn't have sat down to any number of hands, ones that had resulted in him losing nearly all but his shirt and leading to his brother-in-law Rutland bailing him out of those messes.

There'd been the time he'd given his heart to a viper of a woman, who all along had intended their affair to be a spot of revenge against his youngest sister and brother-in-law.

That was his most spectacular mistake of all.

Or it had been.

This latest escapade, however, proved to be his greatest folly, a request that, against all better judgment and reason, he had agreed to last evening.

It was why he was seated in his carriage at the end of the Viscount Wessex's street, doing something he'd done just once in his life—praying.

And for a long while, he rather believed those prayers had worked.

She'd not come.

Rather, she was not coming.

An immense relief, so great, so strong, swept through him the likes of which he'd never before felt.

There was a God, after all.

He'd lifted a hand to knock on the roof when he caught a flash of movement.

Alas, his relief proved short-lived.

Darting quickly, the small figure moved with the stealth of a London pickpocket, and an odd sensation filled his chest.

Bloody hell.

And then she was there. Even as he'd been following her with his gaze, he was unprepared to find her standing outside his carriage below his window. She knocked her hood back to reveal a somber-eyed Marcia.

She had come.

He'd been certain she wouldn't.

She'd been late enough for him to have his doubts.

And following the volatility of their meeting outside the gaming hell, he'd expected she would abandon her plan, as any other woman would have.

But Marcia was not any other woman.

She waved at him happily. "Hullo, Andrew," she said.

With a curse that would have shocked the blackest sinner in London, he opened the door and lifted Marcia inside. It was a mistake. It only brought her body flush with his.

"You're late," he said flatly. "If you're late again, we're all done with this." The last thing he could afford was lurking outside her family's household and being seen with her running into his carriage.

Marcia wrinkled her nose. "You're in a foul mood."

Yes, he was. "Being coerced into helping a young lady sin has that effect on me. Here, put this on." He flicked something at her, and Marcia instinctively shot her hands out to catch the scrap of material.

Her hands were encased in white leather gloves.

He groaned. "What the hell are these?" he asked, tugging the gloves free of her fingers. He tossed the gloves onto the bench beside her.

Marcia frowned. "They are gloves." She pointed to his hands. "The same things on your fingers."

"They are certainly not the same."

"Uh, I think I can see that they are, Andrew." If the rolling of one's eyes had possessed a sound, it would have been contained in this minx's voice.

Grabbing her gloves, he held them aloft. "There's these." He held one of his hands before her. "And these."

She blinked and then drew back. "You're too close, Andrew," she muttered, and then catching his palm in hers, she dragged it closer to her eyes, angling his hand left and right, analyzing it from top to bottom the way a scientist might examine a foreign object.

Then she proceeded to run her fingers along the palm of his hand—his gloved palm, and yet, her touch, feathery soft, gentle, determined, managed to penetrate that material, and his mind grew thick, and his mouth went dry.

All from a lady's innocent touch.

He swallowed hard, or attempted to.

He'd never had an interest in innocent women. In fact, he hadn't understood the reprehensible fellows who bothered with virginal young ladies.

Until now. With Marcia trailing her long, graceful fingers over his hand as if tracing and exploring its contours, it made sense.

This was the manner of temptation that compelled those most wicked of scoundrels. They'd had the right of it all along, with their knowledge of the desire inspired by an innocent's lady's touch.

Then she dragged his hand up and closer, holding it near her mouth, and he sucked in a breath.

"I do not see it," she muttered. "I do not see it." Marcia abruptly shoved his hand away from her face onto his lap. She shook her head. "I don't get it."

I don't get it.

That would make two of them this night.

He gave his head a clearing shake. *Get control of yourself, man.*

This time, wise enough to avoid the temptation that came in touching her, Andrew jabbed a finger first at the glove at her side and then the one he wore. "White," he said. "Black."

She pointed those chocolate-brown eyes up to the heavens. "Yes, I know the color is different, Andrew."

"The white is like a damned flag, Marcia," he exclaimed, his voice climbing to an exasperated near shout. "You may as well be announcing to the damned world that you are there."

Her brow fell, and she reassessed his gloves and then hers. "You know, you are correct. I do see that now. I knew you were the right person for this assignment."

The right person for this...

"Let's get this over with," he muttered.

Lifting his hand, he knocked hard on the carriage roof, and the vehicle lurched into motion.

He braced his feet to steady himself even as Marcia pitched forward.

Andrew shot his hands out, catching her at her waist.

And he instantly regretted it.

Touching her.

The feel of her, slender and... warm, conjured memories of when she'd been in his arms last night, against him, panting and moaning, and—

With a curse, Andrew set her firmly back on her bench and released her, and then curling his hands tightly, he kept them down at his sides.

Angling his head towards the window, he stared out and prayed for a second time, this time praying that he'd not commit the greatest of sins and take her in his arms again.

From the moment she'd awakened that morning, Marcia had been filled with excitement. She'd thought of the wondrous moments she would experience.

But she'd not been able to forget the volatile ending of her exchange last evening with Andrew.

Rejection.

It was fast becoming a familiar sentiment.

Charles.

Andrew.

Andrew was disgusted by her, too.

She'd known as much since she'd raced out of his carriage last night.

And she'd had further confirmation now by the way he'd

recoiled after touching her.

His hands. Those were the greatest clue, however. They were tight fists beside him, as if he were repelled by having touched her.

Marcia felt the sudden urge to cry.

Because she shared that disgust. She knew what it was to loathe her own skin, the skin bequeathed to her by a monster.

And Andrew doesn't even know that, a voice jeered.

What would he think of you if he did know all those ugliest truths about your existence?

That she was a daughter spawned from Satan's own loins, a vile reminder her mother must face every day about that horrific act and that horrific night.

Turning her face, she stared intently at the black velvet curtain, peeling it back just enough to peek out, and the faint hint of crystal pane revealed the glimmer of tears in her eyes. She blinked several times, willing them back, refusing to cry now. Refusing to cry here, with this man.

Since she'd learned the truth, since her mother had finally shared with Marcia the real story about her father, she'd felt... lost. Lost amongst a family and household that had always been a refuge. Her mother was quiet and sad-eyed whenever Marcia was about now. Lord Wessex, the man whom she referred to as Papa, because he'd been a father to her in every sense, and the brother and sister born to her parents... none of them looked at her the way they had before the day her betrothal had died on the steps of St. Helen's Church.

She was destined to always live with her family, because none would marry her now.

And the rub of it was, she didn't want to marry now. She didn't want to trust her heart to any other respectable gentleman.

What was worse—the only alternative left her was to be a burden.

Perhaps it was perfectly fitting, as that was how her existence had begun—as a burden.

She squeezed her eyes closed so tightly they ached, and the pain proved greater than the sting of sadness that had brought the tears, and those drops faded.

"Second thoughts?"

Andrew's gruffly spoken question came with a trace of reluctance, like one who resented or regretted having to speak to her.

She gave her head a slight shake.

The springs of his bench squeaked slightly as he shifted, moving nearer.

She felt his nearness, his broad, powerful form shrinking the space of the carriage.

"It's all right if you do," he persisted with a greater gentleness that brought tears threatening once more as it occurred to her how very desperate he must be to get her to relent… so that he could be free of her. Because even with this man whom she considered a friend, she was still the unwanted.

"It would be the wise decision," he went on, and his knuckles came up to brush the curve of her cheek back and forth, a quixotic caress. His touch was tempting, and the words that continued coming were coaxing, but in a way that belied such a touch. "You've always been wise."

Suddenly, her patience snapped.

Straightening, Marcia slapped his hand away. "I know what you are doing, Andrew."

"And… what is that exactly?" He stared back at her, as wide-eyed and befuddled as he'd been that first time she'd come upon him in her father's offices, wading through the place in search of spirits.

Something about that memory made his disgust with her cut all the more.

"You're attempting to get me to change my mind. You're hoping that I'll free you of your responsibility."

"I'm not attempting to get you to change your mind. I'm *hoping* you do," he said, throwing a single finger up as if he'd made some grand, very different point.

"Well, you don't have to do anything." She firmed her jaw. "I will not force you to be my companion."

"Your chaperone."

She drew back, stung by that correction. *Companion* suggested partner. *Chaperone* made her out to be some child who didn't know her mind and with whom he was forced to partner. "I can ask—"

"Rothesby?" he snapped, his voice cold and curt and angry. "I've already told you, you aren't enlisting Rothesby's help, or the help of any other scoundrel who made your bloody list, Marcia Gray, so let it rest. Now." With that, Andrew whipped his focus towards the window, yanking the curtain back and staring out.

She drew back. A little shiver scraped her spine at the fury emanating from his eyes, and for a moment, she believed his anger was because she'd threatened to go off with another. As soon as the ridiculous thought slid in, she pushed it back. What would Andrew care if she were with any other man?

He wouldn't.

Once more, his concern stemmed from the fact that his brother-in-law, a terrifying fellow to most, was best of friends with Marcia's father. Embroiling Andrew as she had in her plans had only put him in a potential match with Lord Rutland, if he were to find out.

They didn't speak for the remainder of the carriage ride, and miserable at the loss of Andrew's usual joviality and teasing, she counted in her head the passing seconds all the way to 3,469. And all the joy and excitement she'd felt this night vanished as she was left once more with that great big gaping hole of misery in her breast. She felt as lost now as she had for the better part of four days, at sea and hurting inside, all the way to her soul.

At last, they arrived. The carriage rolled to a gradual halt and then stopped altogether.

The driver made no move to get down, and Andrew didn't reach for the door as he had the previous time she'd been in the carriage with him.

Instead, they both sat there in silence. Neither moving.

Because he is still hoping you'll relent. Because he wants so very badly to be free of you and your company.

A strong hand covered her own, and she glanced down at the fingers on hers. His long, slightly tanned digits were testimony of a man who'd shucked his gloves in favor of the sun upon his skin. Her heart quickened.

"I do know you," he said. The anger in his voice was belied once more by the gentleness of his touch, a confusing juxtaposition that her mind couldn't make heads or tails of. "I've known you since you were a small girl playing hide-and-seek amongst your parents' guests at their balls and country parties."

He'd always joined in. A wistful smile pulled at her lips at the memory. He squeezed her fingers slightly, calling her attention back from those musings and bringing her gaze over to his furious one.

"So for you to suggest I don't really know you is disingenuous and wrong, Marcia," he said, handing over a mask.

As she accepted the pretty scrap, it occurred to Marcia, hitting her with all the force of a fast-moving carriage, that she'd offended him when she'd said he didn't really know her. "I've upset you."

"Your opinion that I don't know you annoyed me, yes," he said with a blunt honesty any other member of the peerage would have shied away from. Any other gentleman would have lied, because that would be more polite than arguing with a lady.

She moved her eyes over his familiar face, the angular planes of his cheeks, the firm square jaw harder than she remembered it ever being, the bold slash of his aquiline nose. His was… a beautiful face, slightly harsher and intriguing. How had she failed to note those angles?

"Now, if we're doing this, let's get on with it," he said, yanking his fingers back.

But still he waited, allowing her to decide if and when she was going into… wherever they were. He'd put the choice in her hands, and it was one of the reasons she so dearly loved him as her friend.

Suddenly, the courage that had set her on this course flagged. The idea of entering the world of the demimonde was now real in ways it hadn't been before this day, or even during the course of their ride through London. But the moment she stepped out of Andrew's carriage, she'd enter a wholly foreign world, and nervousness turned her belly over.

She felt his intent stare and knew that he knew her well enough to have gathered the reason for her indecision.

"I am ready," she said quietly.

He nudged his chin her way, and she looked down at the mask he'd given her.

Of course.

Marcia lifted the thing. It was a simple piece adorned with several glittering gemstones that sparkled in the light. He could have gotten her any mask, but he'd brought her this lovely piece.

Questions surfaced at the back of her mind, insidious wonderings about the women who'd worn this article before her, and her belly tightened into a thousand vicious knots.

She fumbled with the strings.

"Here," Andrew murmured, reaching for the mask, relieving Marcia's fingers of it. In one effortless motion, he angled her head slightly and quickly had the protective covering tied firmly in place.

When he'd finished, Andrew paused to assess his handiwork. His eyes locked on her face, and he remained motionless, not so much as blinking.

Unnerved, Marcia touched the corners of her mask. "What is it? Is something wrong?"

"Your eyes," he murmured, as if speaking only to himself.

Her eyes?

"No one will not *not* notice them," he said in that faraway way, and her heart forgot its rhythm. It forgot its sole job was to beat.

"They're… just brown." Her voice emerged as a whisper.

He shook his head and touched a finger to the corner of her mask, lingering at that place just beside her right eye. "They are surely ten different shades of greens and golds and browns, all mixed to make one unique shade unlike any other."

Her breath caught.

Unbidden, her fingers came up and touched his.

That sudden movement—or was it the feel of her hand?—seemed to jerk Andrew back to the moment.

He blanched and yanked his fingers close to his chest as if she'd burned him when she'd touched him.

"I was just saying," he blurted, stammering like a boy who'd gotten caught with his hand in the cookie jar. "Someone might notice because… your…"

"Eyes?" she supplied.

"They're an *odd* shade of brown."

Whatever mad haze had fallen over her lifted.

Marcia wrinkled her nose. "I beg your pardon?" And here she'd thought he'd been waxing on poetic about her eyes.

"They're a lovely enough shade," he said weakly, and also *unconvincingly*.

She pointed her stare at the ceiling. "La, I certainly see how you get your reputation as one of the most charming of rogues," she drawled.

An endearing little blush slapped his cheeks. "I'm not decidedly *not* trying to charm you," he said, slashing his palms up and down in an emphatic sweep that underlined his words. "At all. Ever. As in ever."

"I quite get your point, Andrew," she snapped, unsure why she was so perturbed by his adamancy. This was Andrew. Her friend. And yet, she was. Annoyed. Very much so.

"Er… right." He fiddled with the collar of his cloak. "Now that we've sorted all that out." He lifted a hand and knocked once.

Andrew's driver was there in a moment, drawing the panel open.

Andrew jumped down first, and then as if they were a respectable lord and lady attending a proper ball or dinner party together, he reached a hand inside.

Marcia paused to bring her hood up and into place for further protection, but also because if… when… she saw other people, she'd not be seen wearing this ridiculous headpiece. After she'd adjusted her hood, she placed her hand in Andrew's and allowed him to help her down.

When her feet touched the cobblestones, she did a sweep of her surroundings.

The pavement under her feet was slightly slick and more uneven than the roads in Mayfair. The thick scent of waste hung heavy in the air, making it a chore to draw in a proper breath.

Andrew leaned down, placing his lips against the shell of her ear. "Change your mind?" His breath fanned her skin and tickled her flesh, sending a delicious little tremble from the point of contact and down her whole back in the most wonderful shiver. "Hmm?"

She turned her head slightly, angling her head back to meet his gaze more squarely. His piercing gaze went through her. "N-never." The breathy quaver to her voice laid to waste all her attempts at being a determined woman who knew her mind.

He inclined his head and then held his arm out. "Shall we, then?"

Marcia linked her elbow with Andrew's, and they started forward.

The closer they drew, the louder the noise emanating from a building that was more of a warehouse than a residence.

The moment they reached the front doors, Andrew knocked in a rhythmic, almost singsong tap, hard and loud enough to be heard over the din within.

Reflexively, she stepped closer, expecting him to make some jest at her unease.

Instead, he waited, his focus on the door.

A moment later, it opened.

A giant bear of a man greeted them.

At three inches past six feet, Andrew was a tall man. This stranger had six inches on even him.

He looked Andrew over and briefly glanced at Marcia before wordlessly nodding and stepping aside.

A haze of smoke hung over the room, stinging her eyes, and she blinked several times, both in a bid to ward off the tears and also to see where precisely Andrew had brought her.

Leaning close, Andrew shouted loud enough to be heard over the raucous noise. "Come!"

He looped an arm about her waist, bringing her body flush against his side in a protective gesture, and his touch wrought havoc upon her senses. Together, they wound their way through the building, weaving in and out between guests, mostly men and only a handful of women sprinkled amongst their numbers.

If Andrew had worried about people remarking upon her presence, he needn't have worried. Some several hundred guests' attention was trained intently on the front of the room. The patrons lifted their arms and shook their fists, their shouts all rolling together.

Curious, Marcia stretched up on tiptoe as she walked in a bid to see what commanded their focus.

Andrew continued guiding her closer to the front of the room, and then he held an arm out, gesturing for her to enter the row before them first.

A pair of seated men looked over.

"Waters!" they shouted in unison, loud enough to make themselves heard over the din.

The Duke of Rothesby and the Marquess of Landon. She recognized them easily. Both were notorious rakes and also close friends of Andrew.

"You've brought company," Rothesby remarked over the top of Marcia's head as she settled onto the hard bench beside him.

"Indeed," Andrew said, stuffing his gloves inside the front of his cloak and adding nothing more.

Rothesby gave Marcia another quick glance. "Never tell me *this* is the good fun you saved me from last evening?"

"It appears he took it all for himself," Landon drawled, his voice loud enough to penetrate the shouts filling the arena.

Marcia blushed.

Scooting closer to Andrew so that her thigh brushed his, she looked up.

Two men in a roped-off ring upon an elevated wooden dais circled each other. Arms up, fists close to their faces, they danced about the space.

And then, one of the fighters darted out a quick punch, his blow connecting with his opponent's nose.

Blood sprayed everywhere upon the two fighters, and with a gasp, Marcia reflexively turned her head, burying it against Andrew's shoulder.

It was... horrific.

She stole a peek.

And yet, neither of the men gave any indication that each punch they landed was anything more than a slight nuisance.

When she'd been a small girl, her mother and father had found her a governess, an unconventional woman who'd not snapped a rod against Marcia's back and insisted she stand upright, one who'd not sought to crush Marcia's spirit. Rather, the woman had regaled

Marcia with all manner of fascinating histories and subjects from science to ancient Greeks and Romans, including tales of warriors made to fight within a grand arena in Rome.

Now, watching these two men, bare-chested and barefoot, sparring, Marcia had a glimpse of what those long-ago fights must have been like.

There was a barbarism to the match, and their brutality made it impossible to look away from the raw, virile power of the men, their barrel chests matted with hair and glistening with sweat and the blood they shed.

And Marcia sat more upright and watched, transfixed, alternately fascinated and horrified.

The two men pounded away at each other, trading blow after blow, each strike landing faster, harder, as if each man strove with that next hit to propel his opponent on to death and themselves on to victory.

But neither fell.

Neither faltered.

They remained stubbornly upright, which only whipped the crowd into a greater frenzy.

The fighters danced around the arena with steps graceful enough to rival the smooth glide of London's greatest dancers.

It was nothing short of horrific.

Still, she could not bring herself to look away.

The pair danced closer, so close to where she sat that the sweat flying from their bodies landed upon the skirts of her cloak.

And then, at last, one of the men made a misstep, his left foot dragged, and his shorter-by-an-inch opponent advanced.

Jab, hook, jab, hook, jab, jab, jab.

The head of the poor fellow on the receiving end of those staccato punches whipped all the way back, and he went flying, landing hard on the ground.

As one, the crowd surged to its feet, erupting into triumphant shouts as a uniformed fellow stepped into the ring, took the hand of the fighter still standing, and raised it above his head, declaring him the winner.

At last, it was over.

The fight might have been as short as a minute or as long as an hour, for how well she could make sense of that scene that had just enfolded. Marcia released some of the tension in her shoulders, relieved the violent display was at an end and eager to go.

She looked up at Andrew and found him to be the lone person in the audience not looking at the ring.

He watched her through veiled eyes that did odd things to her chest. Odd that she should develop that sensation only after all these years of knowing him.

Andrew leaned closer. "Tell me, have you had enough, my lady?"

He was pitched slightly forward, as if ready to climb to his feet should she simply say the words.

She knew he would leave his own pleasures here, too, if she gave the go-ahead.

But she'd asked for this, all of this, and to leave now would be to fail. It would mean he'd been right in his belief that all of this was too much for her.

"No," she said with a trace of reluctance, even as a deep part of her wished nothing more than to leave, to have him escort her off so they were away from this place and alone.

Alone?

She stilled.

Andrew gave her a curious look.

"That is, I'm… enjoying the fighting," she finished weakly.

Enjoying the fighting?

She cringed. What an oxymoron.

Andrew inclined his head. "Then we stay."

We stay.

That one particular word hinted at a partnership, which was, in a way, precisely what they were.

Because he'd agreed to her scheme. He'd agreed to assist her in her quest.

Someone approached their bench, and Marcia looked over.

A young woman, her breasts enormous, her generous mouth rouged, and her hips ample, slid over to their aisle.

"Wagers, Lord Waters?"

The woman's husky voice emerged more of a purr, and Marcia

frowned.

"Lucinda," Andrew greeted warmly. "It has been awhile. Entirely too long," he said as he reached inside his jacket and drew out some notes.

The young woman accepted that money, quickly counted it with her long-nailed, curiously painted fingernails, and smiled. "I thought you'd found other"—Lucinda's gaze touched briefly on Marcia before it slid away, the woman dismissing Marcia outright—"interests that had taken you away forever."

"Never, sweet," Andrew said and chuckled.

Never?

Well, now, what was *this*?

Lucinda laughed, a throaty sound that also sounded false and practiced to Marcia's ears, and she folded her arms at her chest and made herself stare intently forward. Anywhere but at Andrew chatting so smoothly with the beauty beside him.

And *sweet*? How casual he was with his blasted endearments.

Marcia's frown only deepened. She might be an innocent by society's standards, but even the most chaste virgin couldn't fail to hear the innuendo there. From the both of them.

A pair of men came through the arena, each taking a place at opposite corners of the wooden dais, each removing their shirts and tossing them to the men waiting outside the ring for them. Marcia's interest, however, remained on the two at her side, visible from the corner of her eye.

Andrew and the entirely too-familiar-with-him beauty.

Lucinda made a show of carefully, deliberately sticking Andrew's money deep inside the deep vee of her cleavage, and damned if Andrew's eyes didn't follow the woman's display.

Marcia's entire being tensed, and fueled with a volatile energy, she proceeded to tap her right foot rhythmically upon the wood floor.

Lucinda leaned in. "Is there anything else I can get you this evening, my lord?"

"That is all." There was a slight, noticeable pause in Andrew's tone. "For now."

Oh, please.

Marcia resisted the urge to roll her eyes. He really was this much of a rogue.

What did you expect?

Her foot stilled its tapping. Furthermore, why should it matter? It didn't.

It absolutely did not.

And then, fortunately, calls were made.

"What are your thoughts, my lady?" That question came unexpectedly from her right side, in a voice raised slightly, and she jumped, looking over to the gentleman.

For one horrifying moment, she believed the duke had heard her silent thoughts, and froze.

His Grace nudged his chin at the ring, and she followed his stare, and relief swept through her.

"It is… fine enough."

"Fine enough," Landon, beside the duke, repeated. "When one is winning, a feat Waters and myself have little experience with." He winked at Marcia and returned his attention to the ring.

The duke's attention remained on Marcia. "I take it you prefer other pastimes."

Unlike the exchange loaded with innuendos between Andrew and his ample wager collector, there was an actual sincerity to the duke's question, and she relaxed some.

"I confess my other interests extend to rapiers and reading."

"Rapiers and reading," he repeated and grinned. "I confess you have me intrigued as to your identity, my lady."

"I am—"

"She is no one." Andrew's sharp tones cut across her response, and she frowned. "She is no one."

At some point, his companion had taken herself off, and Andrew had turned his attention to Marcia's exchange with the duke.

His eyes no longer glittered with the same teasing light that had been there during his back-and-forth with Lucinda. His mouth had gone harder.

Her annoyance stirred. How dare he be boorish to her when he should so easily charm that woman?

Presenting him with a dismissive shoulder, she turned her focus back on the duke.

"You may call me—"

"Do. Not." Andrew gritted out each of those syllables.

"Lady Dorothy."

"Lady Dorothy." The duke and Andrew both repeated the middle name she'd handed them.

She inclined her head.

The duke reached down and unexpectedly caught her fingers in his larger palm. Slowly, he raised her knuckles to his mouth and placed an even slower kiss upon them. "A pleasure, Lady Dorothy."

Instead of releasing her after that respectful drop of his lips, he lingered, his fingers stroking the top of her hand. It was the deliberate stroke of a gentleman confident in his familiarity with a woman and in his ability to elicit a desirous response, and yet…

Marcia cocked her head.

The Duke of Rothesby.

As well as she knew Andrew was as little as she knew the man next to her, a man whom she knew only for the words that had been written about him in the newspapers. He was one of the rogues Society frequently whispered of.

She'd been so very certain that Andrew's touch and whispers earned the dizzying responses they invariably did because he was a rogue, and all ladies responded to all rogues in like ways.

Only with Rothesby, there came none of those shivers she knew when Andrew touched her in a similar manner.

She knew neither why nor what to make of that difference. Because she'd been certain her awareness of Andrew had been merely a product of the fact that he was a rogue. But Rothesby was, too, and she didn't respond the same way to him.

"Enough, Rothesby," Andrew snapped.

"Really, Waters," Landon scoffed. "You'll have the attentions of both Lucinda and the mystery lady? That's bad form."

Ignoring the marquess, Andrew reached over and snatched Marcia's hand from Rothesby's. Then, as gentle as the duke had been, Andrew released Marcia's fingers quickly, letting them fall on her lap.

Hmph.

"Very smooth," Landon said dryly. "Very smooth."

Yes, not only had he let go of her like her hand had spiders crawling upon it, but he'd gone back to staring at the dais with an impatient gaze.

Eager for the next fight.

Oblivious to her, when he'd been only acutely aware of Lucinda. Lucinda, with all her many, many curves.

And why shouldn't he have noted such a woman? a voice prodded.

Unnerved by this sudden concern about where Andrew placed his attention, or rather, on whom he bestowed his favors and attention, Marcia made a show of staring at the two men taking up a place in the ring.

Suddenly, the violent tableaus that played out in this arena seemed a good deal safer than whatever maddening shift had occurred between her and Andrew this evening.

He'd chosen boxing.

Boxing had seemed safer.

There weren't naughty trysting couples and gyrating naked forms and partners exchanging partners. All manner of wickedness and debauchery that were entirely too much for Marcia. That were too much for any innocent.

And he certainly wasn't going to take Marcia to such places and sully her with the extent of depravity that existed, the manner of decadency he'd been partaking of since his university days, but also that he'd been aware of since he'd been a boy well knowledgeable about his father's proclivities.

He'd promised to help her in her quest to take part in the scandalous activities the other half of society partook in. But he absolutely drew the line at those levels of sinning and planned to help her only so much before ending their arrangement.

As such, boxing had seemed safer than the other options. That involved just men pounding each other within an inch of their bloody lives.

What he'd failed to consider was the fact that those same fighters would be bare-chested, or that Marcia would not be horrified by the raw violence but, rather, fascinated by those powerful men.

Her initial horror had since lifted, and she now stared on at the fight, slightly slack-jawed, and Andrew frowned.

Periodically, she shifted in time to the blows that were flying, as if she mentally painted a picture of herself in that ring.

It was not, however, those fighters and her attention on him that merited the gut-twisting annoyance that night.

He observed openly the lively discussion between her and Landon and Rothesby. *Rothesby*, whom she seemed entirely too comfortable with.

In fact, Andrew didn't even attempt to conceal his study of the pair, so engrossed as they were in whatever they spoke about that they wouldn't have noticed Andrew if he were on fire beside them.

Which shouldn't surprise him.

Rothesby was capable of charming every female from age one to one hundred.

And Marcia certainly wouldn't be excluded from those ranks. Marcia, who, for her part, was as comfortable conversing with anyone from wicked rogue to ancient widow.

In that way, the two made a perfect pair with their personalities.

Every coin Andrew spent mattered to him. His finances were on the cusp of disaster. He wasn't in dun territory, but he had enough debt outstanding to be in a bad way soon if his luck didn't turn. As such, each wager mattered. Every bet placed he attended with absolute concentration.

That was before.

Before now, that was.

The current match forgotten, Andrew glared at the comfortably conversing pair. At some point, Marcia had ceased attending the match and devoted all her attention to Rothesby. And Rothesby turned that same intent focus on her. They were as at ease as they would be if they were strolling around Hyde Park or taking a turn down Rotten Row and not seated thigh to thigh at the foot of a boxing ring.

"It grows upon you the more you take part," Rothesby was

saying, his body curved towards Marcia's and hers curved towards his, like they were two damned pieces of ivy growing in the direction of each other, moments away from entwining.

"You mean observe?" Marcia called up to the duke.

"Oh, no… though that does add its own pleasure," Rothesby said. "I mean, actually fighting."

Her eyes widened, and she shifted even closer on the bench, if that were possible. Andrew gritted his teeth.

"You spar?" Marcia asked the duke.

"Oh, yes."

"No more than any other gentleman," Andrew muttered under his breath. The pair, however, would have to be attending something other than each other to have heard him.

"But in this case, I referred to wagering." The duke reached inside his jacket and withdrew a stack of notes.

Rothesby pressed them into Marcia's palm, and then folded her fingers around the offering.

The sight of their interconnected hands, of Rothesby's larger hand on her smaller, delicate one, sent a black curtain of rage descending briefly over Andrew's vision, and he balled his hands into almost painful fists. How dare the bloody rogue put his hands on her? Yes, this was Rothesby, but this… this was also *Marcia*.

"I could not," Marcia murmured.

Rothesby stroked the pad of his thumb in a familiar way over the tops of her knuckles, keeping them closed upon the pound notes he'd given her.

"I insist," the duke murmured in silky tones that sent another wave of fury licking through Andrew, who flared his nostrils.

The only reason for this enraged response was because he'd known her since she was a babe.

"I should not." Marcia offered her rejection a different way, this time a *faltering* rejection, and neither did it escape the other man's notice.

"Let us consider it a gift." Rothesby flashed a grin. "Between friends."

Oh, this was really quite enough.

"She said she could not," Andrew said tightly, and taking Marcia's hand with none of the gentleness his blasted rogue of a friend had shown, he grabbed the notes from her fingers and tossed them at Rothesby's chest. The paper money rained down at the other man's feet.

With that, Andrew turned all his attention back to the match.

A match, by the look of the bloodied fighter Braggert, Andrew was winning.

Good.

He needed a big win.

And the coins he'd spent would bring him a hefty profit.

A big win never failed to cheer him.

That was, until this night.

Feeling stares on him, he looked over.

Marcia and Rothesby both wore matching frowns.

"What?" he snapped.

"You're being rude," Marcia said with her usual bluntness.

"I agree with the lady." Landon made a tsking sound.

Andrew's ears went hot. "I'm not the one taking money from men I do not know."

She gasped.

"Hey now, chum," Rothesby said in a tone better suited to a tutor scolding a recalcitrant charge, and Andrew resisted the sudden need to shift on the bench.

"Yes, no need to be crass," Landon chided.

Now he was getting lectures from Landon. Not that Andrew wasn't deserving of it.

What in hell was wrong with him?

The duke looked at Marcia. "We do know one another now, do we not, Dorothy?"

"That is correct, Evan."

Dorothy? *Evannn?* Since when had Rothesby and Marcia moved to using each other's given names?

Cheers erupted as Maynard was declared the winner. Grateful for the distraction from just how well Marcia and Evan were getting on, Andrew shot a hand up, calling for the bet taker.

Lucinda was there in a moment. "Well done, my lord," she praised in those sultry tones he'd come to recognize as the ones she used when trying to get a fellow to raise his wagering. He had a volatile enough energy thrumming through him that another big wager was due.

As he waited for her to record his bets, Lucinda trailed her fingertip invitingly along the décolletage of her dress.

He sat there, impatient, as he watched from the corner of his eye as Marcia and Rothesby spoke in that engrossed way about…

"… trout. The lakes are well-stocked, but—"

Trout? They were speaking about trout? And fishing?

"My lord?" Lucinda's questioning voice cut across his thoughts.

"That is all," Andrew said. "Thank you."

As in, that was all for this bet and this night, and he'd really had enough of it all.

In fact, he didn't need to stick around to even see if he won. Rothesby and Landon could see to it.

He made to rise.

"Oh, please do wait a moment."

Marcia's plea stayed Andrew mid-stand.

He glanced over.

The minx stretched a thick stack of notes—Rothesby's notes—past Andrew and towards Lucinda.

"I shall take Maynard."

"Maynard is a terrible bet," Andrew said tightly. "He's just fought, and he's exhausted."

Marcia turned a reproachful frown on him. "Well, I believe his adrenaline from fighting and winning is fueling him."

"That is ridiculous," he muttered.

Neither Marcia nor Rothesby nor, for that matter, Lucinda paid him any further notice, busy as they were finalizing Marcia's wager.

After the young beauty had gone, Marcia turned back to Rothesby.

"We shall be partners," she vowed.

Partners.

Andrew tensed.

"I shall like that very much, Dorothy," Rothesby murmured in the husky tones he reserved for seducing widows and wicked women and not Marcia.

Andrew flattened his mouth into a hard line to keep in the flow of words he really didn't wish to heap upon his friend's head.

Partners. Andrew let that word, spoken in Marcia's innocent, bell-like voice, play over and over in his mind.

She'd been intending to approach the other man and enlist his favor, and hell, she would have wound up at this very place.

Or mayhap not.

Rothesby would have likely not balked at taking her to a bloody orgy and watching with her as people made love with more than one partner.

He growled at an image he couldn't shake and desperately wished he could. Because, blast and damn, this was Marcia.

Little Marcia.

Little Marcia, who wasn't so little anymore, but who was still the same girl to him that she'd always been and would always be. And it was why he was so damned bloody protective of her. It was why, against all better judgment, he was here even now.

Shouts erupted, signifying the start of the match.

Maynard's opponent, a taller, broader, more muscular fighter, came out charging swiftly, landing several rapid blows to Maynard's gut in quick succession.

The other man recoiled slightly, but otherwise gave no indication that those jabs had had any effect either way. Instead, he came at Telliers with slower, more methodical, more deliberate blows. He delivered one, two, three, four jabs to the belly and connected the last of the rapid spurt of punches with Telliers' chin, whipping his head back.

With an excited squeal, Marcia exploded to her feet with a rapidity that sent her hood tumbling back, revealing her face in the glow of the heavy candlelight illuminating the arena.

Bright-eyed and rosy-cheeked, she let her own little fists fly as though in so doing she was conferring her strength to the fighter on whom she'd wagered.

In her excitement, she was a sight to behold.

Andrew's gaze snagged on Rothesby.

Rothesby, who made no attempt to conceal his all-out study of Marcia.

Catching Andrew's stare, the duke grinned. "What?" he mouthed, lifting his shoulders in a little shrug.

Andrew touched a finger to the corner of his eye and pointed at the other man. "Watch. The. Bloody. Match," he mouthed.

That silently issued order only brought the other man's head back as he howled with amusement.

Cursing to himself, Andrew returned his attention to Marcia.

At some point, the match had taken a bloodier, more vicious turn as Maynard caught Telliers to him and held him in place as he jabbed away at the other man's kidneys.

Then, in one fluid motion, Maynard spun the dazed fighter away and dealt a quick uppercut to his opponent, catching him under the chin. Even over the din of the crowd, the crack of his jaw shattering reached ringside.

Telliers' eyes rolled to the back of his head, and he staggered back several steps. The fighter fell to his knees and then collapsed, facedown.

The arena roared with the crowd's approval. People stomped their feet almost in perfect unison, their cheers rolling around the room like thunder.

Splendid. He'd lost.

Andrew muttered another curse under his breath and then looked up. "Are you—"

Marcia remained frozen on her feet, her cheeks wan, her eyes rounded, her lashes unblinking.

His loss instantly forgotten, Andrew jumped up. He caught her by the waist and drew her close. "Let's go," he said, and she gave a slight, uneven nod as she allowed him to lead her into the aisle. Keeping her close, he used his body to shoulder a path for them— for her—through the crowded arena, which had swelled with more patrons since they'd arrived hours earlier.

As they neared the exit of the club, the number of patrons thinned.

Andrew opened the door and led Marcia outside.

Even the thick London air proved a cooling balm against the heat from the crush of bodies within the arena.

The moment he closed the door, Marcia drew in several slow,

measured breaths, and squeezing her eyes shut, she tilted her face up, like she'd done as a girl counting stars in the night sky and asking him to help her keep track of that impossible number.

But she wasn't that child anymore.

She was a grown woman.

A woman who tempted.

A woman who enticed.

Not just Andrew, but all men.

There'd been Thornton, who'd won her heart, and now Rothesby, who'd been intent on bedding her.

"Did you enjoy that, Dorothy?" he taunted, his voice emerging harsher than he'd intended as fury at her and Rothesby and at himself lent a sharp edge to it. "Was that everything you hoped for?"

Marcia's lashes slowly lifted, and his chest quickened even as she glowered at him.

She opened her mouth, but he cut her off before she could speak. "And Dorothy?" he spat. "What is that name even?"

Her frown deepened. "It is my middle name," she snapped.

He blinked. "Oh." He'd not known that. It seemed like something he should have known, given how well he knew her.

"It was for my Aunt Dorothy, my mother's godmother."

"I… well, forgive me," he said tightly. "I did not know that."

The riotous sounds within the arena spilled into the streets, a muted background noise to his and Marcia's discussion.

"Is that why you brought me here?" she demanded. Dropping her hands on her hips, she took a step closer. "To scare me?"

He took her lightly by the right arm, and drawing her nearer, he stuck his face close to hers. "Did you not ask me to show you how the demimonde spends their time? You asked for wickedness. Well, this is it. This is what you asked for, Marcia. This is what you asked to see." He pulled her close. "What did you think? We sit around in quiet rooms drinking bloody brandy and whiskey?"

She shook her head. "I… don't know."

And then he kissed her.

Catching her at the waist, he guided her hard against the wall and took her mouth under his even harder.

She stiffened in his arms, and her hands came up… To push him away? Good, she should. Only, he was rake enough that he could admit that and scoundrel enough to revel in the moment she fisted her hands in the fabric of his cloak and drew him closer even as she leaned up into him.

And he was lost.

With a growl, Andrew filled his hands with her buttocks, sculpting that flesh, savoring the feel of her.

And then he remembered who this woman was, that she was an innocent, and yet, even as that reminder of who she was should compel him to release her, it only fueled his ardor. He gentled the kiss, teasing that slightly fuller upper lip that lent her mouth an upside-down pout.

He teased her lips open, and she let him in, welcoming him with a breathy little moan.

"If I were another, I'd be horrified, but I'm not a proper gentleman, Marcia," he whispered harshly between each glide of his tongue against hers. "You think we are friends, but you should know precisely the manner of man that I am."

"I do, Andrew," she said, those enormous, saucer-sized eyes blinking slowly.

Terror filled him at the absolute trust and adoration he spied in her innocent eyes.

Determined to repel her, he gripped her hip and caressed her roughly.

She caught her lower lip between her teeth and then shifted towards him.

And he was lost all over again.

Andrew consumed her mouth, making love to that flesh as he'd longed to, at last acknowledging that want in this moment.

He slanted his lips over hers, harsh and unforgiving in his kiss, and she only moaned her pleasure.

Taking advantage of that slight opening, he slipped his tongue inside and tasted even more of her, dragging her skirts up, and capturing her ankle, he brought it about his waist, anchoring her to him.

Their kiss grew frenzied, a primal mating he was hopeless to gentle, and given the way she thrust herself against him, as if attempting to climb inside him, Marcia didn't wish him to gentle it.

Andrew caressed the bare calf he still gripped in his hand, reveling in the satiny softness of her skin. Had he ever felt skin so fucking soft? Like the finest of spun silk.

There came the click of a door opening, and a surge of noise spilled into the street and into this moment, and he yanked his mouth from Marcia's. The harsh rasp of his breath blended with Marcia's equally noisy, raspy pants.

They needn't have worried. The pair of blokes stumbled past them as if it were the most natural thing in the world for two strangers to be making love against a wall in these streets.

And in truth, it was.

Only, respectable, young innocent women did not visit these places. That reminder was sobering enough to chase away Andrew's powerful hungering to continue what they'd started.

"Come," he said gruffly.

As he led her to his carriage, she didn't speak a word.

Neither of them did through the length of the carriage ride.

Without so much as a parting goodbye, he deposited her near her household, following her with his gaze until she at last disappeared within the safety of her family's fold.

He suspected this marked the end of Marcia's self-edification on the matters of forbidden pleasures. He should be relieved, and yet, as his carriage took him back to his household, he couldn't explain the wave of regret at this being the end of his time with her.

CHAPTER 9

Marcia was meeting Andrew.

It was just Andrew.

The same Andrew she'd known since age nine and with whom she'd swum and fished and played spillikins and lawn bowling. They'd executed endless pranks upon her parents' guests when he'd joined them for summer house parties.

As she prepared to meet him that night for their latest rendezvous, she reminded herself nothing had changed just because he'd kissed her. Why, it hadn't even been the first time. There'd been two. The angry kiss in his carriage. And then the lusty one.

Her heart tripled its beat.

She'd thought numerous times since she'd enlisted his help that he'd been disgusted by her.

Until his kiss outside the arena.

She froze with her fingers on the door handle. Would a man truly repelled by her continue to kiss her?

Yes, the kiss in the carriage had been born of fury, but last night, he'd gentled the embrace and taken his time, and—

Heat flooded her belly, her body tingling at the remembrance of his hands on her. And she'd responded every time he'd touched her.

Mayhap that is because you possess your true sire's wickedness.

The voice at the back of her mind turned taunting.

Mayhap you're just a wanton who'd take and taste wickedness anywhere, and that includes finding pleasure in the arms of a man you've been friends with for years.

Drawing in a shaky breath, Marcia gave her head a clearing shake and focused on changing out of her night dress and into her gown for the evening.

She reached for a serviceable dress, one she donned when she helped her mother garden, and then she paused.

Recalling where she was going and, more specifically, whom she'd be with, Marcia released the dress, and her fingers shoved gown after gown aside.

White. White. White. Off-white. Ivory. White. Pink.

She stopped, staring at the kaleidoscope of pale shades, all indicating innocence. Now all a direct mockery of everything she was, from the blood in her veins to the reason for her existence. Her fingers curled reflexively in the jewel-encrusted gown she'd worn the day she'd made her Come Out.

She dropped that material as if burned. She wasn't innocent. She never would be again. She never had been, for that matter. She was born of sin and evil.

Squaring her jaw, Marcia reached for the only bit of bright fabric before her.

A short while later, wearing a purple gown with her cloak draped over it, she crept to the front of the room, dodging floorboards whose squeaks and groans she'd learned long ago. When she reached the door, she pressed her ear against it and strained to hear any hint of sound. When only silence greeted her, she drew the panel open and headed down the hall.

"Where are you going?

Marcia gasped and whipped around.

Her sister Flora stared back with accusatory eyes.

"To the kitchens," she said weakly.

Flora frowned. "In your *cloak*?"

Yes, her sister was young. Yes, she was innocent, but neither was she stupid.

Marcia's mind blanked, her thoughts stalling as Flora folded her arms and raised an eyebrow.

"I don't like that you're lying to me, Marcia."

"I'm not lying." At least, not well. "And you should be in bed in the nursery."

Her sister ignored that latter reminder. "So I can tell Mother that you—"

"No," she said quickly, her voice rising slightly, and Flora gave her a smug, knowing look.

Marcia bit her lower lip. "I..." Sliding onto the hall floor, she rested her back against the wall and shut her eyes. This was a bloody disaster. She'd been discovered, and if her parents found out she'd been sneaking off, they'd never let her have even the small opportunities to breathe that they did these days.

She felt her sister move into the spot beside her, joining her on the floor, and Marcia opened her eyes.

"I don't like that you are so sad all the time," Flora said softly. Her sister rested her head against Marcia's shoulder, and she leaned her cheek atop the girl's soft curls, which were very much the same shade of blonde as her own.

"I'm sorry, poppet."

"I'm not sorry for me," Flora said, and Marcia heard the frown in her sister's voice. "I miss it for you."

"I'm—" She stopped the automatic apology, recognizing the empty words for what they were.

Flora drew back and angled a look up at her. "But you haven't been as sad these past few days," Flora noted, her gaze entirely too astute for her tender years. "These past days, you've seemed... excited. Like you were climbing out of your skin, but in a good way."

And... she had been.

Marcia wrapped an arm around her sister's shoulders, and they leaned into each other. "You should go to bed, poppet," she said, dropping a kiss on the top of her head.

Flora hopped up. "You... will be all right?"

"I will," she promised. With Andrew as her escort, she had no doubt that her safety would be ensured. What she could not, however, guarantee was that she would continue to evade notice, and though she didn't worry what that would mean for her, she did care about how it could affect her siblings.

With a good deal less enthusiasm than that which had gripped her all day, Marcia made her way outside, finding her way to the end of the street.

The moment she appeared, Andrew opened the carriage door and helped her inside. "Mar," he greeted as if nothing had transpired last evening.

She was grateful for that very casual greeting, for it again felt like nothing had changed between them

As the carriage rolled along for her second night of sinning, she was given pause for the first time since she'd embarked on this quest. If her actions were discovered, if it was discovered that she was joining the demimonde, her sisters' reputations would suffer. That was, her sisters' reputations would suffer *more* because of Marcia. As it was, the latest gossip in the papers speculated that Marcia's mother had made a cuckold of her husband and that none of the children had been fathered by the Viscount Wessex.

She stilled.

All this time, she'd been so fixed on her own hurt and resentment: about how the world now treated her. Her frustration and shame at knowing the man responsible for siring her. She'd been so self-absorbed, she'd not given proper thought to how her mother must feel in all this. Her mother, who'd given her life and who'd only shown her love now found her circumstances splashed upon the pages of newspapers. What misery her mother must be suffering.

And how much more she will suffer if your antics are discovered, and added to those pages...

"Second thoughts," Andrew remarked, and his wasn't a question but, rather, a statement from one who knew her well.

Because he was her friend, she nodded. "I... I am ashamed to say I've not properly thought about what will happen to my family if I'm discovered." It proved she was selfish. With all the sacrifices Marcia's parents had made, she'd repay them with this...

"Society will feed on the gossip, and they will be talked about," Andrew said with his usual bluntness.

He was trying to dissuade her.

As if he felt her weakening, Andrew spoke again, but in quieter, more solemn tones than she'd ever recalled from him. "You don't have to do this, Marcia."

No, she didn't.

She did have to go to polite affairs and be subjected to stares and gossips. "But I want to. I've only ever been respectable, and what has that gotten me?" she asked softly. "If they are going to talk, then I may as well experience what they're all accusing me of." Only, in her voice, she could not hear the same conviction she'd once felt over her decision.

"Tell me this, Marcia," Andrew murmured, leaning across the bench, angling his body closer to hers. That slight movement brought his mouth dangerous close to hers. "Why do you care so much?"

Her senses were all muddled at his nearness, and she had to fight her way through to figuring out the answer to that question: her thoughts disordered for altogether different reasons than before.

"You don't care what people think when they look at *you*?" she asked.

He grinned, the devil's half smile that tempted like that succulent apple in Eden. "Precisely."

Through the dangerous fluttering of her heart, Marcia lifted her eyes to the ceiling. "It's different, Andrew."

"Oh? Because I assure you, people look when I enter a ballroom, and those expressions, are far from favorable."

He was correct on that score, and by his matter-of-fact deliverance, he was unbothered.

"You chose your path, Andrew. I didn't. And they aren't looking at you with pity, and they revel in my fall." She'd felt inclined to point out that key, defining difference.

"They once did," he said softly, so softly she strained to hear and thought she'd imagined that solemn admission from a gentleman so very rarely somber.

"They did?" she asked, her voice faltering slightly.

"Oh, yes. When I first made my entrance at polite affairs, everyone looked at me with the same pity they did my sister Phoebe. I was the pitiable young gentleman whose sire was the worst reprobate in London. They knew my path before I did," he murmured.

She'd always wondered why Andrew danced the dissolute path he had. But he was so much more than his wicked reputation. He was good and loving and loyal to his family and his friends. Her.

He frowned. "Why are you staring at me like that?"

"I just… feel like I know you so much better," she said softly.

An endearing blush spread across his cheeks. "You never knew the reason I am the scandal that I am is because my father was a wicked rotter?"

"I never knew that you became what Society expected of you," she murmured as Andrew now made sense to her in ways he never had before.

His frown deepened as he bristled. "I became what I was always destined to be."

"Because they made you believe that was your future." A life of sin and debauchery.

His features iced over, his expression hard in ways she'd never before witnessed from this man, and a tremble went through her.

In one fluid movement, he slipped an arm about her waist and drew her closer, and she trembled again at his touch.

"You don't want Society's pity, and I certainly don't want that sentiment from you either, Marcia Gray," he gritted out in a furious whisper.

She shook her head frantically. "No! That isn't—"

"You claim you had some grand revelation," he cut her off. "Telling yourself what? That the only reason for my wickedness is because I felt compelled to be so because I was hurt by Society's opinions of me?" He didn't allow her a chance to answer. "You saw me," he said silkily, and then she gasped as he drew her onto his lap and sank his fingers into the curve of her hip.

Her heart thumped… and not from fear, but from the reminder of the kisses and almost kisses they'd shared.

"You see the pleasures I find. I take them because I want them," he whispered against her mouth, his chest moving hard, his breath coming quick against her lips, blending with her own raspy breaths. He moved a sharp gaze over her face. "So do not go entertaining any grand illusions that I am who I am because I was wounded. I am who I am because I'm my father's son."

She knew little to nothing about his father. She'd heard vague whispers, but never details, for when people had begun talking, she'd chastised them or walked away.

Marcia rested her fingertips upon his sleeve. Such tension rolled through his frame, his perfectly contoured muscles jumped.

"I know what it is to share the blood of someone who is evil."

Andrew chuckled, and it was a cold, harsh, mocking sound devoid of mirth, and that rejection cut like a knife, worse than any cut direct she'd been given after the truth of her birthright had been found out. "You just learned the identity of your father. You've had an entire life of being you, Marcia. I knew from the moment I came into this world who and what I'd one day be. They are not at all the same."

She drew back in hurt. "You know nothing," she bit out, hating the slight tremor in her voice.

Andrew stopped caressing her hip, and brought that same hand up to stroke the curve of her cheek. "You want to think that, but you know I'm right. We are not the same, and for you to conflate the two, to speak as if we somehow share something we don't and never will is disingenuous, Marcia."

How had she ever failed to see that ice in his eyes?

Because he'd never turned it on her before.

He'd only ever shown her warmth, and she felt a great need to cry because of it.

He was like a stranger.

His distracted touch slowed, and Andrew moved his gaze over her face. Suddenly, something shifted. His eyes fell to her lips.

He is going to kiss me again.

And she wanted him to. She wanted his lips on hers desperately. She wanted more of this new intimacy she'd shared with him. He lowered his mouth, his breath kissing that flesh first, and her chest quickened.

"You know we are different, Marcia," he whispered and lightly touched his lips to hers in the most fleeting of kisses that wrought only a desperate hunger within her. "You know I am wicked," he breathed between each kiss, "where you are good."

The carriage rolled to a stop.

Andrew set her from his lap and, with no further words passing between them, helped her don her mask.

When he'd finished, he looked squarely at her. "Tell me this,

Marcia. Is this *really* what you want? Or is it mayhap that you *want* to be discovered so the gossips will actually be right in their accusations?"

Starting, she opened and closed her mouth.

Andrew reached over and opened the door. He jumped down and then stretched a hand out to help her.

Marcia placed her fingers in his, and there was something so very natural and warm and… right in the way he folded his gloved fingers around hers, his palm conferring his heat and strength. Her breath quickened, as it did too often with Andrew these days.

He didn't release her hand this time but, rather, twined his fingers with hers and led the way across the pavement and up a handful of stairs to an underwhelming white-stucco establishment.

Unlike yesterday, when there'd been a secret knock, the doors opened as if the person on the other side had been watching for them at the window.

As the man took their cloaks, a rush of noise rolled through the open doorway, slapping Marcia in the face, a blend of boisterous laughter and a cacophony of excited shouts and squeals.

As Andrew spoke in hushed tones to the servant at the front of the room, Marcia peeked around Andrew's broad shoulder, her earlier reservations proving fleeting as her intrigue was restored, to take in the magnificent scene below.

Card tables filled the hall, and hardly a seat remained as lords and ladies, some with masks, and some without, swarmed the gaming floor.

It was not the first time Marcia had seen a card table, having spied them as she'd walked by those rooms set up during proper parties.

But this scene was altogether different.

Grateful for the mask that concealed her blush, she moved instinctively closer to Andrew's side.

The patrons sat with cheroots clenched between their teeth, assessing the cards in their hands around the women on their laps. Many of the men entertained more than one partner. The women were clad in filmy garments that left little to the imagination, the fabric so sheer, it revealed the color of their nipples prodding that fabric. One of those men suckled his partner's breast...

With a gasp, Marcia whipped her attention forward.

The swell of noise in the crowd thankfully swallowed the sound of her shock as Andrew led her with purposeful steps towards the back of the club, finding his way to what appeared to be the lone empty table.

A servant was immediately there, a young woman with midnight curls and a full figure, scantily clad, and bearing a tray of drinks.

"Good evening, Lord Waters," the beauty purred, paying Marcia no notice. "Is there anything I can get you this evening?"

"Two drinks, Linette." He lifted two fingers. Unlike last evening, when there'd been an air of flirtation to his exchange with Lucinda, this exchange was more perfunctory business.

A moment later, Linette set down two snifters of straw-yellow spirits.

"You're certain there is nothing else you want?" Linette whispered in throaty tones, her double meaning clear.

Marcia tensed, focusing her attention on her glass and not on the exotic goddess propositioning Andrew. Why, even her name was luxuriant.

"Perhaps later," Andrew murmured, and with a slight pout, the young woman sauntered off, her hips a-swaying as she went.

Marcia felt besieged by a sudden urge to spit.

Unlike Marcia's, Linette's name was lyrical when spoken. Whereas Marcia's wasn't even really a name but, rather, some ridiculous-sounding, made-up creation from her mother, who'd been desperate to pretend that the daughter thrust upon her was the gift of the man she loved, rather than the devil's spawn.

A woman tainted so much by her blood that even her own fiancé had not been able to bear the sight of her.

Marcia's fingers curled into the arms of her chair, her nails leaving crescents upon the velvet.

"Love?"

Love?

Blankly, she looked up.

Andrew stared back, concern in his gaze, and it took a moment to register that the endearment he'd spoken had been for her.

"Would you like a different drink, love?"

There it was again.

Her heart did a somersault in ways it never had with or because of her betrothed, and it was only because she knew Andrew, and… it didn't make sense. Because friends surely didn't cause other friends' hearts to leap the way hers did now. The way it had these past days with—

Panicked, Marcia tossed back a long swallow… and felt Andrew's stare.

She glanced at him, more than a little afraid that he, with his intuitive way of following her thoughts, knew what she was thinking. "What?"

"You… have drunk spirits before," he remarked.

"Yes." With that, she took another, more leisurely sip and went back to examining Forbidden Pleasures. As the warmth of the drink settled in her veins, more of her reservations melted away. For surely this was only dangerous if she were caught. And Andrew had taken every precaution to ensure her identity was not discovered.

She'd often wondered at the rakes and rogues and scoundrels who frequented these hells. Now, she saw that there was an appeal to them.

Excitement hummed in the air, and the tables buzzed with the possibility of a grand win. And it wasn't… quiet. Why, even the well-attended *ton* events had a measured quality to their respectable noise.

"When?" Andrew's prodding voice pulled her focus back his way.

"Hmm?"

He pointed to her glass. "When did you start drinking brandy?"

She shook her head. "I haven't."

Andrew ran a hand over the side of his cheek. "Marcia—"

"This is my first brandy, as my father never stocks the stuff. You know that. But I've sampled his whiskey and his claret. I don't enjoy them, but neither do I mind them."

"And do your parents know you're indulging?"

Damned if he didn't sound like a reproachful governess

threatening her charge. Her lips twitched, and dropping an elbow on the table, Marcia leaned in. "Andrew, my parents do not know I'm out here with you now, or that I've been sneaking about London. Do you truly believe they know that I sip my father's spirits?"

"They're lax," he said tightly.

She waggled her eyebrows. "Or I'm really just that good at sneaking about."

Grabbing his glass, Andrew held it up. "I'll drink to that," he muttered and touched the edge of their glasses, the crystal clinking.

They exchanged a smile, and it was as though the rest of the room, in all its noisy commotion, faded, and only they two were present.

Andrew's grin flagged, and his lashes dipped as his eyes slid down the lines of her face before settling on her mouth.

He narrowed his eyes, and her heart did that funny thing that had fast become its new normal thing whenever this man was near.

"Wh-what is it?" she whispered, touching her fingertip to the corner of her lip. "Do I have something—"

"No," he said, his voice low and hoarse. "It is fine. You are fine." The column of his throat moved. "More than fine."

He stretched across the table, and her body curved the same way, and his mouth hovered close to hers.

Marcia closed her eyes and leaned up just as he leaned in and—

"Waters, old chum."

That cool greeting brought them swiftly apart. At that familiar voice, she glanced up and froze.

The Earl of Stormont.

Her former betrothed's closest friend peered intently back.

The earlier resolve she'd found in her brandy faded. Heart thundering, Marcia fell back in her seat so quickly, she spilled some of the contents of her snifter.

"Stormont," Andrew returned the greeting in cold tones that made no attempt to conceal his impatience with the other man's interruption.

The earl gave no indication that he either heard or cared about

Andrew's annoyance. Instead, his gaze remained locked on Marcia, and she reflexively touched her mask before realizing the telltale gesture and forced her hands back to her lap.

The earl's gaze narrowed even more. "I was hoping for an introduction to your *latest* companion."

The deliberate emphasis placed on that particular word didn't escape her notice, an emphasis that seemed to serve as a deliberate reminder that Marcia was nothing to Andrew.

She knew she wasn't. She certainly didn't require any reminders from this man, or anyone. But it cleaved her chest anyway.

Suddenly, Stormont flared his eyebrows. "We know one another." That icy pronouncement was directed not at Andrew but, rather, Marcia, and she resisted the urge to shift guiltily on her feet.

Andrew tipped his chair on its back legs and angled his chin up. "Shove off, Stormont."

"That's hardly polite, Waters." Stormont sneered. "Not that I'm surprised."

"Find your own company." Andrew paused. "If you're able," he added with an equal frost to match the earl's. "Coming to my table and insulting me is hardly in good form." Abandoning the casual repose of his seat, he let the chair rest on all fours. "I won't ask you a second time. If you want to play at governess, go find someone else."

The two men were locked in a standoff, and through the tense exchange, Marcia sat absolutely still.

Perhaps there was history between them. Perhaps Stormont's presence had nothing to do with his suspicions that she was the former fiancée of Lord Thornton. And mayhap she needn't worry about him knowing and, in turn, the world knowing and—

Stormont switched his attention back to Marcia.

He peered intently at her. "My lady," he said coolly, and with one last, long look, the earl left.

Marcia's heart thudded against her rib cage as she followed his retreat all the way through the gaming hell to the front of the club and out the door.

"He knows," she whispered.

Andrew gave her a peculiar look, as if there was possibly some other person about whom she could be speaking.

"Stormont," she said, unable to keep the franticness from her hushed words.

"And tell me, Marcia, what if he did gather the truth? What then? Would you wish you'd conducted yourself differently?" Dropping both elbows on the table, he leaned in. "Would you regret that you'd ever set on this path?"

She knew what he was doing and what he was saying without actually saying it. He wanted her to stop this now.

And she should.

She'd realized after her sister had discovered her in the corridor that she could not carry on this way for much longer. The world would speak about Marcia with unkind words and gossip about her regardless of how she conducted herself, but there was hope for her sisters. When Flora had her Come Out in several years, the story of Marcia's bastardy would be a distant memory. But tales of a bastard sister who'd crept about London with Society's most notorious scoundrel and partaken in sinful behavior would be a scandal that lived on long into the future.

She'd end this.

Soon.

After one more night.

She'd have one more forbidden night with Andrew, and then she'd put all of this behind her. And in the years to come, when she remained unmarried with a scandalous reputation only because of her birthright, she'd have the memories of these wicked outings and his kisses to keep her company.

CHAPTER 10

THE FOLLOWING NIGHT, MARCIA FOUND herself trapped.

She was trapped and never getting free.

Her latest cage that night—Lord and Lady Guilford's ballroom.

And she should be grateful. This was the first in all the events she'd been dragged to that she'd not had her parents constantly hovering at her side.

Just then, they twirled past, and she forced a smile that strained her cheeks and waved at her mother and father, whose eyes were not on each other, as they should be, but on her.

Then, mercy of small mercies, they must have believed that false tilt of her lips, likely seeing that which they wished to see because it was easier to do so.

She wanted to leave.

A yearning that had to do with both a need to meet Andrew and so that she might escape the ruthless whispers that followed her everywhere.

Just then, Lady Ella and Miss Scarlett Wilson, a pair of young ladies who'd been presented to the queen the same night as Marcia, strolled past.

Lady Ella snapped open her fan. She concealed her face behind that delicate article, but raised her voice loud enough so that her companion and Marcia might hear her. "She's a bastard, you know."

Miss Wilson giggled. "*Of course* I know. *Everyone* knows. Her family and their friends might host all the balls they wish, but it will not change *what* she is." The pair passed closely, pausing only long enough to look her up and down before continuing on.

Her chest tightened, and Marcia curled her toes sharply into the soles of her slippers, wanting to flee. Wanting to run.

To escape *all* the interest, both from her family and their friends, who sought to rehabilitate a reputation that could not be rehabilitated, and the rest, who found glee in the scandal that surrounded her.

Not for the first time, she looked over her shoulder and peered down at the crowd spilling out onto the dance floor, squinting to make out the numbers on the clock.

She was going to be late.

Andrew would leave, and that would be the absolute end of his consent to help her.

Then she'd be left with nothing but *this*. Gossips gossiping while her parents and friends attempted to protect her from something they had absolutely no control over.

As if sensing weak prey, another pair of busybodies converged upon her. Ladies Patrice Sarver and Persephone Filch. They were older, widowed sisters whose opinions could make or break a young lady. Unfortunately for Marcia, their magnanimity for her had ended the day her scandal had been born.

"No partner for you, eh, Miss Gray?" the white-haired, plumper sister posed, her words a statement more than anything.

Marcia dropped a curtsy and stifled the nasty response she wished to utter. "Lady Sarver. Lady Filch."

Lady Persephone thumped her cane on the floor. "Or should we say Lady Hamilton?" she asked of her sister. "As I see it, the gel should be grateful to have a marquess for her father, even if he is a scoundrel."

Oh, God.

Then she was saved.

Faith took up a place at Marcia's shoulder and glared at her parents' influential guests. "Oh, get on with you now. I don't see either of you being asked to dance," she said, and the two women flushed.

Lady Patrice found her voice first. "You're a rude one, gel. It wasn't bad enough you had the bad ear, you inherited a mouth."

"All the better to point out just how very rude you are."

While the pair sputtered, Faith slipped her arm through Marcia's and guided her off.

"Oh, Faith, you shouldn't have." The sisters would only turn their teeth on Faith, and Marcia wouldn't have her friend suffer because of her.

"Oh, I absolutely should have," her friend muttered, loud enough to earn a curious look from the guests they passed. "I'll not stand by and allow people to speak ill of you." She lowered her voice. "Now, we have to get you out of here. I've told my parents, who've told your parents, we are retiring for the evening," she murmured as she steered them from the room.

Marcia sent a prayer skyward. "You are an angel."

A wry grin tipped Faith's lips up. "Given that which I'm assisting you with, one might argue to the contrary." Once the din of the ballroom had all but faded, Faith brought them to a stop in the empty hall.

Dropping to a knee, Marcia's friend drew open a side table's doors and withdrew a cloak. "Here," she said, handing over the article they'd hidden earlier that night.

Marcia was fastening the deep-hooded cloak when she felt Faith's stare. "What is it?"

For the first time since she'd cooked up her plan and enlisted her friend's help, wary indecision filled Faith's eyes. "You're certain that this is for the best? What if you are discovered? What if you come to harm?" The young woman twisted her hands. "I'd never forgive myself if—"

"I'll be with Andrew," she said simply. He'd never let any danger befall her.

Faith flashed another droll smile. "I believe that is my point."

Marcia scoffed. "Andrew is perfectly safe." Except the memory of his kiss permeated every corner of her mind, leaving her hot inside, and she prayed her friend did not detect the blush burning up her cheeks.

"I daresay that is the first and last time anyone will refer to Waters as 'safe,'" Faith muttered. Her friend glanced about. "Now, go."

With that, Marcia gathered her skirts and bolted off towards the servants' stairs.

Please, don't leave. Please, be waiting.

Because it was a certainty that if Andrew left, he'd not agree for a second time to help her.

He—

A tall figure stepped into her path, and Marcia gasped, all the wind knocked from her as she slammed into that solid wall.

Strong arms caught her, steadying her.

"Forgive me," she said on a rush. And then the rest of the words died on her lips. "Oh."

The dark-haired man clenched and unclenched his hands at his sides. "Hello, Marcia."

She'd been fascinated by his hands from the moment he'd caught her palm for the first kiss he'd ever placed upon it. His fingers had been long, and powerful, and steady. Until now. Now, they shook.

"Charles," she said dumbly, incapable of nothing more than his name.

He looked haggard. Exhausted. Rumpled, even. His sharply chiseled cheeks were covered with several days of growth.

"You…" he began, and when he didn't finish that thought, she stared blankly at him. He swallowed loudly. "Are well?"

A panicky giggle nearly choked her. "As well as a lady can be after being left at the altar."

All the color leached from his cheeks.

He looked miserable. Good. He should be. But also, why should he be? He'd been the one to break it off with her. Oddly, that reminder didn't cut quite the same way it had just days ago. In fact, it didn't cut at all.

Marcia found herself. "Lord Thornton," she said coldly. "If you'll excuse me?" Without awaiting permission, she made to step around him.

"Is Lord Waters dallying with you?" he demanded.

Oh, God. He knew. Stormont had suspected her identity last evening, after all. Heart pounding, Marcia faced him for a second time, grateful for the protection offered by her hood.

His features were strained, a muscle ticking at the corner of his right eye and a pulse throbbing at his jaw. And it occurred to her he was jealous. And yet, why should he be? "Lord Waters is a good friend of my family's," she said, infusing a coolness into her voice.

"Forgive me," he said on a rush. "I know you have better judgment than to engage with one such as Waters."

She frowned. *One such as Waters*? How dare he? Andrew had been a friend to her in every way. For a lifetime, too. She wouldn't let this man or any man disparage him so. "You would dare insinuate Lord *Waters* is dishonorable?" She gave him a once-over. "He wouldn't dally with me." Marcia glared at him. "Nor would he leave a lady standing at the altar."

Charles jerked as if she'd struck him.

But Marcia was not done with him. "For that matter, who I—how did you put it—dally with is not your concern, Charles. Now, if you'll excuse me."

"Please," he said hoarsely. "Don't go." He stretched a hand out. "It was not my intention to insult you."

It was a ludicrous claim for this man, of all men, to make. A laugh bubbled up from her throat. "Which time? This evening or the day of our wedding?"

The remaining color bled from his cheeks. "I am so very s-sorry." His hoarse voice caught and broke. "I need you to know that. I need you to"—he paused, searching for words—"know I regret everything about that day."

She should leave. Andrew waited, and what this faithless man had to say mattered not at all. And yet, she lingered. "Why, Charles?" she asked quietly, and that question came not from the place of agony of that day but, rather, from a desperate need to know how she could have been so very wrong in her judgment about him and his affections.

Charles stared intently at a point just over her head. "I… There was my sister to consider." His tones were peculiarly flat.

"You feared for their reputations should their illustrious brother marry a sullied woman who was beneath him?" She lifted an eyebrow.

"No!" he exclaimed, his voice echoing, and he immediately glanced around to verify they were still alone. When he looked back, he lowered his voice. "It wasn't that. It *isn't* that. I love you," he said raggedly.

"Just not enough," she murmured and attempted to leave.

His features contorted in a paroxysm that sent a chill through her.

She stopped. Something he'd said, a slight omission and yet a significant one, registered. *There was my sister to consider.* Not his *sisters*. Reflexively, Marcia's arms came up, and she rubbed them to ward off the chill. In vain.

Charles closed the remaining distance between them so a handful of steps separated them, and near as she was, she saw the grief and misery etched in the planes of his once-beloved features. "One of my sisters was once… acquainted with Lord Atbrooke."

She stilled, and then her legs trembled underneath her as his meaning took hold.

Oh, God.

Atbrooke had inflicted the same hell he had upon her mother on other women, too.

Including one of Charles's beloved sisters.

She bit down hard on her lower lip. Her entire body trembled. How was it possible to feel this cold and yet have one's palms slicked with sweat?

Her former betrothed stretched a hand out as if to touch her cheek, but then, as if the revulsion of caressing her was too great, he let it fall, and she came whirring back to the moment. "It didn't matter to me that you were illegitimate, you know," he said hollowly. "I would have married you anyway. I just… I couldn't… I didn't know… I…"

Hearing something in those stammered words, Marcia sharpened her gaze upon his face.

But then, Charles took in a deep, unsteady breath. "If… you are running around with Waters, I'd ask you to… stop. To be careful."

She tensed. "Are you threatening me?"

He drew back. "Never," he whispered. "I just do not wish to see you hurt, but I'd never speak ill of you or spread gossip about you. I love you."

He loved her. Odd those three words didn't have the affect they had on her even days ago. "Just not enough," she said softly. But then… "How could you?" she murmured, without judgment.

Pain ravaged his features.

She waited for Charles to say something more. Something. Anything.

For a moment, she thought he might state his desire to wed her after all. Only, there was no relief or joy at the thought. He was a stranger to her.

In the end, she was the one who spoke into the void of silence.

"I am so very sorry," she said, and that apology came from a place deep in her soul, for the hurt his sister had known and for the regret she carried that her existence had wrought another person more pain.

"Marcia," he croaked. "I—"

"You do not need to worry, Charles. Just as you'd not spread gossip about me, I shall not betray what you've shared." That he'd come here, that despite his love and devotion for his sisters, he'd still revealed that most personal, most painful secret to her, of all people, indicated his regard hadn't been feigned.

He was as disgusted by her blood as she was.

Marcia lifted her hood back into place; she turned on her heel and left.

Even as she made her way outside, she found herself suffocating all over again, struggling to get a breath.

At last, she was free.

CHAPTER 11

SHE WAS LATE.

Again.

Unlike the prior time, however, Andrew knew Marcia would be here.

Or he had *thought* as much.

That was, he'd thought as much for the first thirty minutes he'd spent waiting for her. After that, he'd begun to have his doubts.

She'd had a change of heart.

That much had been clear after Stormont had crashed their table last evening.

Nay, he'd seen the first hesitancy before he'd helped her from the carriage.

Following Stormont's exchange, however, something had shifted. She'd been different.

Quieter.

More reserved.

All the way until he'd escorted her home.

Her reason and good judgment had been restored, and all it had taken was the tangible fear of discovery. She had too much sense and reason to continue seeing this through. She'd certainly always possessed far more than Andrew had. The woman he'd known almost as long as she'd been alive would be too clever to tangle herself up with him and visit the haunts scoundrels like Andrew did.

But as he sat there some twenty minutes after the time she'd indicated she'd be here, he felt a different sentiment in his chest.

Something that felt very much like regret.

The moment the thought slipped in, he blanched.

"Regret?" he muttered into the quiet. "Regret." Of course it wasn't regret.

Relief. That was the emotion. It was such a foreign one for a man on the losing ends of many wagers and card hands that it proved nearly indecipherable.

That's all there was to it.

Andrew consulted his timepiece for the tenth time that night, squinting in the dim light in a bid to make out the tiny numbers.

One forty-three.

Nearly forty-five minutes late.

She wasn't coming.

Andrew returned his timepiece inside his cloak and stole one more look outside at streets that still bustled with the lords and ladies attending their respectable affairs.

He'd remain just in case. Just to be certain she didn't arrive so she wouldn't be left waiting in the streets alone.

And then a startled curse escaped him as his gaze landed on a figure staring up at him.

Marcia.

The tight sensation in his chest abated, replaced with a lightness.

Opening the door, Andrew helped her inside. "You are late," he said, making a show of consulting his timepiece. "I told you what would happen if you were again. I almost left," he added after he'd shut the door, and his driver had urged the team on.

It was a lie.

He hadn't had any intention of leaving.

He would have waited until the morning sun had risen.

Instead of rising to the bait, and lighting into him as she would any other time, she remained uncharacteristically silent. She was never silent. "Where were you?"

Marcia fiddled with her cloak. "I was waylaid."

In his peculiar relief at seeing her, he'd failed to note the unusual somberness to the usually always smiling lady. Until now.

Bloody hell. "Your parents?" And it was a much-needed reminder that he was playing with fire.

"No," she said softly, directing her stare at the window. "Charles."

He stilled.

Charles. As in her former sweetheart.

His lip peeled back. "*Charles.*" God, how he hated her use of that cur's name.

"The Marquess of Thornton," she clarified, taking that vile epithet as a question and not the curse it had been. "My former betrothed," she said needlessly.

Hearing her use of the other man's Christian name and knowing there'd been love between them unleashed a visceral feeling inside Andrew. "What the hell did he want?" he snapped, knowing he was being a surly cur but hopeless to control it.

"I believe Lord Stormont suspected it was me with you last evening. Charles asked if I was carrying on with you."

Thornton had approached her, which meant the fellow still cared for her. That realization left Andrew with a sour taste in his mouth.

"I assured him we weren't. I assured him that you are honorable and good to me. He promised he would not betray me," she said on a rush, misunderstanding the reason for his silence.

There wasn't a thing honorable or good about Andrew. If there was, Andrew wouldn't be with Marcia even now.

"Is that all he wanted?" he asked carefully, holding his breath.

Marcia laced her fingers together and stared at the joined digits. "He also wanted to explain why he did what he did," she said, glancing down at her lap.

A visceral, primal rage whipped through him, and not for the first time, Andrew wanted to take Thornton apart. "Well, there is no explaining it and certainly no forgiving it," he said brusquely.

"But there is, Andrew," she said with a greater insistence—and with a loyalty Thornton certainly did not deserve and a devotion that left a tight feeling inside Andrew's chest.

"Absolutely nothing you can say, and certainly nothing Thornton can say, will ever pardon his treatment of you. So do not go about defending him. At least, not to me."

"No," she agreed. "But I can understand why he could not marry me." A trace of sadness glimmered in her eyes.

They arrived at their destination, and he found himself grateful for the sudden end to their discussion about the illustrious Lord Thornton, her former love and sweetheart and a bloody paragon. Only...

"He's not, you know," he snapped, yanking her mask out from inside his jacket.

As he helped her don the article, Marcia stared confusedly at him.

"You speak about Thornton like he's some perfect hero," he said, tying the velvet laces gently at the back of her head. "Like he's an honorable, otherworldly fellow, but he's not. He's a cad and a cur for what he did to you, and that is the only thing that should ever define him in your eyes, or Society's eyes, for all time." He reached for the fabric beside him on the bench and held it up. "Now put this on."

Marcia cocked her head "What—?"

"It's a turban."

"A turban."

He nodded.

Marcia burst out laughing, and it felt so very good to hear her laugh and to see that sadness fade from her eyes. "You expect me to wear *this*?"

"If you expect me to take you along with me, then yes. Yes, I do." After Stormont's visit to his table, Andrew had realized he needed to take even more precautions to ensure Marcia went undiscovered.

"This is absolutely ridiculous. Turbans are for grandmothers and old widows and bluestockings who've never married, with butlers named Cheevers and dogs named Biscuit."

The tension of before gone, Andrew found himself grinning. "And now they're for young innocents who insist on waltzing on the wild side."

"Waltzing on the wild side," she repeated contemplatively. "I very much like that."

"Splendid," he said dryly. "I'm so happy you approve." He jutted his chin her way. "On."

Muttering under her breath, she accepted the turban and pulled a face. "I still don't see why I have to wear this, Andrew," she protested. "I have blonde hair."

"And?"

"And *every* English lady has blonde hair," she said in exasperation.

"Not like yours," he rejoined. "Not glimmering a dozen different shades of spun gold and sunshine."

She'd oft despised her golden curls, longing for something more exotic, something to set her apart from all the other golden-haired misses: a midnight black, a crimson red, even a strawberry shade. Anything.

Only…

Her lips parted, and her heart danced wildly in her breast. The way he'd spoken, she could almost believe the strands were as glorious as he described.

"Spun gold and sunshine," she repeated softly.

The moon shining through the crack in the curtains was bright enough to reveal the bright color that suffused his cheeks.

"You're wearing it, Marcia," he said gruffly, and this time, he wound the turban about her hair with a gentleness that left her weak kneed.

When he'd finished, he paused to assess his work.

She held her breath. Waiting for him to say… something, unsure of what that something was or could be.

"Come." He took her by the hand.

A short while later, he was leading her into Cyprian's Den.

The moment a burly, dark-clad servant drew the front door open, the noise within spilled out, filling the streets with a deafening clamor of laughter and clinking coins.

"Come," Andrew said, pulling her close in a protective way as he slipped an arm around her waist and led her through the club.

As they went, Marcia's gaze took in the disheveled lords, with loosened cravats, clustered around gaming tables. A haze of smoke from too many cheroots hung over the room like a thick London fog. Scantily clad women moved about the room with trays in their hands, offering drinks to the boisterous patrons.

"It is no more decadent than Cyprian's Den," she remarked. In fact, it looked very much the same.

"Ah, but it's not," Andrew whispered, pausing to turn her in his arms and draw her close.

Her entire body trembled, and she tipped her head back to meet his gaze. "I-isn't it?"

"Only on the gaming floors." He shifted, placing his mouth close to her ear so that when he spoke, his lips moved in an accidental kiss. "Off the floors is where the greatest sinning happens. Rooms where men and women or men and men and women and women can meet, sometimes with multiple partners."

She dampened her lips as his words conjured scandalous images in her mind. "In-indeed?"

"Oh, yes. And there are viewing rooms so that others might watch the show. Would you like that, love?" he tempted. "Would you like to visit one of those rooms and view others as they find and give pleasure?"

A wicked ache formed between her legs, the pressure deepening as Andrew shifted so that his mouth hovered close to hers. "Here we are!"

As if he'd uttered nothing more than an observation about the weather, he straightened and motioned to the empty table near them.

Dazed, Marcia blinked slowly, certain that everyone had witnessed Andrew holding her close to him. Alas, everyone in the entire room remained focused on their own pleasures.

He put a hand on the small of her back, guiding her towards the table. "Here," he said loudly, pulling out one of the chairs.

Marcia slid into the comfortable leather folds.

In an instant, a serving girl materialized, and Andrew retrieved two flutes of champagne, handing one over to Marcia.

She took the glass from him, and as he seated himself, she did her best to feign nonchalance. He asked for a deck of cards, and the young woman laid one on the table before bustling off to distribute glasses to other patrons.

All the while, Marcia's heart thumped at the wickedness of being here.

"Well?" Andrew asked. Sitting back in his chair, he reached for the deck of cards, and she was grateful as he shifted away from his earlier naughty talk and on to something as casual as cards. He proceeded to shuffle. "A game of vingt-et-un?"

She nodded. He knew she knew how to play. He'd taught her when she'd been a small girl. Cards were safe.

When he set down the deck, Marcia reached for it, but Andrew covered it with his hand. "You don't come into a place like Cyprian's Den and not wager, Marcia," he murmured in husky tones that sent her heart into a double-time rhythm.

She dampened her mouth. "Wh-what is the wager?" She gave thanks for the volume of the club that muffled somewhat the tremor in her voice.

"I win, and you end this scheme of yours."

Marcia came crashing back down to reality. He was trying to be free of her. Because, ultimately, be it by her family or her former fiancé or the friend before her, Marcia remained someone who was unwanted. "You needn't worry," she said softly. "I've decided this is my last night."

Andrew stilled, his features frozen. "In… deed?" There was a halting quality to that question.

She nodded. Did she merely imagine the glimmer of regret in his eyes?

"A different wager, then," he said quietly. "Since you've agreed to give up your wicked ways, if you win, I'll have to continue putting in appearances at respectable events for each number of hands you beat me."

A startled laugh escaped her. "Surely you'd not risk *that* horror," she said, and his laughter joined with hers.

He winked. "I'm confident in my card-playing skills."

Marcia smoothed her features into a mask of feigned solemnity. "Very well. If *I* win, you shall suffer through visiting polite affairs." She dropped her voice to a whisper. "And what if you win, Andrew?" she teased. "What do you want?"

Or her question had been *meant* to be teasing.

Only, Andrew's gaze darkened, and his golden lashes slipped lower as his stare dipped. His eyes lingered on her mouth, and she felt a wave of heat burn low in her belly.

He is going to kiss me, and I want it. So very desperately.

"If I win, we leave now."

Just like that, the promise of his kiss died.

So her assurance that this was the last night was not enough.

"Best three out of five, Marcia."

Marcia managed a nod. "Very well." She tapped the table.

Not taking his eyes from her, Andrew dealt a card to Marcia, turning over a ten for her and then revealing a seven for himself.

She sat up excitedly, and he dealt her second card.

An ace.

She let out a happy squeal over his curse, even as she fought the niggling of hurt at his annoyed response to her win. "I shan't let you steal my joy at winning," she said, gathering up the cards. Suddenly, she shivered. A chill slipped through her as she felt a stare upon her.

Several patrons shifted, revealing a lone figure seated at a table some seven paces away.

Marcia froze.

Him.

The gentleman stared baldly back at Marcia.

As Andrew shuffled the deck, she made no attempt to look away.

The familiar man was one she'd met but once, some ten years earlier, believing he'd been a friend of her mother's. Innocent as she'd been at that time, she had found herself enthralled by the man with a birthmark like her own.

Automatically, she touched the birthmark on her hand.

He flashed an icy smile. A knowing one. And then, ever so slowly, he lifted his hand. Anyone else would have construed that gesture as a greeting. But then, ever so slightly, he angled his palm to show his matching mark.

Her skin slicked hot and then cold, and nausea churned in her stomach. The ceiling shrank as the walls closed in around her. Her skin crawled. For even with her mask and her turban, he'd recognized her as his own.

Her father. The man who'd sired her. The man who'd raped her mother. The monster whose blood flowed in her veins.

"Marcia?" Andrew's voice came as if from a distance.

She shook her head, incapable of a response when she couldn't even manage a coherent thought.

Her hands quaking, Marcia grabbed her flute and drank down the bubbly brew.

"Hey now," he said gently. "Slow down."

I need to leave.

The pleasure of this night had been tainted with the reminder of who she was.

And yet, she could not make her legs move. Not in the direction she should. Because more than wanting to leave, she wanted to go to him. She wanted to rail at him and rage and pound her fists against his chest and face, leaving him bruised and bloodied and broken, as he'd left her mother.

A loud rush of air filled her ears. "Deal," she snapped, and Andrew cocked his head.

She'd be damned if that man ran her off.

"But…"

"I said *deal*."

Except one could always count on Andrew Barrett, the Viscount Waters, to never do that which was expected of him. With a small frown, he drew his chair forward and leaned across the table. "What is it, love?"

Tears threatened, and she was struck by his innate sense of knowing that something was amiss with her.

The gossip pages wrote about him as a rake who was self-absorbed in his own pleasures, but he'd never been that way with her.

Aware of the marquess's eyes upon them, she gave silent thanks for the shelter Andrew's body now provided, protecting her from the other man's view.

"It is nothing," she said softly.

"I know you," he murmured. "Certainly well enough to gather when something has upset you. Is it because you'll have my company at a polite event?"

Her lips quivered in a smile. "No." Never that.

He lifted a hand between them and traced the pad of his thumb along her lower lip.

Her mouth parted, and a sigh slipped out as her body leaned reflexively toward him and his touch, and that was the power of Andrew, this ability to blot out all noise and darkness so that it was just she and him in the moment.

"Waters, mind if we join you?"

They jumped apart, looking up.

Lord Landon and the Duke of Rothesby stared back with knowing amusement, and the brief, shared connection with Andrew was effectively severed.

"Cards with a single partner is hardly more enjoyable than four." Landon winked and helped himself to a vacant chair.

"Unless that single partner is an intriguing, beautiful woman," His Grace murmured, passing an assessing stare over Marcia that sent heat rushing to her cheeks. "In which case, I'm hard-pressed to stay away." He dropped a bow. "It is so very good to see you again, Lady Dorothy."

Marcia returned that greeting, managing a smile. "Evan."

Andrew frowned. "That won't be…"

Landon had already helped himself to the deck and began shuffling.

She wanted to be alone with Andrew, even in this place where they were surrounded by as many people as could be crammed into the most attended ball of the Season.

But his friends did, however, make for good company, and between their light bantering and Landon repeatedly refilling her glass with champagne, it should have been easy for her to forget the contemptible figure seated at that table across the way, watching them.

Watching her.

And yet, her mind proved unrelenting, painting images and scenes she didn't want, of her mother crying out and fighting Lord Atbrooke as he forced himself upon her. As he sealed her fate and stole her innocence.

"Your turn, love," Andrew was saying, and unthinking, her

movements rote, Marcia tossed down a card.

Whatever card she'd slapped down earned good-natured ribbing and laughter from her card partners. It was as though she were underwater, and the sounds of that revelry were muffled.

Atbrooke picked up his glass and toasted her before downing the contents in a smooth swallow, his smile smug, knowing.

It was the same smile he'd worn when he'd arrived at her Aunt Dorothy's home all those years ago, when Marcia had been innocent and unsuspecting and had seen a smile as nothing more than a smile and failed to note the ugliness contained within that quirk of his lips.

But she saw it now.

And she knew everything, and there was no escaping that knowing, no matter how much she might wish to.

Suddenly, it was too much.

Marcia exploded to her feet, overturning her chair.

"Mar—love?" Andrew's concerned voice came as if from far away, and she was incapable of responding, incapable of seeing him.

Marcia bolted.

CHAPTER 12

SHE'D FLED.

Andrew froze for a moment, staring after Marcia's rapidly fleeing frame.

Nay, she'd not only fled... she'd gone off on her own.

With a curse, he exploded to his feet.

"I'm noticing a trend of the lady passing on your company," Rothesby drawled. "Perhaps you might allow me to take her off your hands, after all."

Ignoring that good-natured ribbing, Andrew scoured the club, frantically searching for her.

His heart thudded a sickly beat against the walls of his chest.

What in hell was she thinking? Didn't she have any idea the danger she might find herself in at this hell?

Amongst the patrons, Andrew caught a glimpse of her satin turban: never more grateful he'd insisted she don that article.

"Waters?" Rothesby called, concerned.

Andrew took off after Marcia as she maneuvered around guests, weaving and sliding between them with the stealth of London's best pickpocket.

Then, he lost her.

Dread tightened in his stomach.

"Mar—" Cutting off that damning shout, he increased his pace.

Not that he needed to bother yelling for her. She'd never hear him above the din of this place.

Andrew shoved his wave through the same crowd Marcia had raced through, elbowing men out of the way, and earning angry shouts from drunken patrons. And then she broke free through the crush, and disappeared down one of the many halls of Cyprian's Den.

Sweat slicked his palms, and he quickened his stride.

Madness tightened its hold over him.

Why in hell had he agreed to take her here.

Why?

Why?

It was a litany in his head as he reached the hallway she'd disappeared down.

Absent of any patrons, silence filled the hall, punctuated by the revelries behind him.

"Dorothy," he shouted, using that middle name she'd given Rothesby. Those unanswered two syllables echoed from the walls. Andrew paused beside the first door, and pressing the handle, let himself in.

A couple in the throes of making love gave no outward indication they'd heard them.

Andrew closed the door hard on those pitchy screams and groans, and continued on to the next room.

With every room, and every tableau he interrupted, his panic spiraled.

"Dorothy," he called again as he entered a fourth bedchamber.

A pair of women, locked in one another arms paused in their embrace. "We could be her." One of the ladies giggled. "Would you care to—?"

Andrew shut the door on the remainder of that invitation.

He reached for the next handle and let himself in.

An eerie silence filled the bedchamber.

White, from the satin wallpaper that adorned the walls to the sheets and coverlet upon the massive four-poster bed, and the filmy gauze covering that hung upon that. The stark color, amidst this house of sin, teased an illusion of innocence. Andrew passed his gaze over the room.

"Dorothy?" he called into the quiet, stepping deeper into the room.

Click.

Relief flooded Andrew as he whipped around. "There…" Andrew went motionless. "*You.*"

"Looking for me, are you?" the woman purred. "My Andrew, all grown up."

It had been years since he'd seen her.

Time hadn't aged her.

The baroness. Marianne, Lady Carew. His former lover. The sister of Lord Atbrooke. And also the twisted woman who'd used him years earlier in an attempt to punish Rutland for his role in seeing her and her brother pay for their crimes.

Just as beautiful as ever. Just as evil as ever.

She was the same voluptuous beauty. She'd been round in all the places a woman should be rounded. A catlike smile still graced her pouty, painted lips. Lips which had been some of the first he'd kissed, but back when he'd believed in love and her interest in him, real. Her midnight curls were so black, they fairly shimmered with a shine of blue upon the ends.

The same woman who'd been a former lover of Huntly had used Andrew as a pawn to hurt his sister Justina. She'd put a bullet in him, and then ultimately been sent away for her crimes.

And she was here, now.

"I'm free," she purred. "Released from that madhouse where you helped put me." Her plump mouth formed a pout. "That was very naughty of you to let them take me away like that."

She was as mad as she'd ever been. It glimmered in her eyes.

"How—?"

"How did I get out?" she countered, anticipating that question. "The gaoler was… very kindly towards me." She smiled like the cat who'd lapped a bowl of cream. "As you can probably imagine why."

Yes, he could. No man had ever been able to resist her. Himself included.

That had been before. He wasn't the boy he'd been.

He narrowed his eyes. "Step out of the way."

Leaning back against the door, so that she was a barrier between him and leaving, Marianne eyed him thoughtfully, and then a coy smile formed on her lips. "I daresay this is the first you've ever ordered me gone, Andrew. As I remember, you were always quite eager for me." Her breath hitched, and she ran a palm down the front of her sapphire-blue silk gown, resting her fingers at the deep crevice of her bodice. "Quite eager."

"I was a child," he said coldly. "And that was before you pointed a pistol at me. Now, move as—"

"Bah, mine was an act of passion." She licked at her lips. "And you always loved my passionate nature." Marianne paused. "As I recall, where I was concerned, you loved all manner of things about me."

Revulsion snaked through him. "I'll not ask you again."

Surprise lit her eyes. "You're meeting another."

Andrew instantly went tight-lipped. Marianne Carew was a ruthless viper. Her discovering Marcia's presence here and his relationship with the lady would only bring problems and danger to her.

"You *are*," Marianne said with a dawning understanding. "You are passing over a night with me in favor of some other lady." She clapped her hands excitedly. "Oh, you must tell me who she is."

The tight quality of that otherwise playful question hinted further at her mercenary nature. And it occurred to him that his disinterest had only the opposite effect on her disinterest. "There is no one," he lied, needing to protect Marcia at all costs. "Step aside, Marianne."

"Do you know," Marianne said, toying a long curl around her index finger, and pondering him contemplatively. "I don't think I shall. Not yet, anyway. You seem to have forgotten how special our time together was." She sniffed as if moments from tears. And then her eyes darkened as she released that strand, and with slow, languid movements, she lowered her bodice. Her enormous breasts tumbled free: the crests rouged crimson as she'd always done.

Back when he'd been a green boy, the sight she made now had driven him to the point of madness with his desire for her. Now, he eyed her with only antipathy and pity.

"Oh, my, you really aren't interested in me, are you?" He heard the challenge there. She palmed her breasts, bringing them together, and closing her eyes, a little moan slipped from her lips.

When he remained completely unmoved, she let her arms fall to her side. "Is it that mouse you were with?" she demanded. "The one you've been squiring about the demimonde?"

He tensed.

Marianne had always possessed the ability to ferret out any weakness.

"I know everything. Everything. I confess… to some curiosity."

He stalked over. "If you'll not move, I'll do it for you."

Her eyes glittered. "Do it," she rasped. "I would like you to, you know." With that, she raced over and crawled onto the bed. Flipping onto her back, she yanked her skirts up, revealing herself to him. "Take me, Andrew. You know you—"

With a sound of disgust, Andrew raced from the room.

"Andrew!" she cried as he let himself out "Don't leave—"

The remainder of her pleas fell forgotten on deaf ears as he bolted for the next corridor, searching for Marcia.

Where in hell could she be?

Rushing through halls of Cyprian's Den, the muted laughter from the gaming hell floor filled Marcia's ears, coupled with the quiet thud of her slippered footfalls.

She continued on, breathless, her lungs burning, and her side aching as she raced on until there was no sound. And only silence.

Slowing her frantic steps, Marcia pressed her ear against the panel, and detecting only silence, she let herself in.

The moment she'd closed the door behind her, Marica's entire body dropped, her shoulders sagging, and she folded her arms around her middle, holding herself tightly and struggling to steady the uneven rhythm of her breath.

There would be no escaping him.

Because escaping him would require that Marcia herself escape, and there was no cutting herself free. There was no disentangling herself from the blood that flowed in her veins or the origins of her birth. She was crafted of evil, and that truth would remain forever unchanged.

And then, as if she'd conjured him of her own thoughts, the door opened, and she stared blankly at him.

The Marquess of Atbrooke. The man who'd raped her mother and sired Marcia.

Of course, he'd found her.

Pushing the door shut behind him, he smiled at Marcia. "Hullo, my dear. It's been… years. Too many."

She recalled that first meeting: back when she'd been innocent and he'd come to call on her mother, and Marcia had smiled and chatted with him as though he were nothing more than a kindly gentleman.

"How did—?" Marcia stopped herself from completing that question.

He answered anyway. "How did I know it was you? I've been watching your townhouse, my dear."

Oh, God.

He'd been lurking outside her home. The place where her mother lived.

"Worry not. I have no designs upon your mother. Anymore," he added, and the bile climbed her throat. "I was hoping to catch a glimpse of you, my dearest daughter." He flared his eyebrows in mock surprise. "Imagine my shock when I saw you sneak out for the first time. As any good father would do, I've since made sure to watch after you when you go out."

Dearest daughter.

That was what she was.

"I'm *not* your daughter," she said, her voice thick. "I have a father. You are not he."

He slapped a hand over his heart. "Ah, but you wound me, child of my loins. I am, after all, the one who knows about your new proclivities, while dearest Lord Wessex remains wholly in the dark."

Fury stole across her vision. "Do not speak so of him. You are not fit to speak his name."

His features formed a mask of wounded affront. "I'm merely speaking the truth. And I find it endearing that you and I should enjoy the same pastimes."

Revulsion snaked through her, and Marcia hugged herself more tightly before she registered what she was doing and noted his cold amusement as he took in her solitary embrace.

Marcia forced her arms back to her sides.

"Yes, yes," he murmured, more to himself. "I would recognize you anywhere, Marcia." He came closer, and reflexively she took a step away from him.

The emotionless, icy grin on his face widened, and this time when he continued forward, she planted her feet on the wood floor, making herself stand tall and proud.

"Sweet, is it not? Like father, like daughter."

Marcia's fingers curled sharply against her palms, her nails digging painfully into her flesh, shredding the skin. She welcomed the sting of pain.

I am going to be ill. She was going to cast up the contents of her stomach right there on his shoes.

"What do you want?" she demanded, proud of that steady deliverance.

"Your mother and her husband have been most unkind to me," he said. "They have run me off and hidden my child from me. They have beggared me, making it impossible for me to make a respectable match."

"They've saved some respectable woman from a future of misery with you. That's what they've done," she said, looking him up and down.

He looked at her and then tossed his head back and laughed. "Oh, Marcia, you have your mother's spirit. She was a fighter, too."

A fresh wave of bile climbed into her throat.

"You asked what I want? I want Wessex and his terrible friend Lord Rutland to stand down," he said icily. "Given the unlikeliness of that, perhaps you would care to remind Lord Wessex that I'm looking to have a relationship with my daughter, unless he'd rather I stay away."

"In which case?"

"In which case I'd expect a small sum of five thousand pounds. To ease my pain in being denied your company."

"You want to bribe my father?" she asked flatly. *And he'd use me as a pawn. He'd use his claim to me to extract money from the viscount.*

"I want you to remind Lord Wessex that your real father would like nothing more than to spend time with my daughter, but I would be willing to forgo my greatest wishes to know you, for the right price," he said silkily. "Otherwise, I can and will be sure to visit his household every day until he grants me an audience with you."

In other words, he'd continue to come to her family's home, reminding her mother of his presence.

As if she can possibly forget, a panicky voice taunted.

It was enough that her mother had to contend with the daily reminder Marcia provided. But having to face him, to look out her window and see him standing outside, requesting entry… And all the papers would write of it. They'd continue to drag forth the gossip about Marcia's mother's past affair with the marquess, when in truth he'd been no lover, but a rapist.

When she managed to find her voice, it emerged garbled. "Stay away from me," she warned. "And stay away from my family."

"You wound me once more," he drawled. Removing his gloves, he beat those white leather articles together. "I'll give you a week in which to speak to Lord Wessex and see those funds transferred to me, at which point you have my assurance that I will not pay my first sweetheart and the daughter she gave me a visit."

"She was not your sweetheart," she hissed. "You, my lord, are a monster. And I am *not* your child."

Suddenly, he surged forward, and Marcia gasped, attempting to retreat, but he gripped her arm hard. "Ah, but you are, Marcia," he whispered. "And you know it." He grabbed her right hand with his free one, his hold harsh and hard and vile, and tears pricked her lashes as she attempted to wrestle free of him. "You see it there on your skin," he murmured, forcing her wrist upward, forcing her to look upon that birthmark she wore, the one they shared. "Why, even in the company you keep and the wicked places you visit, you prove time and time again that blood indeed runs thick." And then, like she were a small child, he released her and patted the top of her head. "A week, dearest." With that warning, he left, closing the door behind him.

Marcia remained absolutely motionless, afraid to move, the world all distorted and twisted in her mind.

Her entire body slumped, and she leaned against the wall behind her, borrowing support, trying to will her legs to work so she could flee this place.

The door opened, and she stiffened. He'd returned.

"Marcia!"

Only, it wasn't him—her father, the rapist and blackmailer—and a giddy relief swept through her, bringing her eyes shut.

"What the hell do you think you are doing?" Andrew demanded, stalking over. "I've had a hell of a time finding you. Do you know the danger—?"

She looked up, and the remainder of that lecture died a swift death.

"Marcia?" he asked, and his tones were instantly concerned. His eyes were, too, and it was too much.

Marcia flung herself at his chest, and Andrew immediately folded her in his arms.

"What happened?" he asked, his voice more than slightly panicked. "Are you hurt?" He ran his palms over her arms, searching for hurts and verifying that she was unharmed.

"N-no," she rasped against his shoulder. At least not in the way he worried about now.

"Hey now, love," he whispered against the top of her head and held her. Just held her, and it felt so very good and safe and wonderful.

This was Andrew, and he was uncomplicated. He was her friend, who'd become even more these past days.

He placed a kiss against her temple, and the tenderness of his lips brushing there brought her eyes closed.

As long as he drew breath, Andrew would forever recall the sheer terror of watching Marcia tear through London's most scandalous and dangerous club and losing sight of her in the crush of men, women, and servers enjoying the revelry. His world had come undone at the loss of her.

Until he'd found her as he'd never before seen her—bereft and empty-eyed and hurting.

Everything hurt inside, and as he held her, he sought to reassure himself that he had her now, also vowing that if someone had harmed her, that person would pay with his life.

She clung to him, holding him tightly, seeming to want to anchor herself in his embrace and find some stability. "My father was here," she whispered, her words muffled against his chest.

Andrew stiffened and then set her away. He looked frantically about.

"Not my real father, Marcus." She folded her hands, looking down at them. "Lord Atbrooke."

He stilled, and his heart thudded sickeningly against his chest. Lord Atbrooke and the cur's sister, Lady Carew, possessed an evil that Satan himself could not manage, and that monster had sought out Marcia. Nor did he think it was a coincidence that he'd been conveniently waylaid by Marianne. This was Atbrooke's sister, after all. "Atbrooke spoke with you," he said slowly, needing to clarify.

She nodded.

"What did he want?" he asked carefully.

"He claims he wants a relationship with me, but he is just doing it because he wants my father to pay him, and I can't have him come around, Andrew." All her words came rapidly, rolling together. "He said he would, but then my mother would have to see him, and I can't allow that. It would destroy her." A pained half laugh, half sob, garbled and raw, ripped from her throat. "It will destroy her. I am his daughter."

Andrew gripped her hard by the shoulders, drawing her close. "You are no such thing," he said sharply, tightening his hold upon her and shaking her slightly, knocking her mask off. How could she see any of Atbrooke in herself? How could she not see she was joy and light and love to the other man's darkness? "Do you hear me, Marcia?"

"But I am his daughter," she said, lifting her ravaged, unmasked gaze to his. "And my mother must look at me every day and see…

him."

"Your mother looks at you and sees you, and there could be no greater joy in the world for her than that."

A tear slipped down her cheek, and he brushed it away with the pad of his thumb. Bending his knees and dropping slightly so he could better meet her eyes, he said, "And you, Marcia, this… guilt you carry, there is no place for it. Your birthright is not a thing of shame unless you let it be."

"if you really believed that, then why do you think your life has been determined by who your father is?" she countered, and Andrew paused.

He'd always just… taken it as fact that he was destined to be his father; he'd been so certain of it. He'd conducted himself precisely as his letch of a father had, and there was something both… freeing and unnerving in realizing that mayhap his life hadn't been just destined because of his blood but, rather, because of choices he'd made, and how he'd conducted himself.

He gave her another light squeeze. "Many women and many men take lovers, and babes are born of those unions. That is just… the way. He was a dishonorable rogue who failed your mother and you. But that is not on you or your mother, Marcia."

"No," she whispered, drawing herself back. "I shouldn't be here."

He'd told her as much from the start of this harebrained scheme. Her belated realization didn't make him feel any sense of real triumph. "No," he said gruffly, catching her by the fingers, determined to get her far away from this place that had brought such sadness to her. He'd never come back, because he'd never see anything here but Marcia hurting and lost. "This place is terrible. Let's leave."

Marcia tugged free of him. "No. I wasn't referring to this place." Then she lifted slow, haunted eyes to his, and a chill stole through him. It seeped through every corner of his being, leaving every spot it touched cold inside. "Alive," she whispered. "I shouldn't be alive."

His muscles contracted. "Do not say that," he ordered harshly, not wanting to imagine a world where she was not in it. She was the one spot of light and good.

Her lips twisted in a sad smile that hit him square in the chest. "You misunderstand me. I… my birth should not have happened." Hugging her arms close to herself, Marcia left his side and perched upon the satin-covered bed at the back of the room. And it was the first time in the whole of his rotten existence that he'd ever seen a woman as desirable as her seated upon a bed designed to make a man think of sinning and yet was unable to think about anything other than what was making her hurt. Marcia stared down at her interlocked fingers as if they contained the answer to existence—her existence. "It was not one that was intended."

Andrew sank to a knee beside her at the foot of the bed. "Marcia," he said gently. "There is nothing wrong with being born of a love affair. There was everything right about it because you came of it," he said insistently, trying to will her to understand that.

A bitter, pained-sounding laugh exploded from her lips. "It wasn't a love affair."

"Then a night of passion," he clarified.

"He was not her lover," she whispered, her voice ragged and broken and faint.

Andrew looked at her askance.

"Lord Atbrooke… He… My mother was not willing," she whispered. She lifted that ravaged gaze to his once more. "His desire was not reciprocated."

Andrew heard the words, and yet, his mind proved sluggish to process their meaning because of the heinousness of what she was saying.

"My mother… She…" Marcia shook her head, as if unable to finish the thought. Her throat moved up and down wildly. "He forced himself upon her."

He stilled, and that cold deepened, adding a layer of ice to the chill inside him. *Oh, God.*

"There was no God in this," she whispered, and he realized he'd spoken those words aloud. Biting her lower lip, she looked at her lap. "I am the unwanted child of that unwanted night. I am the child of my mother's rape." She hugged herself in a lonely, forlorn-looking embrace. "I-I shouldn't b-be telling you this. I-it is my m-mother's secret. But i-it is my secret, too. It's about me, and I can't share it with anyone, and I don't want to because it i-is awful what happened to her, and—"

Andrew drew her into his arms, and she immediately turned her cheek, resting it upon his shoulder. "It's all right," he assured. He knew she needed to speak of it for the impact it was having on her life. "I'll honor your confidence." This burden she carried was so very great for any person's shoulders, and his soul ached that it should be upon this woman's.

She closed her eyes. "It was easier to let you th-think I was ashamed of my bastardy. Because then I didn't have to say… who I am. What I am. My mother being deceived by him was vastly different and preferable to her being raped by him."

And she'd continue to carry this painful, awful secret, her mother's secret, which by default also belonged to Marcia.

A strangled groan shook his chest, and he drew her tighter into his embrace and just held her.

And then the torrent opened.

Marcia sobbed, crying against him, shaking and trembling, and he was rendered helpless by her grief, wanting only to absorb it and make it his so that she wouldn't feel any of this pain, yearning to take all of this from her shoulders and claim it as his own if he could. But that was the one thing he could not do.

So Andrew just held her, absorbing her body's trembling against his and stroking her back.

"Every day my m-mother has h-had to look at me and see m-me and remember that day."

"That isn't true," he whispered against the top of her turban, which had knocked loose in her run through the club.

"It is."

"I know it's not because I know you," he said, drawing back slightly so that he could meet her gaze. "I know because when I'm with you, all I can see is your smile, and I laugh at your jests and listen to your stories, and it is impossible for any person to see anything but you, Marcia."

Her lips parted, and in that moment, she looked at him in a way that no other soul on this planet ever had. Having this woman gaze upon him so—him, Andrew Barrett, the Viscount Waters, dissolute lord and son of a reprobate—alternately left him light inside and riddled with terror.

Marcia threw herself into his embrace once more, and he welcomed the slight weight of her form against him as he folded her close, holding her.

"Thank you," she whispered. "I don't know if what you're saying is right, but when you say it like you did, it makes me believe that mayhap me being born wasn't only evil and bad."

"Listen to me," he said, hugging her harder. "The world is a shite place, Marcia, but not because of you. It is better because of your place in it. Lord knows my miserable existence is certainly better for having you in it."

Her breath caught.

He held her for a long while. Rather, they held each other.

And he knew the moment something shifted between them.

He felt it in the way she went still in his arms, but did not pull away, and he was hopeless to pull away even as he should.

Marcia pressed her cheek against the place where his heart beat, and then she parted his jacket so his lawn shirt proved the only barrier between them.

Andrew trembled, moved by her innocence and the intimacy of that act, one of the most powerful ones he'd known.

"Thank you," she whispered.

He smoothed his palm in a small, soothing circle over the small of her back. "I'm a rake and a scoundrel." He issued that reminder to himself for why it was wrong to want her as he did. "But one thing I'm not is a liar. I didn't say anything to you here that isn't true."

Marcia angled her head back, her eyes meeting his.

Oh, God. He swallowed hard, or he tried to. This was the time to go. To leave. To flee. "Marcia." Her name emerged garbled.

"I want you to kiss me," she said softly, and he froze, certain he'd heard her wrong, that he'd heard only that which he'd wished to hear, because that single thought about the lady had haunted him and tempted him and taunted him for days on end now.

She darted her tongue out, and unlike the bold way in which the women of his acquaintance would have used that flesh to tempt, there was an innocence to the way Marcia trailed that tip along the seam of her lips. "Kiss me?"

And there it was for a second time, a question this time.

Her face fell. "You aren't saying anything."

"Because there's nothing to say, Marcia," Andrew said. "I'm not—"

"Why not?" she interrupted. "I'm not asking you for *more*. Just... another kiss."

Another kiss. Two words that conjured in his mind the other kisses they'd shared, the feel of her mouth, the taste of her.

"Unless you wish for more, too," she said.

Oh, God, save him. She'd said *too*. Indicating she yearned for far more than his kiss... and everything he wished to do with her.

"I just wish to forget."

He understood all too well wanting to lose oneself in another person, just so that, even for a brief moment, one might forget what one was, and had done, and had been, and had seen in life.

A pained-sounding laugh left him, and she bristled. "Do you find this amusing?"

"I find this any number of things, Marcia. Amusing is not one of them. You don't want this," he said, his voice strained.

She tightened her hold. "Don't presume to tell me what I want."

"You are vulnerable. I'm not going to take advantage of that, Marcia," he said, more sharply than he'd intended.

"This isn't about... him or what I've shared. This is about me making a choice of what I want, and I would very much like for you to kiss me, Andrew," she said. And then she drew back, and indecision flashed in her eyes, a different horror. "You don't want me."

It would be both easier and the coward's way to let her believe that. Go figure this should be the moment he found himself capable of some level of honor.

"Oh, I want you, Marcia." Hooding his lashes, he swept his gaze over her. "I want you far more than is honorable or good."

And then, cupping a hand at her nape, he angled her head even as she leaned up to meet his mouth.

He made slow love to her mouth at first, teasing her lips, licking the seam, tasting the corner, and her lips parted on a little gasp, a breathless, captivating sound of her desire, and Andrew used that moment to slide his tongue inside, stroking her flesh with his and kissing her as he'd dreamed of since the first time he'd had her in his arms.

And Marcia came alive.

CHAPTER 13

After Lord Atbrooke had cornered Marcia and threatened her, Marcia had thought she'd never know joy again.

She'd been wrong.

When she was with Andrew, everything felt… right.

And when she was in his arms, everything was right.

Andrew deepened their kiss, even as he searched his other hand along her body, cupping her breast and stealing her breath with that tender but heady touch. And then he moved his search lower, to her waist and then her hip. Gripping her in a hold that was both gentle and possessive, he drew her against him, and she felt the hard ridge of his length.

She felt him and the magic of this most glorious moment, one like she'd never known and would never know again, and—

Then she felt nothing.

She cried out, dazed, as Andrew left her.

Or rather, as Andrew was ripped from her arms.

Blinking, she tried to make sense of what she was seeing—and then prayed she hadn't.

Or wished she could pluck out her own eyes.

Or disappear.

Disappearing would be preferable.

Or being invisible.

Scrambling up, she pushed her skirts down past her knees with hands that shook.

"Bastard," her father hissed. Catching Andrew by the front of his jacket, Marcus slammed him against the wall. Then, drawing his arm back, he punched Andrew square in the face.

"No!" she cried out, and even in the dimly lit room, she caught the streak of crimson that poured from Andrew's nose.

Andrew staggered, but managed to keep on his feet. He gave his head a slight shake. "Deserved that," he muttered, his voice sounding thick and garbled.

"No, you didn't!" she cried and looked desperately to her father. "He didn't," she said more insistently.

"Damned right you did, Waters." Her father buried a fist in Andrew's stomach; this one managed to knock him down.

Oh, God. This was her fault. She'd all but coerced Andrew into bringing her with him and had begged for a kiss he'd been hesitant to give.

Terror for him and the need to protect him from further pain overwhelmed her mortification as she found her feet and flew across the room.

She caught her father's arm just as he would have leveled another blow. "Stop," she pleaded, and when that didn't penetrate, she firmed her voice with a hard resolve. "I said stop, Papa."

Her father blinked, and then as if he'd been burned, he yanked his hands off of Andrew and flexed his fingers several times.

Andrew struggled—and failed—to get to his feet.

Releasing her father's arm, Marcia raced around him and sank to the floor beside Andrew. "It isn't his fault." Oh, God. It was all hers.

"Get away from him this instant," her father thundered.

"I asked him to take me here." She'd begged him and was responsible for all of this. "I pleaded with him to kiss—"

"Marcia, no," Andrew said sharply, denying her the rest of that admission. "Go. Just leave."

As he stood, she searched her eyes over his face, attempting to make sense of what he was feeling.

He should hate her.

She deserved that.

Alas, Andrew had always been a better man than either he or the world had given him credit for. "I am so sorry," she whispered.

"I was in the wrong," Andrew said, and he lifted his hand as if to caress her cheek, and then his gaze slid past her shoulder to where

Marcia's father stood. He let his palm fall to his side.

"Bloody right you were," her father gritted out. "We are leaving." Her father caught her by the arm and tossed his cloak around her, yanking the hood up into place.

Coward that she was, she let him all but drag her from the pleasure hall. She let herself be tugged from Andrew and this place, wanting to put all of it behind her. Wanting to forget Atbrooke and her father's arrival. She wanted to forget it all—except that kiss she'd shared with Andrew.

The moment she and her father arrived outside, the viscount led her by the hand in the same way he'd done when she'd been a child. The driver drew open the door of her father's coach, and her father lifted her gently and set her inside, climbing in behind her.

Marcia had believed there was no greater shame than having all of Polite Society, from friends to acquaintances, witness her being left at the altar.

She'd been wrong.

So very wrong.

This was worse.

In fact, as the driver shut the door, climbed atop the perch of his box, and set the carriage into motion, she was certain this was the absolute worst.

Being discovered in that room in Andrew's arms by her father was far worse.

Seated across the carriage from her father, Marcia huddled on the bench, trying to make herself as small and as invisible as possible.

All the while, the viscount remained tucked in a similar way against the opposite side of the carriage, his gaze firmly on the slight crack in the curtains.

"You called him a bastard," she said quietly.

Her father stiffened, and as if it pained him to do so, he looked at her.

But then, mayhap that was how he'd always felt, deep down. Repelled by her. Hating her with some part of himself for the pain she'd brought to her mother.

Her father stared blankly at her.

"You called Andrew a bastard, but he's not. *I'm* the bastard."

Pain rippled over her father's face. "Marcia," he said, his voice thick with emotion. "I didn't mean—"

She shrugged. "It's fine. I was just pointing out that you were incorrect in casting those aspersions upon Andrew's character." Any of them. Andrew had only ever done what she'd wished, and for that, he had gotten handed a vicious beating. With that, Marcia turned her focus to the passing scenery, the moon's glow so faint it barely lent any light to the inky-black setting of the Rookeries.

"What were you thinking, Marcia?" he asked, his voice laden with pain and sorrow and anger, all emotions she'd never before seen from him and certainly not directed at her.

"I was thinking as I no longer have a reputation that matters that I may as well enjoy life," she said simply.

"But it does matter."

Pain cleaved her chest. "Flora and Maisie," she whispered, remembering once again the reason she'd known she couldn't continue this game. Her brothers would one day weather anything, as all men did. But women weren't afforded those same freedoms.

"Not Flora and Maisie," Marcus said, and a gentleness had returned to his tones. "You, Marcia. *You*," he repeated. "Do you think your name and future and happiness don't matter?"

"I don't have a name, Papa. Not one that is true. Collins was the name made up by my mother, for a man who never truly existed." Marcia's mother had told the world of hero-husband gone off to war all to conceal the actions of Lord Atbrooke. Now, those lies had been found out.

Her father's features whitened. At the mention of her true sire's name?

Marcia sank her fingers into the squabs of her bench. What a sacrifice it must have been for him to love her and care for her when he'd so hated the man who'd given her life. Now, he'd have to contend with Lord Atbrooke's threats and bribes, too.

Unable to meet his eyes, she looked away.

"Marcia," Marcus said quietly, and reluctantly she forced her eyes back to his. "You stopped being a Collins the day I met you." He spoke with a somber insistence. "You stole my heart with your forthright manner and spirit. You are a Gray. You have *my* name."

Her lower lip trembled, and she bit it hard. "Yes." How thoughtless her words had been. This, when he had only shown her kindness and love. "And I've sullied that, too." God, she did not deserve him or her mother.

Her father groaned. "No. That isn't what I am saying."

It might not have been, but that was precisely what she'd done.

She looked down at her lap.

"Marcia, look at me." That gentle command brought her gaze reluctantly up. "Your happiness matters," he said quietly. "Your future matters. You matter. And… running about with a cad like Waters… You deserve more than that."

She frowned. "Andrew is *not* a cad."

A muscle spasmed along her father's jawline. "Do not think to defend him. Not to me. He is his father's son."

"If you believe that about blood, I'm my father's daughter, so then we are a perfect pair, are we not?"

Her father blanched, his facial muscles twisting.

And thankfully, mercifully, they arrived home, saving her from whatever loving assurances he intended to give.

Hockley opened the door, and she hurried to take his hand and let him help her down. Rushing inside, she didn't break stride, heading for the sanctuary of her rooms.

Her heart pounding, Marcia struggled to tug off her turban, and when she failed, she gave up and lay with her back against the door. This was bad. Very, very bad. Her father would never forgive Andrew for this. When it had been only Marcia's fault.

A gentle knock sounded at the door.

Of course she'd be expected to speak on it.

Drawing in a deep breath, Marcia made herself grab the handle and open it.

A frowning quartet stared back at her.

Her siblings, Flora, Maisie, Lionel, and Clarion. All of whom had arrived sporting pretend weapons strapped to their waists.

Her siblings whose reputations she should have put first. Her siblings who would now have Lord Atbrooke in their lives, too. The marquess had insisted he'd stalk their house if the viscount did not pay.

"It is the middle of the night," she said softly. "What are you doing up, little ones?"

"Flora woke us," Lionel said in somber tones.

Clarion shifted on his feet. "What happened?" he whispered.

"Nothing," she said quickly, in an attempt to reassure them.

"Then why are you wearing that silly thing on your head?" Maisie asked. "It's really quite awful. Is that why Papa is upset? Because that's why *I'm* upset."

A strangled half laugh, half sob climbed into her throat, and she buried it behind a fist. "It really is hideous," she said, tossing her arms open.

Maisie came hurtling into the room, and Marcia caught her youngest sibling and held her close.

Clarion remained standing in the doorway, balling and un-balling his hands. "It was Thornton, wasn't it? That's why the whole house is awake." With a black glare, he yanked out his weapon and pointed it at the ceiling. "I *knew* I should have called him out."

Not releasing Marcia, Maisie glared back at their brother. "We agreed I was the better one to call him out."

A familiar quarrel erupted amongst her siblings, who loved playing at dueling. Her brothers entered the room to debate Maisie over who should have that honor.

To be heard over the argument that broke out, Marcia raised her voice. "Thornton has done nothing… this time," she allowed, and her siblings immediately stopped fighting and looked to her. "Furthermore, no one is calling anyone out." *But that isn't necessarily true. Do you truly believe your father will let it go unchallenged that you were at Cyprian's Den with Andrew, and in that bedroom, no less? With him kissing you?*

Her stomach roiled.

"Marcia looks like she's going to cast up her biscuits," Lionel announced, sheathing his sword.

And Marcia *felt* like she was going to cast up her biscuits. "I am fine," she reassured them.

"Then why did Lord Rutland's servant come and Papa shout for his horse and carriage, and why was Mama crying?"

Oh, God. She'd reduced her mother to tears.

What did you expect? And are you really capable of anything but bringing them misery?

Misery that was about to come all the worse when Lord Atbrooke paid a visit, seeking money to stay away from them.

"It is my fault," Flora whispered, and Marcia and her siblings swung their gazes her way. "I was worried after I saw you going out the other night, and I told Papa and—" A little sob escaped her.

"Shh," Marcia said, drawing her sister close. She'd not allow Flora that misplaced guilt. "This is not your fault. It is mine." She'd been the one who'd wronged them. All of them.

As she held her younger sister, and her somber siblings looked on, Marcia stared over the tops of their heads into the flames dancing in the hearth.

What was she going to do?

CHAPTER 14

Well, this was decidedly not good.

Not good at all.

The next morning, Andrew sat on the edge of his bed, the latest note he'd received from the gaming hell owner, DuMond, seeking to collect his debts, forgotten on his nightstand.

What in hell had he done?

He'd almost made love to Marcia.

Innocent, virtuous Marcia.

And it was a certainty that he would have if her father hadn't arrived. Andrew would have slipped her gown off her and explored all of her.

What was worse… he still wanted to. He could not rid his mind of the memory of the feel and taste of her—strawberries and honey, and sweeter than any fruit that equally weak Adam had been presented with in the Garden of Eden.

With a groan, Andrew flopped down on his back and dragged a pillow over his head. A good suffocating. That was what he deserved. It would save Marcia's father the bullet he no doubt intended to put into his black heart.

A knock sounded at the door, and Andrew removed the pillow. "Enter," he called.

His valet ducked his head in the room. "Lord Rutland and His Grace, the Duke of Huntly, are here to see you."

Following Wessex's discovery of Andrew and Marcia, this meeting had been just as certain as the sun rising and setting.

Andrew grabbed his timepiece.

Thirty minutes past five o'clock in the morning.

He'd just not expected it would happen so quickly.

Or that *both* men should be here.

Rutland, yes.

Huntly, no.

His brothers-in-law.

Bloody hell.

What in blazes had he done?

And what in blazes are you going to do?

What you need to do, of course. The voice of honor he'd thought long dead jabbed at the back of his mind. Andrew could—nay, Andrew had to—offer to do right by…

He balked.

He couldn't.

That was another certainty he could add to the list of the sun's patterns and displeased family members.

Because he could not marry Marcia. He'd make her bloody miserable. After all, Andrew hurt everyone who loved him. She'd be no different. It was why he should have never agreed to her madcap scheme.

Andrew groaned.

"I could tell them you aren't receiving visitors, my lord?" Stanley offered, misunderstanding the reason for Andrew's misery.

Yes, at any other time, an unannounced visit by his brothers-in-law would be the source of Andrew's disquiet.

Andrew stared at the ceiling overhead and released a sigh. "We both know that would have no impact, Stanley, but I do appreciate the offer."

From the corner of his eye, he caught the way his valet inclined his head in taciturn acknowledgment.

With a newly acquired understanding for those poor fellows who found themselves making a march to the gallows, Andrew swung his legs over the side of the bed. "Please, tell them I'll be down shortly," he said, heading for his armoire.

As Andrew pulled out garments, Stanley cleared his throat. "Ahem. They said you have no more than ten minutes, or they will commence the meeting in your chambers, my lord."

And they'd do it, too. Andrew cursed. "I will be down momentarily."

After hastily tugging on his garments, Andrew was dressed a handful of minutes later and headed downstairs to his office.

His office, another part of Andrew's inheritance from the miserable man who'd sired him.

Andrew stared at the door.

How many times had he vowed as a young boy to never turn out like that fat, cruel, monstrous man? That had been before Andrew had ultimately realized that he was destined to be him.

It was why he couldn't marry Marcia.

Hell, it was why he couldn't marry anyone.

Or shouldn't.

All things being equal, Andrew was enough of a bastard to realize he'd likely wed at some point, no doubt to a woman who wouldn't mind that he couldn't and wouldn't be more than he was and who would be content with the title of viscountess.

The decision however was made for you the moment you decided to help her sin... a voice taunted.

A sick feeling settled in his gut.

Yes, he knew what was expected of him. He knew what she deserved. Certainly, better than him. But in the absence of that, there was only... he.

"My lord?" His valet's tentative voice cut through those musings, and Andrew gave his head a shake.

Bringing his shoulders back, Andrew pressed the door handle and let himself inside.

Both men were seated in front of his desk. That was good.

Andrew would have expected a volatile rage that kept them on their feet.

"Gentlemen," he greeted jovially as he stepped inside and closed the door behind him.

They stood, their serious eyes following his approach.

Their serious eyes, which contained that all-too-familiar sentiment. Disappointment.

Averting his gaze, Andrew made his way over, taking up a spot on the other side of his desk.

Proving himself the coward he was, he could not meet their stares. He couldn't face more of that disappointment.

"To what do I owe this pleasure?" he said after they'd all been seated.

"Don't do that, Andrew," Huntly gently chided.

Huntly, Justina's husband, who had beggared Andrew some years ago, collecting Andrew's future inheritance and unentailed properties.

"How could you?" Rutland asked in that gravelly voice of his.

The slightly pained quality of that question the marquess put to him was worse.

Andrew would have preferred him icy cold and threatening and dangerous to this.

He stared beyond his brother-in-law's shoulder. "It is… complicated."

With a panther-like stealth, Rutland leaned forward in his seat. "Complicated," he bit out, and Andrew found greater comfort in that anger. "*Complicated*. My God, Andrew you took an innocent young lady to a place of sin and ruined her." A muscle pulsed in the other man's hard jaw. "The daughter of my friend, at that."

"The lady asked me to—"

"To ruin her?" Rutland slammed a hand down on the edge of Andrew's desk in a volatile display at odds with the self-control the marquess was otherwise always in possession of.

Andrew's ears went hot. "She was determined to… to explore certain ends of London, and I—"

"And you were just so very gallant as to see to the chore yourself?" Rutland interrupted, his lips curling in a frosty smile, and then he gave his head a disgusted shake.

"Be that as it may," Huntly interjected, and Andrew looked over to his other brother-in-law. "Discussing why or the details of what transpired will not change them, and that is not why we are here."

"It isn't?" he could not keep from asking.

Wordlessly, both men shook their heads.

A pit formed low in his belly, sitting there like a great, big stone.

Settling back in the folds of his chair and incapable of words, Andrew nudged his chin forward, urging them to say whatever it was that had brought them here.

"I do not believe you are totally without honor, Andrew," Rutland said, with more calm and logic restored to his tones.

"Why, thank you," he said dryly. "I appreciate—"

"I do believe you will offer to do the right thing by the lady."

Andrew's smile froze and then slipped.

And there it was.

It was what he'd already realized at the back corners of his mind.

"I have kept tabs on you over the years, Andrew," Rutland said. "I'm aware that your... pleasures are vast, but that they are reserved for widows and whores and experienced women. Not innocents."

Yes, in that his brother-in-law was correct. As a rule, Andrew had avoided those off-limits ladies. He'd found the idea of dallying with virgins distasteful and had pledged to keep his pleasures to the wantons.

Until now.

"Which begs the question, why change now? Why make exceptions in your usual pursuits this time?" Rutland murmured. "And do you know what I believe—"

"What we *both* believe," Huntly interjected quietly. "There is some fondness on your part for the young lady."

Andrew stiffened. "You are making more of it than there is," he said curtly, determined to disabuse either men of any grand illusions that he was somehow good or honorable in any way. He wasn't.

"Do you care about the lady?" Rutland asked, thinning his eyes into tiny slits as though he searched within Andrew's soul for the answers he sought.

Did he care about Marcia? More than any other person, but because she was unlike anyone he'd ever known and because he admired her and respected her. "I've known the lady a lifetime," Andrew explained. "I care about her in a platonic way, of course." Even as he said it, he recognized the ridiculousness of that false assurance.

"Ah, yes, of course," Huntly drawled. "Because all platonic relationships end with a fellow lifting the skirts of one's friend."

Andrew's ears fired hot a second time, and he fought the urge to wrestle with his cravat. "I didn't have her skirts up," he gritted out. He would have gotten there eventually, had her father not arrived. No doubt that was precisely where Andrew and Marcia had been heading with that kiss. Still, that did not change who he was. "I cannot marry her," Andrew said quietly, as much as for his audience as for himself.

Both men leveled hard looks on him.

Over the years, Andrew had alternately admired and feared the two peers before him. Prior to their marriages to his sisters, they'd been wicked in their own right, and he'd been fascinated by their reputations. Once Rutland and Huntly had married Andrew's sisters, he'd become fascinated by the older gentlemen for different reasons—they'd proven themselves good in ways Andrew never would or could.

"Oh?" Rutland asked, and that single coolly spoken syllable contained a wealth of warning.

But Andrew would not be dissuaded or influenced by either of them. "The lady deserves more than a bounder like me."

"Though I do not disagree with you, Andrew," Rutland said, "the time for what the lady deserves has come and gone. Wessex arrived and dragged her out, and even concealed as she'd been by a cloak—"

"And turban," Andrew felt inclined to point out.

"It will not take much guessing on Polite Society's part the reason his carriage was there and the likely identity of the woman he escorted out," Rutland snapped.

"Are you fine, then, with her being ruined?" Huntly asked, and there was more curiosity to that query than judgment.

Nay. He wasn't. Because Marcia was the one pure thing in Polite Society. The one lady, who didn't share his blood, whom he respected and whose company he enjoyed.

He'd fished with her.

Played spillikins with her through the years.

And then danced with her during her Come Out.

To see her dragged by Society if—when—this new scandal was unearthed would cut him like a knife. Because she didn't deserve that. She deserved so much more. *Especially more than a future with you, but then, what is the alternative?* a voice niggled.

"I think your silence is answer enough," Huntly said gently.

Andrew glanced down at his open palms. "You don't understand. I don't even have anything to offer her." He was in debt: with the money he had squandered years earlier in the hands of the men before him. "I'll make her miserable."

"Undoubtedly," Rutland muttered.

Andrew pounced on that, whipping his gaze over to the other man. "Precisely!" he exclaimed, jabbing a finger in his direction. "You know that. So why would you put her through that?"

"Because the decision was made when you decided to escort her to Cyprian's Den," Rutland said flatly.

Huntly cleared his throat, calling Rutland's attention over. Some silent exchange occurred between the two men, and then Rutland nodded slightly.

"I do not believe you are incapable of good, Andrew," the marquess said quietly. "I've seen enough signs of it within you." Reaching inside his jacket, he withdrew an official-looking document, stamped with the Rutland seal.

"What is this?" Andrew asked.

The other man just nodded, silently urging him to take the packet and look at it.

The moment he did, shock knocked Andrew back in his chair as he stared down at the papers before him.

Nay, not just any papers. Deeds of unentailed lands he'd won… and lost.

His ears hummed, and he remained frozen.

Not just deeds.

It was *all* the money and property Huntly had won from him years and years earlier when, with his previous desire for revenge against Rutland, he'd attempted to use Justina to hurt the marquess. It was also the money and land Andrew desperately needed to cover his debts and establish his future. Only… the euphoria lifted as he was reminded from the hard life he'd lived that nothing was free. "You're offering me my funds and properties back?" he asked carefully.

"If you do the right thing," Rutland said bluntly.

And there it was. Just like that, the bubble of eagerness at what that represented burst. Andrew wanted his funds back desperately, but not this way and not at Marcia's expense. "You are bribing me to marry her?" he asked coldly. Andrew shoved the papers back towards his brother-in-law. "Alas, I must decline."

Huntly's brows shot up. With surprise?

No doubt.

No doubt they'd expected Andrew would sell his very soul for the monies to fund his wastrel ways.

Hell, he was surprised with himself.

It appeared, however, that there was some honor still left within him.

"Ah, but do not think of it as a bribe," Rutland said slowly. "It isn't that at all."

"If it isn't that, then what is it, Rutland?" he asked.

"They are the funds that will be available to you so that you can make both of your lives right. This isn't just about the young lady. It is as much about you getting yourself on a path of respectability and honor… and it will also ensure that Miss Gray does not suffer."

A path of respectability and honor. They were oddly tempting possibilities.

They were novel traits at which his late father—God rot his soul—would have loudly guffawed. But Andrew had found he'd begun to tire of his clubs of late.

It was one of the reasons he'd agreed to help Marcia.

That ennui.

That need for change.

Anything different.

Or that was what he'd told himself.

But with this, his brothers-in-law presented him with the opportunity to not just put himself first but, instead, to put another person, a woman whom he cared about and one whom he'd ultimately ruined. In marrying her, there'd be funds to ensure she was comfortable and safe and secure, and money enough to cover Andrew's debts and… more. Invest as his friends Wakefield and Rothesby did.

That, however, requires you to offer to marry Marcia, a voice taunted.

She wouldn't be so foolish as to agree.

But what if she was?

What if she said yes?

Doing so would allow her the freedom she wanted in life. It would get her out of her household, which she'd been yearning to do, and by her own admission, she'd already loved and lost, so risk to her heart wouldn't be a danger.

Andrew continued to sit there, silently debating with himself. "I will speak to the young lady later this morning. I do not suspect she will say yes."

The ghost of a smile played at the corners of Huntly's mouth. "Oh, I rather suspect she will, Andrew."

The other man might suspect she would, but Andrew knew Marcia was a woman who knew her own mind. He knew her to be clever and logical and far too smart for a chap like him.

"And if she doesn't?" he asked. "What then?"

"Then, it is your responsibility to convince her," Rutland said quietly. "You are a man, and it is time that you either flounder or flourish."

For the first time in a very long time, Andrew felt a kindling of hope for his future.

A short while later, after his brothers-in-law had taken their leave, Andrew found himself in a hall in the Viscount and Viscountess Wessex's townhouse.

His gut churned.

Every muscle in his being knotted.

He was going to do the last thing in the world he should—ask a respectable young lady to marry him. He saw the truth in Rutland and Huntly's insistence. Hell, he'd known as much himself. Whatever he thought about the institution of marriage, and whatever he knew to be his own failings, he also knew that he'd not leave Marcia without the benefit of his name—tattered though it may be. It still ensured her protection and secured her future.

An odd peace settled in his chest.

This was right.

A small figure stepped out at the end of the corridor. He was a serious-looking little fellow. Lionel Gray. "Did you hurt my sister,

Waters?"

Andrew touched a hand to his chest. "I thought we were on a first-name basis, Lionel."

The little boy puckered his brow. "Well, we can be. If you promise you didn't hurt my sister."

"I…"

"Andrew did not hurt me." That announcement came from just beyond his shoulder, and he looked over.

At some point, Marcia had joined them.

He'd expected her to be pale and have swollen eyes.

Instead, she wore the same easy smile she always did around him. Some of the pressure lifted from his chest, and he found himself grinning.

"You are here," she said softly, surprise contained within those three words.

Andrew frowned. "Did you expect I would not be?"

He deserved those doubts, and yet, for some reason, knowing she had doubted him chafed.

CHAPTER 15

Marcia had known Andrew Barrett, the Viscount Waters, since she'd been a small girl, and he'd been a young man still in university.

Over the years, she'd come to know him all the more.

It was why she knew in that moment that her question had hurt him, and knowing she'd hurt him felt like a physical pain to her.

He'd come to see her.

She'd known he would.

Upon her return a few hours ago with her father, she'd gone to her rooms, bathed, and changed into new garments, forgoing a night shift for a dress. She'd been waiting for his arrival, standing at her window and observing the streets.

When the sun had crept into the sky, and night had surrendered its hold to morning, and he'd still not been there, she'd not despaired.

She'd known he was coming.

And he had.

Bruised and battered from the beating her father had dealt him.

Pain twisted in her breast.

Marcia took him by the hand, and he resisted her touch, attempting to pull free. "Oh, do stop. I've held your hand plenty of times before this," she said, tugging him.

His feet remained resolute, planted firmly to the pale-blue carpet that lined her parents' halls. "Yes, but that was before, when you were a girl and…" He dropped his voice to barely a whisper. "Before I was discovered by your father in a bedroom with you in one of the most scandalous haunts in London."

"Fair enough," she muttered. Still, she didn't release her hold of him. "Then it is best you do hurry, lest we're seen."

He hesitated, his features pained as he looked down the hall in the direction of her father's offices.

Then, with a quiet curse, he allowed her to lead him into the closest room.

A parlor.

The moment they entered the room, Marcia closed the door behind them and leaned against the panel, blocking his ability to escape. She folded her arms at her chest. "You're here to speak to my father."

"I'm here to speak to you," he said, startling her with that pronouncement.

Her arms slipped, falling to her sides. "*Me?*"

"Yes." He dusted his knuckles lightly down the curve of her cheek. "You."

Her lashes fluttered as she reflexively turned into his touch, at last understanding why the household mouser she'd befriended responded so when she caressed him, understanding the power of the human touch.

"About what?"

He was here to apologize. That was the only reason he'd rather speak to her and not her father. And she… didn't want that apology. Because that would mean what they'd shared, what they'd done together, had been somehow wrong and dirty.

Suddenly, he stopped that back-and-forth glide of his fingers, and she wanted to cry for the loss of that soothing caress.

"Why, about marriage, of course, Marcia."

About… marriage. *Of course?*

And there it was.

She knew Andrew as well as she knew herself. She knew he was a rogue who valued his freedom and who had no interest in wedding now. With his reputation, perhaps not ever.

Only… She moved her gaze over the harsh, angular planes of his face. "You came to speak to me first?"

The ghost of a smile dusted the corners of his lips. "I didn't ruin your father. I ruined you, and it is your future, not your father's. As such, it seems archaic to not put that question to a grown woman."

"Are you… asking me to marry you?" she whispered.

His grin turned wry. "I am."

He'd defy society's norms and ask her first and not her father? As Charles had done? As all gentlemen did?

In that moment, she lost another large chunk of her heart to the man before her.

Lost her heart?

She'd always loved him… as a friend.

Her mind balked. Her entire being stilled. Her heart stalled.

She'd lost a chunk of her heart to him?

Suddenly, her heart resumed its beat: faster, harder, panicked.

She recoiled. What was this? She didn't *love* love him. Not in that way. Not in the romantic kind of way.

"Marcia?" Andrew asked, the gentle concern slashing through her panicky musings.

"Hmm? Fine," she blurted. Had he even asked if she was okay? "I'm just fine." And God help her, she could not even manage to stop her ramblings. "That's what you were wondering, were you not?"

He opened his mouth, but she couldn't manage to let him get a word in edgewise.

"Or was it the other thing? The… the…"

"Marriage?" he supplied, and the right corner of his mouth kicked up in an uneven grin that wrought more havoc upon her heart. "I didn't think I'd find another person who struggled to get that word out more than me," he said dryly, misinterpreting the reason for her ramblings. Assuming it was because she, like he, abhorred marriage.

Hmph.

Yes, well, that should be a clear indication of the reason she should soundly reject his offer.

After all, it was hardly a promising beginning to accept the hand of a man who, by his own admission, couldn't bring himself to speak the word *marriage*.

Andrew laughed, and the relieved-sounding expression of mirth brought her attention over to him.

"I knew you'd feel that way." He lowered his head, touching his brow to hers.

She frowned. He'd misinterpreted her reaction, and worse, why was he so relieved? "Oh?"

"Because we're friends, and I know you're entirely too clever to wed a bounder like me."

She should be miffed. Hell, she was.

She should remain annoyed with him.

But something in his tone—nay, in those words he'd chosen—gave her pause, tugging at her.

A bounder like me.

That was the light he saw himself in, as a bounder and not much more, when he was so much more.

She knew it because he was her friend. She knew it because she'd known him more years than she hadn't.

Marcia caught one of his hands and slipped her fingers between his the same way she'd done when she'd measured the size of her hands against his larger ones when they'd been children. "You're not a bounder, Andrew."

He stared incredulously at her. "Marcia… I took you to Forbidden Pleasures and Cyprian's Den. I took you to one of the most dangerous fighting rings." Then something shifted in his eyes, a glint darkening in those blue depths that sent her belly aflutter. Andrew lowered his lips close to the shell of her ear, and a breathless giggle built in her throat at the way his breath tickled. "I nearly made love to you."

Her breath hitched.

And there it was, voiced into existence that which had transpired—and what had almost transpired—between them just a few hours ago. "You… did?"

He gave a tight nod.

"I wanted you to," she said softly.

He blanched, his features pulling, and nothing had the ability to douse a lady's ardor quite like the horror in his expression.

Marcia folded her arms at her chest once more. "I *did*. You are skilled in the art of seduction." Even if somewhere, not that deep down, she'd wished it was more for him.

"I was not seducing you," he said, slashing his hands in an upward-downward arc towards the floor. "You are the absolute last, the very last—"

"Those mean the same."

"—woman I'd ever deliberately seduce," he finished over her droll interruption.

Marcia kept her features deadpan. "So you accidentally seduced me?"

"Yes," he exclaimed. "No!"

Marcia laughed and swatted his arm. "I'm teasing. It was just a kiss, Andrew. Only one more kiss we shared." She'd just wanted it to be more.

"Marcia," Andrew began again, his voice strained, and he stole a look at the door. "All of this was a mistake." He spoke in tones more solemn than she'd ever heard from him.

A vise gripped her heart. He'd call everything that transpired between them a *mistake*? In a bid for nonchalance, she rolled her eyes towards the ceiling. "Why, thank you."

"I did not mean to offend you," he said on a rush and proceeded to explain, but as he did, she gave her head a shake.

This hardly seemed a promising start to a marriage.

He was determined that they should be no more than friends.

Well, that was fine. As he'd said, they were friends, and well, friendship was more than most couples had.

Not her parents and not most of her parents' friends.

She went absolutely motionless as an idea slipped in.

And… you would be free of your parents' home.

Andrew offered her a way out of this household, and if Atbrooke thought to use her to access her father's money, then he'd be without that opportunity. There'd be no reason for him to darken this doorstep. Rather, she'd have her own doorstep for him to visit—along with her own servants to throw him out on his arse. There would be no reason to tell her parents and worry them with Atbrooke's presence. Nay, he'd have no ability to leverage her against her parents.

"But I do want to offer," Andrew was saying, bringing her back to the moment.

She dampened her mouth with the tip of her tongue. "Do you believe I'll… say no?"

He blinked slowly, his golden lashes fluttering up and down. "Er…" He scrabbled with his cravat in that endearing way he always had when he was unsettled.

Then it hit her. He'd not believed she'd say no. Was it that he… hoped she would?

Marcia pushed away from the door and started a slow stroll over to him. "You only came to offer me marriage because you expected I'd say no, and you could ease your conscience, knowing you did the right thing, while being saved from actually having to marry me."

By the silence that met her supposition and the guilty color splotching his cheeks, she was on the mark.

Marcia stopped so that just a pace separated them, far enough from him that she might tip her head back and meet his eyes, and she crossed her arms before her.

"I… It occurred to me that you would likely say no." He hesitated. "You… are not? Saying no, that is?"

She'd already taken enough from him. To steal his freedom so that she could secure her own and keep Atbrooke away would be the height of selfishness.

She looked away first. "You don't have to marry me, Andrew," she said softly. "I'll be just fine." She would have to talk to her parents and face down Atbrooke with them. Marcia, however, had ruined too many lives. Her parents'. Her siblings'. She could not be selfish where Andrew was concerned, too. "My reputation was ruined long before last night."

"Your reputation was not. Your name was talked about, Marcia, and by people who don't really know you," he said with a gentleness that he'd always shown her, a tenderness at odds with the image he presented to Polite Society as a cynical, unfeeling scoundrel.

"Don't patronize me, Andrew," she said flatly. "I've been given the cut direct many times. People have actually presented me with their shoulders. They've whispered about me and talked about me, and I've been shunned across ballrooms, even as they treated my father with only respect." There was, in short, nothing the people of High Society could do to her that they'd not already done.

He frowned. "Well, I'm not letting you live in this world without the protection of my name. I was complicit in these antics."

"We both were," she pointed out.

"But then we both know the world is hardly fair where women are concerned, Marcia."

And she fell a little in love with Andrew Barrett that moment. "You deserve more," she whispered.

He frowned. "Wait now. That is my line."

"Actually, I spoke it, and it is mine."

"Yes, but when I speak it about you, I mean it."

"I mean it, too, Andrew. You do. The only reason you were with me was because I asked you to. You didn't want to. You wanted to protect me. I can hardly repay your friendship with the last thing you want." At his puzzled look, she elucidated, "Me."

Andrew frowned.

As a confirmed bachelor, he expected he should feel relieved that she was rejecting his offer.

There should be a great rush of relief.

And yet, there wasn't any sense of relief. He waited and waited, with the Ormolu clock ticking away the seconds, but it never came.

Strangely, it had nothing to do with the fact that her rejecting his offer would result in the forfeiture of his funds and properties.

"What is so very wrong with you that you believe I'm the better catch?" he asked, perturbed that she should so devalue herself.

"Andrew," she said, throwing her hands up in the air with exasperation. "I'm Atbrooke's daughter."

God, he despised that name.

He despised everything about that family.

He'd made the mistake of trusting his heart to Atbrooke's sister, who'd been intent on destroying his sister Justina's now husband.

But having seen Marianne at the club again, he'd realized what he'd felt for her had been a boy's fascination. Whereas Marcia? She was a clever, kind, spirited woman whom he admired.

"I've already told you, Marcia," he said quietly. "You are nothing like him."

"You're saying that because you're my friend." She spoke in the firm, resolute tones of a lady who knew who she was and who'd accepted it, and yet, her gaze slipped to the floor, and she studied the tips of her slippers like they contained the answers to the universe.

Andrew brushed a fingertip along her jaw, bringing her eyes up to his.

"Yes, I am saying that because I'm your friend."

She stiffened.

"Because I would never be friends with one like Atbrooke, and I know you."

Tears filled her eyes, and the sight of that crystalline sheen hurt worse than any of the blows her father had landed on Andrew last evening. "Hey," he murmured, drawing her close in a way that had always felt natural with Marcia.

She turned her face, pressing her cheek against his shoulder as if she couldn't meet his eyes, and he simply held her.

And oddly, it felt... right.

It was strange for him to enjoy holding her in this innocent way that wasn't sexual. And yet, he did enjoy it.

If he'd made that admission to anyone, his reputation would have been destroyed—and rightly so.

He sensed her wavering, and pressed the one reminder which he knew would seal their future together. "There is also the matter of your sisters, Marcia," he said gently, and he felt her tense in his arms.

"I know," she whispered. "It is one thing to have bumbled my future, but to see them suffer because of my actions..."

She drew away a moment later, perfectly composed, and smoothed her palms along the front of her lavender skirts. And secretly, he found himself missing the loss of her weight against him.

"I want to," she said, hugging herself.

He stared confusedly at her. "You want to... what?"

"Marry you," she clarified, and her admission should have sent him running for the hills in terror. So why, then, did his heart move in this odd way in his chest?

Marcia drew in a deep breath. "But it would be selfish of me. I thank you, Andrew, but you are my friend, and because of that, I cannot do this, even if I want to. I cannot steal your freedom."

Andrew frowned. She was resolute and determined to save *him*?

But... blast. That was his role. He was saving her reputation, and giving her his name.

Suddenly, what he'd set out to do this morning—to make her an obligatory offer prompted by his brothers-in-law—shifted, and it became more of a need to protect this woman who was his friend. From Atbrooke's harassment and from the scandal that was surely to come when it was discovered she'd been at Cyprian's Den. And it was only a matter of time before the pieces of a not-so-difficult puzzle were assembled by the patrons who'd spied her father dragging some cloaked woman through the club.

"And what do you think will happen to your name and reputation if it is discovered you were at one of London's most notorious clubs?" he asked quietly.

She hugged herself around the middle. "I'd be sacrificing you to save my siblings."

"It is no sacrifice." And oddly, in speaking those words to her, he found... it wasn't. "You're my friend."

Taking advantage of her silence, Andrew stepped closer and twined their fingers. Drawing them to his lips, he placed a kiss on the top of her hand. "We get on better than anyone aside from my siblings and their spouses that I know of."

"That is... true," she acknowledged, her brow puckering in an endearingly contemplative way.

"And neither of us would enter into a union with any illusions about love."

"That is also true."

She spoke with so much adamance his chest constricted, and he alternately wanted to draw her into his arms to hold her close once more and hunt down her former betrothed to beat the man within an inch of his bloody life for having hurt this woman as he had.

You'll only hurt her, too, a voice taunted. *She may think she loved Thornton, but there will be another. And if you claim her, she'll be denied the true future happiness she deserves.*

He shoved aside those reservations. The time for that had come and gone. Rutland and Huntly were correct on that score.

He couldn't offer her absolutely everything she deserved in a real marriage, but he could give her his name.

"I… confess I have thought some about marriage to you," she shared.

Be it during girlhood or womanhood, she'd always been brutally honest and frank with him. She'd never held back her thoughts.

Mama and Papa are expecting a babe, and my mama told me where babies come from, Andrew, and it is absolutely horrific.

The memory trickled in, pulling a grin from him as he thought back to their lakeside meeting when she'd been a girl. He'd been a young man, pushing her on a swing because even that had been preferable to attending a staid house party he'd joined at his family's urging.

Marcia sent him an arched look. "This is where you are supposed to ask me what exactly I thought about."

Andrew forced his features into a mask of solemnity the level of which she required. "Forgive me. I merely expected you didn't require any urging from me to continue sharing." He inclined his head. "Do continue."

"Well, I thought it could be good fun, as you and I share the same interests."

He cocked his head. She thought they shared the same interests?

"We both like to fish," she said.

Andrew started. Yes, he did. He'd always enjoyed the peace in staking out a spot at a lake, any lake, and he'd done so numerous times with her. "It's been years since I've done that, Marcia," he felt inclined to point out, this time needing to disabuse her of any illusions she might harbor about him possibly being someone different than he was.

She folded her arms before her. "You no longer enjoy fishing?"

"I… enjoy it. I just don't do it."

"We both enjoy card games."

"We don't play the same kind of card games, Marcia," he said gently, recalling the times they'd plunked themselves upon the floor and played vingt-et-un.

Marcia scoffed. "Why, we played vingt-et-un just last night."

"Valid point," he muttered.

Marcia pressed ahead, ticking off all the ways she'd decided a match between them made sense.

"We both hate kippers and enjoy billiards."

"That's true," he concurred. A memory slipped in of Marcia sneaking into the billiards room when she'd been a small girl and he'd been playing at her family's annual summer house party with Wakefield. The oversized table for her then small frame, cue stick in hand as she'd attempted to position it at the felt table… and he and Wakefield giving her tips on how to play. A wistful smile played at his lips.

"Are you attending me, Andrew?" she asked impatiently, snapping him back to the moment. "We both enjoy rising early."

"Only in the country. I'm not so much of a fan of it anymore," he said, feeling inclined to correct her of that supposition.

"Because you're so busy carousing these days."

"That is true."

"Our families get on. We both like children, and rainstorms, and lawn bowling. We're rubbish at singing."

He bristled. "Speak for yourself," he said in mock indignation that pulled a laugh from her.

Marcia smoothed her palms down the front of his jacket the way a devoted, loving wife might do for her husband, and he stared on, fascinated at the glide of her long, delicate fingers.

Friends.

They were friends.

That much was true.

In fact, she'd spoken only truths.

There'd been one, however, that she'd neglected to mention in her innocence.

"We are also compatible in other ways, Marcia," he murmured, touching his lips briefly to the place where her pulse hammered in her neck.

"Y-you are teasing," she whispered, her voice catching, her tone breathless.

"Not at all." Many times with this woman he did tease. Not now, however.

He kissed her briefly, and the minute he covered her mouth with his, Marcia melted against him. Twining her arms about his neck, she lifted herself up and pressed herself close, as if searching for a way to climb inside him.

She opened her mouth for him, and Andrew swept his tongue inside, tasting her sweet flavor of honey, and he drank deeply.

Before he managed to recall where they were, and the reason for his visit, and this discussion.

He shifted back and moved his gaze over her face.

"Are you saying yes, then?"

She remained motionless with her arms still twisted about him, her already enormous brown eyes going all the wider. "I... Why, I rather think I am."

His mind was too tired and sluggish from a lack of sleep.

That was all that accounted for his slow, wry grin.

Except, on the heel of that lightness, reality came rushing in.

Andrew gently disengaged her hands from his person. "There won't be... romantic love, Marcia," he said gently, caring about her enough as a friend that he needed to be honest with her in this. He needed to disabuse her of any notions that would see her hurt in a marriage with him.

"I had romantic love, Andrew," she said as matter-of-factly as any fellow who'd disavowed marriage, and he found himself believing her. "I've no interest in losing my heart again."

Good. That was the very answer he craved in this moment.

"But you will, Marcia," he said, infusing a firmness to those words. "And you'll be stuck with a bounder like me. A fellow not in dun territory, but close." *But you won't be once you marry her.*

Another woman would have met that admission with horror and disgust. After all, she faced the prospect of spending forever with a man who'd squandered the little wealth he'd had on cards and women.

Marcia smiled. "I have a dowry."

He recoiled. "Egads, I'm not marrying you for money, Marcia," he croaked. *Aren't you, though? In a way?*

Guilt swirled.

She patted his hand. "That is honorable of you and generous. Thank you. Though I should also add that marriage to me will be fortunate for you, because I have quite the head for numbers."

Andrew opened his mouth, but then stopped. "Do you?" he asked curiously.

Marcia nodded. "Oh, yes."

It was a detail he hadn't known about her. He knew her in so many ways, and yet, this was a reminder that there were so many mysteries to Marcia Gray, too.

"We're doing this, then," Andrew marveled aloud. And perhaps it was the enumeration on her part, that perfect little list of what they had in common, that made him feel that this wouldn't be such a very bad idea at all. But fear remained.

She gave her head another emphatic nod. "We are."

They were doing this… if her father didn't kill him.

As if her thoughts moved in harmony with his, they both looked to the doorway.

Andrew conceded that a good murdering for nearly making love to Marcia at Cyprian's Den was a fate he absolutely deserved.

And not for the first time that day, real dread filled him.

Which was singularly odd, given that he was about to find himself leg-shackled.

But then, when Marcia had spoken, it hadn't felt that way.

"Second thoughts?" she asked.

If he were smarter than he was, yes, he'd have them.

"About facing your father after being discovered in a bedroom with you?" he drawled in a whisper for her ears alone. "What reservations could I possibly have this day?"

He'd meant to be teasing.

Instead of amusement, sadness touched her every feature as she reached up and gently stroked a finger at the corner of his swollen right eye.

He winced.

"I'm so sorry he did this to you," she returned in a like whisper.

"It's no less than I deserved."

"I was the one who asked you to take me there, Andrew."

"And I should have declined your request, and I certainly shouldn't have… conducted myself as I did."

She paused, that butterfly caress stopping altogether. "And do you… regret last night?" she asked haltingly.

"I only have one regret about being on that bed with you, Marcia."

She froze, their eyes locking.

Marcia darted her tongue out, dampening her mouth, and he followed that innocent but seductive-as-hell gesture. "What is that?"

"That we didn't finish what we began."

And now they would. Because she'd be his wife, and everything that had been forbidden to this point…

Her breath caught.

Andrew took her mouth again under his, crushing her lips in a fierce kiss that he should gentle, but she met him with a like passion, and he was capable only of deepening their embrace, of gliding his tongue along the seam of her lips, following the trail she'd traced with her own moments earlier.

My God, man, you aren't a green boy. This isn't your first time with a woman, but why does it feel that way? Why did it feel as new and as exciting?

He wrenched away, his breath coming hard and fast and ragged to his own ears.

Marcia smiled dreamily, and fears crept back in. The reservations that had been slow to present themselves presented themselves now, reminding him that all the reasons Marcia had given for a match making sense between them were also the reasons that wedding her would be folly.

She was a friend.

And he was destined to hurt her.

Because he wasn't capable of being more than what he was

when more was precisely what she deserved.

"What is it?" she asked.

Even her ability to effortlessly read his moods unnerved the hell out of him.

He forced his lips up. "I am thinking I should get on with meeting your father."

"Would you have me join you?"

He laughed. "Are you offering to keep me safe from your father?"

She nodded. "Yes."

Andrew laughed all the harder, touching his brow to hers. "Thank you for that generous offer, my lady. However, I should see to this myself." As reluctant to release her as he was to face her father, Andrew forced himself to step away and make the trek to the doorway.

"Oh, Andrew?"

He hesitated.

"I should mention my father has company."

Unease formed a pit in his belly. "Dare I ask?" Except he needn't because he already knew. He felt the damned fellow's presence.

"Your brother-in-law Lord Rutland."

He cursed. Of course he'd beaten Andrew here. He'd insert himself in even this? Perhaps it was that the other man feared he needed to be present to ensure Andrew fulfilled the agreement they'd struck.

An agreement that suddenly left him with an odd taste in his mouth and a pit in his belly.

"Now, would you like me to join you?" Marcia offered once more, misunderstanding the reason for his hesitancy.

He forced a smile. "I assure you I quite have it, love."

Marcia gave him a jaunty little wave, and Andrew quit the parlor and headed for the Viscount Wessex's offices.

This was a meeting he was dreading. One, Andrew had sworn to never wed. Two, he'd been caught in a compromising position with a young lady, and by the young lady's father at that.

But adding his blasted brother-in-law into the proverbial mix?

"Splendid," he muttered. "Just splendid."

The servant stationed at the doorway made no effort to conceal his grin.

Yes, because Rutland's reputation as a reformed scoundrel, even all these years later, had preceded him.

As if fearing Andrew might change his mind, the servant stepped forward and knocked once, and pressing the door handle, he swung the double doors wide. "Lord Waters to see you."

Two sets of eyes swung to Andrew.

Andrew ventured into the room.

He'd expected Marcia's father to be seated, had imagined the other man behind his desk, so there'd be at least that barrier between them.

Instead, he stood shoulder to shoulder with Rutland, two men who'd clearly been waiting for Andrew's arrival.

Well, what else did you expect?

The footman quietly backed out of the room.

Andrew got out in front of the meeting. "Brother!" he called jovially. "It is *so* good to see you again this fine morning."

Rutland made no attempt to greet him with anything more than a narrowing of his eyes.

Uneasy as he'd always been around the terrifying fellow, Andrew looked to the one who proved safer in this instance.

Alas, if looks could kill, Andrew would have been a pile of ash burned by that stare, and the viscount's servant would have been summoned to sweep his remnants into a dustbin.

"Do you really think to enter my office smiling?" Wessex demanded sharply. "After how you were discovered, after your latest sins, you should come in here as carefree as Sunday?"

No, Marcia's father was correct on that score.

Andrew inclined his head. "May we sit?" he asked quietly.

Marcia's father tensed, and for a moment, Andrew thought he intended to deny that request.

But then the other man moved behind his desk and seated himself. He gestured to Andrew.

Andrew quickly settled into the leather winged chair opposite Marcia's father. All the while, Rutland positioned himself near Wessex.

Andrew paused to look around the room. How many times

had he invaded the viscount's sanctuary? How many times had he come here only to find Marcia here to keep him company? His gaze landed on the largely empty drink case across Wessex's office.

My father does not drink brandy. Her child's voice from long ago slipped into his memories. That had been the first time they'd met and the beginning of their friendship.

And that friendship is why you really shouldn't go through with this.

Her father was right.

Andrew, however, would receive funds that ensured not only his future but Marcia's, as well.

Marcia, whose ruin was no doubt already being whispered about.

And that friendship was really why he *should* go through with it. Why he needed to.

"Looking for a drink?"

Andrew whipped his focus forward and found Wessex's glare upon him.

He angled his head. Well, at least there would be some hint of pleasantries now. That was a good deal more promising. "No, I—"

"I'm not offering one, Waters," Wessex said sharply. "I'm asking why in hell you're ogling my damned sideboard."

Andrew had opened his mouth to speak when he registered the shadow beside him.

Glancing up, he found his brother-in-law, impressively stealthy for his size, had quit his place alongside Wessex and positioned himself at Andrew's shoulder.

Resisting the urge to squirm, feeling like the boy he'd been when he'd first met the other man, Andrew looked at his brother-in-law. "Would you mind perhaps joining us in a seat?"

"I'm quite comfortable as I am," the marquess said coolly.

"Of course you are," Andrew muttered. Anything to make a chap squirm or remind him of his mere humanness.

Rutland quirked an icy brow. "What was that?" he asked in a silken growl.

Well, to hell with him. To hell with them all. He fought the sudden need to swallow and shook his head. "Nothing at all." Rutland's opinion didn't matter in this moment anyway, not his usual disgust or disapproval. Dismissing the other man outright,

Andrew retrained his attention on the one man whose opinion this day did matter. "I want to begin by apologizing," Andrew said.

"An apology?" Wessex barked, slamming a fist onto the edge of his desk.

His brother-in-law did sit then, a tacit show of support. Yes, Rutland might be disgusted by Andrew and disappointed, but at the end of the day, he'd stand beside him, even when that was the last thing he deserved.

"What were you thinking, Andrew?" Rutland asked, his voice as graveled as always, but gentle in the ways it had increasingly become over the years of being married to Phoebe. He gave Andrew an opening to speak, asking that same question that he had several hours ago.

Andrew bungled his reply for the second time. "I—"

"He wasn't," Wessex snapped.

Andrew bristled. "Hey now. I'll have you know…" Except to say anything more would be to implicate Marcia. It would mean revealing that she'd come to him in confidence and solicited his help. And he'd not betray that trust. He flattened his lips into a line.

Wessex frowned. "What will you have me know?"

"I'll have you know I regret very much what happened," he weakly substituted.

With a sound of disgust, the more respectable viscount looked away.

"I've come to make the situation right," Andrew said, and even as Wessex whipped his attention back towards Andrew, Rutland's features remained impassive, etched in stone.

"And just how do you intend to do that?" Wessex rejoined coldly, in a way that warned.

"I will marry—"

"No."

"—her."

"Marcia won't marry just because she has no other choice. Marcia will marry a good man who is respectable and honorable," her father said.

Andrew couldn't resist. "A man like Thornton?"

The viscount jerked like he'd taken a blow to the belly.

Andrew wasn't through with him, though. "Because, as I see it, the fellow you *did* approve of proved unworthy and broke her heart."

"And do you think you are worthy of her?"

"Hardly," Andrew answered in an instant. He knew he wasn't. "But I also know her wishes should be respected."

Wessex's brows came together, stitched into a single line.

"I already asked Marcia to marry me, and she said yes."

Marcia's father tensed, his entire body jerking as if he'd been shot.

But then, had Andrew a daughter and had a bloke with Andrew's reputation stated his intent to wed his daughter, he'd have responded in a like way. Hell, he'd have probably not bothered with a duel and instead run the bastard through.

"Over my dead body," Wessex thundered, exploding to his feet, and Rutland did the same.

Sliding around the desk, Rutland rested a hand on the other man's arm and spoke a few quiet words to the viscount.

While Rutland and Wessex whispered back and forth, Andrew trained his gaze over their heads, and it occurred to him that Wessex would have preferred to risk death on the dueling field over allowing Andrew to marry Marcia.

Andrew wondered what Rutland's good friend Wessex would say were he to know about the agreement that had spurred him to make this offer of marriage.

At last, whatever Andrew's brother-in-law said seemed to penetrate. The Viscount Wessex nodded once and reclaimed his seat. Rutland remained standing next to him.

It also occurred to Andrew, unlike before, that Rutland had positioned himself as he had to be ready if—when—Wessex pounced for a second time.

That was why he'd come. Not just because of his friendship with Wessex, but because he sought to protect Andrew, as he'd done through the years. Andrew didn't deserve that support, support he expected came solely from Rutland's intent to spare Phoebe pain.

Wessex folded his hands, steepling them under his chin, and he stared over those digits at Andrew, urging him in silence, if not in words, to speak.

"I understand the harm I've done to Marcia's reputation. After that fiasco with Thornton, she can't take any more cut directs, and I would not wish to see her suffer."

There was a long stretch of silence.

He felt his brother-in-law's piercing stare upon him, and discomfited by that probing look, he resisted the urge to shift in his seat.

Suddenly, Wessex barked with laughter. "*You* would not see her suffer?" the viscount said through his empty, frosty laugh. "You would not see her suffer? Well, it appears we are of like efforts in this. However, between the two of us, I'm the only one wise enough to know that keeping her from suffering means keeping you far away from her."

Andrew stiffened.

Only, was Wessex really that wrong? In fact, was he anything but right in this?

Andrew invariably hurt all those whom he cared about. He was his father's son, a wastrel. And it was a certainty that he'd bring that same pain to Marcia, and he'd rather chew off his fingers than do that.

Lord Wessex must have sensed he'd reached him and that Andrew was faltering.

"I know your reputation, Waters," the viscount said more softly, more evenly, his words not steeped in the same rage he'd turned Andrew's way throughout the exchange. "You are a rogue—"

"Were you not one, too?" Andrew interjected.

At his side, he detected Rutland's warning look. Which he ignored.

"As I see it," Andrew went on, "you are the last person to lecture me."

The marquess pressed his eyes shut and shook his head.

"The last person to lecture you? Me, the lady's father?" A ruddy flush suffused Wessex's cheeks. "Trust me, it is *entirely* different. I loved my wife then, and I love her even more now, if possible." He leaned forward. "Can you say you feel the same way for my daughter?"

Andrew grimaced and then, feeling that contortion of his facial muscles, immediately smoothed his features. Andrew didn't believe in romantic love. After Marianne Carew's treachery, he had come to appreciate that there'd only been lust and not love, as was the case in all relationships he'd known and all the relationships he'd ever know, including with Marcia. After all, how else to account for the fact that he could not keep his hands off of her? That even against all better judgment, he couldn't resist taking her in his arms? And yet…

"I care very much about Marcia," he said. And he did love her. As a friend.

Wessex shook his head. "That isn't enough. The man who will marry her will love her to distraction. He'll suffer if it means making her smile. All that will matter is the sound of her laughter, and he'll lay down his life for her every happiness and would trade his soul to Satan to be the one to do so."

Yes, that was everything Marcia deserved. *And you can't even give her half of that.* There were enough deficits in his character and a blackness to his soul that he couldn't be the pure, selfless gentleman her father spoke of.

Wessex dropped his hands to the desk and leaned forward. "Can you be that man to Marcia? Can you promise me you'll give up wagering and womanizing and every immoral thought and replace them instead with thoughts of her and that happiness I speak of?"

Unnerved by the directness of the other man's piercing stare, as much as by his words, Andrew glanced down at his fingers, which at some point he'd balled into a fist. "I will not give you false assurances about being somehow more than a scoundrel. You know exactly what I am. Marcia does deserve more." Andrew lifted his gaze and held Wessex's. "I'm marrying her because that is what she wants and because I'll do right by her."

Fury contorted the older man's face, that emotion ravaging his features and brimming from his eyes. "How much?"

"How much?" Andrew repeated dumbly.

Yanking the center drawer of his desk, Wessex pulled out a page and angrily slammed them on the otherwise immaculate mahogany surface. Then he grabbed a pen, dipped it into the crystal inkwell, and scribbled something onto the sheet. "What is your price?" Wessex demanded, his pen poised over it. "How much do you want to go away?"

Andrew drew back.

Wessex gritted his teeth. "One thousand pounds?"

Marcia's father was offering to pay him off… to leave her. To rescind the promise he'd made to her a short while ago. Andrew curled his hands around the arms of his chair, the wood biting painfully into his palms as he felt another stare.

Rutland's gaze was locked on Andrew's white-knuckled grip, and Andrew made himself relax his fingers, forced them onto his lap in a more casual pose. "No," Andrew said quietly. "I don't want your money." Surprise pulled that admission from him, and perhaps he had more honor than he'd ever believed of himself, because he didn't want those funds, or the ones his brothers-in-law had promised if he'd just offer for Marcia.

"Five thousand."

Andrew pressed his lips into a single line to keep from telling Marcia's father precisely where he could go.

The viscount rested his elbows on the desk, perfectly framing that note. "Thirty-five thousand pounds."

Andrew choked.

Thirty-five thousand pounds? The other man was offering a fortune. It was nearly as much as what Huntly would turn over, but it would come without that string of marriage attached. Andrew could have those monies, and to hell with Rutland and Huntly's hanging his funds and properties over him, and yet…

Andrew went absolutely still.

He could not.

To do so would see him secure, but it would also mean Marcia faced the scandal of that discovery on her own. She'd be ruined, and prey to men who'd never offer her anything but an indecent arrangement.

In that moment he was rocked by the discovery that he did in fact care about another person's happiness beyond his own.

Marcia. He cared about her.

"No," he said quietly.

"Because you figure her dowry is worth more?" A sound of disgust escaped Wessex. "Well, you shan't see a goddamned pence of that money, Waters. Those funds will be tied up for her and her children."

Marcia... and her children.

Just like that, an imagining intruded on what had proven to be a ugly confrontation—a little girl with Marcia's eyes and golden curls. She'd be a handful, that was a certainty, as much a spitfire as her mother. A wistful smile stole across Andrew's lips.

"You find this amusing?" Wessex barked.

Andrew's grin faded, and he leveled a look once more on the enraged viscount. "Despite your opinion of me, no, I do not find this amusing. And that is fine," he said, coming to his feet. "Write the dowry off for Marcia. She can use it as she sees fit. But I'm going to marry her."

Wessex's shoulders sagged, and it was like the life and all happiness drained from the viscount as misery replaced his rage. "You can't do right by her, Waters, because a man like you will only hurt her." He looked away. "Now, get the hell out of my sight."

Andrew brought his shoulders back and bowed.

As he turned on his heel and took his leave, the other man's words, in all their truths, followed him.

CHAPTER 16

SINCE SHE'D BEEN A SMALL girl, Marcia had dreamed of her marriage, imagining what that day would be like and who her bridegroom would be.

She had even arranged her dolls in little seats and pretended that she was marching down the aisle on the arm of Mr. Poppet, the lone male doll in her collection.

She'd been so very sure how that day would play out.

There would be a respectable gentleman who loved her beyond distraction.

There would be tears of joy.

There would be excited laughter and chattering.

She would attend the details of that wedding.

Not so very long ago, she'd had all of that.

Or she'd almost had all of that.

There had been a respectable gentleman, but certainly not one who'd loved her beyond distraction.

This day, her real wedding day, was nothing like any of those imaginings.

Tears. There were plenty of those and sad looks. Those were from her parents, who'd not been able to look her in the eye, which was odd. Given the fact that she was a constant reminder of the man who'd committed the greatest atrocity against Marcia's mother, they should be visibly relieved. Or mayhap that was why it was so very hard for them to look at her. Perhaps they felt guilty about being relieved to have to see her in their house anymore?

"Well, this is grim," Faith muttered from where she sprawled on the pink sofa, one leg stretched over the arm and her lacy white skirts rucked up about her knees. "One would think we were attending a funeral rather than a wedding."

All that was keeping Marcia sane thus far this day were the two friends who'd slept over, spending what would be Marcia's last night in her family's home with her. They'd not left her side.

"I, for one, don't understand what all the sad eyes from our parents are," Anwen said with a frown. New to their fold only just that year, the young lady's family had traveled in different circles.

"Because they don't like Andrew," Faith explained.

"They like him," Marcia said defensively.

"No, they tolerate him," Faith corrected. "Because he is Lord and Lady Rutland's brother-in-law and brother." She creased her brow. "Respectively. And the same with the Duke and Duchess of Huntly, but none of them like him. They see him as a scoundrel, a terrible fellow not to be trusted with young ladies and—"

"Er…" Anwen cleared her throat. "I think I get the point." She gave a less-than-discreet nod Marcia's way.

Faith blushed. "My apologies." She paused. "Now, if you were marrying a fellow like Wakefield, they'd all be on board with the day."

Wakefield, Andrew's counterpart, but also a gentleman who'd been a friend to her over the years—until she'd made her Come Out. At that point, he'd all but disappeared from her life completely.

Andrew had not, however.

Andrew had remained as steadfast then as he was now.

And you are repaying that friendship by locking him into a marriage that he certainly doesn't want.

Her stomach twisted into a thousand knots.

"You are having reservations," Faith murmured, unerringly accurate in her read of Marcia.

"No," Marcia said, though belatedly, and her friends exchanged a look.

Faith pointed to the gold chain Marcia still wore. "It's because you are following the Heart of a Duke."

She really should have taken that silly bauble off, but for reasons she couldn't understand, she'd insisted on wearing it.

Anwen beamed. "Mayhap *Waters* is your true love."

Marcia raised a hand to her breast. Her true love?

Nay, she decidedly did not believe in love. And he was certainly not capable of giving her his heart. Or even his devotion.

She frowned.

She'd not raised that particular point when she and Andrew had discussed marriage, but suddenly it seemed very important that he be faithful to her. The idea of him with another did odd things to her insides, twisting them up in vises and burning like she'd consumed poison, and—

A hesitant knock split the quiet, and they looked up.

Marcia's mother entered the room.

It was time.

"It is time," Faith said, hopping to her feet.

Anwen stood. "Hullo, Lady Wessex."

"Anwen, Faith," Marcia's mother murmured. Still wearing the same sorrowful expression, she looked as Marcia had never seen her, and it was a physical hurt knowing that she was the one who'd wrought this sadness. That was, ultimately, the emotion she was destined to cause her mother.

Mayhap that had been the reason it had been so very easy to accept Andrew's offer.

Or one of the reasons.

Because she could leave and free her parents from the constant reminder of who she was.

The moment her friends filed from the room, the viscountess shut the door behind them.

"I never told you about the day you were born," her mother said softly, leaning against the panel.

Marcia stiffened and managed to shake her head slightly. "No."

She'd never thought about that omission, but now, it made sense. Knowing the truth of how she'd been conceived, Marcia understood why her mother would never want to talk about or relive the day of her birth.

"It was a… struggle to bring you into the world."

She couldn't keep from wincing. "I expect it was." She wanted this discussion over. She wanted it to remain in the vault where unspoken-of stories dwelled.

Her mother pushed away from the door, her features softening for the first time since she'd shared with Marcia the truth about her conception. "Not because of that, Marcia. I will not lie to you." As she'd already done and would have continued to do if Marcia's real father had not stepped forward. "The moment I learned I was with child…" Her mother's voice cracked, and she looked off.

Marcia averted her stare in the opposite direction, unable to let her mind go where her mother's now went, because she hated herself for what she'd brought upon her mother. She hated herself for being foisted on her in an ugly, heinous act.

Warm fingers cupped her face, bringing Marcia's gaze forward.

Her mother held her stare. "I knew only terror, Marcia. But the day I felt you move inside me, it was like a butterfly-soft movement, and it was you, kicking away. I only loved you from that moment on. And when you were born, I didn't see him, because it was impossible to see anything but you." Tears fell down her mother's cheeks, and her voice caught on a sob as she took Marcia in her arms. "I love you."

"I love you, too." Marcia clung to her, as she'd done as a young girl afraid of lightning storms, and she wanted to go back to that. She wanted to go back to the simpler, safer, happier times when she'd believed herself to be the daughter of an honorable soldier whom her mother had loved. But there was no going back. And there was no changing the fact that, no matter how much her mother loved her, she was still a life that had been spawned by a monster.

With a shuddery breath, her mother drew back. "You do not have to do this."

"I know," she said softly. Her parents would never force her. They'd keep her here with them forever if that was what she wished, but they deserved more than that. They deserved freedom from her and the responsibility she'd been.

Marcia's mother moved her eyes searchingly over her face, and a sad smile formed on her lips. "But you intend to do so anyway."

She nodded. "I do."

That pronouncement immediately brought her mother's eyes

closing once more. "For all the ways I was denied a choice by Lord Atbrooke, Marcus was mine. Marriage to him was a decision that belonged to me." Her voice caught. "And I-I hate that you should be choosing to set aside the dream of love."

"But I'm not being forced to do anything, Mother," she said calmly. "This *is* my choice. Andrew is."

Her mother continued her examination, and then she nodded. "Very well," she murmured. She started to turn to go, but stopped, going absolutely motionless, like she'd seen the head of Medusa and paid for that glance with eternal immobility.

"Mama?" she asked, but her mother remained as if in a trance, staring at Marcia's necklace.

Frowning, Marcia touched the pendant that had captured her mother's attention.

"Where did you get that?" her mother asked breathlessly.

Marcia gripped the gold heart. "I… Faith. After Charles ended our arrangement, she gifted it to me. She said…" Her cheeks went warm, and she couldn't complete her sentence regarding the childish talisman they'd professed it to be.

"Its wearer captures the heart of one's true love," her mother said.

Marcia scrunched up her nose. "Not that, per se. Something about—"

"Winning the heart of a duke?"

"You know of it?" Marcia asked.

For the first time in longer than Marcia could remember, her mother smiled a genuine smile that gave her eyes a happy glimmer. "I know of the tale," she murmured, and then she touched Marcia's fingers that still clutched the bauble. "And I wore it a long time ago. Your father… Marcus, gifted it to me once."

Marcia caught the inner flesh of her cheek hard between her teeth and worried it. Knowing that her mother had worn this back when she'd been a young woman nearer to Marcia's age, believing in love and happily ever afters even after the ugliness that had been visited upon her, lent this memento an even greater poignancy.

Her mother patted her hand. "It is going to be all right," she vowed.

She spoke with a confidence about the future that Marcia desperately wished she could feel this day.

She wasn't coming.

She was late.

Andrew knew as much, not because he'd consulted the timepiece heavy in his pocket, but, rather, because his gaze was trained on the hearth near the front of the library, and the timepiece there revealed the rapidly passing moments.

She who'd been left at the altar would leave him.

In that moment, he found himself facing the great swell of dread that had been there since he'd visited her and asked her to marry him.

It had kept him from sleeping, and it had followed him as he'd dressed for the day and as he'd taken up a place at the opposite end of the room to wait for his bride.

It was here now, and it was here with a bloody vengeance.

I cannot do this.

He was the absolute worst future husband.

Marcia's father hadn't been wrong, and neither had Rutland.

Andrew was a bounder. The worst sort of scoundrel.

And she was an innocent in every sense of the word. With a certainty as steady as the turning of the tides, Andrew would hurt her. That was the only way this would end.

Oh, she'd spoken of all the reasons they would be perfectly compatible, and in her matter-of-fact presentation of that list and the items upon it, he'd been able to believe her in that moment.

He'd even been able to hold on to that confidence she'd spoken with during his meeting with Wessex.

It had begun to feel real only after he'd returned home and started on the official end of this marriage business—securing a license and speaking to the archbishop.

And that realness had forced him to confront that he was wholly incapable of being the man she was worthy of. Because he was a cad. He liked his cards, and he liked his women, and hell, he didn't even know if he could be faithful to her. And she deserved fidelity.

Sweat slicked his palms, and he dusted them along the sides of his trousers.

"Second thoughts?" Rothesby said from the corner of his mouth.

Second, third, and fourth ones. Plus some numbers after that.

Andrew, however, knew better than to voice as much before a room full of guests, most of whom now glared at him.

He slid his gaze over to the sharpest glare of all.

The Earl of Wakefield scowled blackly at Andrew, wearing the same stamp of fury on his features as he had when he'd stormed out of Andrew's offices days earlier.

Seated at the end of the makeshift aisle next to his sister-in-law the Countess of Stanhope, Wakefield had been the last guest to arrive.

There came a flurry at the entrance of the room, and as one, all the guests—including Wakefield—looked back.

Lady Faith Brookfield and Miss Anwen Kearsley, Marcia's closest friends, came rushing in.

Andrew tensed as they all but pranced like mice down the aisle, and he braced for them to join him and announce that their friend was, in fact, not coming, delivering the news that would end this farce and save him from a future of respectability.

Only, as they shimmied into the row of seats alongside Faith's parents, the Marquess and Marchioness of Guilford, he felt an odd relief, when the only relief he should feel that day would be if the wedding was called off, and he was spared the leg shackles he was about to don.

Another commotion came at the front of the room.

His mother and stepfather and youngest siblings, George and Georgina, rushed into the room.

His mother and her husband, Nathan, wore somber expressions that made them perfect additions to the company that day.

Bloody hell. Given they'd been traveling, Andrew had anticipated he'd be spared at least the maternal disapproval.

Alas…

His mother held his stare. "Andrew," she mouthed, and he was not so much a fool as to believe that was an affectionate greeting.

He managed a sheepish smile.

His youngest brother, George, and his sister Georgina, however, waved excitedly.

Not all were unhappy to see him.

Andrew stole another glance at the clock.

She wasn't coming.

And he'd not blame her.

There'd be a scandal, but he'd never been one to care much about that.

And this time, there was a rush of relief, because her leaving him at the altar would be the best for the both of them. But especially for her.

He'd be spared from adding one more person to the always growing list of people he disappointed.

He'd not have to bear witness to the day Marcia went from smiling friend to sad-eyed and regretful wife because of some sin he'd invariably commit.

He—

The office doors opened once more, and like a rolling wave, the guests angled in their seats as one.

And she was there.

On the arm of Lord Wessex, whose face revealed no fury or disappointment, instead remaining a perfectly stoic mask.

But the older viscount wasn't who commanded his attention.

Something tightened in Andrew's chest, shifting weirdly at the sight of her.

She wore the ivory silk gown with gold beading along her hem and waist that she'd worn at Almack's the day she'd made her Come Out.

An event she'd insisted since she'd been a girl of thirteen that he attend so they could suffer through the affair together.

A tiara rested on her flaxen curls, giving her the look of a golden Aphrodite, and he drank in the sight of her, her cheeks flush with color, her eyes bright… and smiling.

Aside from George, Marcia was the lone smiling person in the room, and with her approach, the tension left him, the stiffness easing from his shoulders, as for the first time that day, there was an absolute sense of… rightness to this moment. To his marrying Marcia.

It had always been easy with Marcia, and that remained true this day, too.

It was why he needn't fear this moment and this marriage.

Because nothing would change between them.

Not really.

At last, she reached him.

Wessex hesitated for a long while, and then with all the eagerness of the Lord and Savior inviting Satan to supper, Marcia's father placed her fingertips upon Andrew's sleeve. The warmth of her touch penetrated the fabric of Andrew's jacket. Then, after standing for a moment more, the viscount left Marcia and Andrew alone with only Andrew's best man at his side.

"I thought you weren't coming," he murmured for her ears alone, then winced as she discreetly pinched him. "Ouch."

"Do you believe I've the honor of Thornton?" she asked with a frown.

He believed Thornton unworthy of so much as licking the soles of her slippers.

The vicar opened his book and called out to the room at large: "Dearly beloved, we are gathered together here in the sight of God and in the face of this congregation to join together this man and this woman in holy matrimony, which is an honorable estate instituted of God in the time of man's innocency…"

"There is one thing," Marcia whispered to Andrew as the graying gentleman began the ceremony.

Andrew leaned down. "What is that?"

"I need your loyalty, Andrew."

He froze. "Beg pardon?"

"It occurred to me we did not speak about… other women. I do not want you bedding them. I don't want to be cuckolded."

"It was ordained for a remedy against sin," the vicar continued, "and to avoid fornication that such persons as have not the gift of continency might marry and keep themselves undefiled…"

Oh, God. This was the discussion they were having while the wedding took place, and their families and friends watched on?

"A man is the cuckold," he pointed out.

She rolled her eyes. "Well, *that* is ridiculous. Why should there be a name specifically applied to the man to whom a woman has been unfaithful and not the woman?"

"I'm not sure, Marcia," he said in a strained whisper.

Her frown deepened. "Do you mean you aren't sure about the definition, or whether you can be faithful to me?"

Oh, hell.

He fought his cravat for a moment before realizing precisely what he did in front of a room of some thirty-five or so guests. "Marcia, this isn't really the time—"

"I think this is the perfect time," she interrupted, and something in her eyes, the worry there, sent the bells of worry clamoring away in his brain.

This was why marrying her was a bad idea, because ultimately, she had hopes for him, and he'd only let her down.

"May I continue?" the vicar asked.

Out of the corner of his eye, Andrew caught the way Marcia's father, and hell, more than three-quarters of the guests leaned in, as if bracing—hoping—for the moment that Marcia called all of this off.

"You may," Marcia said, lowering her head, and Andrew relaxed his shoulders.

Coward that he was, Andrew made a show of attending the vicar.

"Thirdly, it was ordained for the mutual society, help, and comfort that the one ought to have of the other, both in prosperity and adversity…"

Prosperity and adversity.

The vicar spoke of a partnership between Andrew and the woman beside him. Perhaps it was because this was Marcia whom he'd marry, but he thought that description fit them.

There would decidedly be adversity.

His facial muscles strained, he looked down at the woman beside him and considered the question she'd put to him, and a cold sweat broke out on his skin.

Because he could not do this.

He should not do this.

Marcia would soon have her eyes opened, and whatever childlike opinion she had about his worth, which she had built in her mind like castles in clouds, would be quickly shattered. The illusion would die, the reality coming late to her when it had come quite early for the rest of the people who knew him.

He considered the doorway, but that merely brought his gaze colliding with the sea of angry family members—his and hers—who'd likely drag him back and beat him good for even daring to think of fleeing. That would put him in the ranks with Thornton and make Marcia jilted for a second time.

Or mayhap they'd be content with him running off?

"Are you all right?" she asked softly, and he whipped his attention back to her. "You've gone all… queer."

"Fine," he lied, his voice garbled. That word, spoken in haste, rose above the vicar's prattling on the institution of marriage.

The vicar stopped once more and looked at them.

A flurry of whispers filled Lord Wessex's offices.

"You're having second thoughts," she said, her voice matter-of-fact, but her eyes sad.

It was the first time he was the one responsible for her sadness, and it was an awful feeling that cleaved his chest and shredded him inside. And if he went through with marrying her, the expression she now wore would become a familiar one.

But, God help him, he couldn't deny her anything, even if it was himself. Even if it would be to save her from him… and them.

So he did that which had come too naturally to him over the years. He lied. "Not at all," he said.

"May I continue?" the vicar asked again.

Andrew hesitated a moment more, the last shred of decency he apparently possessed crying out within him to shake his head. Instead, Andrew nodded, and the man of God resumed.

"I require and charge you both, as ye will answer at the dreadful day of judgment when the secrets of all hearts shall be disclosed, that if either of you know any impediment why ye may not be lawfully joined together in matrimony, ye do now confess it."

I'm a wastrel.
I wager too much.
I like drink, also too much.
I've made cuckolds out of husbands and vow breakers out of unhappy wives.
Oh, and I nearly got my sister killed.

"Ye well assured that so many as are coupled together otherwise than God's word doth allow are not joined together by God, neither is their matrimony lawful. At which day of marriage, if any man do allege and declare any impediment why they may not be coupled together in matrimony, by God's law or the laws of this realm, and will be bound and sufficient sureties with him to the parties…"

Andrew stole a sideways look at the audience to his and Marcia's wedding.

Surely one of the people present intended to *declare any impediment.* Because they knew, and they were certainly less cowardly than he was and would speak out.

But no one did.

"Wilt thou have this woman to thy wedded wife, to live together after God's ordinance in the holy estate of matrimony? Wilt thou love her, comfort her, honor, and keep her in sickness and in health and, forsaking all other, keep thee only unto her so long as ye both shall live?"

Andrew's ears hummed, and his pulse hammered under the weight of what he was being asked and what he was committing to.

This was Marcia.

She deserved a man who could be all things for her. Who could love her and comfort her and honor her as she deserved.

Andrew was a selfish bastard.

But he was also a coward, because he knew he'd eventually hurt her, but he could not do so in this moment. Not in this way. Not as Thornton had.

"I will," Andrew said quietly.

Marcia's eyes lit with a joy from within, and he should have withdrawn his consent for that very reason, for the faith she had in him. Because her eyes hinted at more, and that more terrified the everlasting hell out of him. Granted, he'd have the means to see her cared for. But that wasn't the "more" he knew this woman would want. Love. She'd want that.

"So... is that a yes?" Marcia asked.

He looked down and stared blankly at her.

"You vow to keep only unto me, forsaking all others?"

Oh, hell. This again.

"Can we discuss this later, Marcia?" he whispered in pained tones.

She shook her head. "Absolutely not."

"I..." His late father had been a bounder. What if Andrew was destined to become him? "What if I can't be the faithful husband?"

"You can. You just have to commit yourself to me."

She said it so simply, so matter-of-factly, that he stilled, actually believing in that instant that he could, that it really was that simple—because of her.

"I will."

She beamed, and he stared at the tilt of that entrancing upside-down pout of her lips that made him dizzy.

"Wilt thou have this man to thy wedded husband, to live together after God's ordinance in the holy estate of matrimony? Wilt thou obey him, and serve him, love, honor, and keep him in sickness and in health and, forsaking all other, keep thee only unto him so long as ye both shall live?"

"I will." Marcia's answer rang with conviction and lacked none of the hesitancy of which Andrew deserved. And he was humbled in that moment by her ability to speak those words with such truth and confidence because she had that level of faith in him.

And she was the only one.

Even his family didn't believe he could be anything more than what he was. They had no grand illusions.

But Marcia did.

And it was a gift he was wholly undeserving of.

A gift he would invariably squander, as he did everything.

He hated himself in that instant. He despised his future self who'd one day break her heart, which her father had rightly predicted.

"Who giveth this woman to be married to this man?" the vicar asked, his focus sliding from his Bible over to Lord Wessex standing just beyond Marcia's shoulder.

Grief rippled the viscount's features, and for the grim expression he wore, the other man might as well have been attending a funeral.

Which, if Andrew were wedding any daughter of his own to a bounder like him, he could well commiserate with.

"I do," Lord Wessex spoke quietly and twined his hand with Marcia's, passing it over to the vicar.

Without hesitation, Andrew covered her right hand with his, and as he did so, and Marcia's father reclaimed his seat, the minister continued.

"Say after me."

"I, Andrew Barrett, take thee, Marcia Gray, to be my wedded wife, to have and to hold from this day forward, for better, for worse, for richer, for poorer, in sickness and in health, to love and to cherish, till death us do part…"

Andrew pledged his troth, with Marcia following.

"Those whom God hath joined together let no man put asunder…"

With that, it was done.

CHAPTER 17

MARCIA'S WEDDING HAD NOT BEGUN as she'd expected. She'd never imagined the sad-eyed stares and furious ones, just as she'd never imagined the person with whom she'd be standing at the altar would be Andrew Barrett, Viscount Waters.

And yet, after the ceremony, while she and Andrew signed the documents that made their marriage official, guests mingled, and a lightness fell over the room, with guests laughing and smiling, and she could almost believe this day was real.

Her own signatures complete, Marcia stood off to the side, unable to take her gaze from her husband.

My husband.

She played that phrase over several times in her mind, testing the feel of it.

"My husband," she mouthed.

She was married.

To Andrew.

And something in this moment and in the start of a new future with him felt *right*.

Perhaps because he was her friend, and she could trust him not to hurt her. Mayhap that friendship was why they'd always gotten on.

"Many congratulations, Marcia."

The grave felicitations brought her jolting to the moment, and she looked at Benedict Adamson, the Earl of Wakefield.

"Benedict!" she exclaimed happily, taking his hands in hers and giving them a squeeze.

Only, he didn't wear his usual smile, the one he'd always had since their first meeting. He looked as grim as everyone else had during the ceremony.

"Are you happy?" he asked.

"I am," she said automatically, and strangely, she was. Even as this was a marriage of convenience and not born of the romantic love she'd dreamed of, she found herself light inside.

The earl searched his gaze over her face, as if attempting to ferret out the depth of veracity to her promise. "It is my greatest hope that Waters never do anything to hurt you." Sketching a formal bow, Wakefield spun on his heel and disappeared into the crowd.

"What was that about?" Faith's familiar murmur came just beyond Marcia's shoulder, and she looked at her and Anwen.

"Benedict was merely congratulating me on my nuptials."

"He sounded awfully grim," Anwen remarked. "And looks it, too."

As one, they looked towards the serious fellow who'd joined his sister the Duchess of Bainbridge.

"He always looks grim," Faith muttered.

"Be nice," Marcia chided.

"What?" her friend said defensively. "I'm merely speaking the truth."

"I don't disagree." Anwen lent her support to Faith, who gave a nod.

"See?"

"I daresay I'd rather marry a Waters than a Wakefield," Faith declared.

The three friends looked at Andrew, Marcia's new husband.

Her heart did a funny flip at the thought. Or mayhap it was a combination of both the thought and the sight of him.

At some point, he'd finished signing the official documents and had been joined by his mother, stepfather, and youngest siblings.

Only just four, the girl had Andrew's blond curls. She was perched on his hip, her arms about his neck while Andrew spoke to their parents, and there was something so endearingly sweet about his open display of affection for his youngest sibling.

Edine periodically tugged at one of his curls, and each time, he paused in the discussion he was having with his mother and stepfather to smile at her.

It was reminiscent of the care and regard her own father had always shown her, and a warmth filled every corner of her chest.

Suddenly, Andrew dipped Edine backwards, drawing snorting giggles from the girl.

Marcia and her friends sighed.

"Yes, well, I'll allow Benedict does not strike me as one who would go about playing with children," Anwen grudgingly acknowledged.

"He's always been kind enough to us," Marcia felt inclined to point out.

"Mayhap to *you*," Faith said.

She started. "Has he been rude to you?" It hardly fit with the man she'd known over the years.

Color splotched Faith's cheeks. "No," she said quickly, and then her friend's gaze alighted on Andrew and his family once more. "Your husband is looking at you."

There it was again. *Your husband.*

Marcia looked across the room, and sure enough, she found him watching her.

And smiling.

It was his roguish half grin, a captivating, uneven tilt of his lips.

Her heart did that increasingly familiar, funny leap.

Her heart had always responded so to that smile. Hadn't it? This was no new phenomenon.

That was what she told herself, desperate reassurances in an effort to make their relationship the one it had always been and one that had not changed. One where she wasn't completely and hopelessly besotted with him.

Because she could not be.

With his eyes still fixed on Marcia, Andrew said something to his mother and Lord Exeter. The elegantly graying gentleman took the small girl from Andrew and proceeded to tip her upside down as Andrew had done moments ago, and then Andrew started across the room.

To her.

Marcia's mouth dried, and her mind remained scrambled.

And then he was there.

"Ladies." He greeted her friends first, capturing Anwen's hand and then Faith's. "It is a pleasure, as always."

It did not escape Marcia's notice that he directed his words towards Faith's functioning ear. Marcia's heart stirred at the considerate gesture, one her friend had lamented that most members of the *ton* failed to do. Marcia loved him desperately for that kindness, just as she loved him for—

Marcia strangled on her swallow.

Andrew thumped her hard between the shoulder blades. "What's this?" he asked between the determined thwacks. "I cannot have my bride kicking her heels up on our wedding day."

Her friends giggled.

Yes, because he was that endearing.

And Marcia was still not a woman about whom he possessed any romantic imaginings.

Oh, God, I am in bad trouble. The worst.

Not even married a moment, and she was waxing on romantic about Andrew Barrett, the Viscount Waters, from whom she'd practically had to pull a pledge of fidelity at the altar while a man of God officiated and her father at his back.

His smile dipped, as did her friends'.

"We should go. My mother is motioning," Faith said quickly, catching Anwen by the arm.

"No," Marcia said on a rush. "You really don't have to."

Because being alone with Andrew suddenly seemed like a very bad, very dangerous idea.

The butler entered the room and announced breakfast, and Marcia couldn't contain her audible sigh at being saved.

Andrew took her gently by the arm, steering her closer. He lowered his lips close to her ear, and his breath tickled her cheek. Her body quickened as she recalled the last moment she'd been in his arms, an embrace she wanted to know again.

"I daresay it's hardly a good sign to have one's bride frowning on one's wedding day," he said, and then he tweaked her nose the way he always had since she'd been a small girl.

Her panicked thoughts continued galloping wildly in her head. What if that was all she was to him? No different than his younger sister Edine, whom he'd perched upon his hip and brought to laughter, like he managed to pull laughter from everyone.

"I'm not frowning," she said, and Andrew teased a finger along the right corner of her mouth, and her lips parted.

Her belly quickened.

Oh, goodness.

"Frowning again," he pointed out.

How could he, as a rogue, prove completely unaware of the effects he had on her?

"You forget, Marcia," he whispered against her ear. "I know your smile as well as I know your frown."

She caught her lower lip between her teeth. He did know her, but apparently not so well as to gather the reason for her disquiet.

His gaze grew more somber, and he shifted it over her face. "Are you all right?" he asked quietly.

"Yes!" she answered, too quickly, too emphatically.

Andrew gave her a look.

As he'd pointed out, he knew her well enough to identify when she was not herself, though not well enough to realize that her chaotic heart was the reason she was so out of sorts before him.

"You regret your decision," he remarked quietly.

"No," she said, shaking her head. "I… It is just new. All of this is foreign."

He caught her hands, raising them one at a time to his mouth and placing a kiss upon them. "Nothing has to change, Marcia." He spoke with the eagerness of a man who clearly wished for things to remain as they were between them.

"No, you are right."

Except, as he slipped his arm through hers, and they made their way to their wedding breakfast, those assurances she'd given herself melted away.

As Andrew charmed their guests, she couldn't take her eyes off of him. He commanded the room in a comforting way, gesticulating with his hands while he spoke and raising laughter from all parties present. Why, he even managed to pull a grin from Marcia's father, who'd only been grim since he'd discovered them in that bedroom.

Suddenly, the Duke and Duchess of Huntly's youngest babe, Lord William, a boy just one year old, with a tangle of golden curls like his mother and father, erupted into a blubber of tears.

As if on cue, the child's nursemaid came rushing into the room to escort the babe off, but Andrew, in mid-conversation with the earl, reached for his nephew. Naturally and never breaking dialogue, Andrew proceeded to bounce the boy on his knee.

Almost immediately, the babe ceased crying.

Andrew said something to the child, tickling him under the chin.

Andrew was so natural and easy with a babe, a babe who, with his golden curls, conjured an image of a babe who might one day be theirs.

And she wanted that.

As though he had followed the dangerous direction her thoughts had meandered, Andrew looked down at her and smiled.

That smile proved to be the final nail in the proverbial coffin for her.

She felt her lips curling in what she suspected was a stupid smile as, God help her, she found herself as besotted and entranced as any lady who'd ever been seduced by, or seduced by the thought of, Andrew Barrett.

She wanted all of those things with Andrew.

Laughter and love, a family.

Marcia went still, grateful when little Lord William thumped a chubby fist against Andrew's chest, recalling his attention.

She gripped the arms of her chair tightly to steady her trembling fingers.

Oh, God.

This was very bad indeed.

CHAPTER 18

THE MOMENT THEY'D ARRIVED AT Andrew's household later that day, Marcia had not known what to expect.

After she'd been properly introduced to the staff, the lovely, kindly housekeeper, Mrs. Hinkle, had taken Marcia on a guided tour of the entire household, a tour that Andrew did not take part in.

She'd not expected he would, and yet, as she and Mrs. Hinkle made their way from room to room, she found herself wishing he was there with her so she wasn't alone.

Because this was the first—and final—home she'd call her own.

But he did not accompany her. He'd waved her on, and that had been the last she'd seen of him. The day had marched on, with a servant even bringing Marcia supper in her rooms.

She'd only just sought him out and found that he hadn't gone off to one of those wicked clubs where he'd taken her.

Rather, he was here. With his friends, of course.

But still here.

Hovering outside the closed door of his billiards room, she debated what to do.

He didn't want her company.

He'd never professed they would be anything more than friends.

But neither did that mean they had to live separate lives.

These past days with him, as they'd explored the more sinful sides of London he so enjoyed, had proven they were compatible partners, friends. Why, they could still explore all of those same haunts together.

She could be like one of his male chums.

With that resolve in place, Marcia pressed the handle and let herself in.

The room instantly went silent. The three players—Andrew and two of his notoriously wicked friends, Lord Landon and the Duke of Rothesby—stared at her.

For a moment, Marcia's courage flagged as she recalled that she *wasn't* one of his male chums.

Leave. Just go.

But if she went now, then it'd be a certainty that she'd absolutely live her own life while he lived his. And she didn't want that. They were friends, and she wanted that continued friendship.

Before her courage completely deserted her, Marcia smiled and pushed the door shut behind her as she entered.

"Billiards! I confess I've always wanted to play," she said, and Landon and Rothesby sent each other side looks as she skipped over and stretched her fingers up for one of the cue sticks.

She attempted to wrestle it free.

"Here, my lady."

Lord Rothesby was immediately there.

Not her husband.

She didn't want it to matter that this stranger, and not Andrew, had come to her aid.

She smiled and accepted the stick from him. "Thank you."

He returned her smile, his an easy half tilt that radiated with warmth and sincerity, and more of her tension abated… until her gaze went to Andrew.

He did not wear a smile of any sort. Rather, his harshly beautiful features were set in a scowl.

On this, their wedding night.

A wedding night he had opted to spend with his friends.

Unnerved and with an awkward silence hanging over the room, Marcia did a circle of the table.

I should leave.

Andrew gave no indication he wanted her close. Or, for that matter, anywhere near him.

But she was very much a coward, because even knowing he

didn't want her around, she couldn't stand being suffocated by her own silence, lonely and scared, as she'd been since their arrival at his home.

She made a show of studying the table, and while the three gentlemen silently observed her, Marcia brought the cue stick into place.

From the corner of her eye, she caught Landon's smile.

It was, however, Rothesby who took mercy on her.

"It is upside down, my dear. Like this," he explained, and stepping forward, he slid the stick from her fingers and repositioned for her. "If I may?" Even as he asked, he was already helping guide her into the proper stance at the table.

"Like this?" she asked.

Rothesby shifted her forward slightly and murmured his approval. "Like so, my lady. Now, the red ball is the object ball." He guided the stick held between them in the direction of each ball as he named it. "And the white is the cue one. In order to determine who shoots first, players perform a lag." All the while, he retained his hold upon her.

She cast a quizzical glance over her shoulder.

"Each player simultaneously hits a cue ball up the table, bouncing it off the top cushion so that it returns to the balkline." He shifted her stick slightly. "That refers to this area of the table." He traced a gentle circle over the indicated area upon the red velvet table.

The duke proceeded to run through the remainder of the directions of game play and a breakdown of the scoring system.

Andrew remained stonily silent the entire time. Where was his usual mirth?

Probably it's only hit him what he's done, that he's now married.

Shoving aside that taunting voice, she trained all her focus on the game with the duke.

"You, however, can go first, my lady," he was saying, forgoing the lag.

"That is very generous of you, Your Grace. Given we are friends now, however, I trust using each other's more familiar names is permitted?"

Landon slanted a glance Andrew's way.

Rothesby, with a confidence befitting either a duke or a consummate rake, or mayhap both, flashed a wicked half grin that she expected made many a lady's heart flutter. "Far be it from me to reject a young lady's request, Marcia," he murmured and winked.

She braced for her heart to respond in the same way it did when Andrew smiled at her the way this man now did, but God help her, it did not. Even as he took her hands in his stronger, more powerful ones and guided her back into place, her heart remained remarkably steady in its beat.

"Get your damned hands off my wife, Rothesby," Andrew snapped, and she and Rothesby glanced over at him, and this time, her heart *did* pound. "I'll give her the damned lesson," he muttered, stomping over.

In all the years they'd known each other, she'd never known him to be so out of sorts.

Andrew reached for the stick.

Heat filled her cheeks, and Marcia drew it close. "You don't have to give me a lesson if you don't want to," she said archly as Rothesby stepped aside. "Rothesby has quite generously offered to see to the task himself."

"I'll see to it," Andrew gritted out.

Fury blazed from his eyes, and she opened her mouth to debate him and then stopped. Something in those fiery specks in his eyes gave her pause. Why, it was as though he were jealous. Surely he was not, though. Such a thought was preposterous. He didn't care about her in that regard. He'd been clear about that from the moment of his emotionless offer of marriage, and yet, right now, as he shoved Rothesby aside and took her in his arms, she could almost believe he did care about her in that way.

As Andrew positioned the cue, her heart did pound. Dangerously so. And as he held her in a makeshift embrace, guiding their frames in perfect harmony over the table, he drew her arm back.

She trembled.

"Steady," he murmured, and with his body layered against hers, his breath fanning her ear, tickling her neck, the task he'd given her proved Herculean.

Marcia briefly closed her eyes and drew in a slow, steadying breath.

This is just a billiards lesson. It is no different than the one you received from the Duke of Rothesby mere moments ago, and Andrew is holding you only because it's part of his lesson on the game.

She told herself as much. Over and over.

It did not help.

Her body did not understand or care about the difference. At some point, a great shift had occurred in her relationship with Andrew, and their friendship had morphed into something more. Something that made her aware of him in ways she'd not been aware of even her own betrothed.

The stick slid from her fingers, scraping the table.

"Worry not, love," he assured, thankfully misunderstanding the reason for her wayward shot. "Soon it'll become as natural as breathing."

Marcia gave a shaky nod and took in another slow, equally uneven breath.

She forced her focus away from the powerful pull of being in Andrew's arms and allowed him to teach her.

He was methodical in his approach, more matter-of-fact than Lord Rothesby had been, but precise in his directions. With each detail he imparted, he not only displayed the shot himself, but he also helped guide her through the particular motions.

As she stood back, observing his latest lesson, she noted that, attired only in his trousers, white lawn shirt, and boots, he was a sight to behold. The gape at the top of his shirt revealed the hint of tight golden coils that matted his chest.

She'd seen him in even less clothing.

As a girl and then even as a young woman, when they'd swum together at Lord and Lady Rutland's annual summer house parties.

So why should she prove so fascinated, so hopelessly fixed on—

"I propose a friendly wager now that the lady has been sufficiently trained."

Lord Landon's casual drawl pulled Marcia back from her wicked musings, and she studiously studied the table, more than half-certain those present—including her husband—had read the wayward direction of her thoughts.

"How about a match between the happy bride and bridegroom and the remaining bachelors?" Rothesby offered.

Marcia was already making a sound of protest. "I cannot. I would only bring Andrew down."

Andrew slid his spare fingers through hers, interlocking the digits and squeezing lightly, causing her pulse to race. "Worry not. Landon's game play is beneath even that of a first-time player."

She laughed, the expression of her mirth sounding breathless to her own ears. Marcia was thankful that the boisterous, echoing amusement from Andrew and Lord Rothesby and the over-the-top pretend outrage from the earl drowned out that breathy little sound.

"One hundred pounds," Andrew said, tapping the edge of the table and appearing wholly oblivious to the effect he was having on her senses.

Her amusement immediately died. It was a deuced fortune. And on a playful game between friends. "One hundred—?"

Rothesby scoffed. "Five hundred."

Marcia blanched and gave Andrew's sleeve a light tug. "An—"

"One thousand," Landon said.

She strangled on her swallow. "One thousand?" she squawked. "Andrew, that is folly," she said on a whisper.

He took her palm in his once more and dropped a kiss upon the knuckles of first her left hand and then her right. "I have faith in our game play, love."

"Well, that is bloody stupid," she hissed. "Andrew, I've never played, and that really is rude of them to suggest such a wager," she said for his ears only.

"It is a game between friends," he insisted.

"Andrew," she protested.

"Your wife is far cleverer than you, ol' chap," Landon called over. "Heed her advice and make this one of the rare wagers you do forgo."

Marcia frowned in the earl's direction, and he touched a finger to his bow.

"My apologies, my lady."

Marcia tensed her mouth. "Very well," she said tightly.

Rothesby motioned between her and Andrew. "The happy couple may play first."

The happy couple, she mused wryly. How many *happy* couples spent their wedding night with their husband's confirmed-bachelor friends?

"Oh, no." She brought her palms up, holding her stick aloft. "I'd… benefit from watching the game play further."

Rothesby inclined his head. "Let it be a consolation that you took lessons from the best, my lady."

"Andrew is the best?" she asked, perking up, and Andrew gave her a quick little wink.

A wry grin formed on the duke's mouth. "I referred to myself, your first instructor."

"About as memorable for Waters' bride as you are with all the ladies," Landon said and laughed at his own joke, with Rothesby taking that good-natured ribbing.

"Landon, have a care with your mouth around my wife," Andrew snapped.

"Ah, but she is one of the fellows now. Isn't that right, love?" Lord Landon flashed what she expected would be a devastating smile to any other lady and followed it with a wink.

Both left her remarkably unmoved.

Marcia lifted her head solemnly. "One of the fellows," she allowed.

Landon and Rothesby played through, racking up points until the turn switched to Marcia and Andrew.

Her husband drew her close and whispered near her ear, "Just recall your lesson, and remember, it is just in good fun."

Oh, she remembered every one of those lessons. But she had been a girl and not aware of Andrew's body wrapped around hers then.

"Good fun doesn't end with a person standing to lose one thousand pounds, Andrew." She'd intended for her pronouncement to be firm and steady, but it emerged breathy, as her voice became whenever he touched her.

With another wink, Andrew turned his attention on the table

and made quick work of it. Given there were one thousand pounds on the line, she should be attending the game.

But, God help her, she could not keep her eyes off of him.

He was tall and impressive and graceful even in game play. As he brought his arm back for each shot, the muscles of his biceps strained the fabric of his shirt, and her mouth went dry, and she could fix only on that fascinating ripple of material as it outlined his powerful form.

Her husband was a magnificent specimen of masculinity.

My husband.

My husband.

She toyed with those words in her mind, playing them over and over again. The litany became as dangerous as this sudden preoccupation with Andrew Barrett's form.

"Your turn, love."

A startled shriek slipped out, and Marcia jumped at that sudden interruption.

Andrew held the cue stick out, and she accepted it with trembling fingers.

Drawing in a deep breath, she forced her thoughts away from her husband and on to the game. Putting all her attention on the table, she leaned over and let her cue stick fly.

It immediately cracked the red ball, which in turn snapped against the back of the velvet table and sprang forward, colliding with the other balls, which sent two more balls flying. She made quick work of the remaining two, knocking them out in a matter of seconds before setting her stick down.

Silence, to match the one that had greeted her when she'd joined Andrew and his company, filled the room. Only, this proved to be the stunned kind.

"I believe that is one thousand pounds each, gentlemen," she said, dusting her palms together.

Landon released a long groan.

Rothesby tossed his head back and roared with laughter. "It appears we've been swindled by your wife."

Andrew's features were a harsh mask, impossible to read.

"Gentlemen, if you'll excuse me," he said, and she tried to

interpret his tone, but could not.

"Happy to do so before she takes our damned properties," Landon muttered, returning his cue to its proper place on the wall.

Rothesby inclined his head. "Worry not, Marcia. He's merely jesting." He paused. "Landon lost his properties long before you came along."

The marquess flashed a finger, pulling laughter from the duke. But when he looked back at her, there was a new seriousness to the gentleman. Rothesby took her right hand in his and drew it to his lips the same way Andrew had moments ago and gave her knuckles a kiss that lingered as much.

It was also a kiss that left her feeling remarkably flat.

"It was a pleasure, Marcia," he murmured, squeezing her fingers lightly.

A moment later, Andrew's friends filed from the room, and Andrew followed them. For a moment, she thought—feared—he intended to leave the room with them. But he stopped and closed the door behind them with a click that resonated as powerfully as thunder in the quiet.

Leaving Marcia and Andrew alone.

They'd been alone any number of times before this one. Too many to count. Most of those instances had been when she'd been a child and underfoot while he'd been attempting to sneak some peace and quiet for himself.

But this proved their first time alone as a married couple.

Andrew turned back, a scowl stamped on his features.

He was annoyed and disapproving, also firsts for her.

Marcia dampened her mouth. "I've displeased you," she said.

He strode over.

Nay, not strode—stalked. His steps were the languid ones of a lion she'd once observed at the Royal Zoo.

"Oh, no," he murmured, the moment he reached her. "Anything but." He caressed his fingers lightly over the curve of her hip, and her mouth went dry when he suddenly gripped her hard, drawing her close.

"T-truly? B-because you seem angry." Her voice emerged as a breathless whisper.

"Oh, I am not angry," he whispered, placing a kiss on the curve of her neck.

Biting her lower lip, she tilted her head to better open herself to his worshiping mouth. "N-no?"

"Oh, no." Then he slid his palms under her buttocks, scooping that flesh as he pulled her against him. So close, she felt the long line of his erection. "I found myself impressed."

A little laugh escaped her. "You are impressed that I swindled your friends?"

"I'm impressed beyond measure by the ease with which you swindled your *opponents*. Especially those bounders."

Holding his neck, Marcia angled back slightly so she might meet his eyes. "And here I never knew that billiards could be a game that inspires desire. It is—"

He covered her mouth with his, kissing her into silence, and she was happy to surrender the dialogue and herself to him.

Sighing, she let her lips part, and he swept inside, tasting her, and she tasted him in return. All the while, he touched her, his long, strong hands exploring the slight curve of her hip, the flare of her buttocks.

Then, reaching up, he slipped the bodice of her dress down, exposing her bosom to the air.

She gave a little quiver that had absolutely nothing to do with the slight chill that hung in the room.

Andrew palmed her breasts, lifting them gently like he were weighing gold, and then slowly, he lowered his mouth.

A hiss slipped between her teeth, and her legs trembled as he took one of those sensitive peaks between his lips, suckling gentling, tugging at the bud.

There was something so very erotic in the wet sounds of him kissing her in a place she'd not known men kissed before this man.

Closing her eyes, Marcia surrendered herself completely to feeling… and him. She brought her hands up, curling her fingers in his unfashionably long, golden hair, and held him close, anchoring him against her, never wanting him to stop. Not allowing him to stop.

But then he pulled back against her hold, and Marcia made a

sound of protest, but Andrew was merely turning his attention to the other mound, worshiping the other nipple in the same way.

With a little sigh, she closed her eyes and let herself just feel as he flicked his tongue back and forth over that pebbled tip, as he suckled, then stopped, suckled, then stopped.

She grew shamefully damp between her legs, the pulsing there not unfamiliar. The ache was both terrific and terrible, but one she yearned to have assuaged.

Suddenly, Andrew stopped, and she cried out as he straightened, but then he took her in his arms, and kissed her mouth, this time with a greater intensity.

"There will come a day when you regret our marriage, Marcia," he said harshly between kisses that dulled the hint of peril that hung on his words. "But this will not be that day."

She wanted to debate him, to fight him on the point. She couldn't regret marrying him, because she'd married one of her best friends. And she'd come to love him with a woman's heart. But thoughts failed. Her voice failed. Nor was she brave enough to make that profession to him. Not when she also knew him well enough to know such an admission would send him running in terror.

Lifting her up slightly, Andrew perched her on the edge of the pool table.

"Wh-what are you—?"

"Shh," he whispered, gently guiding her down so that the hard red velvet surface was a makeshift mattress beneath them.

She allowed him to lay her back, would have followed him to the bowels of hell in this instant, if he'd so asked.

In any instant, a voice mocked through the dizzying pleasure of being in his arms. Refusing to let the terror of whatever these new feelings were for this man intrude, she pushed them aside and forced herself to focus on this. Only this.

Andrew guided her skirts up slowly. Each swath of skin he revealed to the night air was kissed by that cold and then his mouth.

He trailed those kisses, higher and higher, his lips hot and moist upon her, fueling a fire within.

Her mind clogged by a thick fog of desire, Marcia attempted to push herself up onto her elbows. "Andrew?" she asked breathlessly.

"You are so beautiful," he murmured, his breath stirring the thatch of golden curls at her apex.

And then he kissed her.

He'd kissed her several times. Five times, to be precise, each kiss more potent and powerful than the one to precede it. But none had been like this.

A hiss exploded from her lips, and Marcia shot her hips up off the table. "An-Andrew!" she cried out as he parted her folds and slipped his tongue inside.

He flicked the sensitive nub, teasing it, teasing her. Tormenting her.

"Just feel, Marcia. Let yourself feel only this," he whispered.

Her body went weak, and she lay back, surrendering herself to him completely.

Closing her eyes, she let herself do as he'd urged. *Just feel.*

Every lap of his tongue, every delicious stroke.

It was forbidden and naughty, and she should be ashamed. For surely ladies didn't do this, didn't enjoy this.

But she did, and she felt like she would dissolve into nothing if he stopped.

"Do you like this, love?" His voice, heavy with desire and masculine approval, only heightened her hungering.

She bit her lower lip and nodded, incapable of anything more.

"Hmm?" He licked her, and Marcia gasped, lifting her hips into his tongue.

"Andrew!" she cried out again.

"Tell me, Marcia. I need to hear you say it," he demanded on a harsh whisper.

"I like this," she said with a gasp. Nay, that wasn't sincere or true. "I love it."

With a smile full of raw, primitive male satisfaction, he claimed her with his mouth once more.

Andrew had been with any number of women in his life.

None of them had been innocent.

And none of them had been Marcia.

After this morning, he'd feared that everything would be different between them.

And it was.

In the best possible way.

She was on fire. And he was on fire for her.

She was also close. He felt it in the way her slender body shivered and trembled and in the way she tensed her hips.

And he wanted to give her that greatest of pleasures her body cried out for. He flicked his tongue back and forth repeatedly, alternately suckling that nub and then moving his tongue in and out of her sodden channel.

"You are so wet," he praised between each kiss. He stroked his palms along her long, slender limbs, contoured with muscles from her years of riding.

She whimpered and turned her face towards the wall.

"Look at me, Marcia," he commanded. "There is no shame in this. And certainly not between us. Ever." He held her eyes with his.

Marcia slowly nodded and then arched her hips up, urging him on.

Andrew returned to pleasuring her with his mouth, wanting to drown in the musky scent of her desire. He tortured himself for several moments longer with the taste and feel of her, and then he made himself stop.

Marcia cried out.

Sweat beading his brow, Andrew yanked off his shirt and shucked out of his trousers. Scrambling atop the billiards table, he carried her frame more to the middle and then lay between her legs.

She let them splay wide as he settled himself there.

Slowly, he slid his shaft inside. She was so fucking wet. Drenched with her desire, he was reduced for a moment to the green boy he'd once been, impatient and needing to take her, but he fought to keep from claiming her immediately.

Forcing himself to go slow—because this was Marcia, because this was her first time—he moved with an agonizing slowness, stretching her tight channel with his shaft.

Andrew tamped down a groan.

She was so tight. She fit him like a damned glove, and he'd never felt such a blissful sensation as this.

She whimpered, and he immediately stopped. "Am I hurting you?"

"Only when you stop," she whispered, and wrapping her arms around him, she hugged him tightly, encouraging him to continue.

Andrew groaned, the sound a low, desperate rumble, and reaching between them, he teased her with his fingers even as he remained frozen, partially sheathed. He was determined to raise her desire to a fever pitch.

And he did.

He lowered his head between her breasts and licked a path, placing a kiss on each mark left by his tongue. Then he returned to suckling each swollen pink tip cresting the gentle swells, laving, then sucking. Andrew alternated back and forth until Marcia was keening little incoherent sounds of her desire, blended with his name, and that only fueled his ardor.

He felt her body quiver and knew what she craved, felt in the way her hips had begun to lift up that she was close and that she urged him on.

Andrew moved within her once more, drawing out the same path he'd traveled within her and then rocking forward again, accustoming her to the size and feel of him.

"Andrew," she pleaded, and there was a question coated in desperation.

He thrust deep, and she cried out, her body convulsing, and with a soothing whisper, he cradled her in his arms.

"I'm so sorry, love," he whispered harshly against her ear. "So damned sorry."

Marcia remained with her eyes squeezed tight, her flushed face scrunched up, and he placed gentle kisses upon her eyelids and then continued trailing kisses along the curve of her cheek.

Her lashes fluttered open. "It wasn't so very bad," she said thickly, and it occurred to him that she was attempting to reassure him.

And it was so patently Marcia.

Andrew claimed her mouth in a gentle kiss, and as she sighed, she parted her lips, letting him inside once more to taste of her.

"It has only begun, Marcia." He whispered that promise, and she lifted her lashes.

"It… has?"

He grinned. "Oh, yes." And he resumed his efforts, tasting of her breasts and teasing her with his fingers even as he remained buried deep inside her, even as it took every bit of restraint he possessed to keep from moving. When her hips began to lift reflexively, signaling that it was safe to continue, he did. He drew back and then moved slowly forward, repeating that slow, gentle rhythm until Marcia gripped him, her nails no doubt leaving crescent marks upon his back.

"Please," she begged.

He was unable to deny her anything in that moment.

Just as he'd always been unable to deny her anything.

Andrew thrust and retreated. Thrust and retreated. Over and over.

She met every downward lunge by lifting her hips to meet his.

Sweat beaded his brow as his climax hovered.

"Come for me," he begged, needing her to go first so that he could join her.

Biting her lower lip, Marcia nodded and then stiffened.

Her desire-filled eyes widened with shock, and then screaming to the rafters one word, his name, she came. "Andrew!"

She dragged her fingernails up and down his back, marking him, but he didn't feel it. He was capable only of feeling each sensation as she found her release and surrendered herself so fully and completely to it.

Then she sagged, a final gasp slipping from her lips.

With the echoes of her throaty cries thundering in his ears, Andrew gripped her hips and pumped himself inside her. Gritting his teeth and biting out curses he could not contain, he froze, and with a low groan, he lowered his head to her shoulder and spent himself inside her, coming hard and long. "Marcia," he groaned.

All the while, she held on to him.

He collapsed, catching himself on his elbows to keep from

crushing her.

His heartbeat hammered, clamoring hard in his chest. His ears buzzed from the force of a release the likes of which he'd never experienced.

Never. Never, with all the women he'd bedded, had he felt this sense of completion, and it was just sex. He'd had sex so many times before her. Why did it feel different this time? Why with this woman?

Because it is Marcia, a voice whispered simply in his head.

He stilled.

It is Marcia.

With that, reality came crashing in, as did the truth of what he'd done.

He'd made love to her, cemented the vows they'd taken, atop a billiards table like she was a common doxy. Because he knew absolutely nothing about being with a respectable lady. The women who'd come before her had all been as ruthless in their wants as he. They'd been as knowledgeable, and more, in carnal matters.

But this was Marcia, who'd been innocent and who was good.

And he was only going to muck this up. That much was a certainty. Because he invariably ruined anything and everything he touched. It was a failure of his blood that he could not separate himself from. And now it would touch this woman about whom he cared.

He'd convinced himself that, with the offer Rutland and Huntly had put to him, he could change, refusing to consider until now the obvious truth: what happened if he did not change.

There would be Marcia, hurt, because of him.

Nausea churned in his belly, and he waited until he detected the shift in her breathing, from rapid and ragged to smooth and even, before he disentangled himself from her. Reaching for his jacket, he pulled it closer and removed the kerchief.

As she slept, Andrew gently cleaned between her legs, and when he went to tend to himself, his eyes locked on the crimson stain upon the white material marking her innocence.

Marcia's innocence.

And he'd taken it.

Squeezing his eyes shut, Andrew concentrated on breathing.

He was destined to fail, and yet, this time, he could not.

He had to make more of himself.

For her.

With that, Andrew climbed from his billiards table and collected a slumbering Marcia in his arms. As he set her down in her bed, and lay beside her, sleep eluded him. For he could not shake the feeling of dread at what he'd done.

CHAPTER 19

STROLLING ALONGSIDE THE SERPENTINE, MARCIA and her friends had their parasols propped upon opposite shoulders so they might freely speak with one another.

A dreamy smile played at her lips.

Since their wedding night, she and Andrew had spent every night in the same bed, making love all night… and just before he fell asleep with her in his arms, he called Marcia his *love*.

When he'd spoken that word as he had, breathless and harsh, she could believe he did love her, that she was his love and that these moments between them were more. She wasn't just any woman to him, the next Linette or Lucinda but, rather, someone special, the only woman he needed or wanted.

"Well, I'll be goddammed," Anwen marveled aloud, pulling Marcia back from her musings. "It worked."

Blinking several times, she looked to her friend.

"The necklace," the other woman said, motioning to that small pendant that now hung around Faith's neck.

Faith bristled. "And did you think it shouldn't?"

"No," Anwen allowed. "Only that it wouldn't."

Faith dropped her parasol, snapped it closed, and gave the other woman a gentle thump on the arm, pulling a laugh from Anwen and Marcia.

Though, in truth, as Marcia settled onto the shore of the Serpentine with her friends, it was hard not to be giddy.

When they'd seated themselves, Anwen drew closer. "What is it like?"

Marcia glanced over. "It?"

The other woman rolled her eyes. "*Iiiit,*" she whispered, stretching out that single syllable. "Lying with one's husband. Because from what my mother and sister and the other women in the Mismatch Society whom are married shared, it sounds awful. They assure me it isn't, but I cannot see how any of that can be anything but uncomfortable and painful. And I'm very certain that they are lying to me."

"Anwen," Faith admonished. "Your sister and mother lead a society of women advising other women on matters of intimacy. I daresay they aren't going to lie to you."

"What?" the other woman said defensively. "It wouldn't be unlike our mothers to want to protect us from what it really is like so we don't worry."

Marcia's gaze grew distant as she stared out at the park. "It was… It is… magnificent, as they say," she said softly.

"I knew it," Faith loudly exclaimed, catching several curious looks from passersby. "You are in love with him!"

Another dreamy smile pulled at the corners of her mouth.

"Shh." Anwen sent an elbow sailing into the other woman's side, causing Faith to grunt. "Will you have a care before we are overheard? A lady doesn't wish to have her feelings about some gentleman aired about."

"Ah, yes," Faith said, waggling a finger at Anwen. "But Marcia is wed and—"

"And it's still not anyone's business who she has fallen in love with, and she's given no indication—"

"It is fine," Marcia said softly, and both women immediately ceased fighting and looked at her. "I do love him." She looked off in the distance. "I suspect I always have. For so long, he was just Andrew, my friend, whom I looked to like an older brother. But then, along the way, that changed."

While the two proceeded to argue about their levels of freedom, Marcia twisted her parasol at her shoulder and absently studied the Hyde Park landscape.

There was truth to what Faith had spoken of. As a married woman, Marcia was granted freedoms previously denied her.

Only, she knew precisely what she wanted in life—a real marriage with him.

Because she loved him.

Because she always had.

She knew that now.

"Oh, dear, you have the same look my brother and his wife have whenever they are together," Anwen lamented.

"And isn't that a good thing? That Marcia is in love with her husband?" Faith asked.

"Yes, but does her husband love her—ow." Anwen cried out as the other woman kicked her in the toes.

As if Marcia weren't seated right beside them, Faith cast a pointed look her way and whispered, "Of course he loves her. How could he not?"

How could he not?

Very easily.

He was a rogue who'd likely broken any number of hearts through the years. He'd never professed to love her—not in that way. He made love to her, passionately, but again, he'd had any number of lovers.

And yet...

They stopped at the side of the river. The maid who'd accompanied them, hastened over, snapping a blanket out for them to sit upon.

"Something felt... different between us last night," Marcia confessed to her friends once they'd claimed a seat at the shore, and her friends went silent, staring at her with rapt gazes. "He's not said he loves me, but I think... he might. At least eventually."

Both her friends dropped their chins upon their knees and sighed.

"Why should he not love you?" Faith asked, her tone indignant. "You are perfectly lovable."

"Because he is a rogue," Anwen remarked. "And everyone knows rogues do not fall in love easily." She spoke as one who knew.

"Ah, yes." Faith waggled a finger in the other woman's direction. "But when they do, they make for the very best of husbands."

A shadow fell over the blanket, and they looked up.

A voluptuous, midnight-haired woman, her lush curves wrapped in damp white satin, smiled down at them. She was twirling a parasol propped at her shoulder the way Marcia had moments ago.

With her body blocking the sun as it was, the rays of that glowing orb cast an ethereal glow about her, lending a goddess-like quality to the stranger.

If Eve had come back to take part in a London Season, Marcia rather suspected this was what she would have looked like.

She wore a beautiful, dimpled grin, but something in that grin was false and empty.

Unease traipsed along Marcia's spine.

"May we help you?" Marcia asked softly.

"They may not, but you"—the young woman snapped her umbrella shut and pointed the tip at Marcia—"may. Perhaps we might speak alone?" Her unswerving gaze was icy.

"I…"

"I do not think so," Faith whispered loudly. "We don't know her."

"And you are a scared child?" the woman teased meanly, and then laughed.

Ignoring her, Faith continued speaking. "Whatever it is you care to say to her can certainly be said to us."

As if on perfect cue, Anwen sat up straighter and gave a little nod.

The stranger looked Anwen over—all too briefly—before dismissing her outright and returning all her attention to Faith. "How… charming you are," she said in frosty tones that left little doubt as to how she felt about Faith.

"If you'll excuse us?" Marcia said quietly to her friends.

Her friends gave her a look.

"It is fine," Marcia assured, even though she knew no such thing. "We'll be only a moment."

"Your friend is gauche, Marcia," the woman intoned.

Her friend had only partial hearing. That was not, however, this woman's business. "My friend is loyal and good, and you are a stranger." A cold, mysterious one with icy eyes.

"I am a stranger?" The woman looked stricken. She dabbed at

the corners of perfectly dry eyes. "How that hurts me." She sniffed several times.

Faith and Anwen lingered a moment more. Faith held Marcia's gaze and shook her head slightly. "I do not trust her," she mouthed.

Neither did Marcia.

She waited until her friends had gone, walking along the shore far enough away to allow Marcia privacy, but close enough at hand should she need their help.

"Who are you?" Marcia asked quietly.

"I am Lady Carew, but you may call me, Marianne." Both the title and the name the stranger offered meant nothing to Marcia. "And it is so very lovely to see you, my dear. It is a shame we have not yet met before," the woman said, availing herself of a place on the blanket beside Marcia.

"I am sorry… Do we know one another?"

"We do not. But we should. We absolutely should," the woman said cheerfully, flashing a smile that perfectly dimpled her cheeks. "You see, family should know family."

Warning bells chimed.

"I am your aunt, dearest."

Her aunt?

The only aunt she'd ever known was Aunt Dorothy.

Marcia stilled as the meaning slammed into her.

"It is a shame we have been kept from one another." For a second time, the voluptuous beauty dabbed at the corners of dry eyes and sniffled twice. "My brother Lord Atbrooke is your father."

Marcia went cold inside, that frost touching on every corner of her person, chilling her on the inside and freezing her on the out. "Lord Atbrooke is not my father," she said quietly. Not in the ways that mattered. Marcia knew that now. Andrew had helped her to see that she was more than the man who'd sired her and that night of evil.

Lady Carew's lips formed a pouty moue. "How very rude. Of course he is." She trilled a laugh. "Though he is a bounder with a"—her eyes glazed over as something scandalous and dark lit her eyes—"wicked reputation." She paused. "I understand you have been entertaining yourself at some of London's most scandalous escapes."

She had.

Doing so hadn't made her happy. Andrew had helped her see that, too.

"You think I should disapprove," Lady Carew said. "I don't. Just the opposite in fact, my dear."

"I do not have an opinion one way or another as to what you think about me," Marcia said flatly.

The lady froze and then tossed her head back and laughed. "The kitten does have claws," she praised, patting Marcia's hand. "So perhaps there is more of me inside you. You see, Marcia"—she shifted closer, angling her body so their knees touched, and they faced each other—"so much unites us, dear Marcia. So much." She paused. "That is quite an atrocious name, though," she said with a gentleness that belied the unkindness of that statement. "Your mother really did you no favors with it."

Marcia stiffened. "The name belongs to my father," she said coolly, finding herself and finding her voice.

She might be young and innocent, but she was not incapable of spotting an enemy when she saw one.

"I am so very disappointed that I have not had a chance to meet you before today. We have so much in common."

"What exactly do we have in common?" Marcia asked frostily.

"Why, we share the same blood, and we both share the atrocious, hideous Atbrooke marking." She gestured to the top of Marcia's hand.

Marcia reflexively covered that spot, her mind conjuring the day years earlier when Lord Atbrooke had arrived at Aunt Dorothy's, back when Marcia had been too innocent to understand the power of evil.

"We both enjoy visiting scandalous hells and clubs. And," Lady Carew murmured, letting that word dangle in the air, "we've also shared the same lover."

Marcia's mind went blank. "I don't know what you are—?"

"Why, Lord Andrew, of course," the woman said with a roll of her eyes, as if Marcia had spoken aloud. As if Marcia were capable of joining in this discussion.

Marcia remained still, feeling like she'd taken a fist to the belly. Preferring she had, to this.

The woman wasn't done with her. "He always was such a dear boy." She leaned in and motioned discreetly at her breast. "Dearest Andrew said he did not mind my mark at all. He felt it added to my interest and beauty and was even particular about worshiping it with his mouth." The baroness's gaze grew distant, and her breath grew slightly labored as she touched herself obscenely, as if recalling Andrew's mouth and hand upon her.

Marcia's stomach churned, and all her muscles tensed as jealousy so powerful and real ripped through her, like a poison touching every corner of her person and turning it black within. *That is what she wants*, a voice at the back of her mind reminded. Lady Carew and her brother Lord Atbrooke were cut of the same cloth. *Whereas I? I am my mother…*

That remembrance, that realization steadied her: firmed her.

"Does he do the same for you?" the baroness asked, her voice throaty and ragged. Marcia's hesitation brought a triumphant grin from the other woman. "I take it by your silence he's not even noted your mark, which is good." She let her hand fall from her breast. "In its own way, I suppose," she added, patting Marcia's marked hand. "Tell me, dear niece, is my dear sweet Andrew still as impatient a lover as he always was?"

Even knowing what the baroness intended to do, Marcia could not contain that vicious jealousy as it snaked through her entire being. She curled her fingers sharply into balls.

"Or does he take his time?" The woman's gaze grew distant as if she recalled those past moments shared with Marcia's husband. "Because I taught him to go slow," she said, her voice a breathy whisper. "He was always so eager. Too eager. But he was also an eager student. I taught him to worship my body the whole night through, until the sun rose in a new sky."

"Is this why you've come?" Marcia said, infusing a thread of false pity into her query. "To trade stories about my husband's prowess? How very sad for you. You must miss him dreadfully."

Lady Carew recoiled, and triumph had a satisfying taste. "I don't have any interest in that child," she snapped. "Rather, I thought you might give him this?"

Reaching inside her reticule, she withdrew a folded page.

Hesitating, Marcia glanced down at them—the front page paper from the day she'd been stranded at the altar.

"You see, Marcia," the baroness explained. "We want that money you thought you were denying us when you married Andrew." Her dowry. "And we are determined to have it." The baroness smiled a cold, menacing grin that, despite the warmth of that morn, raised the gooseflesh on Marcia's arms. "We sought those monies from your former betrothed, and he learned firsthand what happens when we're thwarted."

A memory slipped in. Of the night Charles had stopped her as she'd attempted to leave the ball. She'd thought there'd been more he'd wanted to say... and he had. "You bribed Charles?" she whispered.

The baroness preened like she'd been handed a beautiful compliment. "He gave us a rich sum to stay silent about his sister. Alas, he wasn't quick enough with the funds where you were concerned." Giggling, Lady Carew made a show of capturing that sound with her fingers. "We had to teach him a lesson on just what happens if he's tardy with our payments."

Marcia replayed all of that last meeting with Charles. He'd been a man tortured. Ashamed and hurt. And now... it made sense. Because of these monsters. "I believe the word is bribe," Marcia said coolly, finding her voice, and by the slight widening of the other woman's eyes, she'd stunned her with her composure. "You *bribed* Charles. Just as you and Lord Atbrooke were attempting to use me to get money from my father."

"Oh, pooh. One cannot bribe one's daughter." The lady flicked an imagined speck of dust from her gauzy, puffed pink sleeve. "Either way, I'm grateful for my role, as I had the chance to renew my relationship with your husband at Cyprian's Den."

Despite herself, despite the fact she knew what this woman was doing, jealousy bared its vicious teeth. Marcia forced that ugly emotion aside, and kept her features even. She'd not give her the satisfaction.

"Can I help you?"

Marcia looked up, and a powerful swell of relief crested within her breast.

She'd never been more grateful for an interruption.

Benedict stood above them, frowning as she'd never before seen him frown, beating his riding crop against his side.

Lady Carew's eyes went to that strip of leather and gave it—and Benedict—a lascivious look. "No," she purred, rising in a graceful rustle of skirts. "Think of what I said, Marcia," she said, before giving Benedict a more considering glance. "Perhaps another time you might be of service to me, my lord." Hers was an invitation, though as she sashayed off, her hips a-swaying, Benedict gave no indication he'd heard it or cared.

Marcia tightened her fingers on the pages containing this latest bribe.

"Marcia," Benedict said gently as he settled onto the blanket, taking up the spot where her unwanted guest had been. Are you all right?"

How was she?

Enraged. Livid. Teeming with fury.

"You are here," she said, wanting to talk about anything other than the meeting that had just taken place. "I… You did not stay for the wedding breakfast."

Something flashed in his eyes. "I'm sorry. I would have stayed. I had… matters to see to." He glanced in the direction of Lady Carew's retreating form, and when his gaze flew back to Marcia, his eyes were harder than she'd ever seen them.

"How are you?" he asked.

"I'm fine," she lied, her voice sounding odd to her own ears.

"No, Marcia." Benedict gave her a long, searching look, and when he spoke next, he did so with a gentler insistence. "How *are* you?"

And for the first time, the rage slipped, and the misery at this family's hold over her still scraped her raw. Tears threatened.

She blinked furiously, fighting to keep them from falling and to keep him from seeing them.

A slightly pained sound escaped Benedict.

Then Faith and Anwen were there.

"What happened?" Faith demanded, edging Benedict out. "I knew we should not have let you alone with anyone," she said before she'd even allowed Marcia a chance to answer.

"Me?" Benedict sputtered. "I've done nothing."

"Benedict did not do anything," Marcia hurried to assure her friends. It was that venomous viper and her serpent brother. How had she ever worried about the fact he'd sired her. She was nothing like him. She could see clearly now how unfounded her upset had been.

"It was that woman." Faith seethed, slapping her palm against her other. "What do you need us to do?"

"Nothing," Marcia said, speaking over their protestations. "It is fine," she said tightly, not wanting to share what had transpired with them. Marcia firmed her jaw.

Whatever Atbrooke and his sister thought they might get out of her and Andrew, they were sorely mistaken.

CHAPTER 20

SEATED AT HIS DESK, HIS chair tipped back on two legs while Rothesby and Henries, Rothesby's man of affairs went over the details of the arrangement they were putting together, Andrew should be fully attending the discussion.

It was a discussion he'd wanted to be part of for longer than he could remember, but one he'd never had a hope of, because of the state of his finances.

And yet, now that he had those funds at his fingertips and the meeting he'd sought, he could not keep his mind from drifting to Marcia.

She'd invited him to join her and her friends in the park.

And he found himself wanting to be there with her now.

He found himself wishing he had delayed this meeting so that he might have spent the day with her.

Which was utterly preposterous. Theirs was, after all, a match born of convenience, one that had been made to save her reputation and to secure his funds and, with those funds, both of their futures.

So why could he not stop thinking about her?

Because you love her.

Andrew's chair toppled backwards, and he hit the floor hard.

His heart thundering for reasons that had nothing to do with his fall, he stared unblinkingly at the ceiling overhead.

Of course I love her.

But he did not *love* love her.

Not in the romantic way she wished, because he couldn't give a woman that level of love.

But Marcia wasn't just any woman, and their relationship wasn't like the relationships between other husbands and wives.

He groaned. Christ, this was bad.

Two figures peered over him, blocking his view of the white ceiling.

Rothesby frowned. "Waters?"

"I'm fine," he groaned. "Never better."

Scrambling to his feet, he righted his chair and reclaimed a seat upon it. "As you were saying?"

Footfalls pounded outside the corridor, and Andrew heard a familiar voice raised with fury. Andrew, Rothesby, and his man of affairs looked over just as the door exploded open, knocking hard against the wall.

Wakefield shot a hand out to keep the panel from hitting him in the face as it bounced back, and he stormed inside.

With a frown, Andrew came to his feet. "Wakefield. What—?"

"I've come to speak with you," the earl gritted out, his gaze locked on Andrew.

Andrew's frown deepened, and he caught the look Rothesby and his servant exchanged. "This isn't a good time, ol'—"

"Don't you dare 'ol' chum' me," Wakefield barked as two of Andrew's footmen came forward, reaching for the gentlemen. They'd toss him out. But the other man was a friend, and Andrew would never tolerate that.

He lifted a hand, staying the servants. "Gentlemen, if you will excuse us?" he said quietly. "Perhaps we might continue this discussion another time?"

Rothesby and his man of affairs immediately stood.

"Of course," Rothesby murmured as Henries hurriedly stacked his papers, filing them away.

As they took their leave, Rothesby paused to give Wakefield a look. Wakefield, however, gave no indication he saw him. His furious gaze remained locked on Andrew.

Never in all the years that he'd known the other man had Andrew seen him enraged, and certainly never had Andrew found himself the recipient of any such anger.

The moment they'd gone, Andrew motioned to one of the

empty chairs. "Can I get you a—"

"I don't want a damned drink," Wakefield cut him off. He scraped his gaze over the desk littered with the paperwork for Andrew's new investment. "I'm not here to pay a social call."

Andrew flashed a wry grin. "Given your current state, I didn't think it was."

"You are a selfish twat."

Andrew blinked. "I..."

"She deserved more. She deserved better."

Andrew stiffened. So that was what this was about. What Marcia deserved. But then, they'd always been like brothers to her. Or Wakefield had. Along the way, Andrew's feelings for her had grown beyond the fraternal regard he'd always carried and morphed into an all-consuming love.

He froze.

Love.

He braced for the shock and horror that had toppled him earlier. But this time they didn't come. He loved her. He loved being with her and making her smile, and he loved the way she made him smile and—

"Do you have nothing to say?" Wakefield barked, bringing Andrew crashing back to the other man's lecture.

"Undoubtedly," he said solemnly, in complete agreement and without offense. Wakefield knew him as well as his own family, and as such, he knew Andrew's soul had been corrupted and was too dark for Marcia.

Wakefield scowled. "That is it? That is all you'd say? My God, you've taken her to places she has absolutely no place being, places not fit for any innocent, respectable woman."

He winced. So he had discovered the details.

"Marcia has a mind of her own," he said stiffly. He'd not reveal all the details of the arrangement that had ultimately led to their marriage. That wasn't information Wakefield needed or deserved. "I have no intention of discussing my wife with you."

Wakefield's lip peeled back in a sneer. "Ah, yes, your wife. And this from the man who vowed he'd rather spend his days in hell than suffer the constraints of marriage."

The other man tossed out those words Andrew had laughingly thrown some years earlier.

"Things... changed."

"Because you ruined her," Wakefield spat, and his entire body rocked forward. "How very convenient that was for you."

Andrew frowned. "Have a care, Wakefield?" he warned. The other man might be a friend, but there was only so much Andrew would tolerate.

"You tell me to have a care, Waters," the other man scoffed. "You, whose wife is being accosted by your former lovers in Hyde Park while you're busy"—he slashed a hand angrily at Andrew—"doing whatever it is you're doing."

So that was why Wakefield had come. Andrew's stomach flipped over, and he prayed he heard the other man wrong. "What?"

"Lady Carew," Wakefield spat. "She singled out your wife."

Andrew unleashed a curse. He should have expected that night in Cyprian's Den hadn't been the last he'd seen of the viper. That, ultimately, she'd intended to spread her poison, and she'd done just that. *I should have been there with her...* "Marcia—"

"Handled herself with grace and aplomb and strength." His friend answered the rest of Andrew's unspoken question.

Of course she had. But she shouldn't have had to. And she only had to deal with the manner of seedy people in his past because of the manner of man he'd been.

"Why did you marry her?" the earl asked imploringly, as if he'd followed Andrew's guilty thoughts. "Why?"

His friend thought so very little of him. He wasn't the man he'd been. Marcia had helped him see that in himself. That what defined a person wasn't their birthright but, rather, one's own actions, and how one lived one's own life. Andrew's patience snapped. "And what in hell business is it of yours, Wakefield?" he asked quietly. "Why should you care so damned much that you—?" Andrew froze. The truth slammed into him with all the force of a fast-moving carriage, and he drew back, as at last it made sense. "You love her," he whispered.

Wakefield hesitated and then looked away, his silence all the confirmation needed.

Oh, God.

"Why didn't you *tell* me?" Andrew asked, his voice garbled.

Wakefield finally looked back and flashed a sad smile. "Would it have mattered?"

Actually, in the moments prior to everything else that had come so quickly with Marcia, it would have. Until only just recently, he'd been oblivious to the evolution in his feelings for her.

Why, by now she'd likely be wed to Wakefield, who was a better man in every way.

Andrew proved himself the selfish, grasping bastard he was and that Society took him for, because he could not regret that she was his wife instead.

"My timing with Marcia… it was always shite," Wakefield said quietly, studying the hat in his hands. "There was Thornton. After Thornton, well, I attempted to seek her out."

Andrew's mind raced back to that night at Lord and Lady Wessex's ball.

"Someone should check on her… to see if she's all right, and I—"

"But I beat you to it," Andrew whispered.

Wakefield hesitated and then nodded.

If the other man had gone in Andrew's stead, if he'd sat on Wessex's office floor beside her, and they'd shared that moment together, would everything be different?

He didn't want to think of a world where it was.

"I'm sorry," Wakefield whispered. "I'll, of course, not come around anymore. It was never my intention to insult you. Or for you to learn about how I felt."

Andrew held a hand up. "It is impossible not to love her," he said quietly. He'd not begrudge Wakefield for feelings beyond his capability.

Wakefield's Adam's apple bobbed, and he nodded. "I don't deserve your friendship."

"Friendship isn't contractual," he said simply.

The door opened, and Andrew and Wakefield spun their attention to the doorway.

Marcia looked back and forth between them. "Andrew. Benedict," she quietly greeted, finding her voice before he or the earl. "May

I speak with my husband?"

A guilty flush splotched the earl's cheeks as he dropped a belated bow. "Of c-course," he stammered, avoiding her gaze. "Forgive me." With that, Wakefield rushed past her, and closed the door so gently as to not even leave a click in the heavy quiet that hung in the air between Andrew and Marcia.

"Benedict told me you had a visitor at the park," Andrew said quietly. "I am sorry"—he grimaced—"about that." Sorry that his past converged with her future in this way. "I was young."

"You needn't explain your past to me, Andrew," Marcia said simply. "Did you see her at Cyprian's Den?"

His face went hot. "Yes," he said, scraping a hand through his hair. He should have told her. "But I do not want her." Not as he wanted his wife. Nor, did he want anything to do with Marianne Carew.

Marcia came over, joining him. "You aren't responsible for her actions, Andrew." She spoke with a gentleness that sent relief pouring through him. "She gave me this."

Frowning, Andrew made himself take the page from her, unfolding it. He skimmed his gaze over the gossip page taken from the day Marcia had been left at the altar.

"They're bribing us," she said quietly.

His stomach muscles constricted. He should have trusted his exchange with her at Cyprian's Den wouldn't be the end of the lady.

That viper he'd been fortunate to find himself free of, but she'd returned and had spread her poison here.

"They did it to Charles," Marcia reminded him. "When he did not pay timely enough, they revealed mine and my mother's pasts to the world." Her eyes flashed fury. "Or at least their version of our truths."

And they would do it again. They would think nothing of hurting Marcia again.

And whereas he didn't give a jot what they said of him, he knew firsthand how very much it mattered to her. With a curse, Andrew stalked over to the desk, and yanked out the center drawer.

"What... are you doing?" Marcia asked.

"I'm—"

"Surely you don't not intend to pay them?" she asked, her tone equally part horrified and shocked.

Andrew stilled. "Marcia."

"They won't be content, Andrew. They will keep coming back for more and more. Charles is just more proof that they won't. He paid them… to keep a secret in his own family safe, and then they merely switched to bribing him to keep the secrets surrounding my birth silent." She squared her jaw. "The *only* way to defeat people like them is to not be bullied by them."

He searched his gaze over her features, her cheeks ripe with her fury, her eyes flashing. My God, she was brilliant in her strength and convictions.

And yet… he'd also seen firsthand, through the years, the ruthlessness Atbrooke and his sister were capable of. And where he didn't care what they could or might do to him, he did care about this woman before him. "Marcia, I'd not see you hurt," he began.

She swatted his arm. "They can't hurt me. But you granting them power they don't deserve over us, would." Marcia held his gaze. "Promise me you won't, Andrew. Promise me you won't do anything where they are concerned."

"I want to…" he finally acknowledged. "Because I would do anything to keep you from hurting."

Something shifted in her eyes; her face softened, and her lips parted. "Oh."

Some of the tension slipped from him as he dropped the letter, forgotten, and came around the desk to stand before her. "Surely you know how much I care about you," he murmured, stroking the pad of his thumb along her lower lip.

Her lashes fluttered and then she opened her eyes. "Charles cared about me."

Andrew went stock-still, recalling all over that there'd been another whom she'd loved, and who'd loved her in return, and who, had it not been for Atbrooke and his sister, would even now be married to Marcia. Jealousy singed the blood in his veins. "What is your point?" he asked, his tone sharper than he intended.

"He thought to protect me, too, Andrew," she explained. "I don't want that. I want someone who can be honest with me. Do not lie to me. Not as he did."

Someone who can be honest with her. Someone who didn't keep secrets from her…

Like the fact that you were offered a fortune if you married her, a voice taunted. Andrew tensed. For what was a worse secret than that?

But you were going to marry her anyway… as such, it wasn't about the fortune. Not really.

"Andrew?" she prodded, startling him out of the guilty thoughts fomenting in his head.

Andrew caught her hands, and raised them one at a time to his lips. "You have my word, love."

This was different. It was entirely not the same.

That was what he told himself, anyway.

"And you won't give them a pence?" she pressed, having misunderstood the reason for his hesitation.

"Not a single one," he vowed. Nay, with that money he had returned through his marriage to Marcia, he was more determined than ever to make something of himself, so he could care for her and the children they'd one day have together, as they deserved.

And he prayed that he'd not come to regret that decision, or the promise he'd made to her this day.

CHAPTER 21

A WEEK LATER, SEATED IN THE parlor of her new home with her friends opposite her, Marcia should be only content.

The nights she'd spent married to Andrew had been the most magical ones of her existence. Each time, Andrew brought her pleasure the likes of which she'd never known existed.

The mornings, however, she awakened to find herself alone, and he shut away in his office, working on his business matters, like a man absolutely driven.

No, there was no absence of intimacy between them… at night.

His work, however, had now… extended to this evening, and she was being a petulant child, but she wanted at least this time to be theirs.

What did you expect? the voice of reason whispered at the back of her mind.

She had far more than most any other woman in Polite Society. She had a husband who was a friend. And she had freedom to live her life out from under the thumb of overprotective parents. And she had her friends.

"You can always just go join them," Anwen ventured.

"He has business he is working on," Marcia said. Business he was now always working on.

"I daresay he's not the wastrel society says he is," Faith said, and then grunted as Anwen sent an elbow into her side.

Marcia frowned.

"What? I didn't say he was a wastrel. Just that society says he is," Faith said defensively. "I'm merely pointing out that if he were, he'd not be busy as he is seeing to his affairs."

"Well, as I see it, we shouldn't pout," Anwen declared. "We have freedom, and there is something to be said for that."

Her friends nodded in agreement, and even as Marcia belatedly bobbed her head, she knew the truth. She yearned for more than freedom. She wanted everything her mother and father had said she'd been deserving of, but more, she wanted it all with Andrew.

She knew that now.

It was a dangerous discovery to make so very late, particularly after she'd gone and married London's most wicked rake.

It had been one thing not recognizing the shift that had occurred in her feelings for him over the years, denying the change that had befallen their relationship when she'd not been married to him and living with him. Then, when they'd been living their own lives, she'd not had to think about or be directly confronted with the fact that he was Andrew Barrett, Viscount Waters, lover of scandal and sin.

"Marcia?"

The hesitant call of her name brought her head flying up.

Her friends stared expectantly back.

Her mind went blank. They expected something of her, a response. "I…" *Was lost in pitying self-musings, pining for a husband whom I've fallen in love with, but will not fully have.* Not in the way she really wanted him. These were her best friends, and yet, she still found herself unable to share those pitiable thoughts with them.

"Of course she does not wish to go out," Anwen said exasperatedly when Marcia failed to respond.

"And why shouldn't she?" Faith shot back. "Why should she remain bereft and lonely while her husband…" The young lady gave a wave of her hand. "Does whatever it is he's doing?"

Why indeed?

"I'm not bereft," she muttered.

She might as well have not bothered speaking that lie as the other two young ladies launched into a debate, their voices rising as they each strove for her argument to be heard over the other's.

Marcia frowned.

Faith was not wrong. In fact, she was very much right. She was a married woman. Granted, she desperately wished she'd married a man who'd want to spend his days with her—but she hadn't. She had married a man now consumed by work. She'd entered into a logical arrangement, one that would give her a name and spare her siblings from further scandal.

"I want to go," she said, and when she failed to make herself heard over the noisy debate, Marcia cupped her hands around her mouth and repeated more loudly, "I want to go."

That immediately cut across the din of her friends' quarrel.

Both looked over at her, surprise stamped on their features.

Marcia raised her chin. "As Faith pointed out, I have new freedoms."

Faith gave Anwen a triumphant look, and at that silent gloating, the other young woman pulled a face in return.

"And now that I have freedoms," Marcia went on, "that means we have greater freedom, and as such, we would be wise to enjoy it."

A devilish glimmer twinkled in Faith's eyes. "I second that." She put a hand forward.

"I third it," Anwen murmured, resting a palm atop the other young woman's.

Marcia added hers.

A short while later, with her husband's carriage waiting out front, Marcia accepted her cloak from one of the footmen, and draping the garment over her shoulders, she saw to the clasp.

The butler hovered, wringing his hands slightly. "The carriage is ready, my lady."

With a word of thanks, Marcia headed for the door, her friends following close behind.

As Thomaston drew those panels open, they sailed out, and it was the first time since she'd made her Come Out that she ultimately decided what event she would attend.

That was, which *respectable* event she would attend, and there was a heady sense of excitement that came in this not-so-small power she'd attained.

As she reached the front of the carriage, a footman held a hand out, handing her up inside. Anwen and Faith joined her on the opposite bench.

He closed the door with a firm click, and a moment later, the box dipped as he joined the driver, and there came the whistle of the reins, and they were off.

It was a moment of triumph. It was, after all, her first instant of realized freedom.

Or it should be.

Seated on the bench of her husband's carriage, heading to the theater with Faith and Anwen, she should feel only the usual happiness that she did when she was with her friends, only she found that blasted melancholy returned.

"I do say it seems a tad unfair that a lady should go from needing a parental escort one day and being freed of all those constraints the next," Anwen prattled, all but bouncing on the upholstered bench with the same enthusiasm she'd shown since Marcia had rolled up to collect them.

"But it's not the same," Faith said in exasperation. "Marcia is married now. As such, everything is different."

Everything is different.

It was.

Everything had changed.

And yet, at the same time, nothing had changed.

She was still going to polite events, enjoying the company of her friends. But there was not the happy marriage she'd always dreamed of for herself. And worse, there was now this shift in her relationship with Andrew. Now, after they made love, he retreated. There were more barriers than there'd ever been between them. Nay, there'd never been any barriers before. Since that bribe had been put to her and Andrew by Lord Atbrooke and his sister, Andrew had thrown himself into work.

"Marcia?"

Dropping the curtain, Marcia looked across the coach at the opposite bench.

Both friends stared concernedly back, their heads comically tipped in opposite directions.

"I..." She shook her head. "I'm sorry. I was—"

"I was saying I hardly think marriage should make such a

difference in how a woman is treated," Anwen said.

"In some cases, it doesn't change how a woman is treated," Marcia murmured, unable to keep the bitterness from her response. In some cases, one's husband treated one as though she were still the underfoot young girl who'd always made a bother of herself. She thought of the times she'd visited him while he worked, only to find him distracted, absorbed in his business, and not letting her in. She curled her hands on her lap. She'd just not anticipated that he would make love to her and that, after they'd shared the most intimate parts of themselves, nothing would change.

She felt Faith's eyes upon her. "You are unhappy." Hers wasn't a question.

An always, garrulous Anwen instantly went quiet.

"No," Marcia insisted, because surely the only thing worse than being in a loveless marriage—or rather, in a marriage where the love was one-sided—was earning pity from her friends over that state. "I... It is just new and different." Her protestations sounded weak even to her own ears. She forced a smile. "And how should I not be happy? I am with my two best friends."

Both women instantly smiled.

There came a sharp cry from the driver's box, and the carriage lurched to the right.

Crying out, Marcia braced her feet upon the floor to keep from flying forward. Her shriek blended with those of her friends as the conveyance swayed back and forth, barreling forward at a breakneck speed, and then she went lurching back as the driver yanked on the reins.

Faith and Anwen remained unable to hold their places on their bench and toppled forward, landing hard against Marcia.

She grunted as one of the young lady's heads collided with hers.

And then the carriage came to a blessed and complete stop.

But for the occasional groan from her friends, the stillness that followed proved eerie, with an impending sense of danger that hovered in the air just before a lightning strike.

The driver yanked the door open.

"We're all right," she said to Davies. "We..." Marcia's words trailed off as she peered through the tangle of her friends' limbs, and her heart fell. "You are not Davies," she said needlessly.

The big, burly lion of a man flashed a wide grin, displaying a row of uneven teeth. "No, I'm not Davies." He looked from Marcia to Faith and Anwen. "Which one of you is Waters's wife?" he demanded.

Oh, God.

Her friends looked to Marcia, and then scrambled onto the bench, squeezing themselves on either side of her.

Marcia knew precisely who'd sent them. Atbrooke and the baroness had failed in a bribe, and now intended to exact a ransom. "You're a friend of Lord Atbrooke, are you not?"

"A friend of Atbrooke?" The balding stranger tossed his head back and howled with his amusement. "Aye, sure. We're real close."

Anwen lifted a hand up and spoke behind her gloved palm. "I don't think they are really friends."

The man's smile fell, and he scowled. Brandishing a pistol, he pointed it at them, alternating his aim between them. "And oi'm looking to get closer to Waters's wife. Well, now?" he asked impatiently. "I asked you a question. Which one of you is Waters's new wife?"

"That does seem like a bit of a redundancy," Faith blurted, and the burly fellow's attention swung to the two other ladies. "As he's married, and he would not be capable of having a second wife unless his first wife had perished." As soon as those words left her, Faith went pale. "Which she hasn't and doesn't intend to for—"

"Will you shut your mouth?" the man barked. He shot a hand out, catching Faith in the ear that she still was still capable of hearing from. He raised a fist for a second time, but Marcia pushed her friend out of the way, putting herself between Faith and that fist, absorbing this second blow to the cheek.

Pain radiated along her jawline, and dazed, she blinked back the stars dotting her vision.

Marcia made a show of slumping forward, dimly registering her friends' cries as she stretched her fingers towards the warming bricks.

"Now," the man went on, "you're making me angry, and I don't want to get angry. So I'll ask it one more time. Which one of you is—?"

Marcia gripped the brick, and brought it back in a wide arc.

The man abruptly stopped. His eyes went wide, and then rolled to the back of his head, as he slumped to the ground.

"I... did you hit him?" Anwen asked.

She hadn't. She'd intended to.

Unblinking, Marcia stared at the enormous, ginger-headed fellow standing over their assailant. He eyed the brick still clutched in her fingers. "Which one of you is Waters's wife?" he asked in rough Cockney, his tone casual, as if a man did not remain unconscious at his feet, bleeding from his nose.

"That seems to be the question of the night," Faith muttered.

"Well?" he prodded, looking between each of them.

Her heart pounded hard, and Marcia dampened her mouth.

She would not, not now and not ever, allow her friends to be harmed because of her. Marcia shot a hand up.

As soon as she lifted her palm, Faith and Anwen both raised theirs.

"I am," Marcia said quietly, slanting a look at each of her friends, trying to will them to lower their arms.

"No, I am," Anwen said.

"That is untrue, as I am the viscount's wife," Faith added on a rush. She scowled. "And I am going to be very displeased with dear Andrew for the manner of rude friends he's keeping company with, Mr....?"

The stranger puzzled his brow and then grinned again. "Mr. Red."

"That suits him," Anwen whispered loud enough for her voice to ring around the carriage. "He's very red, you know."

"I see that," Marcia said from the corner of her mouth.

Someone behind Mr. Red said something, and the big brute looked back. "I know," he said impatiently and then whipped his attention forward. "You coming with us or staying?"

"Who are you?" she asked quietly.

Just then, the unconscious assailant groaned, stirred, and opened his eyes.

Mr. Red leaned down and punched the fellow once more,

knocking him out a second time. He looked up. "Or you can wait around for this one—"

"We'll go with you," she hurried, and a moment later, Mr. Red joined them in her husband's carriage. There came a sharp whistle, and the black barouche lurched forward.

Her stomach churned, and Marcia drew the curtain back, peering out at the man lying upon the cobblestones. His form grew smaller and smaller. She searched for Davies. "My driver—"

"He's up top with Tavish," the hulking stranger informed her, as if she knew who Tavish was.

"I think Lord Atbrooke needs to find better friends," Anwen said as the carriage rocked and swayed from the precarious speed their new driver had set.

"That wasn't a friend," Mr. Red explained.

"Undoubtedly not." Restless, Marcia let the curtain fall and drummed her fingertips atop her knee. "Who was he?"

Mr. Red shrugged.

Mr. Red, who'd come to her and Faith and Anwen's rescue. Mr. Red, whom she knew not at all, but who apparently knew her husband.

Who could Andrew possibly have as an enemy? There wasn't a thing mean about him. He was always jovial and cheerful and…

And she wanted him here. Desperately.

Her teeth scraped at her lower lip.

Andrew, her husband, was content to keep company with his fellow rakes-in-arms.

Which was hardly a promising start to their marriage.

A marriage that, given the situation in which she now found herself, promised to be as short-lived as her life.

Her breath grew raspy in her ears.

Stop it. No one came to any harm this evening.

She had her friends' lives to consider, her friends who were in harm's way because of Marcia.

It was Anwen who broke the tenuous quiet.

"You were looking for adventure," she pointed out with her ever-present optimism. "Now we've all found it."

Groaning, Faith rolled her eyes.

"What?" the other woman asked defensively. "We have. Why, I cannot expect attending the opera would prove even half as interesting as all this." She paused. "Even if we were alone there."

Faith suddenly widened her eyes, and her cheeks went pale.

"What is it?" Marcia asked uneasily.

The other woman leaned close. "What if he's… with the other man?" she asked in her invariably loud whisper.

As one, she, Faith, and Anwen looked to Mr. Red.

Mr. Red who made no attempt to reassure them.

Faith swallowed hard.

"They are never going to let us venture out alone again, are they?" Faith bemoaned, cradling her ear, and guilt knifed at Marcia.

It was highly doubtful the Marquess and Marchioness of Guilford would ever again allow their cherished daughter near Marcia after this. Nor could she blame them. "You should have let me go," she lamented, and moved Faith's fingers out of the way to inspect her ear. A bruise had begun to form on her cheek.

"And leave you alone?" Faith scoffed. "Absolutely not. Why, there was a greater chance of us commandeering someone else's carriage at gunpoint than in us ever leaving you. Isn't that right, Anwen?"

The other woman gave an emphatic nod. "Absolutely." She smiled. "We are friends after all, and friends do not leave one another."

Friends do not leave one another.

Except, that was what she and Andrew were, and he'd done just that.

Because you went and mucked up your friendship, a voice taunted. *You became his wife when you knew the last thing Andrew ever wanted was a wife.*

She found in that moment, with her carriage rolling on to wherever she was bound for, that she'd lied to herself.

She was never going to be content living a life apart from her husband.

She did want the same devoted and loving union known by her parents, one where they would sooner cut a limb off than be separated from each other.

A bond not unlike the one known by Faith's parents.

Facing the possibility of having her life ended and never seeing him again, she could be honest in acknowledging that she'd married him because she'd wanted to. Because she loved him. More than just the platonic way in which she loved the two women who'd risked their necks for her.

Regardless, she'd never have any of what she wanted if the remainder of this night played out badly.

A surprisingly short while later, the carriage came to a more gradual halt than the previous starts and stops at the hands of their nighttime visitors.

There came the murmur of voices as Mr. Red spoke to the stranger who accompanied him, a man who was still faceless to them.

The door was yanked open, and Marcia and her friends instantly drew back.

"Hoods up," Mr. Red ordered.

As one, Marcia and her friends brought their hoods firmly up into place.

"That's better. Now, get a move on," he said gruffly. Mr. Red caught her at the waist, and he lifted her down with a surprising gentleness. As he helped her friends disembark, Marcia did a study of where they'd arrived... a very familiar place.

"Let's go," Mr. Red urged a second time. "Before we're seen." And she and her friends, side by side and shoulder to shoulder, started towards the club.

"What is this place?" Faith asked in her always louder-than-average whisper.

"Forbidden Pleasures," Marcia murmured into her friend's ear.

The other woman looked upon it with a new interest. "This is that club? I have heard of it and did wonder." A smile formed on Faith's narrow lips. "So there is something good to come out of this night, isn't there?"

"That is one way of—"

"Will you two stop your jabbering until we're inside?" Mr. Red ordered Mr. Tavish, who'd been driving the carriage, assisted a now conscious Davies along. They made their way down a long alleyway that separated the establishment from the building beside it.

The pit of dread in her belly grew to the size of a boulder as he ushered them around back and through a different entrance to the club.

What if she'd traded one assailant... for another? What if Mr. Red was in fact in cahoots with the man who'd struck she and Faith and...

Marcia fought to restrain the rapid spiraling panic.

Entering through the front door would have made this meeting, whatever this meeting was, less ominous. Because then they'd have been surrounded by lords and ladies in the middle of their wicked game play. As it was, no one knew that she, Faith, and Anwen had been kidnapped. Nay, their families, her husband, all expected they were on their way to the theater, rather than here, about to face certain doom.

Trying to order her rapidly clamoring thoughts, Marcia brought her shoulders back and concentrated on drawing smooth, even breaths, attempting to calm herself.

They reached the kitchens, and a handful of men, assembled around a long wooden table, cups of coffee in their large hands, stopped their conversation and looked over the trio of friends.

"DuMond is not going to be happy," one of the men drawled.

The pair of men flanking him broke out into laughter.

Mr. Red went even redder in the cheeks. "Wot? Came upon them being 'napped. Couldn't just leave Waters's viscountess, Flynn."

"It is not Mr. Red's fault," Anwen insisted. "We insisted on coming."

Faith shot an elbow into her friend's side and glared at her. "Because we are each Lady Waters." She gritted out that reminder in Anwen's direction.

The other woman widened her eyes as her mistake was pointed out.

Anwen cleared her throat. "Er, yes, because we are all the viscountess. Isn't that right, Marcia?"

"Yes," Marcia said, with Faith answering a fraction of a second later.

The five men remained silent and then burst out laughing.

"Get them abovestairs," Flynn said between his great guffaws of amusement.

Marcia and her friends fell into step once more as they followed their dark-haired captor through narrow, winding hall after narrow, winding hall and up a flight of stairs and down another, until she was certain they were being walked in a circle.

At last, they arrived at a room.

Mr. Red reached past them and pressed the door handle.

Marcia lingered at the entryway, doing a quick sweep of the masculine rooms that were empty.

"Wait in there," he said, and Marcia jumped, filing in with her friends joining her. "Sit!" he spoke in those brusque, rough tones, and they immediately fell into the folds of a surprisingly luxuriant, leather button sofa. "Wait here, and don't touch anything," he muttered and then shut the door behind him.

The moment he'd gone, restless, Marcia stood and wandered around the rooms they'd been escorted to.

Faith sprang to her feet and made a beeline for the desk.

"He said to sit," Anwen pointed out in a whisper.

"Yes," Faith said. "As in, Mr. Red... who we think is harmless. But it would do well to be sure we know who we are dealing with." Faith set to work tugging at drawers. Each one was locked. "Isn't that right, Marcia?"

Anwen looked to her, and Marcia nodded. Because, really, what did they know this night other than the fact they'd nearly been abducted, and had instead gone off with... two men and brought to one of the most wicked clubs in London.

Marcia did a sweep for sign of a weapon with which to protect themselves.

Unfastening a haircomb, Faith sent the curls, the jewel heart had been holding in place, tumbling around her shoulders. "I have it."

"You know how to pick locks?" A wave of giddy relief filled Marcia.

"Of course," Faith said indignantly, as if she took the greatest offense at having her skills as a thief questioned. "Stand on alert,

Anwen."

The other woman rushed into position, pressing her ear against the door.

As Faith set to work attempting to break into the desk, Marcia did a quick search of the well-appointed room.

Nothing.

Not even a metal poker at the empty hearth.

Fighting her frustration, Marcia went to the red velvet curtains that hung over the window and drew them back to assess the distance to the street below.

Only, she didn't see the street.

The window overlooked the gaming floor below.

Hope rising in her breast, Marcia pounded on the glass, trying to will the patrons to look up.

Alas, the din of the revelry unfolding upon that floor was so loud it reached the proprietor's offices, drowning out her attempts at gaining notice.

Nay, the men and handful of ladies present remained fixed on the cards in their hands or the spinning wheels and felt tables.

A wave of hopelessness swept through her, and Marcia stared out at the gaming hell she'd visited not so very long ago when Andrew had escorted her here.

How she wished he were here now. How she wished he'd accompanied her and her friends to the theater, and she hated the tears that threatened, blinking to keep them from falling.

Then she stopped, her gaze on a table of gentlemen playing faro, but it wasn't the lords whom she fixed on but, rather, the dealer.

The sleight of hand had been so quick that she might have imagined it.

Her own woes forgotten, Marcia tunneled all her attention on the young, scantily clad woman dealing, and Marcia didn't so much as blink.

There it was again.

She rocked back on her heels.

Why, the proprietor was a cheat.

"Ah-hah!" Faith said, her voice triumphant as she got herself inside the drawer.

Quitting her spot at the door, Anwen rushed to the desk and leaned over. "Have you made any progress?"

"I have," Faith said, tugging a ledger out. "Do go back to your job as lookout," she ordered, reading through the book she'd helped herself to. "My goodness," Faith muttered. "There really are some terrible men in London. The number of gentlemen in debt. Lord Hood. Lord Wingate. Lord Landon. Lord Marlow. Lord…" She paused, and hearing something in her tone, Marcia looked over.

"What?" she asked quietly.

Her friend shook her head and ducked back under the desk.

Marcia headed across the room. "Faith?"

There was a beat of hesitation. "Waters," her friend said, and then remaining tucked under the desk, she dropped the ledger atop the desk.

Marcia immediately picked the book up, scanned the pages, and landed on Andrew's name. She promptly choked. Fifteen thousand pounds… Paid. In full.

She stilled.

Not just paid in full… paid in full the day after… their wedding.

Her heart thumped funnily inside her chest.

"Did you find everything you were looking for?" That query spoken from the entry of the room, brought Marcia's and Anwen's attention whipping over to the doorway.

The book slipped from her hands, tumbling back to the desk.

Hell and bloody hell.

"We have company," Anwen whispered needlessly.

Faith, however, without the benefit of full hearing, having returned to her examination of the proprietor's books, remained oblivious to their *host's* arrival.

For there could be no doubting that this tall, well-dressed, smooth-spoken stranger was anything other than the man who commanded Forbidden Pleasures.

"My God, this man must be as rich as Croesus," Faith was muttering to herself.

Marcia cleared her throat. "Ahem."

From under the desk, Faith muttered an occasional word or phrase that rang quite clearly around the room. "Is there even any man not in debt to him?"

Marcia cleared her throat loudly. "I *said* 'ahem.'"

Faith whipped her head up, and there came a loud crack, followed by a groan.

There was a beat of silence and then, "Is he here?"

"He is." The imposing stranger spoke in tones layered with ice and steeped in steel.

Faith hesitated and then popped her head up enough that her eyes appeared over the top of the desk. "Oh hell," she muttered.

Oh, hell indeed.

He came forward with steps to rival a panther's. And they weren't sleek and sexy, like Andrew's but, rather, the primal ones of a man who intended to devour his prey in a dangerous way.

Marcia swallowed hard, and reaching a hand down, she caught the sleeve of Faith's cloak and pulled her to her feet.

He stopped before them.

He moved eyes a shade of blue so dark they were nearly obsidian, back and forth over them. That harsh, emotionless gaze ultimately landed on Marcia. "Hello, Lady Waters."

A chill traipsed along her spine, and she inclined her head, answering that greeting with silence.

"And whyever do you expect I'm not the viscountess?" Faith demanded loudly of the club proprietor, dropping her hands upon her hips. "I mean, her?" She pointed at Anwen. "I might say you can suspect she is not who she claims to be."

Anwen bristled with indignation. "Hey, I take much offense to that."

"What in hell have you brought me?" Mr. DuMond muttered, yanking his gloves off and stuffing them inside his jacket.

"They were being taken," Mr. Red explained.

"I cannot even begin to fathom why," Mr. DuMond said, with a wry shake of his head.

"I beg your pardon," Faith shot back, and the gentleman swung his attention back over to Marcia's friend.

"Faith," she said warningly. Taking a step forward, Marcia placed herself between Faith and the head proprietor, diverting his attention back to her, settling that icy stare on Marcia. "Are you…

involved with those men?"

Mr. DuMond opened his mouth to speak, but Mr. Red inserted his own defense of the gaming hell owner. "Course 'e isn't. The whole reason I was there to save your necks was because Mr. DuMond 'ad me watching after—"

"Enough, Red," the proprietor said crisply, and the loyal servant instantly fell silent.

Marcia attempted to make sense of what he was thinking or feeling or his intentions, but came up empty. His cheeks, nicked and scarred, lent an interesting air to what would have otherwise been a beautiful face. Why, in fact, he might have been any other handsome London gentleman but for the scars that reminded that he was no gentleman, but a man to be feared.

"Escort the viscountess's friends to my sitting room. I wish to speak to the viscountess in private." Mr. DuMond issued that command, and Mr. Red sprang into motion.

"Come on, then, you troublesome minxes. Told you not to touch anything," he mumbled, even as Faith and Anwen raised their voices in protest.

Mr. DuMond looked to Marcia. "Deal with your friends."

"Faith. Anwen," she called over, and her friends went silent. She held their eyes, giving them a look. "It is going to be all right."

"I don't trust him," Faith returned, folding her arms.

"Which one of us?" Mr. DuMond put that question to Faith.

She glared mutinously at him. "Neither of you."

"So you aren't a complete lackwit. As such, I trust you have sense enough to do as you're told, Lady Brookfield."

Faith paled.

"Oh, dear," Anwen whispered.

Mr. DuMond curled his lips in a harsh smile.

"Come along, then," Mr. Red urged.

The moment they'd gone, Mr. Red shut the door, leaving Marcia alone with the notorious gaming hell owner, Mr. DuMond.

In a bid to hide the tremble in her hands, Marcia gave her fingers a task, smoothing the front of her skirts. All the while, she studied the man across from her. He, however, paid her no notice, instead heading over to the sideboard stacked with drinks.

He was tall and broad of shoulder, and his arms strained the constraints of his well-cut jacket.

In fact—she did another sweep of the room—from his appearance on down to the fine Chippendale furnishings, he might as well have been any gentleman.

"Did you know the man who attempted to abduct us?" she asked the moment they were alone, helping herself to the seat across from him.

Mr. DuMond reclined in his seat and dropped one elbow on the arm of his chair. "Do you take me as a man who abducts women?"

It didn't escape her notice that he'd sidestepped her question about whether he knew her would-be abductor.

Unnerved, Marcia stood and meandered back over to the window, examined the crowds below, and waited for her husband's arrival.

CHAPTER 22

THE PAST DAYS HE'D SPENT as a married man proved remarkably different than how Andrew had previously spent his time. Where he'd previously buried himself in wagering and wicked pursuits, Andrew, now in possession of the money he'd once squandered, had flung himself headfirst into different wagers—those of the business type.

And during the night, instead of visiting various mistresses or whores, all his time was spent in the arms of one woman—his wife.

This night, however, after having concluded his business affairs, he'd found his wife… gone.

There'd been a time he'd expected he wasn't a man capable of wanting just one woman. Only to discover how wrong he'd been.

He'd also expected, as a bachelor who'd just been leg-shackled, that he should have breathed a proverbial sigh of relief at finding Marcia off with her friends, and himself in the company of *his* friends.

And yet, as Andrew played a round of whist with Rothesby and Landon, he found himself oddly restless.

"Your wager, Waters," Rothesby reminded, and Andrew, only half attending the hand, tossed down a handful of coins.

Both men folded, with Landon cursing under his breath and Rothesby pushing the impressive pot towards Andrew.

That in itself, those sizable winnings, would have been the sole focus of his notice at any other time.

But not for the first time that night, Andrew found his gaze drifting over to the ormolu clock.

"That has to be the fifth time you've checked the time since we sat for cards, Waters," Rothesby drawled as he scooped up the cards and proceeded to shuffle the deck. "Are we boring you?"

"*I'm* boring me," Landon lamented, saving Andrew from answering. "I do not understand why we're playing at Waters'." He tossed a couple of sovereigns upon the gaming table and placed his wager. "Not when there aren't even eager women about to bed."

"Because he knows his brothers-in-law will cut his life short if he's out carousing mere weeks after he's married," Rothesby said. Adding his bet to the pile, he took a drink. "Isn't that right, Waters?"

Scowling, Andrew eyed his cards. "It isn't their business. We have an understanding." He placed his wager and then slouched in his seat.

Registering his friends' silence, he looked up.

Landon dropped an elbow on the edge of the gaming table and leaned forward, attending Andrew with all the curiosity of London's nosiest busybody. "An understanding?"

Andrew looked to Rothesby. Alas, with the way he stared expectantly back, there'd be no help coming from that direction.

Andrew loosened his cravat. "Marcia is free to live her life as she wishes."

"Which is why you are here, and she is wherever she is?"

She was with her friends, and he was here with these miserable bounders. Picking up his snifter, Andrew gave the contents a smooth swirl. "Precisely. Prior to our wedding, we each agreed that we would carry on our own lives, and there'd be no expectations from either party."

"And you think that is something that will actually work?" Landon asked incredulously.

Andrew frowned. "I know it will."

Rothesby and Landon looked at each other and then burst out laughing.

He bristled. "I'll have you know that she is the one who had her friends to visit tonight, and I—" He closed his mouth, realizing belatedly he'd said too much.

"And you wished to join her, but are instead stuck with us miserable blighters?" Landon drawled.

"That will *never* work," Rothesby informed Andrew, and Landon nodded.

"Rothesby is right. You should have consulted us before you'd agreed to such an asinine arrangement."

"And whyever will it not?" Andrew shot back, bristling with annoyance. "Marcia and I have known one another for a good portion of our lives. There's no romantic feelings involved. She is free to live her life, and I'm free to live mine, and—"

"And you cannot be so stupid as to believe all that," Landon cut him off.

Andrew scowled into his glass. "You don't know anything."

"I know a number of things," Rothesby said, leaning in. "One"—he shot a finger up—"your wife is young and innocent. Two, young and innocent ladies are romantic. Three, said romantic ladies always believe in love."

Moisture slicked Andrew's palms, and he dusted them along the arms of his chair. His friends were both suggesting that when he'd entered into his arrangement with Marcia, he'd deluded himself. Just as he'd fought the truth that had been there plain before him when Wakefield had paid a visit, calling Andrew out as he'd deserved. He'd pushed all those thoughts aside. For if what they suggested was in fact true, then it meant he'd ultimately hurt her. Which was, of course, inevitable. But never had he considered the possibility that he'd break her heart. Not in that way. "She didn't want me underfoot this evening," he found himself needing to add. It had been the first night he'd not spent solely with her. And he missed her.

"Did she say as much?" Rothesby asked.

He paused and searched his memory. "No, but neither did she seek me out." She'd informed him that her friends were coming to visit and had lingered as if she'd intended to say more before ultimately leaving.

"Let me get this straight," Landon said. "You expected your wife would invite you, London's most notorious rogue and scoundrel who married her only because he was forced into the match by her father and brothers-in-law, to give up your usual pleasures to join her?" The other man groaned. "You really are not so very good at reading women, are you, Waters?"

Andrew frowned, and it wasn't the latter affront he took umbrage with. "I wasn't forced into marrying her."

He'd been... incentivized, but that was entirely different.

The uncomfortable lecture was thankfully cut short by the frantic fall of footsteps in the corridor, followed by raised voices.

What in hell?

The door burst open, and his butler stumbled into the room.

"Your servants are rude, Waters," Landon drawled. "All good servants know never to interrupt a game in play."

Ignoring the marquess, Andrew looked to Thomaston.

The servant struggled to get a proper breath. "This arrived, my lord," he said, and it was an indication of the seriousness of the moment that an always in-control Thomaston hadn't bothered with a respectful bow. "I was instructed to give it to you posthaste."

Frowning, Andrew came to his feet and took the note from the other man's hand.

Andrew unfolded it and skimmed the contents, written in a familiar hand.

Waters, you're as rot at watching after your wife as you are at paying your debts. I suggest you come collect your wife.

All the air left him on a swift exhale.

Andrew's body went whipcord straight; every muscle clenched. His fingers curled tight around the edges of the page in his fingers, wrinkling it beyond measure. "Oh, God," he whispered.

"What is it, Waters?" Rothesby asked behind him.

PS: Many felicitations upon your marriage to the lovely viscountess.

His stomach lurched.

Andrew remained motionless for several moments, afraid he'd shatter if he moved.

DuMond had her.

DuMond, the proprietor of one of London's most dangerous clubs, and Marcia was there... alone.

He closed his eyes. *I'm going to be ill.*

"My lord?" Thomaston's hesitant query brought Andrew rushing back, and a sense of calm and purpose stole through him as he gave life to that energy and not the paralyzing fear that came from thinking about Marcia alone with DuMond.

"My horse," he barked, already striding for the door.

"What can we do?" Rothesby called after him.

"She's at Forbidden Pleasures. DuMond has her."

Both men cursed and quickly followed.

"I've already taken the liberty of having it readied, my lord," Thomaston said, trailing after him.

His breath coming hard and fast, Andrew raced through the foyer. The doors hung open, and a pair of footmen stood in wait, anticipating his arrival.

He rushed through and took the steps sideways, two at a time, Andrew caught the reins of his mount from another servant. After scrambling into his seat, Andrew squeezed his mount. "Hyah," he called and kicked his horse into motion ahead of his friends, who still awaited their horses.

As he rode through the streets of London, he kept his gaze forward and attempted to calm his frenzied thoughts. Panicking wouldn't help her. She needed him to be calm. She needed him to have his wits about him.

And yet, a short while later, he was escorted through Forbidden Pleasures, and the sight that greeted him when he entered DuMond's offices was anything but the ominous one he'd imagined the moment that note had landed in his hand.

In fact—Andrew cocked his head—perhaps he'd imagined the threatening tone of the letter he'd received. For Marcia sat at a table across from DuMond and two of the biggest guards employed by the man, doling out cards.

"What hangs at a man's thigh and wants to poke the hole that it's often poked before?" She posed that outrageous question to her card partners.

"Wot?" Creed asked in his booming, always angry-sounding voice.

Marcia paused and glanced up from her hand, blinking innocently. "Why, a key, of course."

The table erupted with laughter.

He'd stepped onto a damned Covent Garden stage. That was all there was to it. There was no explaining any of this.

"Ahem," he said, clearing his throat, and when he still went unnoticed amongst the revelry, he made another attempt. "Ahhhem."

Marcia glanced over, and her eyes brightened. "Andrew!" she greeted, jumping up.

In an instant, the levity died, and as the three men looked squarely at Andrew, the façade of a friendly game between friends might as well have been an imagining he'd conjured in his head.

"Waters," DuMond said silkily, and with slow, unhurried movements, he came to his feet.

Flynn and Red turned dark looks on Andrew. "Took you long enough."

"Hey now." Marcia made a sound of disapproval. "There's no need for that," she chided and took a step towards the head guard.

Andrew's body jolted, and a shaft of fear ran through him. "Marcia, come over here now," he said quietly.

"It is fine, Andrew," she spoke as if she were soothing a nervous child.

"I said come over here, Marcia," he repeated, fighting for calm and control.

DuMond leaned a hip upon the table and arched an eyebrow. "Are you issuing orders in my offices, Waters?"

"I'm issuing an order," he said tersely. "To my wife. Marcia," he urged again.

She folded her arms. "I'll have you know I do not appreciate being ordered about any more than Mr. DuMond enjoys it."

"Bloody hell, Marcia," he gritted out. "This is not the time for this."

"I believe this is the perfect time for it."

Instead of waiting for his headstrong bride to do as he'd demanded, Andrew took a hurried step towards her, and then he stopped, the air exploding from his lungs, and slipping in a noisy hiss through his teeth. "Marcia," he whispered. The glow of the candles bathed her face in a soft light, illuminating the bruise on her left cheek.

Marcia's fingers came up to touch that spot, and she winced.

A black curtain of rage fell across his vision. "I'll kill him," he growled, and with a roar, he charged for DuMond.

DuMond's men instantly had weapons drawn and trained on him.

"He is not speaking of you!" Marcia exclaimed, gripping his arm and tugging at it. "He is speaking about the ones who did this," she repeated, and feeling dazed, he blinked several times. She was here. She was safe. "Isn't that right, Andrew?"

His relief proved fleeting. Every muscle in his body tensed as he registered the weapons trained on him… and Marcia.

His pulse hammered, and fear pumped through him. Memories of the past merged with the present, of another gun held by Marianne Carew and pointed at his sister and then the blast of a gunshot. Only this time, it was Marcia in harm's way.

And it was because of him, once more.

He struggled to get control of his rapidly careening thoughts. Terror had no place in this moment.

DuMond shot a palm up, and his soldiers took that silent cue, holstering the weapons.

"Why don't you have a seat, Lord Waters?" The other man spoke in those silky, menacing tones. "Lady Waters."

This time, Marcia looked to him, and there was so much trust—far more trust than he was or would ever be deserving of—in her eyes, it hit him like a kick to the gut. He drew out one of the upholstered gilded chairs for her.

DuMond snorted. "How lovely."

"I told you he is polite," Marcia said as she settled herself into the chair as comfortably as if they had joined members of Polite Society for tea and biscuits. "Did I not?"

DuMond's guards erupted into laughter.

"Your wife continues to speak your praises, Waters," DuMond remarked as he motioned with one hand to his henchmen.

The burly pair filed from the room, leaving the three of them alone.

"I explained you weren't deserving of that devotion," DuMond said casually as he fetched a drink and carried it over. He motioned to the open chair beside Marcia. "Would you not agree?"

He wholeheartedly agreed. He'd known it all along.

"Of course he does not agree," Marcia said, her voice ripe with indignation. "He's perfectly kind and good and—"

"Marcia," Andrew said quietly. He looked to DuMond. "I hardly think abducting the wife of a peer is good business?"

DuMond narrowed his eyes. "Is that what you think?"

"Andrew, Mr. DuMond did not abduct me," Marcia spoke chidingly, and Andrew took his gaze from the proprietor and put his focus on his wife. "He saved me and Faith and Anwen."

Andrew shifted his gaze from DuMond to his wife and stared blankly at her. His stomach muscles seized for a second time. He'd not only put his wife in danger, he'd put her innocent friends in danger, too. "I was nearly abducted but it was not Mr. DuMond—"

Atbrooke and Marianne.

He'd known that failing to pay off Atbrooke and his sister would have only put he and Marcia in the siblings' crosshairs, and had an obligation to be looking more closely after her, for when they ultimately struck. And they had. And Andrew hadn't been the one to stop it. But, rather, DuMond.

Andrew closed his eyes.

"Be warned, Waters," DuMond spoke coldly. "I've been tolerant with you this evening, because of your wife." He narrowed his eyes on Andrew. "The only reason you were given entry this evening was because after years, you've finally settled your debts to me." He paused, that stretch of silence deliberate and taunting. "Coincidental timing with your marrying Lady Waters, would you not say, gentlemen?" he asked of his henchmen.

The enormous guards chuckled. "Indeed," the taller-by-an-inch fellow said. "Very coincidental."

Andrew felt Marcia's gaze on him, and his ears went hot.

"Yes, your marriage proved beneficial to the both of us," DuMond drawled, earning laughs from his men. Andrew's stomach muscles spasmed. "And from what I hear from other gaming hell proprietors round town, I wasn't the only one."

Andrew's pulse pounded in his chest, and his mouth went dry.

"I'd speak with my husband, Mr. DuMond," Marcia said softly to the proprietor.

The gaming-hell owner flashed a cold look at Andrew, and then with a single flick of a hand, urged his men gone.

The moment he and Marcia were alone, he looked to her. Andrew's stomach dropped, along with his heart.

Her eyes remained locked on him.

Pale as he'd never seen her. Her features frozen.

"Where did the money come from?" Marcia tipped her head sideways a notch. "Did you use my dowry to pay off your debts?"

"No!" that denial exploded from him. "I'd never." That would remain untouched; for her.

"Then… how did you suddenly find such a sum? Was it a mere coincidence that you've paid off your debts after we married?"

He heard the thread of desperation in her question; one that begged him to tell her that truth. Only, that truth, would be a lie.

Oh, God.

Marcia rocked back on her heels. Understanding filled her eyes. "Someone *did* offer you money to marry me," she whispered. "Didn't they?"

"Marcia." He could not form a single, coherent thought, the tightness in his chest making it impossible to focus on anything other than her.

"You don't deny it," she said, her eyes stricken.

No, he didn't. Because he couldn't.

Andrew, coward that he was, desperately found himself wishing to follow DuMond and his men from the room. He wanted to be anywhere that wasn't here in this moment. Andrew remained motionless, unable to move, unable to get a proper breath through his tightly constricted lungs.

She had gathered the truth. Of course she had. She was clever. She'd have always figured it out.

But she'd deserved to know.

"Marcia," he tried again.

"I should have thought you might have mentioned if you were receiving money to marry me," she remarked, her voice pitched.

Oh, God. He briefly squeezed his eyes shut. "It didn't seem important," he said hoarsely. This moment, his life, their life together, were spiraling rapidly away from him, and he was helpless to put back together the pieces of them.

"Didn't seem important?" Marcia cocked her head.

And there it was.

His heart thudded a painful beat against his chest. His mind blank, he fought his way through the fog, to stream together words that would make this right.

"Who?" she demanded.

"You needed security. You needed my name. I would have never left you in such a way," he entreated, willing her to believe him, and it was the truth.

Marcia angled her chin up. "That isn't what I asked."

No, it wasn't.

"My brothers-in-law... I lost money to Huntly years ago," he said, his voice hollow, his explanation meandering. "They held on to it for me. Kept it safe." Because they knew you wouldn't. They knew you were a wastrel and worthless. Unable to meet her eyes, he looked briefly away. "Rutland indicated they would return those monies and properties if I... if I..."

Marcia stared expectantly at him.

Andrew made himself complete the admission, owning that sin. "If I married you."

Marcia froze, and then her face fell; her eyes going wide and stricken, she hugged her arms around her middle. "Oh, my God."

"Please, Marcia," he begged, striding over. "It wasn't just about the money." *At all.*

"Don't!" she cried, her voice pitchy and shaken, and the sound of her suffering gutted him from the inside out.

Andrew stood motionless, allowing her that space she craved, forcing himself to watch her fight her way through the tumult. Then, Marcia sucked in a deep, shaky breath. "I knew nothing about the arrangement between you and Lord Rutland," she said softly, smoothing her hands down the front of her skirts.

Andrew closed his eyes. He was going to lose her. Nay, he'd already lost her.

"Did you think those details didn't matter, Andrew?" she pressed when he remained incapable of anything but silence. "Hmm? Did you think I wasn't entitled to the knowledge that you were *bribed* to marry me."

"I wasn't bribed," he rasped. He opened his mouth to say as much, to save himself and their marriage at any cost. "I was offered—" A fortune to *not* marry her. To tell her might salvage some of her feelings for him, but that would only bring hurt to her relationship with her father.

Marcia's golden brows came together. "Yes?" she prodded him, her voice containing the same desperation that gripped him now.

And, in this instant, Andrew discovered he possessed some shreds of honor still, after all. "I *was* offered money." He finished the thought, letting it remain incomplete. "But it isn't how it looks."

The hope in her eyes went out. "But you must admit it certainly looks nefarious, does it not?"

"Yes," he said, his voice hoarse. "I can certainly see that." He found his legs and strode over to her, but the look she cast his way froze him.

He'd never before seen such ice in this woman's eyes.

Not even when she'd been speaking about the man who'd sired her, or the man who'd jilted her.

And it was a sentiment she now turned on Andrew. Because *he* was deserving of *that*.

And it cut him to the core.

God, what a mess he was making of this. All of it. "But that isn't it at all. I wanted you to be happy and knew… I knew…" Andrew closed his eyes. He'd known he'd ultimately break her heart. As her father had predicted. When he opened his eyes once more, he met her gaze, and the pain in her eyes cut through his heart. "I thought I made you happy, too. I cared about you. I *wanted* to marry you," he begged. It had always been Marcia. There'd only ever be Marcia.

"How much was returned to you?" she asked coolly, completely glossing over those assurances he'd given.

Andrew winced, hesitating. "Enough to cover my debts and then some beyond that. Some fifty-five thousand pounds and unentailed properties I'd lost."

Properties he'd lost in poorly placed wagers. It wasn't every day a man was confronted with the mess he'd made of his life.

Marcia inclined her head. "Well. That is quite a fortune, and now that you have those monies, you're free to spend your days playing with your investments, and not spending time with the wife you didn't really want."

"No!" he rasped, her words hitting him like a kick to the gut. "I want to spend my nights and days with you, Marcia," he said, willing her to understanding, imploring her with his gaze and his words and everything in him. "You helped me see I'm different than my father, and the day you came back from the Serpentine… I committed myself to being a better man and making something worthwhile of myself and funds so that I could care for you and the children we will one day have." Little blonde-haired girls with her spirit and tenacity.

And for a moment, he saw her waver, felt her softening, and he found hope. "Marcia, I love you."

"Do not," she rasped, her voice breaking. "Just… do not."

Andrew closed his mouth, holding back the rest of the profession that was a day late. He *did* love her. He always had. It had, however, taken him all of almost forever to realize all the ways in which he loved her.

He needed her to know. To trust him in this.

Andrew tried again. "In retrospect, I see where I should have mentioned all of this… Marianne… Rutland and Huntly."

Tears filled her eyes and then slipped silently down her cheeks, crystalline trails that broke his heart all over again, and he took a step closer.

"It was only about you," he whispered, catching those tears with his thumbs and brushing the drops away. "I only wanted you." He knew that now. He suspected he always had.

And then, with the grace of the most regal of queens, Marcia pulled away from him, tipped her chin back a fraction, and nodded at the door. "My friends are waiting for me."

"Of course," he said dumbly.

As Andrew started after her, he scarcely dared to breathe for fear that he'd break apart and would never be able to put the pieces of himself back together.

A short while later, Andrew, after depositing his wife's garrulous friends at their respective households, he and Marcia returned home.

The moment they reached the foyer, she climbed abovestairs, without so much as a glance back.

Andrew stared after Marcia, following her entire, slow, regal retreat: wishing he had the words to make this right, and alternately proving a coward for welcoming a reprieve… because he didn't know what to say.

His relief was short-lived.

"His Lordship, the Marquess of Rutland, is here," his butler said without preamble as he accepted Andrew's cloak. "Along with Her Ladyship's father, the Viscount Wessex. I've shown them to your offices, my lord."

Of course, Rutland, with his eyes and ears all over London, would have gathered what had transpired this night.

Bloody splendid. The goddamned cherry on the end of this bloody night.

Turning on his heel, Andrew headed for his office.

The moment he stepped inside, his gaze moved quickly from his stoic brother-in-law to the ashen gentleman at his side.

"She is safe," he said quietly as he closed the door behind him.

"She is safe?" Wessex repeated, and then his shoulders sagged, and he sank onto his haunches. "She is safe." He repeated those three words like some sort of mantra to call himself back from a place of terror.

Uncomfortable with that display of emotion, that weakening that bespoke the depth of the father's love for the cherished daughter whom Andrew had inadvertently put at risk, Andrew headed to the sideboard and poured himself a drink.

"I'm taking her."

Had the other man bellowed those three words, they couldn't have packed more power than they did in that quiet, calm deliverance.

Andrew stiffened, and drink in hand, he turned back. "I beg your pardon?"

"As you should. My daughter was nearly killed this night." Wessex clipped out each syllable of each word. "I am taking her home with me."

"You think to take my wife?"

"She's not some damned possession of yours, Waters," the older viscount bellowed. "She is my daughter. She is mine and my wife's greatest joy, and I obviously knew you were never worthy of her, but I'll not stand by and let her be hurt because you can't properly care for her."

Andrew squared his shoulders. "You are not taking Marcia anywhere," he said quietly, and Lord Wessex drew his shoulders back. "That is, not if she does not wish to go." He'd not keep her here against her will. But neither would he allow anyone—her parents included—to make decisions for her. "If you speak to her, and that is what she wishes, I will not stand in her way."

He felt Rutland's piercing stare on him.

Tension filled the room.

Wessex glared at him, and then without another word, he let himself out.

The moment he'd gone, Rutland lit into him. "I told you to marry the lady, and instead of looking after Wessex's daughter, I'm getting word from DuMond that he's saved her from being abducted?" his brother-in-law hissed.

"Having your eyes all over London watch me, are you?" he spat.

"Damned straight I am," Rutland snapped. "And be glad I am, or else your wife would have found herself dead or worse."

Andrew slammed his untouched tumbler of whiskey down hard enough to break the glass. "My wife was in danger, and your first order of business was contacting her father?"

"Yes, it was," Rutland bellowed, and Andrew rocked back. It was the first time he'd seen the always composed and in-control marquess lose his temper. "Because she is also Wessex's daughter, and someday"—he looked Andrew up and down—"given your reputation and how you were discovered with the lady, you'll find yourself with a daughter, and you'll understand."

"She's my wife," Andrew barked.

Rutland took a step closer. "The same wife you so easily offered to turn back over to her father?" he taunted.

He drew back. "I did not," he said, indignant. "That is not what I did at all." He'd been allowing Marcia to make the choice.

"The lady is your wife, and I'd suggest you start *acting* like it," Rutland said quietly. "For I am not giving you blind loyalty, Andrew, because you are not deserving of it. You've done nothing to prove yourself reliable."

At any point in his life.

Rutland might as well have spoken that harsh truth aloud.

"And yet, with all my many flaws"—and there were many, Andrew agreed—"you still coordinated my marriage to your best friend's daughter." He couldn't manage to keep the bitterness from slipping in.

"Because you ruined her, Andrew," Rutland said flatly. "Because I knew Wessex would duel you if you did not, at the very least, offer her marriage, just as I knew you wouldn't shoot Wessex. You'd have defaulted your shot, and my wife, your sister, would be grieving your death," he said, as ruthlessly methodical in the determination he'd arrived at as he'd always been. "Furthermore, with Miss Gray's reputation and the scandal already surrounding her, she was never going to find a respectable husband, and I had hoped…" The fight seemed to go out of Rutland. He gave Andrew a sad look and then shook his head. "I had simply hoped you might rise to the occasion."

Andrew fisted his hands at his sides. The reason Rutland had supported the match was because he'd sought to save Andrew's life and also because he'd believed there wouldn't be another more deserving man coming behind him for Marcia. And in that, both of them had stolen from Marcia the future that she deserved. "I have risen to the occasion since I married Marcia," he said quietly. He'd given up visiting his old haunts. He'd stopped carousing and drinking. "I've changed." His lip curled in a sneer. "Have your men not told you that?" But then, would it really matter? To Rutland, to the world on the whole Andrew was and would always be the same person he'd always been. Only, Marcia had seen more in him. Marcia had opened his eyes to his own worth. Marcia, whose love he'd also lost. Andrew sank into the folds of his chair, and stared blankly out.

Rutland was right.

Andrew had failed Marcia this night.

He was deserving of that condemnation and rage from Marcia's father.

Feeling his brother-in-law's gaze on him, he looked up. "I trust you've another lecture for me," Andrew said tiredly. The good Lord knew he deserved it.

"The opposite," his brother-in-law said gruffly, returning to the front of the office, he claimed a seat across from Andrew. "I want to talk."

Andrew quirked an eyebrow.

"I want to be here for you," Rutland explained, and that offering, but rather, of an ear came so unexpectedly, so welcome, the words tumbled from Andrew.

"I bungled it all. All of it. Marcia learned about the offer you made me, and now she thinks my motives were driven by something they weren't."

"What were they driven by?" Rutland posed that question quietly.

"Love," he said without hesitation. "I love her. I didn't realize it when you asked me to offer for her. I knew only that I cared about her. I always did, but this…" He touched a hand to his heart. "I've never felt this way about any woman or any person."

"Like you'd give your life to see her smile."

"If I could," Andrew said, his throat spasming. "And it hurts so damned bad," he whispered, his voice breaking and his fingers shaking, and he dropped them to the table.

"Then tell her."

"I tried," he said tiredly. Slumping in his chair, he looked beyond Rutland's right shoulder. "But I expect you can see how she would see I'm not the most reliable in terms of trustworthiness."

"Wessex intends to take her back home with him this evening," Rutland said with a gentleness Andrew couldn't recall seeing in the other man.

Oh, God.

Andrew wouldn't survive this. And that was just fine, because he didn't want to survive it.

"I thought, given she is your wife, that you would wish to know that."

Andrew's eyes slid shut. "Thank you," he said, because he was expected to say something, but every other damned response eluded him.

His brother-in-law sat forward. "Andrew, no one wronged your sister more than I did," he said quietly, unexpectedly. The marquess didn't share an iota of himself or his past or details of his life or marriage with anyone, and yet, in this instant, he did with Andrew. "I stole her virtue to trap her, and by all rights, she should have spent every one of her living days hating me, but she doesn't. She didn't. She forgave me. And I can't explain that. Somehow…" Rutland turned his palms up. "Somehow she loves me, and if Phoebe managed to forgive me and trust me with her heart, then I have to believe Marcia can extend those same gifts to you."

Andrew dragged a hand down the side of his face. "It's not the same."

A wry grin formed on Rutland's lips. "It's never the same when it's *you* feeling this. Trust me. But it is. Men are flawed, terrible, complicated creatures who manage to make a muck of everything." He leaned forward and dropped his right elbow on the table. "But somehow we find our way. And do you know how?"

Andrew shook his head.

"Because of love. Because there are women who are complex and wonderful and capable of loving us all despite all our limitless flaws, and they—and that emotion—make us better people. Not perfect," Rutland clarified. "But better. It is up to us, however, to decide if we will be better people, and I know you are capable of that, Andrew."

Yes, Andrew had finally come to see that he was more than the tainted legacy of his bigamist father. He saw he could be a better man. Marcia had helped him see that in himself.

Only, what if that realization had come too late to save his marriage to the only woman he'd ever love?

CHAPTER 23

Marcia left with her father that night.

She needed to see her mother.

As such, she returned to her childhood home: so very certain there wasn't another conversation she wished to have heard less than one about the origins of her birth.

She'd been wrong.

This one hurt just as bad.

Only in different ways.

Because of the person responsible for this hurt. Because she'd trusted him. Because he'd been her friend and then her lover. And because she loved him.

She'd been hurt before.

But never, never had the hurt felt like this.

Her entire body ached.

So this was what true love felt like, like one was being shredded into a million broken pieces.

Curled on her side in the same bed that she'd known for the past ten years, Marcia stared at the beveled mirror across the room and her reflected visage. Her cheeks were swollen and red from all the tears she'd cried that afternoon.

When her life had fallen apart, Marcia had run to the home of her childhood, a place that represented safety and happiness.

Only, that illusion had been shattered weeks earlier, and she was now left with only reality.

She wanted to go back to safer times, when she was ignorant of her past and when Andrew had been her friend and not the man she loved beyond all reason. Because then she wouldn't hurt like this. Because she would have laughed and rolled her eyes when she'd learned the truth and understood that there had been so very many women in his life, even the heinous one whom Marcia shared blood with. And then it wouldn't hurt like she was being ripped slowly to pieces.

Biting her lower lip hard enough to taste the metallic tinge of blood, she welcomed the pain.

Her mother rubbed small circles over the small of her back.

"I'm miserable," she whispered as her mother sat on the edge of the bed beside her.

"Do you want to talk about it?" her mother murmured.

Marcia hesitated, because saying yes would feel like a betrayal of the man she loved despite everything she'd discovered that night. Another fresh wave of tears filled her eyes, and she nodded.

Like she was the child of years ago when she'd suffered her first real loss with the passing of Aunt Dorothy's pug, Marcia sat up and hurtled herself into her mother's arms and just wept.

Her mother folded her close, and Marcia cried all the harder. It felt so very good to be held by her mother.

Only, her mother could not make this better.

As a grown woman who now knew the cruelties life was capable of, Marcia saw that no hug could erase a hurt like this. A hug could bring comfort and warmth, and that was enough. She took solace in that discovery.

When her tears trailed off to shuddery hiccoughs, Marcia rested her chin on her mother's shoulder and took comfort in the small, soothing circles as her mother rubbed her back.

"You love him."

"Beyond all reason," she lamented.

"Alas, I fear that this is what true love is." Marcia heard the smile in her mother's voice. "When one is happy, there is no greater joy, and when knows hurt, it cuts sharper than a blade."

Marcia bit her lower lip, torn between wanting to share all and none of it. Despite all that had transpired with Andrew, and this newfound discovery that she loved him, she knew how the world viewed him, and she wanted to protect him from further judgment, even from her family.

Especially from her family.

But this was her mother, the mother who'd given her life even when the decision had been forced upon her. She could have treated Marcia with disdain and hated her for what she represented, but she hadn't. She'd loved her unconditionally and openly and had been only ever good to her.

So Marcia told her mother everything, beginning with the plan she'd cooked up and Andrew's initial resistance. She shared her run-in with Lord Atbrooke and the threats he'd made, and how, after all that, Andrew had held her and kissed her and helped her to see beauty in herself despite the man who'd sired her.

A heavy silence followed.

"Charles was a terrible bounder," her mother finally said, unexpectedly.

"He… had his reasons." Marcia sank onto the mattress, sitting beside her mother. "Charles confessed Lord Atbrooke… hurt someone he loved very much."

Her mother paled. "Oh," she said, her voice weak.

There was another pause.

It wasn't a question. "I don't blame him," she said tiredly. Not wanting to talk about Charles. Because this wasn't about her former betrothed.

"If he'd loved you, he would have given you his name. He would have stood beside you. Andrew never cared about any of the gossip."

A wistful smile stole across her lips. "He never did." Nor had he cared about who fathered her.

"I always marveled that he should have been so very good with you when you were a girl. He cares you about you, Marcia. I do not doubt that."

No, she didn't, either.

He'd not wanted to help her in her scheme, but in the end, had done so, in order to protect her. And in that, in forcing his hand, she was the one who got him caught. And he'd never blamed her. He'd taken full ownership.

"He insists it wasn't just about the money," Marcia said into the quiet. She laid her cheek against her mother's shoulder, and her mama stroked the top of her head the same way she'd done when Marcia had been a small child.

"Do you recall when you were a girl, and we'd first come to London, Marcia?"

She nodded, the thrill of leaving the country and seeing the Town still fresh.

"Do you recall when we almost left…?"

A memory tripped in. "Papa came."

"Lord Atbrooke had threatened me, too. I was so scared, I took you and left," her mother said. "Marcus stopped our carriage… and he stopped me from going. He insisted I stop running, and face the future with him. And… I'm not saying Andrew wasn't wrong in this. He absolutely is. But I do know, running away, will solve nothing. If you love him, and he cares for you, that you can find a future together."

She did love him.

And more, she did want a future with him.

Thoughts of them together traipsed through her mind, like a slowly changing kaleidoscope of memories—their first meeting in her father's library when she'd been a girl, and he'd been trying to sneak spirits; their meeting in that same library after Charles had jilted her; the moment he'd taken her in his arms and just held her and reminded her of her worth; their wedding day—

Tears filled her throat, and she swallowed painfully around a new swell of emotion.

"You can always trust that your father and I will welcome you back if it means you will be safe and happy."

Safe and happy.

Both of which she always felt with Andrew.

Marcia closed her eyes.

The memories from just a short while ago all played and replayed in her mind.

Andrew, stricken as she'd never seen him. His eyes haunted as he'd pleaded with her.

There'd not been guilt there, but grief. She'd seen her own emotions reflected in his eyes, this man whom she knew so well.

I needn't have married you. I was offered those funds even if you declined my offer.

He would have had those funds free and clear even if he did not marry you, a voice niggled. A reminder born of her own desperation. Or was it? Was it desperation to see what she wished to see and not in fact some hint of proof that he'd married her because he'd wanted her?

Had she fallen so completely head over toes in love with him that she sought to convince herself that he carried some affection for her?

"I wanted you to be happy and knew... I knew... I thought I made you happy, too. I cared about you. I wanted *to marry you."*

As he'd spoken those words, she'd wanted to believe him. She'd wanted it with every fiber of her soul.

Marcia drew in a deep breath.

She knew what she needed to do. Nay, what she wanted to do.

Escorted home a short while later by her father, Marcia went in search of her husband.

Her husband.

Andrew, who had made love to her so beautifully and so magnificently and—

And who'd received a fat purse for marrying her.

As she went from room to room looking for him, those ridiculous romantic musings flew from her head in a moment. Restless, she strolled through the silent household that was now hers. An eerie silence greeted her, made all the more ominous by the shadows that danced upon the walls and carpeted floors.

Quickening her steps, Marcia headed for his office.

She paused outside, lifting a hand to knock and then stopping.

Did she truly have to knock?

A detail she'd not sorted out, a question she'd not thought to ask. Or mayhap one didn't ask such questions before marriage. Mayhap one asked them after one spoke one's vows? Or perhaps one didn't ask at all? Perhaps one simply figured it out as one went along.

Either way, she was needlessly reminded all over again about this great shift in her existence.

Closing her eyes, she rested her forehead against the smooth, cool surface of the panel. She'd been destined to feel all these things with whomever she'd wed. She'd have certainly felt them with Charles, as Charles had been a stranger to her but for two months of her life.

"Ahem."

Gasping, Marcia straightened.

"My apologies, my lady," Thomaston, the kindly butler said. "If you are looking for His Lordship, Lord Waters is outside in the gardens."

"Thank you, Thomaston," she said softly.

Marcia headed down to the kitchens.

As was the way with all efficient cooks, several covered trays sat out. After she'd availed herself of a wooden plate, Marcia removed the lid of one and proceeded to fill her dish with an assortment of bread and pastries.

With her filled plate in hand, she headed from the room and resumed her journey.

She reached the double doors leading to the gardens and let herself out.

A rush of chilly night air greeted her, and yet it proved welcome. The crisp coolness of the evening chased away the uncomfortable warmth of the household.

Marcia drew the door shut behind her and assessed the grounds.

The gardens were a tangle of overgrown plants and flowers in desperate need of tending.

And that was when she found him.

She stilled.

Her heart knocked funnily against her chest.

The little cloud of white cheroot smoke that formed a halo of sorts above his head had given him away.

As Thomaston had said, Andrew was here.

Marcia started forward.

❦

She'd left.

He'd watched from the windows, his soul crushed, and his heart dying as she'd allowed Wessex to hand her up.

And with her had gone his every reason for living, and smiling, and laughing.

Only, she was… back.

He felt her before he heard her.

A pad filled with notes rested beside him, his charcoal pencil atop it. Andrew had set aside his work and given his attention to nothing other than the heavily clouded London sky.

He waited for her to call out a boisterous greeting, as she'd always done.

He wondered if it would be the singsong greeting she sang sometimes when she saw him, or whether she'd sneak forward and burst upon him, attempting to scare him with her stealthy approach.

In the end, she did none of those things.

She moved quietly, her steps careful in ways that were unlike her.

She'd changed.

She'd never been cautious around him.

With their marriage, he'd gone and changed her.

His gut clenched at the realization.

But it was Marcia.

She had come back.

Which meant she'd not left him.

Yet.

"Marcciaaaa Grayyy. Marcia Grayyyy." He sang that song for her as much as for himself.

"Andrew Barrettt. Andrew Barreett," she returned in that same tune in her same discordant little way.

Despite all that had haunted him this evening, he found himself smiling.

As though that greeting they'd used so often with each other had broken her out of the melancholy that had hovered like a life force in the gardens, Marcia, her hair plaited, wearing a modest wrapper, dropped down onto the ground beside him.

She set the plate down on the ground beside her and pushed it closer to him.

His gaze went to the items heaped upon the wood dish: a Banbury cake. A ratafia cake. An almond-jam tart.

His heart tripped its beat.

They were... all of his favorites. Surely that meant something. Surely...

Surely you're seeing what you want to see.

"You should be resting," he gently chided.

"I was unable to sleep," she confessed, resting her chin atop her knees. She stared out at a pair of dunnock birds hopping along the overgrown earth. Distractedly, she reached for something on her plate—one of the biscuits—and proceeded to pick off little pieces to toss them at their nocturnal visitors.

He tensed. "You are certain DuMond and his men did not harm you?" Because if they had, he'd end each of them, viciously, painfully.

"I wasn't hurt by Mr. DuMond or his men," she assured him. "Atbrooke's man was the only one who harmed me."

His gaze went to her swollen cheek. "You were hurt by that cur..." His throat worked. "And by me."

Anything could have happened to her, because of Andrew. Terror sluiced through him all over again.

Marcia glanced down at the remaining piece of biscuit she held, and when she spoke, she directed her softly murmured words at it. "I went to speak with my mother this evening."

To ask if she could come home? Of course, Lord and Lady Wessex would allow it. And in so doing, they'd steal his every joy. His chest hitched painfully. He couldn't form a response. Not a single one.

Marcia looked up. "My father asked for me to come home... to stay. For good."

As in forever. As in, leave Andrew.

He took a draw from his cheroot, letting the acrid smoke fill his lungs and then exhaling a white plume. "Is that what you want?" Ah, God. How was he able to get that question out in a voice so steady? How when he was splintering apart inside?

Marcia moved closer. "Is that what *you* want?"

He wanted her. He knew that now. He could be honest enough

with himself and acknowledge that he wanted her in his life, and though his mind and soul shied away from the word *love*, he'd gone half-mad when he'd imagined her hurt… or worse. But he proved himself less selfish than he'd believed.

"I want whatever it is you want," he said quietly. It was a lie. Selfishly, he wanted her in his life, always and forever. But he wasn't so selfish that he'd insist she remain with him. He'd give her up if that was what she wished. Sucking in a ragged breath, Andrew took another draw of his cheroot. He slowly exhaled.

Marcia pulled pieces off that slice of bread, doling them out to the pair of birds, who eventually tired of the offering and took flight with their last crumbs. Dropping the remainder of her biscuit onto her plate, Marcia dusted her palms together. "Were you unable to sleep?"

"No," he said. Andrew dumped the ashes at the end of his cheroot onto the graveled path.

Marcia followed his movements and then wordlessly reached for that smoke.

He frowned as she rescued it from his fingertips and studied it for a moment.

Marcia held his gaze and took a draw from the cheroot and then promptly dissolved into a choking fit. Tamping down a grin, he thumped her lightly between the shoulder blades. "You don't want that," he said, slipping the scrap from her fingers. "It's vile."

"You smoke them."

"You're not me, Marcia."

She was good and pure and innocent.

And you're corrupting her.

Her being abducted and now being out here smoking cheroots with Andrew were proof of that.

"Do you want to return to your clubs?"

"No," he said with a rapidity that came only from truth. Somewhere along the way, it had all become tedious. Empty.

But he'd also spoken with a speed that apparently left her disbelieving. "I could continue to join you," she said with more of that hesitation. "As I have done before. If that is what you want."

"I don't want to do that." Not anymore. Tonight, having nearly lost her had proven how empty and miserable his life had become. He paused. "Is that what you want?"

Her eyebrows came together. "I…"

"What do you want, Marcia?" he urged when that sentence meandered off to that place where other incomplete thoughts went to die.

"I really haven't given it much thought," she confessed, glancing down at her hands. "I'd not really thought beyond…" The clouds parted overhead, allowing the half-moon to claim a spot in the sky, and a soft light descended over her face, illuminating her blush.

"Beyond?" he prodded.

Her color deepened, and she studiously studied her palms like they contained the answers to life.

"Falling in love."

His smile froze, and his gut clenched.

She lifted her eyes to his, and he remained immobile, unable to say anything, because really, what was there to say? At last, she was being honest about what she dreamed of—romantic love. And he loved her. Madly, desperately, and completely, and yet he'd told her, too late. He'd told her too little.

Try again.

"Marcia, I—"

"What is this?" she asked, the patent curiosity that was so hers ringing in her question. Reaching over, she picked up his notepad. She flipped through the pages, skimming as she went, before settling on the last page. And he found himself relieved by that shift away from this tumult of emotions inside.

"They are plans. This is… what I've been working on."

"Plans?"

"You'll find my estates have fallen into some disrepair." He should have attended them far sooner, but he'd chafed at addressing the details after his inheritance had been snatched from him when he'd been a boy and held in safekeeping, as Rutland had called it. "I had the idea to invest in several ventures that have proven profitable for Rothesby."

Marcia angled her body so they faced each other. "What type of ventures?"

Just like that, with her genuine interest and the ease with which she spoke with him, the tension melted away, and he found himself speaking with her as he always had.

And it felt so damned good.

"Steam," he said.

She cocked her head.

"They say it is the wave of the future and that it won't be long before the locomotive completely transforms transportation, making the carriage obsolete and becoming a major mode of travel."

"What is a locomotive?"

"You don't know what a locomotive is?" he asked, and she shook her head. "Oh, Marcia." He shifted so they faced each other, and his knees touched hers. "They are magnificent. They run because of a high-pressured engine. They began by hauling coal from local mines—"

"And you think they will soon haul people?" Her voice rang with amusement and some of the same excitement that matched his.

"They already are. Men—"

"And women."

"Men and women have been riding horses since the dawn of time, and as such, a change is long overdue."

"And you wish to be part of that change?"

Now he could be part of that change, because it was a wager of a different sort. A wager on the future and innovation and invention. "I will be," he said quietly. "I want to be part of... something," he confessed, feeling her eyes upon him. He raised the cheroot to his lips and took a deep inhale, looking out at the tangle of weeds choking a rosebush. "My sister Phoebe and her husband have traveled. They've seen the world, the Cook Islands. As has my mother and her husband. Hell, my youngest brother, who is not even nine, has done so. And I'm left asking, what have I done? What have I done that has any meaning or value or significance?" They were thoughts he'd never before considered because he had been so consumed by his own gratifications and sinful pursuits that he'd not stopped to think about what his life had been or would become.

Unsure what to make of the way she looked at him, he said, "You think I'm being ridiculous."

"Not at all," she said with an rapidity that rang only of truth. "I'm thinking that you are wise to look to the future and admirable for pursuing something different than you've ever done."

He heard the wistful quality in her words.

The same wistfulness that matched the time he'd found her at the side of her family's lake, lamenting the fact that she'd never beat the young boys present in a swimming race.

"Are there any things you wish to do, Marcia? Because the world is now open to you in ways that it was previously closed as an unwed lady," he pointed out.

She chewed at her lower lip. "I… haven't given it much thought."

He caught her right hand that continued to fiddle with her skirts, stilling that restless gesture, and she looked at their joined hands and then up at him.

"You should, Marcia," he said quietly. "You should think about what you want, and you should take it, because you deserve it."

Her lips parted slightly, and the heavy quiet of the midnight still magnified the little sigh that escaped her. When her eyes went soft, his mind balked at everything he saw there.

Andrew swiftly yanked his hand free, unnerved, because he couldn't let his mind go to that level of a relationship with Marcia. He couldn't let them go there. Only hurt awaited on the other side.

The disappointment she was helpless to hide radiated from a gaze that had always been so very expressive, and it served as proof for him to worry about their marriage becoming anything more than what it was.

Clearing his throat, Andrew grabbed his notepad and jumped up. "It is late," he said quickly and helped her up. "You should retire."

"Yes." She lingered. "But I don't want to." Marcia lifted her eyes to his. "I want to stay here with you."

She wanted to stay here with him.

Did he merely imagine the double meaning to those words, that she wished to remain in his home and wanted to be in his bed. And for the first time in his life, he wanted more from a woman. He wanted so much more with Marcia, but he was desperate enough to take whatever she was willing to offer him.

Andrew looped an arm around her waist, and with a breathy sigh, she was already melting against him.

Their mouths were on each other, and all the emotions of that night consumed him, desperation fueled by the relief of knowing she was unharmed lent an intensity to their embrace.

"I nearly went mad tonight, Marcia," he rasped between kisses, "imagining what they would do to you."

She clung to him, returning that kiss. "He didn't. I am fine," she promised. "I am here with you, and I am not going anywhere."

She was not going anywhere.

Exalted by that avowal, Andrew deepened their kiss.

There was a desperation to their lovemaking, an unbridled rawness to every slash of his lips against hers and in the hands they roved over each other.

Andrew caught her under her buttocks, filling his hands with that supple flesh and drawing her against the long line of his erection.

Marcia whimpered and moved rhythmically in a gyration as old as time.

He should gentle this meeting. Even though they'd made love over and over this week, she was still a lady.

But she wouldn't allow him to slow. "Please," she begged, and he guided them down onto the ground. Shoving her skirts up, he lay between her legs and plunged himself inside the warmest, wettest sheath he'd ever entered.

Crying out, Marcia arched her back and neck. "Andrew!"

"You are so wet for me," he praised as she lifted her hips in time to his.

When Marcia cried out again, Andrew joined her in her surrender, shouting his release to the skies above as he came inside her. He continued thrusting, ringing every last drop of pleasure from her, and then he collapsed, catching himself by his elbows and framing her body with his.

They remained that way, locked in each other's embrace, their chests heaving and their breaths coming in fast pants, until it settled into a smooth, even rhythm. And still, they just remained that way. Holding one another.

A better man would let her go. He'd let her pack her things and go back to her parents' home.

When she went, she'd steal his very reason for smiling and living. He loved her.

He'd never be worthy.

But mayhap it wasn't about being worthy. Mayhap it was, as Rutland had said, about being the best version of himself that he might be, not just for her, but for him. He loved her, and he needed her to know that, and then if she still did—

His mind shied away from that.

She couldn't.

She had to know.

She had to stay.

"I love you, Marcia," he whispered, resting his brow atop hers, so their eyes met, willing her to see. "I love you, and want you in my life." Her eyes went soft. "If you go, I'll be destroyed, and I'll deserve it," he said, his voice harsh and guttural. "But I'm selfish enough to beg you to stay with me."

"You cannot lie to me again, Andrew," she said softly.

His heart beat hard against the walls of his chest. "What are you saying?" he whispered.

"I'm saying that I love you, Andrew," she said simply. "I always have, and I want ours to be a real marriage."

A sob tore from his chest as he caught her to him, dragging her into his arms, and holding her close. "I love you."

"But there can't be any more lies," she said a second time.

He opened his mouth to deliver that pledge: in truth, and one that would ensure she remained with him... forever.

But stopped.

For... a lie of admission was still a lie. He'd known that before, and had kept from her the details.

"Andrew?" her voice, his name, emerged haltingly from her lips.

"There... was a discussion that took place between your father and I," he said, carefully choosing his words. "However, it is not my place to share those details."

Worry darkened her eyes. "Andrew…"

Andrew kissed her, and reaching down, he teased her center with his fingers.

She bit her lip hard. "A-are you trying to d-distract me?" He caressed that sensitive nub, ringing a gasp from her.

"Is it working?"

Moaning, Marcia gave a juddering nod.

"We are going to take this slow, love," he promised. "I'm going to make love to you all night."

And he did.

EPILOGUE

THE FOLLOWING MORNING, WITH THE servants bustling about her bedchambers, removing dresses from her armoire and laying them on the opposite side of Marcia's bed, her trunks sat out, nearly filled.

Her lady's maid and several other young servants hurried back and forth from the armoire to the bed, neatly laying out the gowns to be packed.

Her brothers brandished hatpins like sabers, even as their sisters stood at the mirror, trying on Marcia's bonnets.

The two girls looking adorably childlike in the too-large-for-them headwear they'd donned.

Marcia smiled on wistfully, recalling the days when she'd tried on her mother's things in quite the same way.

How fast time went.

One went from being a young girl playing at life, to a grown one actually living it and wishing for the simpler, less painful, and less complex times of long ago.

"Ohh, I like this one," Maisie said in her singsong voice. She wagged the wide-brimmed poke bonnet.

"Let me see!" Flora reached for the article, but Maisie snatched it close.

"You are seeing." The younger girl stuck her tongue out. "You're trying to take."

"To try."

"To take!"

The girls raised their voices in a rapidly spiraling quarrel.

Their mother rushed over. "Poppets, we do need to pack those."

Maisie held the article protectively close to her chest. "Marcia would want me to try them on. Isn't that right, Marcia?"

It was impossible to not smile at her younger sister. It was always impossible not to smile because of all of her siblings. "I do not see the harm in them trying them on," she allowed, hopeless to deny them anything. "As long as they take turns," she added. "In fact, if you do a very good job of it, then I will let you each keep one."

Happy cries erupted from her sisters, and she managed her first real smile since she'd left the park.

Only…

Her smile fell.

She loved her siblings to the moon and beyond, and yet, she'd also thought nothing of putting their reputations in harm's way with her pursuit of pleasure.

How selfish she'd been.

How self-absorbed.

Grief and pain and shame about her birth had all been the reasons for her recklessness. That, however, did not pardon her from doing as she'd pleased without proper regard for how it could affect their futures.

Yes, there'd only been strong whispers from the *ton*, based on even stronger speculation following her father's flight with her from Cyprian's Den and then her hasty marriage. But the scandal remained, and her brothers and sisters deserved so much more.

She stared at her sisters as they played, boisterous in the gift of innocence afforded only a child. They didn't know the truth surrounding the circumstances of Marcia's birth, but they would one day learn that Marcia had been sired by another man. Society had already begun to speculate about the origins of their own births, and for that reason alone, Marcia should have done everything she could to conduct herself in a way that was above reproach, so one day, there were not more whispers they need contend with.

Her mother rested a hand upon her shoulder.

Marcia glanced over. "I am so sor—"

"They will be fine," her mother interrupted and gave her arm a light squeeze. "They will find people who love them and respect them despite everything, and if they do not, well, then, they will be better without those people in their lives."

Marcia caught the inside of her right cheek between her teeth. She didn't deserve that grace. From any of her family.

Just then, the door opened, and Thomaston announced Lord Wessex as if they were meeting in a formal parlor. "You wished to"—every set of eyes swung to the father at the entryway of the room—"see me," Marcus said, his voice slightly garbled. It took but a single glimpse to know he decidedly did not wish to talk. "I can wait belowstairs until you're... finished!" he said on a rush, hurriedly moving to close the door.

"Not at all," Marcia said, hopping up. "I came so I might speak with you." Amongst other reasons.

When her father turned his gaze back on Marica, his features wore the same strain they had when she'd been a girl wondering aloud how babes were made.

Her father cast a desperate glance at his wife.

"Sorry," she mouthed in return; though the little shrug Marcia's mother gave was anything but commiserative. With a handful of words, the elder viscountess dismissed the servants, and her children.

Marcia's siblings promptly groaned. "Do we have to leave?" Maisie wailed. "I haven't even tried on the rose-covered bonnet."

"There will be time enough for that," their mother said soothingly, as she personally escorted each of her younger children from the room.

"Well, do not be long," Lionel said, as he followed at the back of the sibling line. "I was in the midst of a serious sword battle at sea with Clarion." The rest of the young boy's words were muffled as their mother pushed the panel closed behind them, so that only Marcia and her father remained, and a quiet alongside it in her childhood chambers.

Marcia broke the silence. "Andrew said I should speak to you... about a matter that occurred between you and him. My husband would not break your confidence."

"That... is generous of him," the viscount murmured, earning a censorious look from his wife. "What?" he said defensively. "I'm not being sarcastic, but truthful rather. It… is generous."

"And perhaps you might tell your daughter just why that courtesy her husband extended you *is* so *generous*?" Marcia's mother said, showing absolutely no mercy, and no quarter.

Marcus flattened his lips into a hard line and gave a slight nod of his head. He took a deep breath. "I paid Andrew a visit prior to his coming to offer for you. I… made him an offer of my own," he said quietly.

Her heart thumped funnily against her rib cage. "What did you offer him?"

Marcus hesitated.

His wife gave him a pointed look, urging him to speak.

"Fifty-five thousand pounds," he finally said, and Marcia rocked back on her heels.

The night she and Andrew had been discovered, and Marcia ruined, Andrew had been offered two fortunes: one to marry her, and an equally sizeable one to not. "You offered him a fortune to marry me," she whispered. Andrew would have received fifty-five thousand from walking away from her, keeping those monies free and clear and remain a bachelor. But he'd not chosen that. He'd chosen… her. So much love for him swelled again in her heart.

That great dunderhead. Why hadn't he told her?

Because even with your father's ill opinion, he'd been determined to protect the other man. Because knowing her as he had, Andrew had rightly gathered such a discovery would have brought resentment between father and daughter.

"Please," her father entreated, misunderstanding the reason for her quiet shock. "I thought… I wanted you to be happy, and I feared he couldn't, and…" He stretched a palm out. "I would have done anything, Marcia. Anything."

Marcia pulled herself back from her musings, and looked to her father. "I love my husband," she said bluntly. "He has been a friend to me for years. He treats me as an equal in our marriage." Just as he'd treated her as an equal prior to it. "He makes me happy. And I'll not tolerate him being treated as somehow less by anyone." She firmed her gaze on him. "And that includes by my own father."

Tears gleamed in her father's eyes. "I'm sorry," he said, his voice ragged. "Please, forgive me."

"Of course I forgive you, Papa." She paused. "That is, as long as you promise to treat Andrew with only respect and kindness in the future."

Her father nodded, and Marcia rushed over, even as he opened his arms, and they hugged one another. From the corner of her eye, Marcia caught the way her mother's shoulders sagged with relief. "You have my word," he said against the side of her head. "I love you, Daughter."

Daughter.

A watery smile brought her lips up. Yes, that was what she was… his daughter. "I love you, Papa."

The door exploded open. "Are you done?" Lionel called as he skipped back into the chambers. "Because it sounded like you were, and I made the decision it was time to return."

A laugh exploded from Marcia's lips, melding with her father's as he set her from him.

"It is myyyyy turn." Flora's raised voice cut across the other siblings.

"No, it is mine," Maisie insisted, dancing out of her sister's reach.

"Girls," their mother scolded, and she clapped her hands lightly.

To no avail.

"Let Flora and Maisie have the bonnets," Lionel declared. "I shall take"—he brandished one of her hatpins and pointed it towards his brother, Clarion—"her *daggers*."

"They are not daggers," their mother bemoaned, and patting Marcia distractedly once, she rushed off to interject herself between her two sons, now in the midst of a game of bloodthirsty pirates.

Alas, her mother's efforts proved futile as her sisters joined in the melee.

Suddenly, the door burst open a third time.

Marcia gasped as Andrew came hurtling in, out of breath like he'd run a long race. "Thomaston said you were packing. Why are—" He did a sweep of the room, taking in the small army of Grays. "You…" he finished in a bewildered murmur. "Are you going somewhere?"

Silence greeted him, so loud that Marcia heard the thundering of her own heartbeat distinctly in her ears.

The lull lasted just a moment, as all quiet did when Marcia's siblings were about.

Flora skipped over. "We aren't going somewhere," she said in a singsong voice. "Marcia is. We're just packing her up."

"You aren't packing," Lionel shot back. "Mama and Marcia are. You're just playing with Marcia's bonnets."

The little girl stuck her tongue out.

Her brother followed suit.

Marcia's father laid a hand on each of the quarreling children's shoulders.

"And Marcia isn't packing," her younger brother piped in happily.

Andrew's eyes flew to the boy. "She isn't?" he whispered.

Lionel gave his head a big shake. "Nope. She is *leaving*."

Looking stricken, Andrew's gaze flew from Marcia's father to Marcia.

She trembled under the force of emotion in his eyes.

"Of course, he knows she's leaving," Flora intoned with the complete breeziness of a child delivering words despite not knowing their meaning. "He's her husband."

"Well, he wasn't here," Lionel groused. "How should I know if he knows? I assumed he was packing, too."

Andrew looked over the tops of her siblings' heads and gave his head a befuddled shake. "What is happening?" he mouthed.

Marcia was… going somewhere.

Upon his return from a meeting, Andrew had gone home only to be informed his wife was abovestairs packing her trunks.

Andrew tried to draw in a breath, the ragged inhale noisy in his ears even as it melded with the raised voices of Marcia's siblings.

All the while, his gaze remained locked on her, and she was so very still, watching him. But he couldn't identify the emotion in her eyes now, not like he'd always been able to identify it. That was because, before she'd married him, her eyes had been invariably filled with the same happiness her siblings now exhibited. It was just one more thing he'd cost her.

Marcia's mother cleared her throat. "Andrew," she said quietly.

Blinking slowly, he looked over. "My lady," he returned, adding an equally belated bow. "Wessex," he added.

The older viscount inclined his head. "Andrew."

Andrew. Not Waters.

That was… promising.

Marcia's mother offered him a warm smile. "I believe, given your marriage to my daughter, we might dispense with that familiarity," she said gently.

It was a generous offer, considering all he'd done. But then, mayhap it was easier for her to make that offer knowing her daughter would be leaving him, and this would be the last he would see of her.

His gaze went to Marcia once more. Marcia, who was as still as he'd ever seen her. More still than he'd ever believed her capable of being.

"Andrew, you look very rumpled," Flora remarked. "Does he not?" she asked of her siblings, and each nodded their agreement. Flora switched her attention to Marcia and their mother. "Doesn't he look rumpled? Like he—"

"That is enough," their mother murmured, sweeping over and catching Flora by the hand. "Come along," she said to the remainder of her children as she took Lionel's palm in her spare one. "Let us leave Marcia and Andrew alone."

"But Andrew only just *arrived*," Lionel whined. "And Andrew loves to play pirates. I'm sure he'd like to join us while Marcia finishes her packing."

"I'm certain Andrew will play with you some other time," Lord Wessex assured his son.

As the four pairs of little gazes went to Andrew, his chest constricted. For Lady Wessex's had been a false offer, made because of a need to remove her children. After all, he'd not have the privilege of being part of their family. Not in the way he wished, as Marcia's husband. Grief crested and threatened to drag him under.

"Isn't that right, Andrew?" Lord Wessex prodded.

"I… I expect we will play together sometime in the future," he said, his voice thick.

Lady Wessex gave a pleased nod. "There you have it. From Andrew's mouth itself. Now, come along, little ones," she urged for a second time. She relinquished the hands she held to add another clap, as she and Lord Wessex gathered their younger children. "I trust Marcia would like to speak to Andrew."

"About what?" Lionel chimed in. "Why can't they talk with us here?"

"Because they're talking about the fact that Marcia is packing," Flora said in an exasperated way, and as the noisy siblings filed from the room, Andrew might have smiled, if everything hadn't hurt inside.

After the children were ushered out, Lord Wessex shut the door in their wake with a quiet click, leaving Marcia and Andrew alone.

The moment she'd gone, Andrew and Marcia spoke at the same time.

"Andrew—"

"Marcia—"

He stopped and gestured to her. "Please, you go ahead."

He'd give her the first word, his soul, his heart, and anything and everything she wished if she'd just give him a chance at a new beginning.

She shook her head, and her gaze dipped briefly to take in his wrinkled garments. "You were gone this morning," she said softly. "And I thought—"

"I was meeting with my brothers-in-law this morning," he said on a rush, determined to fight for her and their marriage. "That is why I was locked away. I requested their help in dealing with Atbrooke and his sister. Huntly's good friend, Lord Chilton's brother is an investigator, and I wanted to be sure I employed people to… see that they are dealt with, and you safe," he finished weakly, forcing himself to quit his rambling.

Marcia darted her tongue out and trailed the tip over her lips, dampening her mouth, a mouth he ached to kiss. The only mouth he ever wanted to kiss.

She'd quite ruined him beyond all thought for any other woman.

He stopped before her, only a pace away, and she tipped her head back enough to meet his gaze.

"Andrew, I—"

"Why are you packing?" Andrew blurted.

She narrowed her eyes. "You don't... think I'm leaving you?"

"No!" he exclaimed. He tugged at his cravat. "You... aren't. Right?" Andrew stretched a palm out, caressing her cheek with his fingers. "Because, damn it, Marcia, I'm a selfish cad, and I want you in my life forever. I love you. I love you as I never believed myself capable of loving another person, and not because I don't believe in love, just that... I never thought I would experience"—he gestured frantically at himself—"this."

"Andrew—"

"I love you, Marcia," he said, his voice hoarse as he interrupted her again, needing her to hear him and know everything in his heart. "I have never loved anyone the way I love you." He touched a fist to the center of his chest. "It's a love that consumes me and alternately awes me and terrifies me. And I never knew I could feel like this."

Her lips trembled, and he took another step closer, trying to persuade her with his words and his eyes to believe in him. To trust in him. "But I do. When you're with me, I'm capable of only smiling and laughing, and I want to be a better man, not just for you, but because of you. Because you helped me see that I'm not my father, and I've made a muck of so many things." He knew he rambled, his words coming quickly, and he paused only long enough to drag a shaky hand through his hair.

"I'm not leaving you, Andrew," she said, exasperation rich in her voice. Marcia took his hands in hers. "When I was a girl, my mother... She left the viscount. She thought it was for the better, to spare him from Lord Atbrooke. He put that fear in my mother and attempted to drive a wedge between her and Lord Wessex, just as he and his sister attempted to drive a wedge between me and you." Her eyes hardened, and she firmed her jaw. "I would never leave you, Andrew. I told you that last evening, and it is not changing. I love you," she said simply.

He remained motionless, afraid if he so much as moved slightly or breathed, he'd find this was only a dream conjured of his own yearnings. "But you are packing," he whispered.

"Yes," she murmured, drifting over to him, and then she stopped so close, he could breathe in the lemon and honey scent that clung to her. "You said several times that your siblings and sister have been to the Cook Islands and that you have never gone, and I sent word to your parents asking if they might help me coordinate travel arrangements. I thought we might have a proper honeymoon."

"A honeymoon," he said dumbly, incapable of doing anything more than echoing her.

She nodded.

"A honeymoon," he repeated.

She'd arranged for a honeymoon trip for them, to a place she recalled him speaking of, and she wished to make a journey to those islands with him.

Emotion crested in his throat, and joy and relief swept through him. Tears stung his eyes. Andrew blinked several times, and when he opened his eyes, he found Marcia's worried gaze on him, indecision in her expressive features.

"You do not like the idea?"

He shook his head, and her face fell.

"You misunderstand," he murmured, his voice thick. "I love it." He nodded. "It is perfect. Just perfect."

Marcia stilled, and then as he opened his arms to gather her close, she launched herself into his arms.

Andrew pressed a hard kiss against her temple. "I never want to be apart from you," he rasped.

"And you won't. I fear you are quite stuck with me, Andrew."

"And I never want to be unstuck from you."

She laughed, giddy with joy, and he found laughter spilling from his lips.

"Well, I never want to be *unstuck* from you," she said.

He kissed her. "And you shan't," he promised. "We shall be together forever."

Marcia slipped her fingers through his, twining them and bringing their joined hands to her heart. "Forever."

He raised her knuckles to his mouth, placing a tender kiss upon them. "Forever."

THE END

Coming to the World of Heart of the Duke:

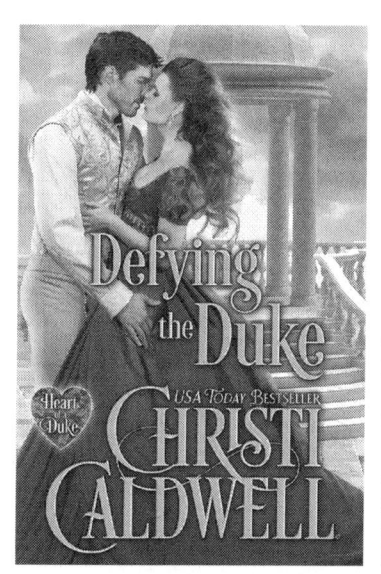

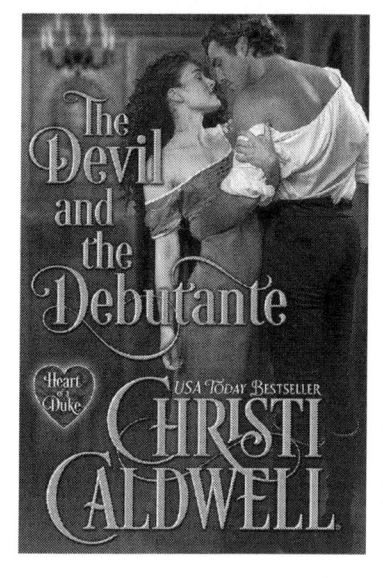

- Defying the Duke
- To Marry Her Marquess
- The Devil and the Debutante
- Devil by Daylight

OTHER BOOKS IN THE HEART OF A DUKE SERIES
BY CHRISTI CALDWELL

TO HOLD A LADY'S SECRET
Book 16 in the "Heart of a Duke" Series by Christi Caldwell

Lady Gillian Farendale is in trouble. Her titled father has dragged her through one London Season after another, until the sheer monotony of the marriage mart and the last vestige of Gillian's once-independent spirit conspire to lead her into a single night of folly. When her adventure goes so very wrong, she has only one old friend to whom she can turn for help.

Colin Lockhart's youthful friendship with Lady Gillian cost him everything, and a duke's by-blow had little enough to start with. He's survived years on London's roughest streets to become a highly successful Bow Street Runner, and his dream of his own inquiry agency is almost within his grasp.

Then Gillian begs him to once again risk angering her powerful father. The ruthless logic of the street tells Colin that he dare not help Gillian, while his tender heart tempts him to once again risk everything for the only woman he'll ever love.

To Tempt a Scoundrel
Book 15 in the "Heart of a Duke" Series by Christi Caldwell

Never trust a gentleman…

Once before, Lady Alice Winterbourne trusted her heart to an honorable, respectable man… only to be jilted in the scandal of the Season. Longing for an escape from all the whispers and humiliation, Alice eagerly accepts an invitation to her friend's house party. In the country, she hopes to find some peace from the embarrassment left in London… Unfortunately, she finds her former betrothed and his new bride in attendance.

Never love a lady…

Lord Rhys Brookfield has no interest in marriage. Ever. He's worked quite hard at building both his fortune and his reputation as a rogue—and intends to enjoy all that they can offer him. That is if his match-making mother will stop pairing him with prospective brides. When Rhys and Alice meet, sparks flare. But with every new encounter, their first impressions of one another are challenged and an unlikely friendship is forged.

Desperate, Rhys proposes a pretend courtship, one meant to spite Alice's former betrothed and prevent any matchmaking attempts toward Rhys. What neither expects is that a pretense can become so much more. Or that a burning passion can heal… and hurt.

BEGUILED BY A BARON
Book 14 in the "Heart of a Duke" Series by Christi Caldwell

A Lady with a Secret… Partially deaf, with a birthmark marring her face, Bridget Hamilton is content with her life, even if she's been cast out of her family. But her peaceful existence—expanding her mind with her study of rare books—is threatened with an ultimatum from her evil brother—steal a valuable book or give up her son. Bridget has no choice; her son is her world.

A Lord with a Purpose… Vail Basingstoke, Baron Chilton is known throughout London as the Bastard Baron. After battling at Waterloo, he establishes himself as the foremost dealer in rare books and builds a fortune, determined to never be like the self-serving duke who sired him. He devotes his life to growing his fortune to care for his illegitimate siblings, also fathered by the duke. The chance to sell a highly coveted book for a financial windfall is his only thought.

Two Paths Collide… When Bridget masquerades as the baron's newest housekeeper, he's hopelessly intrigued by her quick wit and her skill with antique tomes. Wary from having his heart broken in the past, it should be easy enough to keep Bridget at arm's length, yet desire for her dogs his steps. As they spend time in each other's company, understanding for life grows as does love, but when Bridget's integrity is called into question, Vail's world is shattered—as is his heart again. Now Bridget and Vail will have to overcome the horrendous secrets and lies between them to grasp a love—and life—together.

To Enchant a Wicked Duke
Book 13 in the "Heart of a Duke" Series by Christi Caldwell

A Devil in Disguise

Years ago, when Nick Tallings, the recent Duke of Huntly, watched his family destroyed at the hands of a merciless nobleman, he vowed revenge. But his efforts had been futile, as his enemy, Lord Rutland is without weakness.

Until now...

With his rival finally happily married, Nick is able to set his ruthless scheme into motion. His plot hinges upon Lord Rutland's innocent, empty-headed sister-in-law, Justina Barrett. Nick will ruin her, marry her, and then leave her brokenhearted.

A Lady Dreaming of Love

From the moment Justina Barrett makes her Come Out, she is labeled a Diamond. Even with her ruthless father determined to sell her off to the highest bidder, Justina never gives up on her hope for a good, honorable gentleman who values her wit more than her looks.

A Not-So-Chance Meeting

Nick's ploy to ensnare Justina falls neatly into place in the streets of London. With each carefully orchestrated encounter, he slips further and further inside the lady's heart, never anticipating that Justina, with her quick wit and strength, will break down his own defenses. As Nick's plans begins to unravel, he's left to determine which is more important—Justina's love or his vow for vengeance. But can Justina ever forgive the duke who deceived her?

One Winter with a Baron
Book 12 in the "Heart of a Duke" Series by Christi Caldwell

A clever spinster:

Content with her spinster lifestyle, Miss Sybil Cunning wants to prove that a future as an unmarried woman is the only life for her. As a bluestocking who values hard, empirical data, Sybil needs help with her research. Nolan Pratt, Baron Webb, one of society's most scandalous rakes, is the perfect gentleman to help her. After all, he inspires fear in proper mothers and desire within their daughters.

A notorious rake:

Society may be aware of Nolan Pratt, Baron's Webb's wicked ways, but what he has carefully hidden is his miserable handling of his family's finances. When Sybil presents him the opportunity to earn much-needed funds, he can't refuse.

A winter to remember:

However, what begins as a business arrangement becomes something more and with every meeting, Sybil slips inside his heart. Can this clever woman look beneath the veneer of a coldhearted rake to see the man Nolan truly is?

To Redeem a Rake
Book 11 in the "Heart of a Duke" Series by Christi Caldwell

He's spent years scandalizing society.

Now, this rake must change his ways.

Society's most infamous scoundrel, Daniel Winterbourne, the Earl of Montfort, has been promised a small fortune if he can relinquish his wayward, carousing lifestyle. And behaving means he must also help find a respectable companion for his youngest sister—someone who will guide her and whom she can emulate. However, Daniel knows no such woman. But when he encounters a childhood friend, Daniel believes she may just be the answer to all of his problems.

Having been secretly humiliated by an unscrupulous blackguard years earlier, Miss Daphne Smith dreams of finding work at Ladies of Hope, an institution that provides an education for disabled women. With her sordid past and a disfigured leg, few opportunities arise for a woman such as she. Knowing Daniel's history, she wishes to avoid him, but working for his sister is exactly the stepping stone she needs.

Their attraction intensifies as Daniel and Daphne grow closer, preparing his sister for the London Season. But Daniel must resist his desire for a woman tarnished by scandal while Daphne is reminded of the boy she once knew. Can society's most notorious rake redeem his reputation and become the man Daphne deserves?

To Woo a Widow
Book 10 in the "Heart of a Duke" Series by Christi Caldwell

They see a brokenhearted widow.

She's far from shattered.
Lady Philippa Winston is never marrying again. After her late husband's cruelty that she kept so well hidden, she has no desire to search for love.

Years ago, Miles Brookfield, the Marquess of Guilford, made a frivolous vow he never thought would come to fruition—he promised to marry his mother's goddaughter if he was unwed by the age of thirty. Now, to his dismay, he's faced with honoring that pledge. But when he encounters the beautiful and intriguing Lady Philippa, Miles knows his true path in life. It's up to him to break down every belief Philippa carries about gentlemen, proving that not only is love real, but that he is the man deserving of her sheltered heart.

Will Philippa let down her guard and allow Miles to woo a widow in desperate need of his love?

The Lure of a Rake
Book 9 in the "Heart of a Duke" Series by Christi Caldwell

A Lady Dreaming of Love

Lady Genevieve Farendale has a scandalous past. Jilted at the altar years earlier and exiled by her family, she's now returned to London to prove she can be a proper lady. Even though she's not given up on the hope of marrying for love, she's wary of trusting again. Then she meets Cedric Falcot, the Marquess of St. Albans whose seductive ways set her heart aflutter. But with her sordid history, Genevieve knows a rake can also easily destroy her.

An Unlikely Pairing

What begins as a chance encounter between Cedric and Genevieve becomes something more. As they continue to meet, passions stir. But with Genevieve's hope for true love, she fears Cedric will be unable to give up his wayward lifestyle. After all, Cedric has spent years protecting his heart, and keeping everyone out. Slowly, she chips away at all the walls he's built, but when he falters, Genevieve can't offer him redemption. Now, it's up to Cedric to prove to Genevieve that the love of a man is far more powerful than the lure of a rake.

To Trust a Rogue
Book 8 in the "Heart of a Duke" Series by Christi Caldwell

A rogue

Marcus, the Viscount Wessex has carefully crafted the image of rogue and charmer for Polite Society. Under that façade, however, dwells a man whose dreams were shattered almost eight years earlier by a young lady who captured his heart, pledged her love, and then left him, with nothing more than a curt note.

A widow

Eight years earlier, faced with no other choice, Mrs. Eleanor Collins, fled London and the only man she ever loved, Marcus, Viscount Wessex. She has now returned to serve as a companion for her elderly aunt with a daughter in tow. Even though they're next door neighbors, there is little reason for her to move in the same circles as Marcus, just in case, she vows to avoid him, for he reminds her of all she lost when she left.

Reunited

As their paths continue to cross, Marcus finds his desire for Eleanor just as strong, but he learned long ago she's not to be trusted. He will offer her a place in his bed, but not anything more. Only, Eleanor has no interest in this new, roguish man. The more time they spend together, the protective wall they've constructed to keep the other out, begin to break. With all the betrayals and secrets between them, Marcus has to open his heart again. And Eleanor must decide if it's ever safe to trust a rogue.

To Wed His Christmas Lady
Book 7 in the "Heart of a Duke" Series by Christi Caldwell

She's longing to be loved:

Lady Cara Falcot has only served one purpose to her loathsome father—to increase his power through a marriage to the future Duke of Billingsley. As such, she's built protective walls about her heart, and presents an icy facade to the world around her. Journeying home from her finishing school for the Christmas holidays, Cara's carriage is stranded during a winter storm. She's forced to tarry at a ramshackle inn, where she immediately antagonizes another patron—William.

He's avoiding his duty in favor of one last adventure:

William Hargrove, the Marquess of Grafton has wanted only one thing in life—to avoid the future match his parents would have him make to a cold, duke's daughter. He's returning home from a blissful eight years of traveling the world to see to his responsibilities. But when a winter storm interrupts his trip and lands him at a falling-down inn, he's forced to share company with a commanding Lady Cara who initially reminds him exactly of the woman he so desperately wants to avoid.

A Christmas snowstorm ushers in the spirit of the season:

At the holiday time, these two people who despise each other due to first perceptions are offered renewed beginnings and fresh starts. As this gruff stranger breaks down the walls she's built about herself, Cara has to determine whether she can truly open her heart to trusting that any man is capable of good and that she herself is capable of love. And William has to set aside all previous thoughts he's carried of the polished ladies like Cara, to be the man to show her that love.

The Heart of a Scoundrel
Book 6 in the "Heart of a Duke" Series by Christi Caldwell

Ruthless, wicked, and dark, the Marquess of Rutland rouses terror in the breast of ladies and nobleman alike. All Edmund wants in life is power. After he was publically humiliated by his one love Lady Margaret, he vowed vengeance, using Margaret's niece, as his pawn. Except, he's thwarted by another, more enticing target—Miss Phoebe Barrett.

Miss Phoebe Barrett knows precisely the shame she's been born to. Because her father is a shocking letch she's learned to form her own opinions on a person's worth. After a chance meeting with the Marquess of Rutland, she is captivated by the mysterious man. He, too, is a victim of society's scorn, but the more encounters she has with Edmund, the more she knows there is powerful depth and emotion to the jaded marquess.

The lady wreaks havoc on Edmund's plans for revenge and he finds he wants Phoebe, at all costs. As she's drawn into the darkness of his world, Phoebe risks being destroyed by Edmund's ruthlessness. And Phoebe who desires love at all costs, has to determine if she can ever truly trust the heart of a scoundrel.

To Love a Lord
Book 5 in the "Heart of a Duke" Series by Christi Caldwell

All she wants is security:

The last place finishing school instructor Mrs. Jane Munroe belongs, is in polite Society. Vowing to never wed, she's been scuttled around from post to post. Now she finds herself in the Marquess of Waverly's household. She's never met a nobleman she liked, and when she meets the pompous, arrogant marquess, she remembers why. But soon, she discovers Gabriel is unlike any gentleman she's ever known.

All he wants is a companion for his sister:

What Gabriel finds himself with instead, is a fiery spirited, bespectacled woman who entices him at every corner and challenges his age-old vow to never trust his heart to a woman. But…there is something suspicious about his sister's companion. And he is determined to find out just what it is.

All they need is each other:

As Gabriel and Jane confront the truth of their feelings, the lies and secrets between them begin to unravel. And Jane is left to decide whether or not it is ever truly safe to love a lord.

Loved By a Duke
Book 4 in the "Heart of a Duke" Series by Christi Caldwell

For ten years, Lady Daisy Meadows has been in love with Auric, the Duke of Crawford. Ever since his gallant rescue years earlier, Daisy knew she was destined to be his Duchess. Unfortunately, Auric sees her as his best friend's sister and nothing more. But perhaps, if she can manage to find the fabled heart of a duke pendant, she will win over the heart of her duke.

Auric, the Duke of Crawford enjoys Daisy's company. The last thing he is interested in however, is pursuing a romance with a woman he's known since she was in leading strings. This season, Daisy is turning up in the oddest places and he cannot help but notice that she is no longer a girl. But Auric wouldn't do something as foolhardy as to fall in love with Daisy. He couldn't. Not with the guilt he carries over his past sins… Not when he has no right to her heart…But perhaps, just perhaps, she can forgive the past and trust that he'd forever cherish her heart—but will she let him?

The Love of a Rogue
Book 3 in the "Heart of a Duke" Series by Christi Caldwell

Lady Imogen Moore hasn't had an easy time of it since she made her Come Out. With her betrothed, a powerful duke breaking it off to wed her sister, she's become the *tons* favorite piece of gossip. Never again wanting to experience the pain of a broken heart, she's resolved to make a match with a polite, respectable gentleman. The last thing she wants is another reckless rogue.

Lord Alex Edgerton has a problem. His brother, tired of Alex's carousing has charged him with chaperoning their remaining, unwed sister about *ton* events. Shopping? No, thank you. Attending the theatre? He'd rather be at Forbidden Pleasures with a scantily clad beauty upon his lap. The task of *chaperone* becomes even more of a bother when his sister drags along her dearest friend, Lady Imogen to social functions. The last thing he wants in his life is a young, innocent English miss.

Except, as Alex and Imogen are thrown together, passions flare and Alex comes to find he not only wants Imogen in his bed, but also in his heart. Yet now he must convince Imogen to risk all, on the heart of a rogue.

More Than a Duke
Book 2 in the "Heart of a Duke" Series by Christi Caldwell

Polite Society doesn't take Lady Anne Adamson seriously. However, Anne isn't just another pretty young miss. When she discovers her father betrayed her mother's love and her family descended into poverty, Anne comes up with a plan to marry a respectable, powerful, and honorable gentleman—a man nothing like her philandering father.

Armed with the heart of a duke pendant, fabled to land the wearer a duke's heart, she decides to enlist the aid of the notorious Harry, 6th Earl of Stanhope. A scoundrel with a scandalous past, he is the last gentleman she'd ever wed…however, his reputation marks him the perfect man to school her in the art of seduction so she might ensnare the illustrious Duke of Crawford.

Harry, the Earl of Stanhope is a jaded, cynical rogue who lives for his own pleasures. Having been thrown over by the only woman he ever loved so she could wed a duke, he's not at all surprised when Lady Anne approaches him with her scheme to capture another duke's affection. He's come to appreciate that all women are in fact greedy, title-grasping, self-indulgent creatures. And with Anne's history of grating on his every last nerve, she is the last woman he'd ever agree to school in the art of seduction. Only his friendship with the lady's sister compels him to help.

What begins as a pretend courtship, born of lessons on seduction, becomes something more leaving Anne to decide if she can give her heart to a reckless rogue, and Harry must decide if he's willing to again trust in a lady's love.

For Love of the Duke
Book 1 in the "Heart of a Duke" Series by Christi Caldwell
by Christi Caldwell

After the tragic death of his wife, Jasper, the 8th Duke of Bainbridge buried himself away in the dark cold walls of his home, Castle Blackwood. When he's coaxed out of his self-imposed exile to attend the amusements of the Frost Fair, his life is irrevocably changed by his fateful meeting with Lady Katherine Adamson.

With her tight brown ringlets and silly white-ruffled gowns, Lady Katherine Adamson has found her dance card empty for two Seasons. After her father's passing, Katherine learned the unreliability of men, and is determined to depend on no one, except herself. Until she meets Jasper…

In a desperate bid to avoid a match arranged by her family, Katherine makes the Duke of Bainbridge a shocking proposition— one that he accepts.

Only, as Katherine begins to love Jasper, she finds the arrangement agreed upon is not enough. And Jasper is left to decide if protecting his heart is more important than fighting for Katherine's love.

In Need of a Duke
*A Prequel Novella to "The Heart of a Duke" Series
by Christi Caldwell*

In Need of a Duke: (Author's Note: This is a prequel novella to "The Heart of a Duke" series by Christi Caldwell. It was originally available in "The Heart of a Duke" Collection and is now being published as an individual novella.

It features a new prologue and epilogue.

Years earlier, a gypsy woman passed to Lady Aldora Adamson and her friends a heart pendant that promised them each the heart of a duke.

Now, a young lady, with her family facing ruin and scandal, Lady Aldora doesn't have time for mythical stories about cheap baubles. She needs to save her sisters and brother by marrying a titled gentleman with wealth and power to his name. She sets her bespectacled sights upon the Marquess of St. James.

Turned out by his father after a tragic scandal, Lord Michael Knightly has grown into a powerful, but self-made man. With the whispers and stares that still follow him, he would rather be anywhere but London…

Until he meets Lady Aldora, a young woman who mistakes him for his brother, the Marquess of St. James. The connection between Aldora and Michael is immediate and as they come to know one another, Aldora's feelings for Michael war with her sisterly responsibilities. With her family's dire situation, a man of Michael's scandalous past will never do.

Ultimately, Aldora must choose between her responsibilities as a sister and her love for Michael.

BIOGRAPHY

Christi Caldwell is the *USA Today* bestselling author of eleven series, including Wantons of Waverton, Lost Lords of London, Sinful Brides, Wicked Wallflowers, and Heart of a Duke. She blames novelist Judith McNaught for luring her into the world of historical romance. When Christi was at the University of Connecticut, she began writing her own tales of love—ones where even the most perfect heroes and heroines had imperfections. She learned to enjoy torturing her couples before they earned their well-deserved happily ever after.

Christi lives in the Piedmont region of North Carolina, where she spends her time writing and baking with her twin girls and courageous son.

For more information visit www.christicaldwell.com.

Printed in Great Britain
by Amazon